Weatherbury Farm

A Sequel To Thomas Hardy's
'Far From The Madding Crowd'

Patricia Dolling-Mann

iUniverse, Inc.
New York   Bloomington

Weatherbury Farm

A Sequel To Thomas Hardy's 'Far From The Madding Crowd'

IUniverse books may be ordered through booksellers or by
contacting:

iUniverse
1663 Liberty Drive
Bloomington, IN 47403
www.iuniverse.com
1-800-Authors (1-800-288-4677)

ISBN: 978-1-4401-0409-1 (pbk)
ISBN: 978-1-4401-0410-7 (ebk)

Printed in the United States of America

Contents

Chapter One
Oakdene

AFTER A LONG SCORCHING summer, the days gradually began to shorten; trees displayed a panoply of colours at the lower end of the spectrum, announcing the close proximity of the season of mists and mellow fruitfulness. Persons involved with the land whatever their station, peasants and farmers, land owners and tenants, all prayed fervently that the weather would hold good until the last of the harvest had been safely gathered in, which would, Deo Volente, certainly be within the next day or two.

A strikingly attractive, middle-aged woman, hair just beginning to show minute streaks of silver-grey stood still, sparing a precious minute from her prosperous busy life, in order to glance across to the adjacent meadow and the fields beyond. The panoramic view, changed only by the seasons and not by man across the centuries, was visible only from the kitchen window of Weatherbury Farm. The front of the house provided the only other pleasing vista; a square, grey stone paved area, leading to a curved lawn encircled and enhanced by colourful herbaceous borders of varying lengths, and several orchards now abundant with fruits, plump and ripe, begging to be harvested.

To the right of the stone built Jacobean Manor, stables abutted the building forming a sizeable stone-flagged courtyard; on the left side a huge barn had been built some hundred years after the original building, using the existing edifice as a party wall.

The woman smiled with pleasure at the vision on the horizon. Her three, now nearly grown up children, chased each other playfully like long-legged colts, alongside and around their father as he strode purposefully along the white heath path before turning sharply into the lane across the meadow which would lead them to Oakdene and Bathsheba.

Gabriel, pausing a moment, raised his eyes towards the great bulk of the house. It was necessary to form a shield with the palm of his hand for the bright orange light was sinking slowly on the horizon and the farmhouse kitchen facing westwards reflected the sun's rays making it virtually impossible to see through the lattice window at such a distance. It was hard to break the habit of a married lifetime and it must be said he had no wish so to do. Accordingly the farmer did as he always did for he hoped to catch a glimpse of his adored wife before she saw him, a game they both played and laughed about for who could truly know who saw who first. He was rewarded with a wave as Bathsheba, seeing her family approaching, left the warmth and sanctuary of her kitchen so that she could fling open the door to welcome them.

Adam, who had sprinted on ahead was first through the door but then he always had to be first in everything he did. Bathsheba suggested it was because he was her first born but he would more than likely have been exactly the same had he been the last to be born as his father had been quick to point out. Now, at eighteen, he had already grown a good three inches taller than his father and had inherited his mother's colouring and dark brown hair. Surprisingly, his facial features were the only part of him which showed who had fathered him. His slimness helped to give him an air of elegance which contrasted oddly with the stolid swarthiness of the farm workers he had been working with during the long days of summer. In spite of the intense heat of the sun, it had been an unusually warm season, the youth had remained pale of complexion but not unhealthily so.

He would shortly be going up to Christminster College where he had decided quite on his own volition that he would read for a degree in the classics with a view to becoming a schoolmaster or possibly a writer or maybe even both for he was overtly ambitious. He hadn't seemed to mind the taunts of "sissy" from some of his schoolfellows, most of who were to become engineers, scientists or farmers. Of course some would stay on their fathers" farms learning, as indeed their fathers before them had done, as they went along, by trial and sadly sometimes error but all with a view to doing a man's job.

But Adam Oak was not of that ilk and his parents, knowing their son as they did, would not have dreamed of trying to discourage the boy from doing something they knew he had set his heart on. Perhaps they would one day regret that lack of guidance for already there were signs of a wilfulness that could lead him into trouble if an unsuitable path should be chosen.

Sheba, after reluctantly relinquishing her arm from the crook of her father's elbow, the girl being as fond of her father as a daughter could be, hugged her mother. They looked more like sisters than their true relationship for the daughter was the possessor of the same English Rose colouring and the same dark brown hair as her mother but at seventeen years of age was still an inch or two shorter than her parent and would more than likely stay that way. A rather intense child, her father often teased her about her love of reading and called her a bookworm. They always knew where to find Bathsheba the younger for the library was her favourite room apart from her own boudoir.

One day she would perhaps go to train for a teacher but there was plenty of time for that. Gabriel secretly hoped she would meet a nice, suitable young man when the time was right, not too early and not too late, marry and have a large family, he being a real family man himself.

Gabriel looked at his two women standing close together and felt a familiar warm glow which seemed to spread pleasantly from his stomach to his toes. He was sure he was the envy of the whole of Wessex for hadn't he, not only one of the largest, most successful properties but was head of the cleverest, handsomest family for miles around.

'Where's Matt? I thought I saw him with you a moment ago.'

Gabriel sat down, as he did every night, on the wooden rocking chair they had bought and cherished since their marriage eighteen years earlier. The couple had gone to Weatherbury market on the first Saturday after the ceremony with the sole purpose of buying for Gabriel a chair he could call his own. Woe betide any of the children if they tried to commandeer the precious chair. Often they would vie for the seat especially when they were very small but as soon as their father put in an appearance they would scatter. It was known simply as father's chair and they quickly learned to respect the fact.

As usual he removed his boots, spread out his legs and wriggled his toes as if he wasn't sure whether or not they may have stopped functioning after spending all day imprisoned in the brown leather boots made by Jacob Heather, the most experienced of the many village cobblers.

'Gone to check on Prince. He thought he had a bit of a cough when he took him out early this morning; I suggested it was the dew getting to him; told him not to worry but you know what he's like with all the blessed animals.'

'That boy should take his bed to the stables,' Bathsheba laughed. 'I hope he hasn't forgotten 'tis the special pre-Harvest Home supper this evening, Gabriel. Did you remind him?'

'He'll be along, when he's good and ready. There's nothing you or I can say will hurry him, as well you know, Bathsheba.'

'Well its mostly cold fare for supper tonight so I suppose it doesn't matter over much, though as we've guests it don't seem polite for him to be late.'

Bathsheba tutted to herself knowing full well that Gabriel would side with the boy if necessary. Besides it was rather good that he was interested in that side of the farm as they seemed to be moving over more and more to livestock. Animals were more reliable than crops, not depending so much on the weather as it were, although this year being so glorious they were bound to make a good profit especially with the corn and barley.

Maybe they would postpone any changes just yet. She must pin Gabriel down and have a proper discussion about the future of Upper Weatherbury farm. He left the bookwork and the running of the business side of the farm almost entirely to her these days although he had always been, and he would be the first to admit it, more of a practical man than an academic. He had never found excitement in working out balance sheets or fulfilment in making a profit as his wife did but he was clever in his own way, self-taught as he was; how else could they have such clever children but Gabriel was an outdoor man, you only had to look at his healthy, lithe body and ruddy complexion to see that at no more than a glance.

When old James Everdene had died many years ago, it was to Bathsheba, his niece, that he had left all his property there not being a male heir. Although there had been some ups and downs in the past, Bathsheba, alone, had managed the property successfully and was well known in the locality for being a hard-headed business woman.

After the tragic murder of her first husband, Francis Troy, by William Boldwood, a neighbouring farmer who was obsessed with love for her, Bathsheba had given herself time to recover from the shock of those dreadful events before she and Gabriel had tied the knot. The tragedy had been twofold because the unfortunate Mrs. Troy had thought for a long time she was a widow, her missing husband's clothes having been found on the deserted beach at Lulwind Cove. It wasn't until he arrived unexpectedly at the very Christmas party in which she was to announce her engagement to William Boldwood that she had known he was still alive. When he had forcefully tried to claim his wife, the distraught farmer Boldwood had lost control, grabbed a gun, and shot Francis Troy through the heart.

When Bathsheba had eventually realised how much she cared for the ever faithful Shepherd Oak, she was more than happy to accept his proposal of marriage and it hadn't taken the couple long to settle into their steady, contented life together, sharing a love which many waters cannot quench, nor the floods drown.

Chapter Two
Good News, Bad News

LIDDY HAD BEEN HELPING Bathsheba for most of the afternoon to prepare the food for the guests although their work was simply that of arrangers as Maryann Money had done all the cooking on the previous day. The celebration was small compared with what would take place in the Great Barn on Saturday but it was still a much looked forward to date on their calendar. It was a chance to meet friends and neighbours in a relaxed way after the last hectic days of summer and harvest; a chance to congratulate or commiserate with fellow farmers about prices and profits, a chance to discuss plans and hopes for the coming year.

On Saturday the ale and cider would flow freely and there would not be the time or the inclination for serious discussion as everyone would be intent on letting their hair down, making sure they and their employees had a good time, although the latter would need little encouragement. This evening was an employer's evening, Saturday more an employee's time.

Guests began to arrive even before the stroke of seven, they were a punctual lot these farming types, always eager for an excuse for a social gathering especially when there was bounteous good food thrown in, but, there was still no sign of Matthew. Not unduly alarmed, for it was not unusual for Matthew to forget the time, Bathsheba agreed to wait until they were almost ready to sit down before she sent Adam to bring back his brother.

Doctor Theodore Melksham and his new wife Harriet had arrived just before the old grandfather clock in the hall struck seven bells and were the first visitors of the evening. He had been married before but had been a widower for many years, the father of two adult sons now also doctors. One, Teddy, had decided to specialise in surgery and was at present abroad gaining valuable experience, Albert was doing post-graduate research into the cause and treatment of the dreaded cholera at one of the big London Hospitals.

The first Mrs. Melksham had sadly died in a riding accident soon after the twins" fourteenth birthday. Everybody assumed the doctor would never marry again for their love was somewhat legendary but, last year, some ten years after the tragic accident, he had introduced his new young love to the villagers at the Harvest Home. There were whispers at first, some not as kind as they might be for the young woman was some twenty years the doctor's junior. Some were unkind enough to suggest she might be more suitable as a wife for one of Dr. Melksham's son's rather than become their stepmother.

A few months later, apparently oblivious to all the gossip and without undue ceremony, the elderly man and his young bride were married at the local parish church by Vicar Hansworth.

Bathsheba liked Harriet, finding the difference in their own ages no barrier, for the new Mrs. Melksham showed a maturity that defied her years. The talk amongst the villagers that the doctor had done a bit of cradle snatching was sour grapes for the most part as the doctor was well respected and his judgement largely went unquestioned. Already, after such a short time the talk was becoming old hat. Locals were heard to say 'The good doctor deserves to be happy after all he's been through,' quite forgetting it was they who had raised the objections in the first place.

Bathsheba hugged Harriet and drew her into the kitchen. There had been speculation among the women at Oakdene that Harriet was pregnant as she had appeared unwell at times in the past few weeks. Bathsheba wanted to be the first to quell the rumours if they were untrue.

Harriet's brown eyes were sparkling like the jewels on the stretched forefinger of all Time and she had never looked more beautiful.

"Tis true then, Harriet?'

The pregnant woman smiled. 'Yes. By Christmas time I shall be able to give Theodore a very special gift.'

Bathsheba hugged her new friend. It would be pleasant to have a birth at that special time of the year and secretly she hoped it would be a boy. Seemed right somehow. Why they might even ask her and Gabriel to be God parents.

'Shall we tell everyone at supper, Harriet? Of course if you'd rather wait.' Bathsheba began.

Again Harriet smiled. 'I don't think there's much point in waiting. I can't keep it a secret much longer,' she said patting the slight bulge which her wide sash could not quite disguise. ' These things have a habit of announcing themselves, don't you agree?'

The two women laughed knowingly. One had already experienced such a happy event several times but occasionally couldn't help wondering if she would really like to go through it all again. Bathsheba, on the whole, decided perhaps not. She was happy with her family and it felt complete. Two sons to carry on the family name and a delightful, intelligent girl.

What more could a woman want, besides, lately she had been having signs that it was a bit too late to add to her family.

The last guests were arriving and soon the oak panelled living room was buzzing with lively conversation. Gabriel stood with his back to the crackling log fire, his face ruddy from the heat. The crystal chandeliers had been lit early and now sparkled and glittered as the dusky shades of twilight descended on the gathered throng.

Bathsheba raised a quizzical eyebrow at her husband. In answer he shook his head indicating that their youngest son had still not put in an appearance. A few minutes later Bathsheba saw Adam disappearing out of the room and she guessed Gabriel had sent him to the stables to bring Matthew back.

The long refectory table, resplendent in snowy white cloth, was laden with cold meats and home grown salad vegetables. It was an informal affair where everyone would help themselves apart from the soup which Liddy and Maryann would serve hot when everyone was seated.

Liddy no longer lived at the farm since she had married Fred Bateman, the bailiff from a neighbouring farm, although she was happy to help out whenever she was needed. Bathsheba and Liddy had been friends for a long, long time and shared many memories both happy and sad. Sometimes they would sit over their tea cups for longer than they should, reliving the old days although there were a few they would both prefer to forget.

Mary Cross, whose husband had recently left her for the pretty young barmaid at The King's Arms in Casterbridge, did most of the housekeeping with the help of Fanny and Maria her twin daughters. Gabriel had suggested they move into the lodge as they had to move out of the cottage when Fred Cross absconded. It was a condition of employment that the cottage was tied to the job.

The girls were the spitting image of their absent father and Mary found it hard to reconcile the fact that, every time she looked at her daughters (for they were a constant reminder of the good times she had shared with her husband), she may never see her beloved Fred ever again. Of course she insisted that she would never take him back to all who bothered to enquire, even if he did have the gall to show his face at Oakdene again but deep down she knew she would. She loved him and had confided as much to Bathsheba who was able to sympathise having been in a similar situation for hadn't her first husband been in love with another. Not only had he loved another but had been the father of a bastard child. The tragic outcome had softened the blow for Bathsheba for who could feel anything but sorrow for the dead Fanny Robin and her stillborn child?

Bathsheba had insisted she did not need a live-in housekeeper in spite of Gabriel's advice that she should and it seemed to work well especially now the children were grown. Most of the cleaning of the huge old house was taken care of by Temperance and Soberness Miller. They had jumped at the chance of what they regarded as promotion, more so when Gabriel had offered them Nest Cottage for their life time. Bathsheba could rely on the two "girls" for they lived up to their names and had even vowed never to marry. Now in their forties it was unlikely they ever would.

The main topic of conversation at supper this evening was the merging of the two farms over to the east of the county for old Farmer Barnes was retiring and he had decided to sell at long last to William Tilbury of Long Thatch. George Barnes had a vested interest of course as Agnes his orphaned granddaughter would be marrying into the Tilbury family next year. Funny how things seemed to work out without too much help from mere mortals, Gabriel had said when he'd heard the news of the old man's sickness which had forced him to retire.

'I believe our friend Dr. Melksham has some good news he wishes to impart,' Gabriel stood at the end of the long table, glass in hand raised ready for a toast.

Theodore stood up proudly, his old friend Gabriel opposite to him. 'I'd like you all to raise your glasses to my good wife Harriet for she is to present me with a child before the year is out.'

There were cheers from everyone. Nobody was surprised except perhaps the good doctor himself. He sat down a little overwhelmed by the response of his neighbours and friends.

'Father!'

The dining room doors were flung open with very little regard for the effect it would have on the assembled company.

A distraught Adam clutched at his father's arm.

'Steady on boy. Whatever's the matter?'

Bathsheba was already at the door. 'It's Matthew, isn't it!'

Adam appeared shaken, his pale face now ashen.

'I think he's been kicked or something. He wasn't moving. I couldn't wake him.'

'Adam. Adam, calm down. Dr. Melksham and I will go and see what can be done. I'm sure it can't be serious. Matthew knows what he's doing.' Gabriel tried to reassure his oldest son to no avail.

The small party made their way quickly to the stables where they could see Matthew curled up in a heap in the corner.

Dr. Melksham examined him quickly and diagnosed a mild concussion brought about by a blow to the head.

At the doctor's prodding, Matthew began to stir.

'Keep still, boy. Try and tell us what happened.'

Matthew could see a sea of faces above him and as he tried to move there seemed to be twice as many. He sank back on the hay and tried to remember what had occurred.

'Let's get him back to the house. There's little I can do for him here,' the doctor instructed.

Carefully, four men made a stretcher with their arms interlaced like a lattice, so that Bathsheba could help her son, who had lapsed back into a state of unconsciousness, into a comfortable position on the makeshift stretcher. Crab-like the men made their way back to the farmhouse where only a short while ago everyone had been laughing and singing. As they entered the hall there was a deathly hush as the guests waited anxiously for news.

Catching a glimpse of Bathsheba's pale, anxious face, Harriet hurriedly left her seat at the dining table in order to offer whatever comfort she could. Her husband raised his eyebrows discreetly as she looked at him questioningly. The situation didn't look too good.

The four men gently laid the still, unperceiving form of the boy on to the chaise-long in front of the blazing fire. The doctor quickly unbuttoned the boy's shirt and began a more thorough examination than he had been able to do in the cold stables. Although Matthew stirred once again he was unable to talk and quickly lapsed once more into his previous state of unconsciousness.

Unable to contain herself any longer, Bathsheba asked tearfully, 'Is he going to be alright, Doctor?'

Dr. Melksham looked up briefly. 'I'm sorry, Bathsheba. Until he regains consciousness, I really cannot tell. He appears to have received a blow to the head but whether it is serious or not only time will tell.'

The doctor's wife drew her friend to a chair and urged her to sit down. She touched Gabriel's arm as they passed. He hadn't taken his eyes off his son for a minute until now. 'I think a spot of brandy might be a good idea, if you wouldn't mind Gabriel.'

'Of course. Yes. Good idea.' He turned to Liddy who had joined them for news to relate to the guests. 'Would you be so kind, Liddy?'

'Of course. Can I get anything for you, doctor?'

The doctor replied without looking up. 'Another blanket and a hot water bottle if you please.'

'Yes sir.' Liddy scurried from the room in order to complete her task as quickly as possible.

'Well, Gabriel, I've completed the examination and you will be pleased to hear, your son has no broken bones.'

Bathsheba lifted her head from the cradle of her hands. 'But why is he still unconscious, Dr. Melksham? Shouldn't he be awake by now?'

'I'm sure he'll be alright in a little while, m'dear. Young boys are extremely tough y'know.'

His reassuring tone did little to comfort the distraught mother.

'Sip this, Bathsheba. It will help.' Harriet handed her the glass Liddy had just bought.

The burning liquid made Bathsheba cough, she being unused to strong liquor but it did offer a small thread of comfort. As she did so, Matthew sat bolt upright.

'What's happened? How is Prince? Why am I in here? I should be at the stables.'

'Hush my man!' Dr. Melksham instructed. 'You've been involved in an accident. You must lie still. Can you tell us what happened?'

Bathsheba, her face now wreathed in smiles, asked Harriet to please inform the guests that her son was now out of imminent danger.

A sigh like a gentle breeze wafted round the room as they discovered Matthew was suffering only minor injuries for in that short time whilst the rescuing team were busy the company around the table had decided that the poor boy was at the worst dead or at best with both legs gone.

As they later found out, the accident had been Matthew's own fault because he had entered the stables quietly, startled Prince, causing the horse to rear backwards. In trying to get out of the way, Matthew had knocked his head on a slanting oak beam effecting him to be concussed. The poor dumb animal had merely looked on. Gabriel was pleased he would not have to use his gun on Prince for he knew Matthew would never have been able to forgive him.

The party continued until the early hours, the guests reluctant to leave the warmth and hospitality of the old manor. Outside the stars were glitteringly bright, suggesting perhaps a very early frost.

Gabriel reassured his wife, 'We'll not have frost this side of Michaelmas nor a good many weeks after.

Bathsheba said she was glad. In spite of being born and bred a country girl she hated the winter and the cold. If by magic she could have introduced tropical climes to Wessex then she would have.

Arms entwined about each other's waist the couple made their way up the wide oak staircase to the privacy of their boudoir.

'I'll just look in on Matthew before we settle down,' Bathsheba whispered to Gabriel as they paused outside their youngest son's door.

'Don't be long then,' Gabriel squeezed his wife's arm.

Matthew was sleeping peacefully, snoring a little every now and then.

Bathsheba closed the door quietly and was soon undressed and in bed next to her husband. She breathed a great sigh of relief as she snuggled up close to Gabriel. How could she have borne it if Matthew had been killed? She shuddered involuntarily.

'You alright, Bathsheba?'

'Yes; oh yes. I'm just thinking how lucky we are. Gabriel, should we perhaps encourage Matthew to follow in Adam's footsteps, you know, go to university?'

Gabriel by this time was almost as dead to the world as his son was in the next room for he had now been awake well past the first four acts of day. 'Yes, of course, Bathsheba,' he murmured sleepily.

Bathsheba smiled to herself. That's half the battle. One down, one to go.

Chapter Three
A Native returns.

'GUESS WHO'S GOING T'BE the new shepherd!' Andrew Smallbury was always at the forefront when there was any news worth the telling.

Jan Coggan's two sons were in Oakdene's far orchard gathering fallen apples to sell at Weatherbury market. Although there was an abundance of fruit and prices were lower than last year, both Mark and John knew there would be an eager crowd, travellers who'd come from far flung corners of Wessex, ready to bargain for the apples or barter for other sundry items, be they anything from milking stools to bundles of furze.

Since cider making had ceased at Oakdene, Gabriel had generously said they could help themselves to the mellow fallers. What he didn't know, or at least the farm workers were unaware that he knew was that a little shake of a branch or two would help good, plump apples to fall to the ground of their own accord. If one put a basket beneath the said tree in order to catch the falling fruit then it was either good luck or good judgement or both.

'Don't you want to know?' Andrew was not getting the interest he had anticipated.

The young men had heard through their father, Jan, who was Gabriel's confidante, who the new shepherd was to be but had been sworn to secrecy in case there were objections among the labourers, as strictly speaking he was all but a stranger. Local jobs usually went to local men unless they had been hired at the bi-annual hiring fair when they could have travelled a considerable distance. Even so, newcomers were often likened to a cuckoo in the nest and had to prove themselves before they were accepted.

Mark and John enjoyed teasing the carter's son as his sense of humour was somewhat limited to laughing at the plight of other people rather than at himself. They couldn't miss this God sent opportunity to give him a taste of his own medicine and waited to see Andrew's agitation at their apparent lack of interest, he being a hot tempered being. They didn't have long to wait. Soon the fiery-haired long streak of pump water was doing a jig around the apple basket, hopping first to the left and then to the right as if he was engaged in some ancient, medieval fertility rite.

'You need the fiddler to keep you in step,' Mark played an imaginary violin which further incensed the impatient Andrew.

He took a swipe at the fiddler who ducked as he was expecting the action, with the result that Andrew, wrong footed, landed head first in the apple basket.

The two boys were doubled up with mirth by this time and didn't notice the shadowy figure, hidden as he was by the lush greenness of the laurel hedging, observing what was going on.

Benjamin Tallboys was eager to see what Farmer Oak's workers looked like. He believed that much could be discerned from watching a person's behaviour without their knowledge. In his guise as shepherd he was hoping to educate these poverty stricken labourers so that they might fight together for a decent wage. He had been living in the neighbouring county of Somersetshire for the past eighteen years and the last time he had had contact with Gabriel was when the good shepherd himself was making plans to emigrate to California. That Gabriel had decided to abandon his plans and marry Bathsheba had come as no surprise to the new shepherd.

He had been about when Gabriel was first taken on as shepherd at Weatherbury farm, just as a casual worker for the haymaking, but he had come to know Gabriel well and was well aware of the strength of his feeling for the beautiful woman who, after dispensing with her untrustworthy bailiff, had run the farm herself.

Gabriel had updated him with the news of Bathsheba's marriage to the handsome dragoon guards sergeant and the subsequent tragic outcome. News had travelled as far as Somersetshire but Benjamin Tallboys had heard various accounts none of which matched exactly what Gabriel had told him but then that was what gossip was about. A minor disagreement can become that major condition called war after several times of telling. Who is it who has not heard of Chinese Whispers?

That the farm workers were a simple folk who did not often complain, worked hard and made a living as best they could, there was little doubt, but they deserved better and if Benjamin Tallboys was to live up to his reputation then he would see that they eventually got what was rightfully theirs. In his opinion the only way up was through education and knowledge. All he had to do was convince his fellow men likewise, convince them they had the right to a decent standard of living at all times, not just at the whim of the gentry.

Old Jan Coggan had told his sons who the new shepherd was to be. What he hadn't told them for fear they would blab all over the village was that with the express consent of Gabriel Oak, Benjamin Tallboys was to carry on where his uncle

George had been forced to leave off. Not exactly as militant a man as George had been, quite the reverse for he was known to be a gentlemanly man, Ben intended to set up a night school where anyone who wanted to better themselves would have the opportunity.

Gabriel had agreed to fund the project for the first year, then it was up to Ben and the students. Such is the dedication of a man excited by a new idea which is backed by an influential colleague, Ben knew he would succeed. Maybe his name would go down in history the way his uncle's had. Although Ben wanted recognition he was of that rare breed who wants to help his fellow man without monetary reward. If that came later then he would not of course object.

He was pleased with his observations. The boys were high spirited, not cowed down as he'd half expected they might be. It'd take a lot of spirit to do what would be necessary and with the fervour of John Knox, Benjamin Tallboys vowed to bring increased knowledge and opportunity to this particular part of Wessex, the place in which he had been born five and thirty years ago, left and now felt had been urged to return by some unseen, powerful force.

It was certainly opportune that Fred Cross had decided to leave shepherding at this particular time but Ben had a deep empathy with Mary Cross, his own wife Elizabeth having recently left him. Of course it wasn't exactly her fault for she had died in childbirth but Ben hadn't wanted her to take the risk as she was never strong having been struck down with an obscure fever when she was but a few years old. He hadn't even got the child to care for. The good Lord had seen fit to take her as well.

'Come on, Andrew Smallbury! Help us pick the rest of this fruit off the ground and you can have a part share in our gains,' Mark instructed.

Andrew picked himself up, assumed a haughty air, and did as he was bid. If they wanted to pretend that they knew everything then he was not going to play their silly games.

'Our father told us t'other day arter he'd bin to see the master about something or other. Don't ye take on so, Andrew Smallbury or you'll fall down with an apoplexy or something just as unpleasant.'

'What did your father have to say about the new shepherd, Mark Coggan? I've never heard of him in these parts afore.'

'He just said he's a gentlemanly man with forebears in these parts and thought he would have done better than shepherding with his edication.'

Andrew Smallbury wasn't satisfied. 'D'ye think he'll stay long hereabouts?'

'Goodness, let the man have a try at the job before you get rid of him,' John joined in.

The trio made their way back through the orchard picking up the odd apple or two they had somehow missed on the way. They were all looking forward to Saturday, for a Harvest Home at Oakdene had become legendary. The Saturday market should show them a good profit too. Pity Mother Coggan would need most of it but there should be enough to enjoy a glass or two of ale at the Bucks Head.

Benjamin Tallboys made his way back through the orchard, skirted round the edge of the meadow which bordered Oakdene's gardens and strode along the same path that later Gabriel would tread upon on his way from the hay fields. He hoped to catch his old friend but if he didn't they would meet later as arranged over a glass or two of ale at the King's Arms in Weatherbury. Gabriel had promised to look out for some suitable establishment where he could set up the institution. He hoped there wouldn't be any opposition from the gentleman farmers who employed the labourers. Some of them were against educating the peasants for fear they would become dissatisfied with their lot. The Martyrs of Tolpuddle lived on in the minds of some of the Wessex landowners. They didn't want any repetition of what had happened then. The labourers themselves may well ask; Cur valle permutem Sabina Divitias operosiores? if they had the knowledge.

Ben knew he was taking a chance but having decided on a course of action he was determined not to give in easily. At least not without an effort which would rival Hercules.

Chapter Four
Two men and a plan

GABRIEL, AFTER SOME CONSIDERATION, had chosen the King's Arms as the place most suitable for his rendezvous with Ben Tallboys for the simple reason it was not often frequented by his own employees. Gentlemen of a certain breeding were usually to be found there; farmers and landowners, merchants and artisans in the main. Occasionally one would find a local small trader who had hopes of attracting the more wealthy as potential customers but usually they preferred to mix with their own kind where they felt more comfortable and in their own words, "don't have to watch our P's and Q's.

No one seemed to know for sure how this had come about but there had been some speculation over the years. It could have been something to do with the fact that the ale was slightly higher in price than that to be found at the Bucks Head. True it was a fair walk to obtain the cheaper beer but many villagers would rather walk several miles than pay what they regarded as over the odds for their bevy.

John Jacobs was a jovial landlord. He'd have a joke with the best of them but he would not allow the fiddle to be played after a certain time of night. This also did not go down well with the more gregarious of folk often to be found among the lower classes. However it was the perfect place for discussion, be it the price of grain, speculation on the new trade unions which were beginning to spring up all over the place, or a deep philosophy about the meaning of life with the emphasis on how to improve a person's lot and it was the latter that Gabriel Oak and Ben Tallboys had on their agenda this evening.

The inn was divided into several small rooms the like of which could be seen in many village inns throughout England during the reign of Queen Victoria. Gabriel and Ben sat at a table not too close to the blazing log fire for although it was autumn and the nights were now cool, the two outdoor types could not abide to be over-heated. So, their table just inside the door was comfortable if you didn't count the minor bump or two to the table as some clumsy customer pushed the door open, in their exuberance, a bit too wide.

'Have you decided on the place yet, Gabriel?' Ben was eager to get started now he had almost completed his observations.

'Wouldn't ye like to settle in first, Ben. Get to know folk a bit. There's no hurry, y'know. They'll trust you more once they know you.'

'I don't expect a rush to my door as soon as I announce my plans, Gabriel. These things take time as well you know. For that very reason I should like the meeting place to be fixed as soon as possible.'

Gabriel smiled somewhat wryly. He wasn't sure if his old friend realised just what he was taking on. They were a bit stick in the mud were the locals and most had an abhorrence of change. What a commotion there had been when the navvies had arrived to dig the ground to prepare for the railway. Why, the crowd had become near riotous at one demonstration and had needed to be quelled by the local police force who had needed to seek reinforcements from Casterbridge and Kingsbere.

Still, they had come round in the end and now several of the more affluent enjoyed the excitement of the new form of travel and a trip to the seaside town of Budmouth, a little over ten miles from Weatherbury, was now in the realms of possibility for many people previously excluded from such travel.

'I've had a word with Parson Hansworth and he's agreed for you to use his front room parlour at the vicarage, as long as you can guarantee there will be no noisy fiddling and no singing, dancing or blasphemy.'

Benjamin threw back his head and laughed so loud that several bystanders, who had been deep in conversation at the bar, turned their heads to see what was so funny. They were keen to share the joke but Gabriel put up his hand as if to ward off any forthcoming enquiries, shaking his head as he did so. They quickly understood that it wasn't a joke to be shared.

'Singing and dancing are definitely not on the agenda you can be assured, Gabriel.'

Ben quickly got over his outburst which was partly due to his vision of Parson Hansworth laying down the law and partly to the fact that he had consumed several jars of ale.

'There is one other proviso.' Gabriel hesitated.

'Go on, man. Spit it out.' Benjamin Tallboys could be very outspoken at times even if he was speaking to his betters although usually he was most respectful. Why, he doffed his cap to the squire the same as any other man in these parts.

'You have to teach whatever verse from the bible the parson deems suitable depending on the time of year and "twill be entirely at his discretion,' he said, echoing the parson's very words.

Ben didn't see that as a problem although he did think the parson was off-loading what was rightfully the job of the preacher. But all in all it was a small price to pay for the use of the room and Benjamin was a god-fearing man, had been brought up to read the scriptures and knew them reasonably well. It certainly wasn't a problem. He rubbed his hands together gleefully.

'When can I start, Gabriel?'

The two men rose simultaneously as if drawn upwards by some invisible scarlet thread.

'Sunday then, Ben, after the morning service.'

'Sunday it is then!'

They shook hands causing the other occupants of the bar to think both men had clinched some very profitable business. 'Twas true in a way but not in the way those business men who had only pecuniary gain uppermost in their minds would have guessed.

Bathsheba was alone when Gabriel arrived back at Oakdene. Several of her near neighbours had been to visit, for once a week Bathsheba would have an evening of poetry reading taking the opportunity to arrange the gathering when she knew Gabriel would be otherwise engaged. Much as he liked reading, he did not share Bathsheba's newly acquired passion for works of the bards.

Usually it turned out to be a time to catch up on the local gossip or at least to discuss the local news in much the same way as the men did at the King's Arms. Sometimes there was little poetry reading actually performed. Tonight had been different for the woman had just started to read the Lucy poems of Wordsworth and Coleridge. It was Harriet's idea for she used to teach at a finishing school in Exonbury and she had told her new friends how much the young ladies had enjoyed them.

Gabriel was tired and didn't wish to be drawn into a long discussion on the merits of the Lakeland poets.

'If you would just like to read me one verse, I'll be satisfied.' The husband yawned widely and settled himself in his chair prepared to listen.

Bathsheba opened the book and began;

'She dwelt among th'untrodden ways
Beside the springs of Dove
A Maid whom there were none to praise
And very few to love.'

'That's beautiful, Bathsheba. I don't mind listening to another verse of that.'

Gabriel loved to listen to Bathsheba for she had a very pleasant tenor to her voice and was particularly accomplished musically. He settled back in his familiar chair ready to be lulled into a sleepy oblivion.

Bathsheba continued. When she reached "But she is in her Grave, and Oh! The difference to me." Gabriel sat upright.

Thinking it was her reading of the poem that had disturbed her husband, Bathsheba reached over and patted his arm preparing to apologise.

'It's alright, Bathsheba. It just brought back memories of Fanny Robin for some reason. I can't say why.'

'I had the very same thoughts earlier. 'Tis strange the way some things are so evocative. Perhaps it was the mention that Lucy had very few to love. Fanny Robin was sadly alone when she died for you can't call the workhouse a friendly place to be.'

'We must make sure nothing like that ever happens to our children, Bathsheba. There! That poem has made me rather maudlin and morose and I came home in quite a different frame of mind. I said I didn't wish to enter into a discussion about poetry. It always seems to affect me in this way.'

Bathsheba looked up at her husband remembering the words he had said to her many years ago.

Do you remember, Gabriel, what you used to say to me when we were first wed?'

It was as familiar as the sunrise and now he repeated the phrase.

'When I look up, there you be.'

Now, Bathsheba repeated that comforting phrase.

The couple laughed, forgetting their previous fit of melancholy.

'Let's go to bed and I'll tell you about the plans Benjamin Tallboys and I have made this evening.

The poetry evening had ended when the shadows of twilight began to fall. The ladies had gathered up their books and headed for home as the reddening sun cast long shadows across the heath, for no one enjoyed being out after dark, at least not alone. Bathsheba was glad she was at home for she loved Oakdene almost as much as she loved those dearest to her. As she reached the borders of sleep, she hoped, quite irrationally, that she would never have to choose between the two but if she should she would have to rely on providence to be her guide. In her innermost mind she felt sure that day would never come.

Chapter Five
No Work on the Sabbath.

THE LATE-MEDIEVAL CHURCH AT Weatherbury had escaped so far the attention of the improvement zealots although the architectural change which was sweeping the land like the wind, from which no hiding place could be found, was sadly destroying the ancient characteristics of many country churches. Some alterations to the twelfth century tower had been carried out; it had been widened in the thirteenth century and heightened in the fifteenth century. Now, on this first Sunday after the harvest had been safely gathered in, the grey stone walls resounded with,'Come ye thankful people come',and other favourite harvest hymns as the congregation gave thanks for the successful harvest.

Everyone within the blessed place had their own good reason to thank the Lord. Full barns equated with full stomachs and an assured income for farmers, regardless of how hard the coming winter months might be. For the labourers, there would be a good chance of full employment and therefore full bellies for them and their families.

Generally speaking it was a happy throng who emerged from the church. They shook hands with Parson Hansworth, passing him in single file as he stood resplendent in his white cassock, winged sentry-like, in the shadowed Gothick porch on that sunny October morning.

For most of the men of the parish it had been something of an effort to attend the early morning service for they had taken advantage of the freely flowing ale and cider at the Harvest Home on the previous evening. Those who had partaken of the lethal metheglin were suffering most. One or two who we shall not call by name but of whom the parson had made a mental note failed to turn up. They were not in the best of health in spite of caring wives plying them with the latest cure for sore heads. As a last resort, the oldest one of the afflicted had tried "the hair of the dog that bit" to no avail except he was now sleeping the sleep that is the friend of Woe.

The Harvest supper and dance in the Great Barn had been a rowdy, rip-roaring success. Gabriel proclaimed it was the best one ever, but then he always did.

Bathsheba, as she always did, had asked him to check the hayricks and he had been able to reassure her with a knowing smile, 'All safely covered.'

It had become as much part of the ritual as arranging the fiddlers and preparing the food. Since the awful storm which had taken place, why it must be twenty years ago now, the checking and re-checking had become a habit they dare not break for fear of challenging the fates. Although Bathsheba and Gabriel laughed at their own obsession, deep down they knew, as everyone with the smallest grain of common sense knew, just how disastrous a sudden storm could be. All their profits could quite easily be lost as they nearly had been all those years ago. Once the ritual was over they could relax and enjoy themselves and that is exactly what they did.

Young Bathsheba was particularly happy. Her new, pale blue dress of the finest shot silk showed off her budding charms to perfection. Gabriel, on seeing his daughter daintily descend the wide oak staircase, had likened her to a royal princess, causing her cheeks to change from delicate pink to fiery red.

She had danced most of the evening with Adam's friend, George Abbot. They had first met several years ago when George and Adam had been new boys at the Casterbridge Grammar school. Gabriel, inquisitive about the kind of boy who attended the school, he never having gone to such a school, had invited George and his family to a meal at Oakdene in order to get to know his son's new friend. He had approved of George immediately and had formed a long and lasting friendship with his father, Joseph Abbot. It wasn't too long before Bathsheba and Louisa Abbot had also formed a long and lasting sisterly friendship. Fortune had indeed been smiling on them all, the day the two boys had met, for the two families were now inseparable, sharing many of the usual ups and the downs of life in a farming community.

In spite of the difference in their personalities, they were like chalk and cheese, the two boys had surprisingly also remained friends. Adam, when given the choice, preferred not to exert himself physically but George loved the outdoors and was to follow in his father's footsteps, eventually taking over the running of the family farm. He had just started a course of study at the Royal Agricultural College, Corinchester and would help his father run Acorn Farm, two hundred acres of chalky downland between Abbots Cernel and Godwinstone, as soon as he was qualified. Already he had suggested his father buy one of the new steam threshing machine to cut labour costs and speed up the whole procedure. His father had promised to think about the purchase but was not one to make hasty decisions. He had promised to discuss the proposition with Gabriel in the next few weeks. They might decide to share the cost as that seemed to be the latest idea according to George.

Now had come the time for the parting of the ways for the two young men. Adam was off to Christminster in two day's time in preparation for the start of the Michaelmas term and really couldn't wait to start on his studies and meet like-minded new friends. He had very few qualms about leaving his old friends in Weatherbury and its environs.

Outside Weatherbury church the worshippers gradually dispersed to go their own ways. Sunday being a day of rest for most folk, they meant to take advantage of the good weather, which still held although a few grey clouds were just beginning to appear on the horizon. It wouldn't be long before the rains came, and once they started summer would be well and truly over.

Sheba promised her mother she would be back in time for the midday meal and quickly made her way down the forking gravel path which led either through the lych gate and to the village beyond or if the left fork were chosen then the back of the church could be reached. She had noticed George Abbot take the left fork and now as she skirted round the corner of the ancient building she could see him deep in conversation with Adam. They were sitting irreverently on a crumbling, grey tombstone in the corner of the churchyard.

George stood up as Sheba approached.

'Good morning, Bathsheba. I was just bidding farewell to your brother.' He smiled, raised his hat and turned as if to go.

Sheba blushed with pleasure at the use of her full name. Everyone had called her Sheba for as long as she could remember. As her father had pointed out, it was less confusing to have one Bathsheba and one Sheba in the house.

'I was hoping to have a word, George.' Sheba suddenly realised she had no idea what it was she wanted to say to the handsome youth. For years she had been conversing with George with ease. Now her feelings had undergone a subtle change, a change she didn't immediately recognise, and she felt nervous and tongue-tied. On the spur of the moment she invited George to see Westy's new puppies.

'I'm afraid I can't just now as father's waiting for me,' the youth apologised.

George would dearly have liked to stay a while with this pretty young girl he had so recently begun to admire but he knew his father would not tolerate lateness so it would have perforce to be some other time.

Thinking he wasn't at all interested in her, a despondent and somewhat embarrassed Bathsheba seized her brother's arm and demanded that he look at the puppies.

Too surprised to resist, Adam went along with his sister.

Once out of earshot, Adam turned to Sheba, 'What was that all about? Matthew's looking after the dogs. Can't you ask him?'

'It was nothing. Really!' she emphasised. 'I just thought George might like to have one of Westy's puppies when they are grown big enough.'

Adam had noticed the delicate blush on his sister's cheeks and as daylight dawned he decided kindly not to persist with his questioning. He suddenly realised that his little sister was fast becoming a beautiful young lady. He would have a quiet word with George if he got the chance but he was doubtful whether the opportunity would arise. He would probably not see him until the Christmas vacation as their colleges were miles apart. They were both going to be extremely busy with the promising new life which lay before them, too busy to give more than a passing thought to their old, country way of life.

When brother and sister arrived back at Oakdene, Adam's trunk had been placed in the Great Hall ready for collection. Sheba felt a funny twingeing sensation in the pit of her stomach as she realised she would not see her brother at all for the next few months. They didn't always see eye to eye but there was a strong bond between them and impulsively Sheba turned and hugged her brother.

'Hey, what's all this about?' Adam was a little discomforted at his sister's sudden show of affection. He didn't know quite what to do so he turned and ran up the wide staircase, taking the steps two at a time like a gazelle in flight in an attempt to hide his embarrassment.

Bathsheba, hearing the commotion, called for a little peace and quiet, reminding them that it was the Sabbath. Sheba shouted an apology and left the Great Hall for the sanctuary of her boudoir. She didn't want to be questioned about her morning's activities for fear of giving away her feelings for George. She knew she would be teased unmercifully by her family if they knew she had a crush on George Abbot. Why, horror of horrors, he might even get to hear about it and then what would she do? Sheba decided she would have to be very careful whenever George's name was mentioned in future for she seemed totally unable to control the tell-tale blush which rose unbidden to her cheeks.

As she lay in her bed that night, Sheba made a decision. As George was obviously not interested in her then she would never marry. She would ask her father to arrange for her to go to the teacher training college in Melchester as soon as possible and then she need never see George again.

It was a dark night, the once bright moon now obscured by heavy clouds. The rain, which had threatened earlier, had put in an appearance and Sheba listened to the pitter patter of the rain drops as they fell gently on her window pane. Later on there would be a storm but Sheba was ignorant of that fact for she was soon fast asleep, safe in the arms of Morpheus.

Chapter Six
A Turn for the Better.

OAKDENE WAS STRANGELY QUIET now that Adam and Sheba had gone away. Matthew was at school all day and when he got home he would oftimes join his father in the fields where there was always plenty of jobs needing and waiting to be done. Any spare time he did have he would spend at the stables with Jacob Millson the groom or in good weather he'd be out in the countryside riding his beloved Prince who had now quite recovered from the shock of seeing his master hurt.

Sheba had sought safety in business.

It had been decided that as her dearest wish was to become a teacher, the family had consulted with Harriet as she had before her marriage worked as a mistress at Exonbury College, Sheba must spend a year at the finishing college prior to going to Melchester for her formal teacher training. Happy at this decision, Sheba had sent for the necessary books immediately, happy to keep her mind occupied and delighted at the prospect of moving away from Oakdene so soon.

So engrossed in her preparation for the new course was she that her mother found it difficult to persuade her to put down the new literature even when a shopping trip to Casterbridge had been deemed necessary.

Much as she loved the house and her family and would undoubtedly miss them all whilst away on her studies, the thought constantly uppermost in her mind was the morning when George had rejected her. It did not occur to her for one minute that the young man in question might have been genuine in his reason for not accompanying her on her expedition to see the puppies. Her youthful innocence and inexperience were to blame but Sheba still had a young head on her young shoulders and could not be expected to have the reasoning power and maturity of her elders.

If only George shared her feelings, Sheba had explained to her beloved Westy on the day prior to her leaving Weatherbury she would have been happy to have stayed at home, helping her mother with the daily tasks and joining in with the social life of the village as she had done all summer; she would have been content to wait until George returned to Acorn Farm for good. Her single resolve now was to become a good teacher, perhaps starting a school in some deprived part of Wessex which as yet had no such establishment.

Maybe that was what the fates had decided for the young Bathsheba. Only time would tell.

Several days later, history was seen to repeat itself for there in the Great Hall stood a large trunk waiting for collection. This time its destination was in the opposite direction to Christminster; the new carriage service would take the container west, to Exonbury. The very next day the owner would follow, to begin the exciting journey, which she hoped would remedy the heart ache she now felt; stop the disease before it was too late, and bring its own rewards.

Bathsheba guessed there was more to Sheba's hurried decision than pure altruism. Her instinct told her that her daughter was in love but unless Sheba chose to confide in her there was little she could do. The mother consoled herself with the fact that although her daughter felt she was destined for a life dedicated to helping others, only when she had tried this new way of life and realised it was not her destiny, would she return to Oakdene and carry on the life her parents desired for her.

It was now Michaelmas and Gabriel had been right as usual about the weather as there had been no sign of any frost so far, although the nights were dropping in fast, and it was quite chilly in the evenings and early in the mornings. Often the mist would obscure from view the trees in the orchard until well after breakfast.

Matthew had been a new boy at Casterbridge Grammar school for the past few weeks and just as Adam had settled there and made new friends so had Matthew. Already he was talking of a career as an animal doctor which came as no surprise to his parents so recently Gabriel had made it his business to ask the head teacher about the qualifications necessary for such a career. The master had assured Gabriel that there was plenty of time to make arrangements as Matthew would be at the Grammar school until he was at least sixteen years of age then they would decide. As Gabriel had told Bathsheba later when reporting on the matter, there was no doubt in his mind that Matthew would "take to animal doctoring very well, when the time came".

As Bathsheba began to show signs of the empty nest syndrome Gabriel suggested they have "a bit of a party" or maybe "go to the fair at Budmouth". Cheered up at the prospect she invited their good friends, Theodore and Harriet Melksham and the Abbots, who when replying in the affirmative asked if they might bring along two guests so that they could combine business with pleasure.

'Who are the Godwins, Gabriel?' Bathsheba had heard the name but was not acquainted with the family.

'They live over at Martinsham Hall. He's the Godwin of the firm, Martin and Godwin; you remember, they make steam engines?' Gabriel paused to see if his wife did indeed remember.

Bathsheba nodded. 'I've heard of the firm. Didn't they build that new model village t'other side of Casterbridge, Gabriel?'

'That's how he got his knighthood so 'tis said. I've heard they're a very decent sort of couple though. No airs and graces and the like in spite of them being so wealthy, and titled.'

'Thank goodness for that. I can't abide people who pretend they're better than they are,' Bathsheba was emphatic in her denouncement of the pretentious.

Nevertheless, she decided to make the evening special, buying a new dress and taking extra care with her hairdressing. She had been feeling a little more tired than usual but had put it down to the extra energy required to put into operation the new plans they had made. Of course the sadness at losing two of her siblings may have had something to do with her feeling of sadness and malaise.

The decision to increase the dairy herd at the expense of some of the arable land had meant an inordinate amount of organisation making Bathsheba wish at times she had left things as they were. Perhaps she would have a chat with Dr. Melksham after dinner if the opportunity arose. There were so many new medicines available these days that he was bound to recommend something she could take. Best not to mention it to Gabriel as it was bound to turn out to be nothing serious and she knew he would only worry.

The opportunity did not arise because when the men and women met up again after the cigar smoking and the port drinking, the conversation was dominated by Gabriel's plan for all four couples to go to the fair at Budmouth at the coming weekend. As well as a hiring fair, Gabriel, Joseph and Cornelius needed new workers, so they would again be able to combine business with pleasure. Cornelius had recently opened another factory, which made high-class carpets, and he needed men to work the massive looms. The wages were good, better than working on the land and Gabriel and Joseph showed some concern that the men might prefer factory work and then they would find it difficult to get labourers. Although said in jest there was an underlying concern in the statement.

There would be entertainment and sideshows for the ladies to enjoy, and the men of course once the business of the day was finished.

'Sir Cornelius and Lady Emma Godwin are two of the nicest people I've ever met, Gabriel.' Bathsheba was enthusiastic in her praise of their new acquaintances.

'I'm surprised we've never met them before,' Gabriel's forehead was furrowed in his puzzlement making his thick greying eyebrows almost meet. 'I did hear he was hell bent on buying up small farms over in the west but he never approached me. I should have sent him packing if he had.'

Bathsheba laughed at her husband's fierceness. He so loved Weatherbury farm; nothing short of an act of the good Lord would make him give up his precious land. How she loved her man. Why she wouldn't change him for all the Sir Galahads in Kingdom Come wherever that might be and she told him so. The feeling was mutual.

'You looked beautiful this evening, Bathsheba.' Gabriel was helping his wife to unpin the hairstyle she had so carefully prepared earlier.

'Don't I always?' She replied teasingly.

In his reply, Gabriel, although not a man given to indulging in hyperbole, made no bones about how well he thought his wife always looked.

'As pretty as the Lady Emma?' Bathsheba wanted to know. Emma Godwin, only a little younger than Bathsheba, was still a strikingly handsome woman and must have been overwhelmingly beautiful in her youth. Knowing she'd been looking a bit pale and feeling a little tired of late, Bathsheba really would have felt better had she been able to have that word with Doctor Melksham. However, after an excellent meal with particularly pleasant guests, and enough good wine she was feeling much more like her old self but a little reassurance from a loving husband wouldn't go amiss.

Gabriel was not sure how to put into words what he wanted to say without upsetting her. He decided to be blunt.

'You have looked a bit tired lately my dear. Perhaps you should have a word with Theodore Melksham tomorrow.'

'Now, now, Gabriel. I'm fine. 'Tis true I've been a little bit under the weather but I'm alright now,' Bathsheba assured him. 'Come,' she invited taking his arm. 'I'll show you how well I am.'

Soon convinced, Gabriel blew out the candle satisfied. He wouldn't know what to do without Bathsheba. Why, it was too awful to contemplate. He was glad she had managed to convince him that she was back on form. They both fell asleep happy; both were looking forward to the future with eager anticipation.

Chapter Seven
Education on the Agenda

BATHSHEBA WOKE SUDDENLY FROM a dreamless, uninvaded sleep blaming the noisy cockerel for waking her at the crack of dawn. Not wanting to wake Gabriel who hadn't yet been disturbed by the cacophony and was sleeping soundly, she crept quietly from their bed, picking up her wrap as there was now that familiar nip of Autumn in the air. It was scarcely dawn and from the oriel window on the landing Bathsheba could see the Moon on the wane. The cockerel, who had ceased his crowing temporarily, and the birds, who had not yet woken from their nests in the leafy arbour, effected a ghostly quiet which pervaded the old manor house creating an atmosphere of eerie expectation.

Shivering, Bathsheba decided to make her way to the kitchen to see if Maryann was up and about. As she reached the top of the staircase a wave of nausea swept over her causing her to clutch at the newel post for support. Recovering quickly she grinned to herself, "That'll teach me to over-indulge."

In the kitchen, Maryann had already lit the monstrous black range and the warmth enveloped Bathsheba as she opened the door. Again the same feeling of nausea engulfed her and she swayed, leaning on the door jamb for support this time. Recovering quickly once again, she made her way to the old cook's chair which stood in its permanent position by the fire. Seeing her mistress in distress, Maryann poured a cup of tea and offered it to the pale looking woman.

'There Missus, drink that. You'll soon feel better,' Maryann said kindly. She had given birth to seven children, four of whom were still alive and she knew pregnancy when she saw it.

'I'm afraid I rather over-indulged last evening, Maryann. We had such splendid guests that the time just slipped away without any of us realising it and the wine flowed altogether too freely.'

Maryann was nonplussed. Did her mistress really think it was the wine that was to blame for her condition? She decided to humour Bathsheba, after all she was the mistress and time could be relied upon to tell the truth.

'When would you like breakfast, Ma'am, that is if you're feeling better?'

'Usual time, Maryann. Mr. Oak will want to be off on time and there is Matthew to consider.'

'Young master's had "is, Ma'am. Gorn off to the stables. Said as "ow he wanted to ride Prince before school now the nights are dropping in.'

'But it's hardly light yet, Maryann. What is he thinking of?' Bathsheba vowed to put her foot down where the young man was concerned, or at least ask Gabriel to put his foot down. He was asking for trouble riding before dawn.

Gabriel turned over sleepily putting his arm out to give his wife the customary cuddle. After groping about for a few seconds, he realised the distaff side of the bed was empty. Bathsheba seldom arose before him so, assuming something was amiss, he left the comfort of the tester and made his way downstairs. Bathsheba was just on her way up.

'Where've you been? Is anything wrong?'

Bathsheba shook her head and immediately wished she hadn't for the nausea struck again.

'O, Gabriel! I'm afraid the wine did me no good at all. I shall avoid intoxicating liquor in the future,' Bathsheba vowed.

Many times Gabriel had echoed the very same sentiments so he was able to empathise with his wife. 'You'll be alright in a few hours. Why don't you go back to bed?'

Bathsheba agreed for once and without argument returned to their boudoir thankfully. She was a little perplexed as she was usually unaffected by wine. Maybe it was the salmon she had eaten. She wasn't sure but was glad later that morning to feel well enough to visit Dr. Melksham.

'How long have you had the symptoms, Bathsheba?' Dr. Melksham enquired kindly.

'The tiredness a few weeks, Theodore, the nausea is new.' Bathsheba suddenly realised as she talked to the doctor what it was that was wrong with her. The earlier symptoms which had led her to believe she was getting too old to have any more children had been misleading in the extreme. Now she breathed a great sigh, partly with relief that it was nothing serious after all and partly with dread. Did she and Gabriel really want to increase their family at their time of life? She wasn't sure about her own feelings and she certainly didn't know how Gabriel would react.

'Well, Bathsheba,' Dr. Melksham began.

'I'm with child, aren't I?'

'You most certainly are, Bathsheba,' the good doctor was beaming. 'It will be just after Harriet gives birth. How splendid. The children will grow up together.'

Bathsheba nodded in agreement. She had to get out of the room, as quickly as possible. She needed time to think.

'Yes,' she agreed distractedly putting out a hand to shake the doctor's own. 'It will be ...er, nice for them.'

Bemused and not a little bewildered, Bathsheba made her way back to the sanctuary of Oakdene but diverted to the summer house. It was little more than a wooden hut built for the children to play in on rainy days but they had long since ceased to use it. Now it was a haven, a refuge, where she could deliberate on the astounding news.

Gabriel was late home that night. He had met with Benjamin Tallboys in the Kings Arms after work and had stayed much longer than he had meant to.

Once again the men sat at the usual table just inside the door. When they had been served with their measures of ale, Gabriel put his arms on the table and leaned across eager to hear whether the first meeting had been successful.

'What news, Ben?'

'Nothing dramatic, Gabriel. Only three turned up and one of they didn't stay for more than half an hour. Made some excuse about his wife being worried if he was late.'

'Sounds a bit feeble to me,' Gabriel was disappointed. 'What about the other two? They coming back then?'

'Oh, yes. They're as eager for the fray as Richard the third was to do battle so much do they want to improve themselves. Both said they'd had practically no education as money was so short when they were boys.'

'Am I to know the names of the new scholars,' Gabriel was inquisitive. 'I promise not to tell anyone if that's what they wish.'

'I can't really keep names secret although the men would prefer it that way. I think they fear reprisals from their employers if news gets out they're trying to better themselves.'

'I understand, Ben, but it's not to be a secret society, is it.' The question was rhetorical and Gabriel was serious. There was more likely to be trouble if there was gossip. Much better to be open about what Ben was offering.

'We'll discuss it at the next meeting, Gabriel. Why don't you drop in yourself?' Ben invited.

'Good idea. I'll do that. That's if I won't be intruding.' The last thing Gabriel wanted was that Ben should think he couldn't trust him.

'We've arranged next Monday. Shall we see you then?'

'I think that'll be alright. Now, Ben, are you going to tell me just what you hope to teach these new pupils of yours?'

The discussion went on at length which is why Gabriel was home later than usual. Ben explained how he planned to play it by ear a bit as he wasn't sure what the interested parties wanted to learn or more to the point how much they already knew. Some would have received some form of education, maybe even have attended school for a few short years. At the very least some may have learned to read a little from attending Sunday School.

'The most important thing, Gabriel, is that they learn to read and write. Then they stand a better chance of getting on in this world.'

Gabriel agreed. He was happy to leave the organisation to Ben Tallboys. He was a capable fellow and able more than most to express himself clearly.

'I'll be off then, Ben. But I'll have a word with the Coggan boys, make sure they come along with me next Monday. Young Andrew Smallbury can come too. He could do with a bit of educating,' and as an afterthought,' and anyone else I can persuade.' Gabriel laughed then stood up as the landlord called time.

Ben sat and finished his ale. He was surprised Gabriel was so keen. It was doubtful whether he realised that there may be trouble if his plan came to fruition. Maybe he should put him completely in the picture. He was fond of old Gabriel and the last thing he wanted was to cause any animosity amongst the local farmers. But, he was a man who had the courage of his own convictions and he hadn't spent years planning an Agricultural Labourers Union only to give up if it meant hurting a few friends. If it should come to that then he would be saddened but if that's what it took, so be it.

Bathsheba was already asleep when Gabriel eventually crawled into bed. He kissed her gently trying not to wake her. It was the fair tomorrow and knowing she'd been a bit off colour decided a good night's sleep was just what she needed to put her to rights.

Having undressed by the light of the Moon, he failed to see the hurriedly scribbled note on the table next to the bed. It said:

'Wake me when you come in. I have some important news!'

B.

Chapter Eight
Incident at the Fair.

BATHSHEBA WAS UP FIRST for reasons which were now apparent to all but a few in the household. Unfortunately, the expectant father was numbered among the ignorant for the simple reason that in doing his wife the favour of letting her sleep when he arrived home late he had failed to see her note asking him to waken her. In so doing he had inadvertently done himself and her a gross disfavour for the news Bathsheba wanted so badly to share with her husband remained unsaid.

It was the morning of the Budmouth fair and Bathsheba was busy once again in the warm kitchen of the farmhouse, this time making arrangements for the forthcoming outing and picnic. Maryann had laid out various cold meats and cheeses; they were wrapped in muslin cloth ready to be packed into wicker hampers. The bread was still baking in the oven so would be deliciously fresh for the lunch-time repast. Gabriel had chosen the wine and put out the kegs of ale. Bathsheba shuddered as she noticed the beverages standing proudly on the dresser waiting to be packed. To think she had been so naive as to think it was alcohol that was responsible for her nausea.

'Feeling better, today, Ma'am?' Maryann enquired placing a brimming cup of tea on the table next to her mistress.

'Thank you Maryann; a little better except for this wretched sickness.'

'Well, 'tis only to be expected, if you'll pardon the pun, Mrs. Oak, ma'am.'

'Does everyone know that I'm with child, Maryann?' Bathsheba was taken aback. She hadn't realised the astute cook had been aware of her condition. She felt a little foolish that she hadn't realised it herself.

The cook reminded Bathsheba that she herself had given birth to a number of children and had helped many a neighbour in their hour of need. "It's a common enough condition and truly the first thing a woman knows if things aren't as they should be, if you know what I mean.'

'Yes,' Bathsheba hesitated, 'But I'm at the time of my life when...,' she didn't know how to explain to this down-to-earth woman who she felt knew more than she did herself.

'You mean the change, Mrs. Oak? You're a bit young for that, I should think.'

Obviously, Bathsheba thought, but decided to change the subject.

'Are there any sweetmeats for the hamper, Maryann?'

'I put them in a separate container as I thought they might get tainted by the cheese as 'tis so ripe.'

'Thank you. Is breakfast ready now?'

'I'll bring it to table in about ten minutes, ma'am, if that's alright.'

As Bathsheba climbed the stone steps which led from the kitchen to the oak panelled dining room the glare of the sun through the round window over the door threw long beams across the dark hallway. Dust motes floated in the beams and

Bathsheba paused, suddenly reminded of her own mortality. The phrase "ashes to ashes, dust to dust" went round in her head like a fairground ride. She sat down on the worn leather porter's chair in the hallway wondering whether the unexpected pregnancy was affecting her mind.

The dining room door opened noisily, startling her out of her reverie.

'We're just off, Bathsheba.' Gabriel pecked her cheek as he passed. He was already at the dairy in his mind.

'Gabriel,' his wife began. She really must tell him about the baby, the sooner the better.

'I haven't forgotten 'tis the fair. I'll be back in good time.' he promised as he disappeared out of the door closely followed by Matthew who was on his way to school in Casterbridge.

I must have been in the kitchen longer than I thought. O well, I'll tell him eventually. I suppose another day doesn't matter all that much. I'll tell him tomorrow, she promised herself on her way to the dining room.

The friends had arranged to meet at the Ring, just outside Casterbridge on the Budmouth road. When Gabriel and Bathsheba arrived the others were already waiting. The Godwin carriage was to transport all four ladies, Cornelius and Theodore. Gabriel and Joseph would go on ahead on horseback. It was a fine October day and had the leaves not taken on the colourful Autumn hues of some great Turnerish work of art it could easily have been mistaken for a day in summer. It was a delightful ride to the seaside town of Budmouth as Cornelius had seen fit to order an open topped landau. The conversation quickly became animated as the travellers drew near to their destination. Everyone, without exception, was looking forward to the forthcoming entertainment. For a short while Bathsheba forgot her worrying, pregnant, condition.

Harriet was looking extremely well and it wasn't until Emma asked when the child was due that Bathsheba remembered her own plight. She felt her face blanch and immediately became aware of the look of concern on Harriet's face. Bathsheba put a finger to her mouth indicating she wanted no talk of her own condition at this stage. Perhaps many people already knew or had guessed but in fairness to Gabriel she refused to talk about it to anyone until she had discussed it with the expectant father.

They could hear the noise and smell the acrid odour of the steam engines long before they arrived at the fairground. It was a popular happening and carriages seemed to be arriving from all directions. So that the ladies would not muddy their frocks unduly the liveried carriage driver put them down on the white path just inside the field gate. The three men who had business to do went off promising to be as quick as possible. They too wanted to enjoy all the fun of the fair. Gallantly, Theodore offered to escort the ladies, knowing he would receive many envious glances from his fellow men, at the bevy of beauty around him

The ladies were keen to try their luck at the hoopla so off they went, leaving the men to go about their business in the next field where folk who were seeking employment were milling about. Theodore reluctantly agreed to try his luck at throwing some hoops and to his and the stallholder's amazement secured for himself a prize. Louisa, Bathsheba and Harriet were unlucky because their lack of height was something of a handicap. Emma, the tallest by far, at her third attempt won a little porcelain ornament, which pleased them all.

Bathsheba noticed an advertisement emblazoned across a nearby tent, SEE THE SMALLEST MAN IN THE WORLD, so off they all went to gaze on some poor unfortunate fellow who was childlike in stature but had the wizened features of an old man. Harriet wasn't happy at the sight so they soon left to make their way to the refreshment table.

It seemed there would not be time to do everything everyone wanted to do so by mutual consent they decided to split up into two groups. Harriet would accompany her husband as she wanted to see his prowess on the shooting range. She managed to persuade Louisa to go with them with the promise of a prize for her, assuming Theodore was as good with a gun as he professed to be.

That left Bathsheba and Emma free to walk around the various stalls trying their hands at anything they fancied.

'Have you ever been on a carousel, Bathsheba?' Lady Godwin enquired of her new friend.

'Not since I was no more than nine or ten,' Bathsheba laughed. 'Have you?'

Emma said no she'd never got around to it and suggested they be daring and have a go now before they were too old.

'Yes! Let's go. We've another half an hour before we have to meet the others.'

The noise of the traction engine was deafening but this only added to the excitement of the carousel. Emma climbed on to a white-painted pony with blast-beruffled plumage; Bathsheba chose the bird next to her which just happened to be a multi-coloured cockerel, its plumes flashing red and gold in the sunlight. Soon the full-hearted music started once again growing louder as the ride gathered momentum. The ladies clung to the golden barley sugar poles as if their very lives depended on it.

As Emma's pony began to rise and fall, she looked out over the blur of faces watching the ride. They began to whirl faster and faster until Emma's eyes could no longer follow them and she had to look away. She glanced across at Bathsheba whose face had turned a ghostly white but it was impossible to make herself heard above the din of the engines and the music. Emma clutched at the pole with both hands, trying to signal to her friend to do the same but it was too late. Bathsheba had felt the now familiar feeling of nausea, could feel her hands slipping but could do nothing about it. The din pounded her ear drums as she swayed knowing there was little she could do to prevent herself from falling. The last thing she remembered was the sky whirling above her and the awful, familiar sensation of falling she'd experienced occasionally but only in her dreams.

The ride was stopped almost immediately but Bathsheba had lost consciousness by this time. Soon an anxious crowd gathered around the unconscious woman lying on the ground. As the authoritative voice of Theodore shouted, 'Let me through, I'm a physician. For goodness sake let me get to her!' the crowd parted like the sea at the command of the Lord.

Emma was bending over Bathsheba, gently waving some sal volatile under her nose in a vain attempt to revive her stricken friend. The tiny red stain which suddenly appeared on Bathsheba's pale yellow dress was spreading quickly like melting snow.

'She seems to have injured herself, Dr. Melksham. Near the top of her leg. See, she is bleeding.' Emma was at a loss as to know what to do.

Theodore realised immediately what had happened but was reluctant to say in front of the huge dense crowd which had appeared as if from nowhere.

'We must get her home. She needs urgent medical treatment.'

'I'll get Roberts to fetch the carriage. It will be quicker to take her to Martinsham Hall.' Emma had forgotten her anxiety in the need for prompt action.

'Yes, I'll travel with her. Could you stay and tell Gabriel what has happened?' The doctor asked his wife who, on hearing the commotion had caught up with her husband and friends.

'Of course, Theodore.' Harriet was happy to move away from the crowd, to make her way back to the refreshment tent where they had arranged to meet at tea time.

Once in the carriage, Bathsheba began to stir. The rocking of the carriage was jarring on her already painful abdomen and she couldn't stop herself from crying out.

'It's alright, Bathsheba.' Emma held her hand, 'We'll soon have you comfortable at the Hall.'

Bathsheba lifted her head a little and at once saw the blood red stain on her gown.

Sobbing she turned to the doctor, 'Do something please,' she begged. 'I don't want to lose it.'

Theodore took hold of his patients hand. 'Try to stay calm my dear. Getting in a state will do far more harm than good as I'm sure you realise.'

As realisation dawned Emma gasped for it brought back unhappy memories she would rather have forgotten for ever. She too, long, long ago had been through a similar devastating experience. At least she could empathise with her new friend and make sure she received the best medical treatment money could buy.

It was hard to find words which would adequately express the grief she felt for Bathsheba but she tried. 'I'm so sorry Bathsheba. I shouldn't have asked you to ride on the merry-go-round.'

'It's not your fault, Emma. Really! Tell her Theodore.'

'She's quite right, Lady Godwin. You couldn't possibly have known.'

'You must stay at the Hall until you are quite recovered. I insist.'

Once in the spacious bed-chamber, tucked up in the grand four-poster kept only for very special guests, Bathsheba felt a little more comfortable. The sedative the doctor had given her helped. But she was consumed by an awful feeling of guilt. What had she done? She knew she should never have risked a ride on the carousel and wondered now how she could have been so irresponsible. What was Gabriel going to say? As much as she was longing to see her husband she couldn't bear it if he blamed her for the loss of their child.

Chapter Nine

Sojourn at the Hall, Resolution and Independence.

AFTER FOUR LONG DAYS of mental pain and physical discomfort Bathsheba began to feel a little better. Lady Godwin had insisted on her being seen by a physician from London to give his expert advice on Bathsheba's condition. He simply repeated what Theodore Melksham had said. Bed rest, light nourishing meals plenty of beef tea and the stricken woman would be back to normal in a week or two.

Physically this was true but Bathsheba had still not plucked up enough courage to tell Gabriel the truth about her infirmity. In the event it would cause a rift between them for Gabriel had heard rumours that his wife was pregnant and had quelled them with vehemence.

On the fifth day Bathsheba was sitting up in bed with a breakfast tray across her knees when there was a knock at the door. She had seen very few people since the incident at the fair, the doctor had forbade visitors except very close relations but many of her friends had sent messages of sympathy.

'Come in,' she answered surprised at the earliness of the caller.

It was Emma who, in spite of her status, always seemed to be up and about early.

'Bathsheba, I've something I feel I must speak of and I don't quite know how because I don't wish to offend you.'

'Whatever can it be?' Bathsheba was intrigued. Surely she wasn't going to be turned out of her comfortable abode so soon.

'It's about your condition. My dear, there have been rumours going around that you have miscarried and I'm afraid Gabriel will learn of it from other sources. If you'll forgive my interfering in what is an intensely personal matter', Emma paused reluctant to upset her friend but felt the circumstances dictated she must, 'I think you really must explain the circumstances of your illness when he visits today.'

Bathsheba put down her cup carefully and looked up at her befriender. 'Don't you think I haven't tried,' she burst out angrily. It was alright for the Lady Emma to come in giving orders. Much as she liked Emma, Bathsheba remained a little in awe of the woman. However in this instance she was right and Bathsheba had to agree.

'I'm sorry, you're right of course. I'll tell him today, I promise.'

Emma smiled. 'Is there anything you would like?'

No, I'm being looked after like a princess, quite spoiled. Why I won't want to go home.' Bathsheba managed a Mona Lisa smile.

Emma left and went about her business of organising the evening's entertainment leaving Bathsheba to rehearse her speech to her husband. At the end of the morning she was no nearer to knowing what she would say than she had been three hours earlier.

There was to be a small dinner party at the Hall in the evening as the Honourable Sarah Godwin was returning from a sojourn to see her two brothers who lived in the Midlands. The London physician had said Bathsheba may get up and join in the party as long as she was careful not to over exert herself. It promised to be quite an occasion but she must speak to Gabriel before they sat down for the meal; as soon as he arrives, she vowed.

As it was such a fine day, the weather was once again warm for the time of the year, Bathsheba dressed carefully with the idea of taking a turn around the grounds of the delightful Elizabethan mansion. Surrounded on all sides by swards of green, the house had been much altered since it was built in the fifteen hundreds when Queen Elizabeth the first was on the throne of England. Starting off as little more than a country manor it was now of vast proportions. Huge alterations had been made during the eighteenth century when there was a craze for "modernising" country houses and a wing was added to either side of the house. During the nineteenth century a wide veranda was added to the back of the house, complete with stone balustrade, giving the building a more elegant appearance.

The landscaped gardens looked the same as when they were planned and laid out by Capability Brown but as they had matured over a hundred years some of the trees were now of gigantic proportions. Just to the west of the house and approximately a hundred yards from the main building the Godwins had built a beautiful glass and metal summer house looking for all the world like a very miniature Crystal Palace. At Lady Emma's wish the gardeners had created a fernery underplanted with spring bulbs followed later in the year by summer bedding. A truly glorious place to take a break from the madding crowd.

Bathsheba was sitting in the summer house when Gabriel caught up with her. He was already dressed for dinner and with a shock Bathsheba realised she had only a short time to change out of her outdoor clothes and put on her own finery.

'How are you, Bathsheba?' Gabriel asked kissing her tenderly.

'Much better. It's so good to be out in the fresh air.'

'You must be careful not to overdo things, you know,' Gabriel furrowed brow reflected his concern. 'Has the doctor said what caused you to be so out of sorts my dear?'

Bathsheba put her hand to her breast, trying hard to bring some order to her rapidly beating heart. The unpleasant sensation which felt like the fluttering of a panic stricken caged bird made her want to get up and run, to escape from the summer house which had changed from a place of refuge to a claustrophobic prison.

'Gabriel.'

'Yes?'

'I have a confession.'

Gabriel's eyebrows shot up in amazement. 'Have you? Whatever can it be?'

'Please tell me you won't be disappointed in me, Gabriel?'

Bathsheba shifted, uncomfortable now on the wooden seat which surrounded the round walls of the summer house.

Gabriel put his arm around his wife assuring her he loved her very much and nothing she could say would change that.

'I was pregnant, Gabriel. I miscarried. I'm so sorry!' Rivulets of tears streamed down her pale face.

Gabriel withdrew his arm, shocked and was for a few seconds speechless. The silence lay heavy between them, broken only by the shrill crying of peacocks as they paraded proudly in the grounds.

Bathsheba tried in vain to dry the tears but somehow they just kept flowing.

'Bathsheba,' Gabriel hated to see his wife so upset. He didn't care at this minute what she had done. He loved her for what she was as he had done since the day they had first met on Norcombe Hill. He reminded her of this fact. 'Please don't take on so. You'll make yourself ill.' He handed her his large red-spotted kerchief. 'Use this. They little lace ones are very pretty but don't mop up a flood very well.'

Bathsheba managed a watery smile remembering quite inappropriately the day Gabriel had first proposed. His offering then had been a baby lamb and she had arrogantly turned him down thinking he wasn't good enough for her. How mistaken can poor mortals be!

'That's better! After the flood, the sun rises, calm and bright.' Gabriel echoed Wordsworth's poetic words much to his wife's delight.

Bathsheba's smile lit up her whole face. 'That's from Resolution and Independence isn't it?'

' Mm. You see, I do remember some of that poetry you read to me.'

They hugged each other fiercely declaring a love which only the young proclaim to know about.

'Come, we must get ready for dinner. Let's show these people we can ride any storm.' Gabriel rose pulling Bathsheba to her feet. 'I've really missed you Bathsheba. How soon can you come home?'

'I think I've relied on these good people long enough. Tomorrow it shall be, Gabriel,' his wife declared.

It wasn't until much later that Gabriel finally confessed how disappointed he had been that possibly the last chance to have another child had been denied him. Now wasn't the time. All he wanted was to see his dear wife returned to full health and back at Oakdene.

The large dining room at Martinsham Hall was magnificent in its lavish decor. The Godwins had lived at the Hall for almost twenty years and during that period had worked on restoring the many-roomed mansion to its original style. Tonight, as the small dining room, a friendly place of no more than thirty feet square, was in the process of being re-hung with a deep red Chinese silk brocade, Bathsheba had peeped in on her first outing downstairs to admire its splendour, they were to eat in the large dining room. Entrance was gained through rich mahogany double doors and guests were announced formally then shown to their seats by blue and gold liveried footmen. It was not an affair Gabriel and Bathsheba were used too and both felt a little uncomfortable to begin with.

Cornelius, now presiding proudly over the splendid display of gleaming silver tableware and immaculate Sevres china, greeted everyone personally as they were announced, shaking their hand cordially. Emma sat opposite and to his right sat a pretty dark-haired woman who was being introduced as "the Honourable Sarah Godwin". Bathsheba was puzzled. Sarah looked similar in age to Emma but was not at all like her in looks. What was the relationship she wondered? She conversed with the Godwins as if she was on very familiar terms. Later Bathsheba found out through conversation with her host that she had been the adopted daughter of Cornelius and Emma for many, many years although how it came about remained a mystery. It did not seem polite to enquire too closely.

The food served that night made the harvest supper look like a peasants" picnic such were the delicacies dished up. Sometimes Gabriel was unsure what exactly he was eating but if taste was anything to go by and surely that was what mattered then he cared not a jot for the label the dish had been given.

Experiencing a taste sensation such as he'd never known before Gabriel was surprised to hear his name repeated twice from the head of the table. He looked up wondering what was the reason for such repetition and caught the eye of his host.

'I'm sorry, Sir Cornelius. I was enjoying the,' Gabriel was at a loss as to know what to call the delicacy.

Emma saved his face for, smiling, she joined in, 'It is a new recipe from France, Gabriel, the recipe is somewhat complicated but I'm sure Mrs. Marsden, our head cook, will oblige Mrs. Oak with the details for your cook should she require them.'

'Why thank you, Lady Emma.' Gabriel looked across at Bathsheba who replied with a knowing wink.

'As I was saying,' Cornelius went on, 'I hear you have plans for educating the peasants, Gabriel. How are they progressing?'

Somehow Cornelius managed to incorporate an unexpected respect to the label peasant as if he were on their side. Gabriel was nonplussed knowing little about the Godwins so decided to play it a little cautiously until he knew the man better.

'Very well so far, Sir but I'm not directly involved you know. 'Tis true I'm putting a small amount in to the fund but 'tis Benjamin Tallboys, my new shepherd, who is the brains behind it all.' Gabriel smiled at his pun and a wave of laughter floated round the table. Suddenly everyone seemed interested in what Gabriel had to say.

'Vicar Hansworth has agreed to let the front room of the vicarage for a small fee and Ben is to teach in his own time. There haven't been many takers yet but we are hopeful.'

Sir Nathaniel Martin, Cornelius's partner, joined in. 'How are the squires and the like taking it? Has there been any opposition, Gabriel?'

'No, not yet.' Gabriel had not anticipated that the conversation would turn in this direction. He had hoped it was not widely known amongst the gentry but he should have known there can be no secrets in such a place.

'Good,' Sir Nathaniel replied with a nod towards his partner. 'Let's hope it stays that way.'

Emma, always the perfect hostess, realising the conversation could become heated, suggested that if everyone were replete the men might like to retire to smoke whilst the ladies withdrew for their coffee.

The drawing room was littered with sofas and chairs of rich design. In the far corner there was a grand piano and Lady Emma sat down to play for her guests. It was a relief for Bathsheba as the excitement of the evening was beginning to take its toll of her slowly ebbing strength. She played the pianoforte herself and could recognise the tune Emma was playing. A favourite of hers and Gabriel, she complimented her hostess on her prowess.

'The Moonlight, is one of my favourite pieces and if I may say you played very well.'

'Well, it wasn't always so. When Cornelius first bought me the instrument, it was at the Great Exhibition you know, I could play very little. But, I persevered and now it is a pleasure to play,' Emma explained.

'Did you really go to the Exhibition at the Crystal Palace, Lady Emma?' Bathsheba was intrigued. She would like to have seen the sight for herself.

'Believe it or not it was during week one of my honeymoon,' Emma laughed.

Bathsheba was impressed, not for the first time. The Godwins were surprisingly unpretentious for their station. I could really get to like these people, Bathsheba thought realising at the same time it was unlikely they would meet very often once she had returned to Oakdene.

Chapter Ten
Return to Oakdene.

AS THEY DROVE UP the lane which led to Oakdene, Bathsheba breathed a sigh of relief at the familiar landscape. The trees in the orchard were fast shedding their orange and gold leaves making a deep russet carpet on the ground. Martinsham Hall was, she had to admit, glorious in its splendour but Bathsheba had grown to love the old farmhouse and to her there was simply no comparison. Smoke billowed out from the tall chimneys and she imagined the warmth and comfort of her drawing room, feeling an anticipated thrill take hold of her as she envisaged the sofa where she could relax and be her own self once again as she never could at the Hall.

The large landau Lady Emma had insisted she use had ensured a comfortable journey but as the footman handed her out of the carriage she felt as if she had been set free. Oakdene was so familiar, so comforting that tranquillity seemed to exude from its grey stone walls. Bathsheba wondered if it had a similar effect on other people and meant to ask at the first opportunity. As she walked up the wide stone steps to the old oak door an unexpected pleasure assailed her for it was flung open by Sheba who, having been informed of her mother's sudden illness had asked to be allowed home for a few days. Her eyes sparkled with unshed tears of joy at the sight of the pale-faced Bathsheba.

'How are you?' Sheba enquired concerned at the pallor of her mother's face.

'I shall be quite well now I'm home again Sheba,' the mother replied reassuringly hugging her daughter. 'It is so good to see you my darling but your father didn't tell me you would be here.'

'I asked him not to. You see,' Sheba explained, 'I thought you would insist you would be alright and didn't need me.'

'You're probably right, Sheba. I wouldn't want to drag you away from the college, you having been there such a short time.'

'I knew that's what you'd say!' Sheba declared with a single clap of her hands, 'That's what I told father.'

'Well you're here now and very pleased I am too.'

Sheba was quite correct. Bathsheba wouldn't have dreamed of sending for her daughter. Anyway she was almost fully recovered now but if she were honest she did feel a little bit low and Sheba's company was just what she needed; needed to be reminded of the family she had, rather than dwelling on what might have been. She didn't know whether to tell Sheba the real cause of her sickness. It wasn't a subject they had talked about in any depth, Sheba being so young and unmarried. Bathsheba decided she would tell her daughter the truth if and when the time was right. There was no need for her to know.

The log fire was burning brightly in the pleasant sunny south-facing sitting room just as she had imagined. Bathsheba contrasted the difference between the opulence of the house she had been residing in for the past few days and the shabby comfort of Oakdene. Her feet up, on a worn tapestry footstool,

Bathsheba leaned back against the brightly embroidered cushions on the Chesterfield. Her sigh of relief was audible to her daughter who sat opposite.

'Pleased to be home, mother?' It was an unnecessary question. As Bathsheba relaxed, the tiny lines in her face which Sheba had noticed for the first time when she greeted her mother at the door, even though it was only a matter of weeks since they had been together, seemed to have virtually disappeared.

'Oh yes. I do so love Oakdene. I don't know how you can bear to be away, Sheba.'

'I must admit it's nice to be back, but mother, I have my life ahead of me. I need to see what life is like away from Weatherbury,' Sheba tried to explain. 'It's not that I don't love the place,' She didn't know whether to tell her mother about George but it was still painful and the time wasn't right, 'but.' She paused.

'It's alright, Sheba. I understand. I was young once you know although it does seem rather a long time ago.'

Sheba laughed, the tension of the moment quickly dissipated by her mother's apparent understanding. She stood up to ring the bell for tea. It was the panacea for all ills and they both felt they could do with a little light refreshment.

'It's good to see ye home, Ma'am,' a smiling Maryann nodded towards Bathsheba as she carefully placed the tea tray on a small table next to Sheba. 'Will ye be mother?' Maryann enquired of Sheba. Realising what she had said she felt her face redden and she turned towards the door.

'Thank you, Maryann. You don't mind, mother?' Sheba looked towards her mother who was looking decidedly uncomfortable. 'or would you like to lie down for a while? I'm sure Maryann wouldn't mind bringing a tray to your room.'

'Indeed Ma'am, I don't mind at all,' replied Maryann glad of the distraction.

'No, thank you. I'm quite alright and I beg of you not to make so much fuss?' Bathsheba bravely fought the tears which threatened to spill down her cheeks. She had an awful empty feeling at the pit of her stomach, a dreadful sense of loss. Why did I have to go on that wretched merry-go-round she asked herself for the umpteenth time? Would it have made any difference? She would never know for sure. The doctor from London had said it may have happened anyway but she couldn't stop blaming herself and in a way she felt, quite unreasonably that the Lady Emma should share the blame. It was she who had suggested the adventure.

Sheba watched her mother anxiously. She wasn't herself at all. At a loss as to know what to say to comfort her she offered to read to her.

'That would be lovely dear,' Bathsheba replied.

Sheba went to the table and picked up the book she had been reading before she'd heard the carriage approach.

'We're studying Mr. Wordsworth and Mr. Coleridge at the college, mother.' Sheba said excitedly. 'One of the new ones we have been reading is Intimations of Immortality. Shall I read a verse or two?'

Bathsheba smiled. It would seem to be a case of like mother, like daughter. She nodded and leaned back once more, having regained her composure, prepared to be entertained.

> 'But there's a tree of many, one,
> A single field of which I have looked upon,
> Both of them speak of something that is gone:
> The pansy at my feet
> Doth the same tale repeat:
> Whither is fled the visionary gleam?
> Where is it now, the glory and the dream?
>
> Our birth is but a sleep and a forgetting:
> The soul that rises with us, our life's Star,
> Hath had elsewhere its setting,'

Sheba glanced up from the book to see how her mother was enjoying the reading and was horrified to see silent tears streaming down her face.

'It's just the beauty of the poetry dear,' Bathsheba prevaricated, 'but I am a little tired so I shall go to my room and rest. Perhaps you would like to read to me again later, perhaps this afternoon?'

Sheba nodded, 'Of course, mother.'

Poetry is like music, her teacher had said, it evokes images and memories which although oft times bring pleasure can also bring a sadness far beyond human expectation.

It was quiet in her boudoir. Only the twittering of the birds in the trees outside the window broke the stillness and quiet of that Autumn day. Relaxed now and dozing a little, Bathsheba was suddenly awakened by a commotion which seemed to be coming from the direction of the orchard. She lifted herself up from the bed and peered into the gloom of the afternoon. Although it had been such a bright morning, storm clouds had gathered making it difficult to see through the trees. She could however hear voices which seemed to be raised as if in anger.

Opening the window she could make out several male forms, one of which danced about as if on hot coals.

Bathsheba rang the bell alarmed at what seemed to be signs of trouble. In all the years they had lived together at Oakdene, she and Gabriel had never had more than a cross word with their employees, never had to dismiss anyone.

Sheba, who had been in the kitchen, heard the bell and offered to go to see what her mother wanted. Maryann, busy as usual and somewhat reluctant to converse with her mistress under the circumstances had agreed with alacrity.

'What's going on, Sheba? There seems to be an awful commotion coming from the direction of the orchard.'

'One of the Coggan boys said that a cottage on Acorn Farm has been burnt down, mother.'

'And whose would that be?' asked Bathsheba curiously.

'I'm not sure but one of the Coggan boys says it must be a warning of some kind.'

'What nonsense,' Bathsheba cried. 'It more than likely to be an accident.'

They later found out it was far from being an accident, on the contrary, it was an act of destruction albeit with a good reason. It had been thought by the group of labourers watching that the cottage had been set on fire deliberately and the family rendered homeless simply because the cottager was no longer needed on the farm. The new steam threshing machine was the reasoning behind the judgement.

Gabriel was brim full of the news when he arrived home. After greeting his wife, for he was indeed very pleased to have her reinstated at Oakdene, he explained, "Tis getting to be common practice now. The new machinery is so clever and quick it is making man redundant on the land.'

'And elsewhere, "twould seem,' put in Sheba who had been listening to the conversation.

'What, do you know about such goings on, Sheba?'

'We were discussing at college, father, the impact that such mechanisation would have on agricultural workers and Miss Norman reminded us of the Luddites.'

'That was a very long time ago. We live in more enlightened times now, surely?' Gabriel was surprised at his daughter's knowledge of such things.

'Miss Norman said that Farmers and landowners were burning the cottages so the workers would have nowhere to live and have to move on. Then they wouldn't think of wrecking the new machines.'

'She's a clever lady, your Miss Norman,' Gabriel admitted. 'but I can't see Joseph Abbot stooping to such measures. Anyway, he hasn't actually bought a machine yet; 'tis just in the planning stage.'

It did make sense to render the workers homeless but was hardly humane surely. Gabriel was nonplussed. 'Well it won't happen on this farm!' he declared, standing up as if addressing the congregation, thumbs hooked in his waistcoat, 'and I shall make sure all my regular workers know their jobs are safe.'

Bathsheba clapped her hands. Her husband was so fierce in his commitment he was almost funny but she was so proud of him.

'I shall go and see Ben Tallboys. This very night. Find out if he knows what's going on. If they can burn down cottages, why the good Lord only knows what they will do to him if they think he's causing trouble.'

It was a sad state of affairs and one which could lead to much unrest on the farms if something wasn't done and quickly. Gabriel hurried to the King's Arms that night hoping to see his new shepherd. The way things were going, Monday might be too late.

Chapter Eleven
Commotion at the Inn,
Quae Curia.

As GABRIEL DREW CLOSE to the Kings Arms he could hear the hum of raised voices even before he reached the open door. The bar was crowded and it looked as if someone were holding court as all heads were pointing in the same direction. Squeezing past the table where last week he and Benjamin had discussed their optimistic plans, Gabriel caught sight of Joseph Abbot for it was he who commanded everyone's attention.

'So you see,' he was explaining, 'the cottage was almost derelict. It simply wasn't in my financial interest to renovate it.'

A voice close by obviously was not satisfied for it asked, 'What about the tenant? Where will he and his family live now?'

Joseph's reply was emphatic. 'They were casual labourers and their work was done. No more than that.'

To uninitiated ears it seemed a plausible reason to fire the cottage. There was much ooh-ing and aah-ing but gradually the hubbub subsided and the crowd began to disperse. Stepping down from the brass bar rail where he had been perched, Joseph crossed over to where Gabriel had managed to secure a seat.

'I hear there's been some trouble, Joseph.'

'The trouble is, Gabriel, no one round these parts likes change. They feel threatened by the new machinery and are panicking if you ask me. I don't think they believe me. Not entirely anyway.'

Joseph's red face told its own story. The man was uncomfortable with the position he had found himself in, accused of deliberately making a family homeless. It was true; he had indirectly made the family homeless but not in the way he had been accused. Gabriel had known Joseph and his family for many years and he didn't believe that he would be intentionally malicious. He always treated his workers fairly, that was one of the reasons the two men got on so well, their policies were similar, so Gabriel tried now to reassure his friend. 'It'll all blow over in a day or two, Joseph, you mark my words.'

Joseph was not convinced. He had heard of other farmers firing cottages for the very reasons he had been accused of and felt he had been naive in the matter; should have thought it through, foreseen the trouble that might be caused by his action. He stood up, shrugged his shoulders and made as if to go, 'I'll be off then Gabriel, my regards to Bathsheba.'

'Thank you Joseph, I'll give her your regards. She's feeling much better now.'

Joseph sat down again. 'I'm sorry Gabriel, but what with all the fuss I quite forgot your dear wife's plight. It's unforgivable of me. I'll ask Louisa to visit tomorrow. Perhaps you would both like to come to supper on Saturday?'

Gabriel felt sorry for Joseph. The events had really upset the man and he was quite unlike his usual cheery self.

'Fine with me. I'll look forward to Saturday. Better ask Louisa to confirm with Bathsheba when she sees her tomorrow though,' Gabriel laughed diffusing the tension a little.

'Good to know who your friends are,' Joseph put his hand on his friend's shoulder as he bade him farewell.

As Joseph left, Benjamin Tallboys joined Gabriel. 'I was hoping to see you, Ben. Sit down,' Gabriel invited.

'Is there something troubling you, Gabriel?'

Several of the men at the bar were looking in their direction. 'We can't talk here, Ben. Come outside.'

The two men walked round to the back of the inn, past the stables, where there was a small knot of men playing with the devil's playthings by the light of a lantern, until they reached a hay barn. They perched themselves on some bales of straw so they would be comfortable and more able to concentrate on their discussion.

It was gloomy in the barn but there was just enough light from the moon to see an outline. The scampering of small animals at the back of the stacked bales suggested to the men they were in the company of field mice.

'The cats will soon give them a run for their money,' Gabriel said solemnly, nodding towards the back of the barn. He lit his pipe, inhaling deeply several times and blowing out clouds of smoke with each breath continuing this performance until he was satisfied that the pipe was well alight, then spoke again.

'I don't mind telling you Ben, I can't help worrying about the feeling of unrest there is about these days.'

'I share your concern, Gabriel, but why especially now? It's been a good harvest; there'll be plenty of work through the winter.'

'This is not the first cottage to be burned down,' he raised his hand as Ben was about to interrupt, 'I know Joseph Abbot is innocent, I've known him long enough to believe what he says, but the labourers are scared. That means they're ready to believe the worst.'

'Well, I think 'tis not without good reason,' Benjamin leaned forward pressing his fingers together as if in prayer, 'but I'm on their side as well you know. I can understand why they're so worried.'

'It's not them I'm worried about just now, Ben Tallboys, 'tis you. If the gentry get wind of what you're trying to do then they'll stop at nothing to get rid of you. I should think they'll jump at the chance to use you as a scapegoat, blame you for the unrest. It will let them off the hook.'

Benjamin knew exactly what Gabriel was trying to say. It wasn't the first time he'd come up against opposition from the upper classes, heaven above knew that, but it wouldn't put him off and he reminded Gabriel of the commitment he'd made the other night.

'Anyway, burning cottages is not directly my business, at least not that they will see it that way. I just want to give the men a chance to better themselves. It doesn't mean they will necessarily be better off materially but you know the old saying, "educate the fathers and you educate the sons". That's what I want.'

'I know that and you know that, 'tis other folk we have to convince,' Gabriel acknowledged nodding his head

Benjamin leant back against the hay. The two men sat in silence for a while, each thinking his own thoughts about the subject of education and the betterment of the human race. Ben was the first to break the silence.

'I think we should explain what we're doing, Gabriel. Put out some pamphlets or something like.'

Gabriel was amazed. Had his friend gone completely mad? He laughed thinking it was meant to be some kind of irony. Benjamin looked serious enough; surely he didn't mean it. Gabriel looked hard at the man. 'You're not joking are you?'

'No. I'm not. You see it's like this. If I advertise what it is I'm doing then I'll not be blamed for something I've nothing to do with, if you see what I mean.'

Gabriel was a little confused and said so.

'If I'm open and above board, they'll think it's alright. That's the way their minds work.' Benjamin's tone had taken on a slightly derisive air. 'But, Gabriel, I can't afford to be connected with trouble, at least not the violent kind. That'll get us nowhere. Don't you agree?'

Gabriel nodded. Perhaps Ben was right. There was no sense in antagonising anybody if it could be avoided.

'Alright then. Let's do what you suggest. How shall we go about it?'

Benjamin Tallboys stood up, placing his thumbs in his waistcoat pockets as if to balance himself. 'I'll tell you what I'll do. I'll have a word with the printer in Casterbridge and see if he'll do a poster or two and maybe a few pamphlets as well. He owes me a favour so he may do them for nothing.'

'Yes, Ben. Do that. Let me have a look at them before you display them though, won't you.'

The two men shook hands. It was a good night's work and they both left the barn far happier than when they had entered the place.

Halfway up the track they heard scuffling and then a shout and a thud. Looking at each other they made for the place where earlier some men had been gambling with dice. It seemed like the game having finished they had started talking about the allegations against Joseph Abbot. As Gabriel and Ben were to find out later, one man was for and three men were against the farmer. It wasn't long before the three men, brimful with drink, started picking on the one who was on the side of Farmer Abbot. The three men were too much for the single fighter and he was soon overcome.

Gabriel recognised the man lying on the ground as one of his own workers. He bent over to him and was shocked to see the man was badly hurt; on the surface he had just a few cuts and bruises but when they tried to rouse him it became obvious he was out for the count. The two men looked up unsure of what to do next.

'Well, we can't leave him here, Ben. Let's see if we can get him on to that bale of hay over there.'

They carefully lifted the prostrate figure and placed him in a more comfortable position. He was heavily built and it took them all their time to lift the unconscious body on to the hay.

'I'll cover him with that horse blanket over there, Gabriel, if you'll pass it to me, then I'll go and get some help.'

'No, you stay with him, Ben. I'll go.'

As Gabriel approached the King's Arms he could hear the sounds of crashing glass. He hurried into the bar and was immediately engulfed in a major fracas. There were tables over-turned and splintered glass everywhere. Not stopping to ask questions and knowing he it was unlikely he would receive any help from anyone there he hurried out again into the cold night air. It was obvious the fight had spread to the inn although how it happened Gabriel wasn't sure.

Looking back towards the barn he caught sight of two shadowy figures. One man appeared to be leaning heavily against the other.

'Who's that?' Gabriel shouted.

There was no immediate answer so Gabriel went towards them.

''Tis you Jake Harbutts. Is that young Will you've got there?'

The two brothers were well known for their pugilistic tendencies and it wasn't the first time they had been blamed for instigating a fight.

They were now full of remorse. 'I'm sorry, Mr. Oak. "Twas the drink. We didn't mean for old Luke to get hurt.'

'It looks as if young Will has come off nearly as bad as Luke. Is he alright?'

'He'll be alright in the morning, Mr. Oak.'

'Well, Luke Houseman didn't look to good when I saw him last', Gabriel told them. 'In fact I'm just on my way to get some help.'

As he spoke he saw Ben supporting Luke and they were making their way slowly towards him.

'He came round almost before you were half way up the lane, Gabriel, so we thought it best to get indoors.'

Benjamin and Gabriel took him to the inn where they could better see the damage which had been so cruelly inflicted on him. Fortunately, the fight had stopped as quickly as it had started. All that was left was a few broken tables and a glass littered floor which the landlord was busy clearing up muttering as he did so.

'Looks like we were wrong in our first estimation, Gabriel. He's not that seriously injured.'.

'Like to explain what that was all about, Luke Houseman?' Gabriel invited.

'S'alright, Mr. Oak, sir. They just got a bit carried away.' It was clear the injured man was not going to give anything away voluntarily.

Gabriel tried again. 'Luke, was it anything to do with what went on earlier?'

Old Luke Houseman was a loyal employee of Gabriel Oak and he was torn between telling his employer the truth and letting his so-called friends down.

Gabriel tried again, impatient by this time. 'Luke Houseman, will you please tell me what is going on?' The man glanced up at Benjamin Tallboys.

'It's alright, he's one of us,' Gabriel assured the worried looking man.

'They two said as how Farmer Abbot did it deliberately, fired the cottage I mean, sir, and it wouldn't be long before you did the same, Mr. Oak. I wasn't "aving that an" I said so. Then the next thing I knew I were on the ground.'

'Thank ye for that, Luke, I'll talk to the men in the morning.'

Luke Houseman turned to go, now much recovered. 'I don't think they'll believe you, sir.'

'Leave it to me, Luke. You get off home now. By the way, was the older Harbutts involved?'

'Only at first. He soon made his way back to the inn. Why do you ask?'

'It doesn't matter just now, Luke. You get on home.'

Luke Houseman made his way up the lane leaving Gabriel and Ben to bid each other farewell.

'What was going on in the King's Arms Gabriel? I could hear the noise right down the lane.'

'My guess is that once Joseph Abbot's supporters got to hear about what happened there was a set to. Old John Harbutts could never keep his mouth shut.'

'I might have known he'd be involved. I would have given Luke more sense than get involved with them.' Ben sounded surprised.

'Well, he wouldn't normally I'm sure but he could never resist a challenge even if it's only dice. I'm off now, Ben, so I'll wish you G'night.'

'G'night, Gabriel.'

The two men parted each going in a different direction. It had been quite an evening one way or another and Gabriel wasn't looking forward to the morning. Ever a peace loving man, the thought that his own workers could even think he would treat them unfairly had upset him more than he would admit even to himself.

Bathsheba was waiting for him when he arrived home eager to hear what all the fuss had been about. Maryann had told her a version but Bathsheba knew her housekeeper could be relied on to get her facts a little twisted if not entirely wrong.

'Well, was it true. Gabriel?' Bathsheba wanted to know.

'Partly.'

His wife gasped with astonishment.

'No, he didn't do it to get at the labourers, of course he didn't.'

Bathsheba breathed a sigh of relief. 'What happened then?'

Gabriel related all that had happened at the Kings Arms that evening.

'Poor Luke. He wouldn't hurt a fly.' Bathsheba was full of sympathy for the old man, 'But fancy him fighting on your behalf, Gabriel.'

"Tis a nasty business and I for one will be glad when I've put the men's minds at rest.'

Bathsheba nodded in agreement. For years they had run the farm without trouble. How tiresome it was to be put out by a monstrous piece of machinery which they hadn't even bought yet.

'What do you think of investing in a steam threshing machine, Gabriel?'

'I shall have to have a serious discussion with Joseph as soon as possible,' Gabriel said. 'Oh, I nearly forgot. Louisa Abbot will be here tomorrow afternoon to ask after your health and Joseph suggested we have supper with them on Saturday. Shall I leave the arrangements with you, m'dear?'

'Yes. It'll be nice to see Louisa. I haven't seen her since the Budmouth fair. Yes, Gabriel. By all means leave it with me. Perhaps Sheba will be able to join us.'

It was good to see Bathsheba looking better. Life would be good once they'd sorted out the disturbance hereabouts.

'You go on up, m'dear. I'll just have a night cap then I'll join you.'

Chapter Twelve
The Path of True Love

SHEBA WAS SURPRISED TO find herself enjoying her short holiday at Oakdene. Even a few weeks away from home had allowed her to see her "problem" with a new perspective. Her mother seemed to be recovering well so whatever had caused the sickness could not have been serious. She would allow herself a few more days at home before going back to the sanctuary of her Exonbury college.

When Louisa Abbot invited her parents to supper on Saturday and insisted that of course she must come too, Sheba thanked her politely and said she would look forward to it very much. She loved Acorn Farm almost as much as she loved Oakdene and with the absence of the cause of her sorrow there would be a chance to enjoy the enveloping comfortable atmosphere of the old farmhouse, and she may even get to hear news of George. Not that she was really interested of course, but he was an old friend and it was to be expected that she would

ask after him; also it would be an opportunity to show off one
of the fashionable new gowns she had purchased recently.

They had been at Exonbury College only a few weeks
when she and her new friend Jayne had been invited to
take part in a sight-seeing trip to include the new arcade of
shops which had recently been opened in the city. Neither of
the girls had ever seen such exciting displays before. Jayne,
born and brought up in a small village in Devonshire, was a
dashing looking girl; bright blue-eyes, apple-pink cheeks and
golden ringlets, she was the epitome of Alice Liddel who had
experienced, according to Mr Dodgson, so many adventures
in Wonderland. Indeed, whilst in the company of Jayne, Sheba
had come to expect the unexpected.

Seeing the wonderful display of gowns in the window,
the wilful Jayne had persuaded their chaperone to allow them
to enter the shop to inspect the merchandise resulting in an
order for two gowns apiece, to be delivered as soon as possible
to the college.

Excited as children in a toy shop the girls had enjoyed
choosing the cloth from the many assorted bales laid out
in rows like Catherine Wheels. Next the style had to be
chosen which was of the very latest as the shop employed a
dressmaker recently trained in London. Lastly the colour,
which was perhaps the most difficult, there being all the lovely
hues of the rainbow and more besides. For their ball gowns,
they had chosen from different ends of the spectrum, Jayne
a dark red velvet and Sheba a deep violet shade of the lush
cloth. After considerable debate, the girls had left the choice
of trimmings to the expert having given her some indication
of their preferences.

When the gowns had finally arrived at the college the other
young ladies, gathered around for the opening ceremony, were
frankly envious and announced that they in turn must visit
the shop to place an order. Sheba had left Exonbury before
the outing had been arranged so she would have to wait until

she returned to college to see what had been the choice of her friends and acquaintances. Without a doubt they would be on show at the end of term Ball to which she remembered now she was expected to invite a partner. Perhaps her mother would be able to help with that as she wasn't sure who to ask. Jayne's brother had written offering himself as a partner but Sheba had refused feeling she would be uncomfortable with a stranger. If only George, but there Sheba cut her dreams short, knowing it was pointless to allow herself to pursue that line of thought.

'I've just peeped in to see how Sheba is progressing,' Bathsheba told Gabriel as they prepared for their outing to Acorn Farm. She explained how Sheba and a friend had shopped in Exonbury. Tonight she was to wear one of the new gowns she had purchased there.

'She's looking better than when she left here even though it was such a short time ago,' Gabriel noted. 'More colour in her cheeks. That college life must suit her, although I'd have thought being indoors most of the time would have reduced her complexion.'

Neither parent had mentioned the state of their daughter's health before although they hadn't failed to miss her unaccustomed quietness a few days before she'd left Oakdene for her adventure into Devonshire. It was good to see her restored to her normal temper and Bathsheba told her husband so.

They were both ill-prepared for the vision that was awaiting them in the Hall. Sheba had put her hair up as Jayne had taught her and was wearing a circlet of forget-me-nots around the crown. Her striking lapis lazuli gown was of the very latest style, which showed her tiny waist and décolletage to fine advantage.

Gabriel thought what a pity it was that George would not be home this evening. Although he'd said nothing to his wife he thought Sheba and George would make a good match. And, what an advantage there would be in joining the two farms. Adam seemed set for a career in an academic world and Matthew was still determined to lead the life of an itinerant veterinary. Well, if it was meant to be it would happen but it wouldn't hurt to encourage the two young people surely.

The carriage was waiting and Gabriel helped his two beautiful companions up the steps wrapping a blanket around them both as the evenings were cool now that autumn was well under way. He sat opposite them smiling.

'You look happy, father,' Sheba remarked.

'Wouldn't you like to know what it was I was thinking?' he teased his daughter.

'If you would like to tell me, father,' Sheba rejoined.

Gabriel laughed out loud. 'I'm not sure whether I should tell you.'

'Then it must concern me,' Sheba declared.

'You're quite right. It does concern you.' he paused for effect as both ladies looked at him expectantly, then continued, 'I was thinking about you and George Abbot, if you must know. What a good looking couple you would make.'

Sheba felt her face blanch and was aware that her mother had turned her head and was now watching her closely. She had the feeling that her mother suspected George was the reason she had wanted to escape from Oakdene although she had said nothing at the time.

'Oh, father, what nonsense. George is like a brother to me. There simply couldn't be anything between us. It would not seem right.' Sheba protested quickly and vehemently causing Bathsheba to think perhaps her daughter did protest too much.

The family in the coach remained silent for the remainder of the journey but it wasn't long before they were rattling over the cobbled driveway which led, by way of a tunnelled archway formed by the intertwining branches of two huge oak trees, to their destination.

As soon as they reached the front door it was obvious from the selection of carriages on the drive that there were to be more than the one or two guests they had previously been led to believe would be there.

'Isn't that the Godwins'' landau, Gabriel?' Bathsheba enquired of her husband.

Before he could answer a group of young people leapt out of the carriage immediately in front of theirs. Two young gentlemen and a pretty raven-haired beauty in a gown of rich gold brocade walked up the steps in front of them.

Sheba was horrified for she had recognised the taller of the gentleman leading the threesome was none other than the son of the house. Bathsheba had also noticed and stealing a quick look at her daughter saw the look of discomfort as she recognised George. Putting an arm on Sheba's as if to support herself she whispered, 'It looks as if it's going to be an entertaining supper party tonight, Sheba.'

Recovering her composure quickly, Sheba smiled, 'You're quite right, mother. Shall we go in?'

There must have been at least twenty people in the drawing room when the Oaks were shown in. Bathsheba had been right about the Godwin carriage. Sir Cornelius and Lady Emma were holding court in the centre of the room. The discussion centred around the recent unrest but apparently Martin and Godwin had been trouble free so far and Sir Cornelius was extolling the fact.

Gabriel quickly joined in. It wouldn't hurt to become friends with this fair minded businessman and now was as good a time as any to forge the friendship.

Joseph Abbot turned to greet Gabriel shaking his hand. 'You're just in time to give us your opinion, Gabriel, on what we see as scare-mongering among the labourers. Do you think there is any cause for alarm?'

Gabriel shook his head. 'I don't think there's much to worry about at the moment, Joseph. The men are just a bit worried, that's all.'

Sir Cornelius joined in. 'From what I can gather, the wages have been reduced on some farms. This is causing ill feeling among the men who are having to suffer lower wages.'

'So you agree it has nothing to do with my burning the cottage, Sir Cornelius?'

Theodore Melksham joined in, 'It seems wages are a slightly higher in the factories and this is making the men look hard at the work they must do in the fields to earn what must seem in comparison a pittance.'

Sir Cornelius nodded, 'It certainly is a problem and not one that will be solved easily.'

The supper gong sounded just as the debate showed signs of becoming heated.

Sheba had managed to avoid George and his friends so far. She had made straight for the sofa where Harriet Melksham, blooming in her advanced state of pregnancy, was seated. Now they both rose to go into the supper room where the table, which would not have looked out of place at St. James" Palace, had been laid. Everyone had been allotted a place. This was not unusual but had not been expected on this particular occasion it supposedly being a small gathering.

Sheba was placed next to the raven haired beauty she had seen earlier. George sat directly opposite and introduced her. 'I'd like you to meet my friend Bartholomew Westley and his sister Adeline.'

Sheba shook their hands and forced a smile. 'I'm delighted to meet you. Did you meet George at Corinchester, Mr. Westley?'

'Indeed I did, Miss Oak, and now I hope to stay at Acorn Farm for several weeks whilst George and I work on a new project.'

'May I ask what the project entails, Mr. Westley?' Sheba enquired, deliberately avoiding George's eye.

'I'm afraid I'm not at liberty to divulge the facts, Miss Oak, as until we have completed the work we cannot be certain of its success.'

Sheba was not a little confused but supposed they had good reasons for their secrecy. No doubt in time she would discover more.

Sheba looked across at Adeline Westley and caught a quizzical look in her adversary's eye. 'How long will you be staying, Miss Westley?'

Adeline Westley turned to George and smiled up at him. 'Oh, for a few days I should think. That is if I'm welcome, George?'

George smiled back at the enchantress. 'I would be delighted if you would stay for as long as you can spare, Adeline. You know that.'

So, Sheba thought, they are on first name terms. That was quick allowing that he had only met her at the beginning of the new college term.

Adeline addressed Sheba. 'I expect you are wondering how George and I met, Miss Oak.'

'I assume you met through your brother, Miss Westley.'

'Well, in a way. But you see, my father teaches at the college and always makes it a habit to invite new students to tea as soon as possible. He insists it helps them to settle in more quickly. I, of course help with the entertainment. That is how George and I became acquainted.'

'I hear you are at college in Exonbury, Miss Oak,' Bartholomew Westley turned towards his neighbour.

'Yes, I'm hoping to train to be a teacher when I've completed my studies there. Do you have an ambition, Miss Westley?' Sheba enquired politely.

Adeline Westley blushed a becoming shade of pink. 'Oh, I expect to make a good marriage. I have no need to work for my living.'

It was Sheba's turn to blush. George surprisingly came to the rescue. 'Sheba has no need to work, Adeline. But she does have a vocation.'

That's told her, Sheba thought, pleased. Endeavouring not to show her pleasure she turned to Bartholomew and said boldly, 'And what is your ambition, Mr Westley.'

'It is of the self same mettle as my sister, Miss Oak. I too hope to marry well and run my own farm. Not in that order you understand,' he said with a short laugh.

'Then I hope you both fulfil your ambitions, truly I do.'

'And you yours Miss Oak,' Bartholomew inclined his head towards his neighbour.

Sheba was dying to ask George what his ambitions were but thought it would seem slightly ridiculous having known him for so long. Adeline did it for her.

'Now it's your turn, George. What do you hope to gain from life?'

The question had been re-phrased and George answered in the same vein. 'As much as I put in. That's all.'

'Well said, my friend,' Bartholomew Westley laughed. He had known George Abbot only a short time but already they were as close as brothers. He had a vision of George and his sister together. They made a handsome couple and she could certainly do worse. He decided at that moment to do all he could to encourage the friendship. It would help if he became further acquainted with Miss Oak. She had known George for a long time. Maybe she would put in a good word for his sister.

'When will you return to Exonbury, Miss Oak?'

'As my mother has made an excellent recovery, I shall return next week.'

'Then perhaps you will do me the honour of accompanying me to an evening's entertainment at the New Theatre in Godwinstone before you go.'

Adeline grabbed George's arm familiarly. 'Let's make it a foursome, George? What fun we will have.'

Whether Sheba or George entirely agreed was ignored. Plans were put into action immediately and the outing arranged for the evening before Sheba left for Exonbury.

The remainder of the evening was pleasantly spent, the guests enjoying the ladies singing and playing. Gabriel was persuaded to play his flute accompanied by Lady Emma at the piano. Not too much money had been lost at the bridge table. The Abbots were pleased with their social evening knowing it would be repeated in a short while although it would probably be without the young people as they would soon be back at their various homes and colleges.

On the way back through the dark, now barely recognisable, country lanes, the trio who had set out in optimistic mood were returning in much the same frame of mind, that is except for one. Sheba was trying hard to think of an excuse for not going to the theatre next week but try as she might she could think of nothing. She toyed with the idea of saying an evening at the theatre was not to her taste but it sounded so priggish and anyway, George already knew how much she liked drama. No, what could not be cured must be endured she supposed. And, she acknowledged to herself later, Bartholomew Westley did appear most agreeable. Not unlike her favourite hero, Mr. Fitzwilliam Darcy in looks, only Bartholomew was much more gregarious.

Chapter Thirteen
News from Christminster; a visitor.

ON MONDAY MORNING TWO letters arrived at Oakdene via the mailcart. One was addressed to Mr. and Mrs. Oak, the script being instantly recognised by the recipient as her eldest son's flamboyant scrawl. The second was addressed to Miss Bathsheba Oak and postmarked Exonbury.

The family had finished breakfast earlier than usual as Gabriel had urgent business to attend to in Casterbridge and had needed to make an early start. He had muttered something about Benjamin Tallboys and the vicar but had been in too much of a hurry to explain. Matthew, as usual, had ridden out and had breakfasted in the kitchen in spite of his parents" warnings not to ride until dawn had completely broken. Their advice had been to wait until after sunrise but impatient Matthew knew better. He would as soon run a mile to see a fire such is the impatience of youth.

Bathsheba and her daughter were lingering over a last cup of tea as this was Sheba's last full day at home, when Maryann brought in the mail. The letter from Adam was unusually long for him.

'What news, mother? Is Adam well?'

'He seems to have taken to the academic life like a duck to water. Most of what he writes describes the college architecture, the building style and its environs. There is an excellent description of his own college. Would you like me to read it to you?'

Sheba nodded. If she had been born male she would have chosen a similar course to Adam and she now showed an avid interest in her brother's lifestyle at Christminster.

'He invites us to attend the Carol Service at Queen's Chapel.' Bathsheba paused whilst she scanned the letter.'

'I'll miss out the architectural description as you will see the buildings for yourself when we visit next. That'll be during the week before Christmas, Sheba. We shall of course attend the Carol Service. I've heard it's rather special. You'll be able to come with us I hope?' Bathsheba had forgotten temporarily that Sheba had her own life to organise now.

'I'm sure I'll manage it, mother. I might invite Jayne. Do you think Adam would mind?'

'I would think not, but may I suggest you write to him and enquire, Sheba.'

Sheba nodded. 'Do carry on, mother. Does he say what his room is like?'

'I'll read out the next bit.

'I share a room, which is approximately twice the size of my room at Oakdene, with a fellow called Christian. We have a single bed; both of us are by a window as the room is on the corner, a desk and a small wardrobe each and share a rather large mahogany drop-leaf table which dominates the centre of the room. Our large west-facing lattice window overlooks the Isis. They tell me I'm particularly lucky to have a room with such a splendid view but then my room-mate is the nephew of an earl! I suppose it helps to have friends in high places!

I spend many thoughtful hours upon the window seat under the large lattice and have already written a small volume of poetry which I hope will be published in due course. My course of study is everything I expected and more besides. Mother, I am happy! Father, I hope you will one day understand."'

Sheba smiled. 'I'm so pleased Adam has settled in so well. You must miss him a great deal, mama.'

'I do and I miss you too but it does my heart good to see you both gaining experience and achieving some measure of independence.'

Matthew put his head around the door. 'I'm off now, mother. Goodbye Sheba.' He blew a kiss and was gone.

They both laughed. Bathsheba had almost completely recovered physically from her sad loss and it was good to see her back to normal so quickly. Sheba wondered if her mother would ever have another child but decided not to risk upsetting her by asking so instead she asked,

'Have you been to the New Theatre in Godwinstone, mother?' It had been built only recently with funds donated by the Martin and Godwin Company and is the talk of the town as seats are both comfortable and affordable.

'No, not yet. Your father has promised we shall go but I'm not sure when it will be. Remind me to ask him, Sheba. Perhaps if you say you have enjoyed yourself it will inspire him to make an effort to buy tickets for us.'

Sheba promised and found she was looking forward to the outing although she was unsure what the travelling players would be performing.

'Do you happen to know what is being enacted, mother? Bartholomew Westley didn't say and I didn't think to ask.'

'I'm afraid it will be a surprise, Sheba as I can't remember what was on the poster in Casterbridge when I was there last.

I know it was a Shakespeare play but which one I cannot say. Wait a minute, I think... no, I don't want to tell you wrong so I'll say nothing. What arrangements have you made?'

'The party will be here after supper, about six thirty and we shall travel to Godwinstone together in the Abbot chaise.'

'Then we'll have supper early. I shall go and arrange it at once.

As Bathsheba left the room Sheba opened her letter. It was from Jayne with the latest news from the college. The gowns had arrived and everyone was in raptures over them. Jayne was missing Sheba and couldn't wait for her return. She wrote, "Give my kind regards to your mother and tell her I hope her health has improved enough to allow you to return very soon."

Sheba smiled. Jayne was a dear and she was missing her. It would be good to get back to Casterbury once this evening's performance was over.

The party arrived on time to collect its fourth member and was soon on its way to the theatre in Godwinstone. The play they were to see was "A Midsummer Night's Dream', Sheba's favourite, so she was pleased she had decided to accept Bartholomew's invitation.

It soon became obvious by the way Adeline kept glancing across at George that she was very much taken with the young man. Sheba vowed to not allow herself to be disturbed by his attention to the beautiful sister of her companion. Instead she turned her own attention to Bartholomew who was sitting directly opposite to her in the coach making it easy to converse.

'Tell me, Mr Westley, are you a devotee of Mr Shakespeare? Sheba leaned across in an intimate way making sure her words were directed at Bartholomew and not George.

'To tell the truth, Miss Oak, I haven't seen a play since I left school. My time has been taken up with study, as I'm sure you can imagine.'

Sheba was a little disappointed. So, Mr. Westley was not to be a soul mate. 'What a shame. I adore literature in all its various shapes and forms.'

Bartholomew quickly realised that if he was to make an impression on Bathsheba Oak he must show some interest in her favourite subject.

'Of course, it's not that I dislike literature, Miss Oak, it's purely a lack of time which prevents me reading a great deal I assure you.'

Sheba was a little consoled so she smiled and leaned back in her seat. Perhaps I shouldn't judge him before I have had a chance to get to know him, she thought. Adeline was laughing at something George had said and Sheba couldn't help wondering if it was really that funny. She'd never seen anyone flirt so outrageously before and was thankful the journey was but a few miles long.

The theatre was impressive. Not large by city standards but beautifully decorated with silk hangings and etchings of recent performances. The deep-red velvet cushioned seats matched the curtains framing the lyric stage. The programme listed the players but as they were a travelling company the names were unfamiliar to the party. Their seats were to the left of centre giving them a splendid view of the stage and Adeline quickly organised them so that Sheba led the way followed by Bartholomew then herself and lastly George.

The play quickly got under way and the party of four along with the rest of the audience were soon engrossed in the exploits of the four lovers on stage. The path of true love which never runs smooth was very much in evidence that evening. How much Sheba was able to empathise with Hermia only she knew. However, now deep in the forest, the arrival of the rude mechanicals temporarily stayed the solemnity of the plot as they amusingly argued over which part they should play in their own Greek drama. As the lion roared Sheba could see Adeline clutching George's arm in mock fear. Bartholomew had noticed it too and wished Sheba would do the same but it hadn't taken him long to realise that she was not of the same ilk as his sister. He stopped himself. What was he thinking of? His intention in cultivating a friendship with Bathsheba Oak was to encourage a deeper friendship between his sister and George Abbot. All the same he found himself becoming more and more attracted to the serious-minded, intelligent, beautiful girl sitting next to him.

On the way back there was much discussion of the drama which had been enacted on the Godwinstone stage.

'It is such a romantic play, don't you think, Miss Oak?' Adeline asked of her companion. Without waiting for an answer she carried on whispering but loud enough for George to hear, 'Don't you wish you could procure some of that love potion? What fun we could have.' As she stopped speaking she looked across at George who had the good grace to blush ever so slightly.

Sheba was pleased when the carriage at last reached Weatherbury. Altogether the evening had been rather pleasant and Bartholomew an attentive companion. On the spur of the moment as he handed her out of the carriage she mentioned the ball at Exonbury college. 'I hope you don't think I'm being too forward Mr. Westley but I would like to invite you to my college ball.'

This is better than I could have hoped, thought Bartholomew, and accepted with alacrity. 'I'd be most honoured, Miss Oak.' He bowed his head slightly. 'Perhaps we could make a foursome of it. What do you say?'

'Er, I'm not sure how many guests I'm allowed to invite but I'll let you know, if I may?'

Adeline had overheard the conversation and put her head out of the carriage window. 'Do say it's alright, Miss Oak. George and I would love to come, wouldn't we George?'

Once again Sheba felt as if she had been manipulated into a situation about which she could do very little unless she told an outright lie, as the number of guests were not limited as far as she was aware and certainly her parents would be unable to attend as they had a prior engagement.

'Thank you for a pleasant evening, Mr Westley. I'll be sure to let you know as soon as possible.' They shook hands and as the carriage disappeared into the shadows Sheba sighed. I really will be pleased to be back at Exonbury. Life is far less complicated there, Sheba thought, as she climbed the stairs to her boudoir.

It had been an interesting evening though. The play had been, as it always would be for her, wonderful in the true sense of the word. Still thinking about the love story as she drifted off into sleep she mused on the multi-layers of the story and wondered, not for the first time, how on earth William Shakespeare had conceived such sparkling dialogue. She supposed that was what was meant by genius. Unless one was also a genius perhaps one would remain unable to understand fully the complex meanings. At the moment she had difficulty understanding the ordinary goings on of real life never mind the complexity of fiction.

She dreamed that night that she was Hermia. Her father was insisting she marry Demetrius but she couldn't because he loved Adeline. It was hardly surprising that Demetrius had the features of George Abbot. In her dream she could hear Adeline laughing as she offered her a love potion. She was about to take it when she was awakened by the acrid smell of smoke. Peering out of the window into the early dawn she could see clouds of smoke coming from the barn attached to the main house.

Obviously others had been awakened because she could hear footsteps rapidly descending the staircase. Wishing she was still dreaming, Sheba dressed quickly and joined the small throng who had gathered to help the fire fighters. It looked as though there was no stopping the blaze as it gathered momentum. Soon it would reach the main house.

Soon, red tongues of flame could be seen through the dense pall of smoke which billowed high into the early morning air, causing folk for miles around to look up and wonder what was on fire.

Gabriel, who had organised teams of firefighters many times was soon in control and gradually they reduced the angry flames to a sullen glow and finally to extinction but not until part of the main house, mostly the kitchen area, had been severely damaged. It would mean the family moving out for a time whilst the roof was repaired but apart from the inconvenience would not cause too much hardship.

Gabriel would stay on to supervise the work and in spite of his mother's concern, Matthew would also stay. In the end, Bathsheba decided to move into one of the nearby cottages so that she could keep an eye on her menfolk. She really didn't relish another stay away from Oakdene so soon after the last one.

There was no doubt, Oakdene was like a magnet to the Oaks. It seemed to hold on to them whatever happened.

But for Sheba it was time to go. Her college course could wait no longer although she was reluctant to leave her mother as the fire had caused her to be a little aggrieved. She had offered to stay but Bathsheba insisted she would be better out of the mess and had even managed to laugh when she said it. Sheba had hugged her mother insisting that she must not overdo things. Bathsheba had promised as she waved her daughter on her way.

Chapter Fourteen
In the Name of Progress...

THE DAMAGE TO THE old farmhouse house was not nearly as severe as had first been suspected. Some parts of the kitchen were out of action for some time as that was where the fire had started and not, as was first thought, in the barn. They would never know for sure how the fire started but were able to surmise due to the severity of the blaze that a spark from the open fireplace had spat its ire on to the hearth rug where it may have smouldered for several hours before finally igniting. When Maryann had vacated the kitchen there was but a small ember left glowing in the powdery grey ash.

The cook distinctly remembered checking, as indeed she always did, making sure the guard was firmly attached to the ancient brass fender before she took her leave around ten thirty. The barn being as it was, attached to the kitchen area of the house and sharing a wall, it was not long before the heat had been sufficient to ignite the carefully baled hay stored in the barn; hay which had on occasion generated enough heat to set itself aglow.

It didn't seem fair, Bathsheba commented to her friend Harriet on her now almost daily visits to the doctor's house. With all the care she and Gabriel took over securing their crop, making sure it was decently covered in all weathers, the barn should have been the safest place. The new insurance would take care of some of the lost profit but not all. Now Bathsheba had good reason to be pleased they had decided to go over more to dairy farming. Last year would have seen over half of their hard earned profit gone up in smoke. In the event it was little more than a third.

Harriet was getting restless as her time grew ever nearer and she was often heard to say that she would be glad when it was all over. Those who didn't know her well would have reason to think she was sorry she had got herself into her pregnant state. Although she thought, and her husband agreed, she should have a further few weeks to wait she felt deep inside it would not be that long. Bathsheba, seeing her friend blooming and excitable, felt twinges of regret that she had lost her own child in such a tragic fashion only a few short months ago. She still felt guilty at times but had at last ceased blaming Lady Emma Godwin.

It was as if Harriet had read her thoughts for she queried, 'Have you seen the Godwins lately, Bathsheba?'

'No, at least only in passing. Lady Emma gave one of her regal waves to me as she passed by in her Landau whilst out shopping in Weatherbury last week. Have you seen them?'

'We were invited to supper a few days ago but I really didn't feel up to it so we regretfully had to decline the invitation. I dare say we will be invited again in due course especially now they are patients of Theo's we shall need to be sociable although I must admit I find it no chore as they are such a delightful couple and Lady Emma shows enormous empathy with my state of health.'

Harriet grinned as Bathsheba nodded vigorously. They both knew the rules of the game and didn't mind playing in the least.

'Have you heard from your absent children, Bathsheba?' Harriet took a delight in hearing news of the Oak family as there always seemed to be something interesting happening.

'Adam's recent letter from Christminster declares he is still ecstatically happy. I only hope it lasts!' his fond mama declared with a smile. 'We shall be visiting the college next week. It is a pity you are so near your time, Harriet. We would have dearly loved you to accompany us. Perhaps next time?'

'I can certainly be there in my imagination though, Bathsheba. Theodore was at Christminster as you know, and never tires of telling me tales of his escapades. I feel as if I have been there myself sometimes. And Sheba; how is she?'

It was now several weeks since Sheba had returned to Exonbury. From her letters she seemed settled and happy.

'Sheba had a visit from young Bartholomew Westley last week. He is to partner her at the college ball, Harriet. He seems a pleasant enough young man and is known by Joseph Abbot of course. I must admit I thought it was George Abbot who was her raison d'être but it seems I was mistaken. I could have sworn that was the reason she wanted to leave home so quickly but she never said as much and I didn't ask.'

Harriet shifted about in her upright chair trying to find a comfortable position. 'Oakdene is completely finished now, I take it?'

'Yes, thank goodness. I took the opportunity to have a brand new cooker fitted which is a bit bigger than the old one. Maryann was most unhappy to begin with but now swears she couldn't possible live without it. She says it's easier to light and she absolutely delights in not having to suffer the smoke from the old black monster. Personally I prefer the old range. I suppose I'd got used to its peculiar little ways.' Both women laughed. It was common knowledge that Weatherbury folk did not like change even when it was in the name of progress.

'You don't talk much about Matthew, Bathsheba. Is he well?'

It was true. Bathsheba didn't talk much of her youngest son. He was a law unto himself and didn't seem to require much contact with humans. Apart from school and meal times he was totally absorbed in the stables having just acquired a new full grown horse of sixteen hands. Not that he neglected Prince. He would be with them until it was time for the knacker's yard. As Bathsheba explained to her friend, 'Matthew must be descended from Saint Francis of Assisi. Tis said he and the animals were as one and Matthew is the same. I'm not at all sure how he will cope with being an animal doctor though as he can't bear to see them hurt.'

'His satisfaction will come in the healing skills he will acquire, Bathsheba. Never you mind.'

Bathsheba supposed her friend was right. Her children never failed to amaze her and she felt a glow of pride as she recalled their accomplishments so far. She had every reason to be proud of them and hoped she would have reason to continue to be proud of them.

'It will be your turn soon, Harriet.'

'I really can't wait,' Harriet replied, rising with some considerable effort as her friend made for the door having heard her carriage arrive.

'Will I see you at my poetry soiree on Thursday, Harriet?'

'I'll do my utmost to be there, Bathsheba.' She kissed her friend goodbye and felt a now familiar twinge of pain in the lower regions of her back as she leaned forwards. She really would be glad when it was all over.

'We'll be reading from "Songs of Innocence and Experience",' Bathsheba explained. 'Do you have a copy of Blake's poems, Harriet?'

'As a matter of fact I do. I'll bring it.' The two women hugged each other before Bathsheba climbed into the waiting carriage.

As the carriage drew near to the cobbler's shop in Weatherbury, Bathsheba noticed a crowd milling around outside. It was a favourite meeting place for the women of Weatherbury, a place to exchange gossip, but there seemed more men than women today. Why aren't they at their work, Bathsheba thought? Tapping on the roof of the carriage she ordered Caleb to take her to where the noisy crowd was gathered.

She could see that it was Benjamin Tallboys who was holding forth, as he stood balanced high on a wooden chair, like the vicar in his pulpit. Bathsheba paused to listen.

'So you see, if you join the union you'll at least have some protection,' he explained above the noisy mutterings of the congregation.

'They'll never put up with it. It'll be certain dismissal for anyone who joins,' a voice from the front retorted with scorn.

Mr Tallboys was ready for the comment. 'That's where you're wrong, Andrew. We've moved on apace since the martyrs. Mr Oak has given me his word that joining the union will not affect you in any way whatsoever.'

There were groans and comments of disbelief as the men discussed the latest bit of news.

Bathsheba was surprised to hear Gabriel's name mentioned but when she thought about it, it seemed reasonable as her husband and Ben Tallboys had been collaborating for some time about better conditions for the workers. She had to admit she thought it was mainly about teaching the labourers to read and write but from this evidence it had gone much further.

Bathsheba turned to get back into the carriage. She would talk with Gabriel tonight. She felt a little aggrieved that he hadn't told her all the details of his plans. Then the awful thought crossed her mind that perhaps this was Mr. Tallboys" idea and her husband was unaware of what exactly was going on.

As the carriage drew away from the scene, a horseman went riding by. To her surprise, she saw that it was Gabriel. So, he did know what was going on. Bathsheba didn't know whether to be pleased or angry. She had always felt in charge of Weatherbury farm even though Gabriel organised the manual labour and day-to-day workings on the farm. She had never really accepted joint ownership and still ran the place in much the same way as her Uncle Levi Everdene had all those years ago, before he had died and left the farm to his niece.

Now, as the carriage rattled up the uneven cobbled drive, she took time to look at Oakdene. From its outward appearance very little had changed. Even the fire had caused need of little in the way of restoration. The only concession to progress was not to do with the building, that remained the same, it was the parterre in front of the house which had been reorganised to form rose beds and swards surrounded by tangled masses of summer flowers which at this time of the year were very little in evidence, it being the middle of winter. On the whole though, the old place was fundamentally unchanged and would remain so for a long time to come if she had her way. None of this so called progress for Oakdene. Bathsheba smiled to herself. She was as guilty of resisting change as any of her neighbours.

It was after nine when Gabriel finally arrived home. Bathsheba teased him, 'If I didn't know you better I'd be sure you were visiting another woman.'

Gabriel knew very well his wife was teasing for they loved each other as much now as they had on their wedding day and often reminded each other of the fact but he couldn't help feeling a little guilty that he had neglected her of late. He was so taken up with affairs of the farm and his collaboration with Benjamin Tallboys that the time seemed to slip away like sand through the fingers or a handful of dust.

Once again Gabriel had met his friend at the Kings Arms where they had discussed at length the recent turn of events. Benjamin was finding it hard going trying to convince the men they would not be discriminated against simply for joining the union. Some of them had, with some reluctance, at last joined his evening classes and were progressing well. After only a few weeks Andrew Smallways had pumped his teacher's hand in his excitement at being able to write his own name for the first time. But, when Ben had introduced the subject of trade unions he had met with a wall of silence. Incredibly, it appeared no one wanted to become a member even when their teacher had explained it was for their own good. There seemed to be a great gulf fixed between them.

Gabriel explained to Bathsheba, 'They're so behind the times it's unbelievable. You'd think the Tolpuddle Martyrs were transported only last year instead of more than forty years ago.'

The frustration he was feeling was plain to see. 'I don't know what to do, Bathsheba. I've called a meeting in the square after church on Sunday. If I can't convince them then, I shall give up!'

Bathsheba knew as well as he that would not be the case but she sympathised with him and promised her support. She would try, at her poetry soiree, to introduce the subject gently at first, just to see what the other women thought. All she had to do was convince her fellow females that what Gabriel and Benjamin were doing was the only way forward. Remind them that people have no hopes but from power.

Gabriel hugged his wife. She never failed to amaze him. Whenever he looked up there she was. To think, if it wasn't for Boldwood committing his dark deed all those years ago, she might still be married to Sargeant Frances Troy of the Dragoon Guards. He shivered involuntarily. Bathsheba took his hand in hers. It was a moment of telepathy. Together they could conquer the world, there was no doubt about it. However for the time being all they needed was to please each other and at this they had become expert. Tomorrow there would be problems to sort out, perhaps even resolve if they were really lucky but tonight was theirs, they had an urgent need for each other, and they made the most of it.

Chapter Fifteen
Two Contrary states.

BATHSHEBA CHECKED THE SMALL round table, where she had placed several copies of Blake's poems acquired from the Weatherbury Reading Room only this morning, tweaking the ecru lace cloth so that the pattern of roses hung in such a way to be pleasing to the eye.

With Christmas only a week away she was a little surprised that so many of her friends had agreed to attend this last session of the year. With all the preparations for the festive season gathering momentum it was a time of furious activity. For herself she was glad, to pause, to enjoy the time to relax away from the hustle and bustle and she guessed her guests must feel the same.

The atmosphere in the drawing room lent itself pleasantly to the event to take place. The logs on the fire blazed gently giving off an aroma of apple as they hissed. The huge Christmas tree, so recently introduced by Prince Albert into this country and as yet unadorned, for the trimming would take place on the eve before Christmas day, stood rooted in the corner giving off its distinctive pine smell. The odour from a large glass bowl of Chrysanthemums in the centre of the table added to the mix of perfumes in the room.

Mrs. Cross had arranged the Queen Anne chairs in a semi-circle. Gabriel's rocking chair stood slightly aloof from the rest. This is where the lady of the house would preside and start the proceedings. It was the hostess's prerogative to choose the poetry until the interval and to commence the reading.

Bathsheba sat in the rocking chair and opened her own copy of Blake's poems. She had decided to start with, "The Shepherd" as it seemed appropriate. She didn't necessarily agree that "the Shepherd's lot" was always sweet and neither would her friends but the sentiments were pleasant enough and it was a gentle poem to start the proceedings. It also seemed appropriate for the time of year.

Bathsheba wondered now, as she waited for her first guest to arrive whether she had been correct in asking Lady Emma Godwin if she would like to attend. Lady Emma had written straight back accepting the invitation "with great pleasure" and had seemed genuinely pleased to have been invited. She had asked if Lady Sarah could join them and Bathsheba had of course agreed.

Harriet was the first to arrive looking a little tired and very heavy but otherwise blooming.

The friends greeted each other with a hug. 'How are you, Harriet? Come and sit down, do.'

'I didn't think I'd make it, Bathsheba,' Harriet explained smiling. 'Every morning when I awake my first thought is "will it be today"? But still I go on.'

Bathsheba nodded with complete empathy. 'Do you think it wise to be away from your home, Harriet?'

'That's what Joseph asked but I managed to convince him that I could be home in a matter of fifteen minutes. I have taken the liberty of keeping my carriage under cover in your stables, Bathsheba. I hope you don't mind. And, nothing is likely to happen in that short time, don't you agree?'

Bathsheba actually didn't agree but decided to humour her friend. She well remembered how each day seemed to drag as she drew near her time with all three of her children, even though she was busy with farm work. She forced herself not to remember the fourth pregnancy. It was still very painful and whenever Gabriel asked her, as he often did, if she was sure she had recovered fully she would insist that she'd never felt better but they never talked of the possibility of having another child.

Eliza Hansworth the vicar's wife was next to arrive. It was the first time she had wanted to join the ladies as previously she had insisted, when invited by Bathsheba, that she had far more important things to do than become involved in such trivialities as poetry readings. When told, Gabriel had remarked that he could see little difference in psalms and poetry and Mrs. Hansworth was not averse to reading the psalms out loud in church. Bathsheba did not take up her husband's challenge to define the difference between psalms and poetry if indeed there was any but thought it might be an interesting topic for a later ladies" poetry evening.

Surprisingly, in the previous week, Eliza Hansworth had approached Bathsheba to ask specifically for an invitation which had caused a little curiosity and much speculation among the longer serving members of the group. Someone was heard to suggest that perhaps the interest shown by Lady Emma Godwin had something to do with Mrs. Hansworth's sudden decision as it was well known that Vicar Hansworth sought a higher post than vicar of a relatively small parish like Weatherbury.

Even before Mary Cross had announced her properly Eliza Hansworth had breezed into the room, black silk dress ballooning like a ship in full sail, taking the chair in the centre of the semi-circle so she would be sure to sit close to one of the more eminent guests. Bathsheba raised an eyebrow to Harriet who hid a smile behind her lace-gloved hand.

Bathsheba greeted the latest arrival cordially, handing her a poetry book.

'No thank you, Mrs Oak. I shall listen only if you do not mind,' her tone was precise and clipped.

Bathsheba would dearly have loved to say she did mind but her breeding would not allow it. Instead she insisted it was of course at the members own discretion whether or not they chose to read out loud or merely listen. Somehow Bathsheba managed to make only listening appear derogatory but the thick skinned woman missed the cynicism completely.

The Ladies from Martinsham Hall were next to arrive followed quickly by Louisa Abbot. After formal introductions were completed Lady Sarah and Lady Emma sat either side of the vicar's wife to her obvious pleasure and delight. Liddy would be joining them after refreshments had been served as she had kindly offered to help Maryann serve even though the latter had insisted she could manage perfectly well thank you. Bathsheba knew Liddy felt uncomfortable in the presence of such distinguished guests and had only agreed to attend at all because Bathsheba had been so persuasive.

As soon as everyone was seated comfortably, Bathsheba began reading;

'How sweet is the Shepherd's lot!
From the morn to the evening he strays;
He shall follow his sheep all day,
And his tongue shall be filled with praise.

For he hears the lamb's innocent call,
And he hears the ewe's tender reply;
He is watchful while they are in peace,
For they know when their shepherd is nigh.'

There was applause all round. Eliza Hansworth looked at first one and then the other to see the reaction of her neighbours. She desperately wanted to be correct in her etiquette, to make an impression on the Ladies present, it was almost painfully embarrassing to observe. One might almost feel sorry for the woman if she wasn't so pretentious.

Bathsheba agreed to read two more of the "Innocence" poems before the break for refreshments and had already chosen "Laughing Song" because it was so jolly and "A Cradle Song" especially for Harriet. Again the applause resounded around the room as she finished with;

'Infant smiles are his own smiles;
Heaven & earth to peace beguiles.'

There was a tap on the door announcing the arrival of the refreshments. Whilst the company partook of the fare Lady Emma offered to play on the pianoforte a pleasing, jolly piece by Mozart. Bathsheba had wanted to bring up the subject of the workers and the unions but as it was important for Lady Emma to take part she had to put it off. Instead she was forced to listen to Eliza Hansworth fawning to Lady Sarah about what an excellent job the vicar was doing for the Weatherbury inhabitants.

Then the chance that favours the prepared mind occurred. Mrs. Hansworth was singing further praises of Vicar Hansworth to Lady Sarah and everyone else who would listen when she mentioned how kind he was to let Benjamin Tallboys have the use of a room at the vicarage to educate the peasants.

Bathsheba seized the opportunity to put her case. 'I do so agree with you, Mrs. Hansworth. Mr. Tallboys is doing a splendid job. In fact he is trying to persuade the men to better themselves.'

'Oh yes. And I agree entirely. The labourers should be taught to read and write. How else can they benefit from the Good Book?' She turned to Lady Emma who had finished playing the lively concerto and had rejoined the group having been superseded by Lady Sarah who couldn't wait to escape from the vicar's wife.

'Don't you, Lady Emma?'

Emma Godwin nodded her agreement. 'Not only from the Good Book though, Mrs. Hansworth. There is a certain amount of knowledge to be gained from the bible, I endorse that, but there are many other sources of knowledge you know. For instance, there are other excellent books one can read and we can also learn a great deal from listening to those who are better educated than ourselves. Don't you agree?'

Mrs. Hansworth nodded her agreement but looked slightly taken aback. She didn't expect Lady Emma to be on the side of the peasants thinking her status gave her ample reason to be above that sort of thing. She couldn't have been more wrong for Lady Emma continued, 'I also think it is a splendid idea if the men are better educated and especially if they decide thereafter to join in the union movement. What do you think, Mrs. Oak?'

This was the chance Bathsheba had been waiting for. She hadn't expected Lady Emma to be so completely on the side of the labourers though. It was a pleasant surprise and she made the most of it.

'As a matter of fact, Lady Emma, I was hoping to broach the subject after the readings this evening.'

'Let's discuss it now! What had you in mind, Mrs. Oak?'

Bathsheba glanced across at Lady Sarah who responded quickly, 'I'm happy to carry on playing, Mrs. Oak, as I've no wish to become directly involved.'

Putting down her delicate china cup, Bathsheba began, 'I'm not sure how much everyone here knows about the union movement. I know Louisa and Harriet are aware of the position of the workers. Perhaps I'd better start by asking who doesn't know what's going on.'

Bathsheba looked round the assembled group. Liddy had now joined them having served the refreshments. She asked, 'What exactly is the union movement all about, Bathsheba?'

'It's about workers having a force behind them; to see they are adequately rewarded for the work they do; to see that the conditions in which they do their work are amenable to the job.'

Liddy nodded her head. 'I see. It sounds reasonable to me. Is there a problem?'

There was a chorus of yesses as the women all wanted to explain to the naive Liddy exactly what the problems were. It was Lady Emma who gained the floor.

'It's simply this,' she explained. 'The men are frightened that their employers will refuse to keep on anybody who joins a union because of the demand for higher wages.'

Liddy responded quickly. 'I see, Lady Emma, and I can understand that. But, is it true? Have they good reason to be concerned? Your husband is a wealthy landowner; how does he feel?'

'He's all for the unions. He's a fair minded man, although I say it myself.' She looked pointedly at Mrs. Hansworth as she spoke who having been singing her own husband's praises herself all evening now realised Lady Emma had noticed. Embarrassed, she had the good grace to look down at her feet.

Liddy continued. Whilst the other woman were happy to let her speak she would carry on. 'I've heard tell that your husband, Sir Cornelius, pays above the odds anyway. Naturally he would go along with the plan but what about the farmworkers. They're the ones who could suffer most, surely.' Liddy had grown quite red in the face by this time.

Bathsheba joined in, 'You see Liddy, 'tis the farmworkers who need the union, not necessarily the factory workers, although I do believe Martin and Godwin are exceptional in the way they treat their workers. I've heard that in the cities factory work can be every bit as grim and hard as work on the land.'

The women had become so engrossed in the topic of conversation no one but Lady Sarah had noticed Harriet's discomfort. The pregnant woman was leaning against the pianoforte where Sarah Godwin had ceased playing in order to try to persuade her she should go home.

Bathsheba left the group and joined her friend. 'I'll call for the carriage, Harriet. You really should be at home. You don't look at all well.'

Harriet agreed willingly to let Liddy go for the conveyance. The sporadic discomfort in her lower back had been steadily getting worse all evening. The pain seemed to be more at the front now and although she should have a little longer to wait she felt the birth was imminent.

'I'll come with you, Harriet,' Bathsheba insisted.

'You can't leave your guests, Bathsheba. I'll be alright.'

'Then I really must insist Liddy accompanies you, Harriet.'

Liddy was happy to go along. It wouldn't be the first time she had assisted at a birth.

'Come along Mrs. Melksham,' Liddy said kindly 'I'll see you safely home. Will the doctor be there?'

'Unless he's been called out, he'll be at home.' Harriet was becoming a little confused as the pain seemed to take over her entire body.

The ladies" group had ceased conversing and all eyes were upon the expectant mother. All, with the exception of Lady Sarah Godwin who for some reason of her own had remained a spinster, knew what Harriet was going through and all wished they were able to do more for her.

'Would you like to take the Landau, Mrs. Melksham? It will much more comfortable than the governess cart you came in.' Lady Emma offered kindly.

Assuring her she would be perfectly alright, Harriet, with the help of Bathsheba and Liddy made her way to the front door where her own carriage awaited.

'Be sure and let us know when the child is born, Liddy,' Bathsheba instructed as the carriage pulled away in haste.

'I will, I will,' cried Liddy as the carriage drew away, under the oak tunnel and down the long drive to the main Weatherbury Road.

The women returned to the drawing room but none wished to continue the discussion. All thoughts were with Harriet. Everyone would be pleased when the happy event had taken place. Dr. and Mrs. Melksham were a popular couple and there would be much celebrating at the announcement of the new arrival.

By the time Gabriel arrived home, the guests had all gone and the house was quiet once again. Matthew had had supper with a friend and would not be back until the following day so Gabriel found Bathsheba sitting alone in his chair reading when he arrived at about ten o'clock.

He was eager to know how the talk of the unions had been received.

'I think the Godwins are in favour of union membership,' Bathsheba was able to report. 'I'm not sure where Vicar Hansworth's wife stands. She seems to want to impress the Godwins so she may not raise objections, which of course means we will have the support of the vicar.'

Gabriel smiled. 'They're too much like social climbers to be committed Christians if you ask me. It don't seem right for the vicar to be that way inclined. Still, as long as they don't make trouble, I'll not complain.'

Suddenly there was a great clattering at the front door as if the caller was chased by the devil himself. As Maryann had retired to her bed, Gabriel answered the call.

'Oh, Mr. Oak, is Bathsheba still up?' A distraught Liddy, big round tears coursing one another down her nose, pleaded.

'Why, yes, Liddy. Come in.' He took her arm and guided her to the drawing room.

Bathsheba had risen and was at the door to see what all the commotion was about.

'Liddy? What is it?' Bathsheba sat the woman down gently. 'Tell me! Is it Harriet? Is she alright?'

Liddy was weeping softly now. 'She had a fine baby boy, Bathsheba. Everything was fine and then suddenly,' Liddy was having difficulty speaking. 'Suddenly there was a great gush of blood and Mrs. Melksham just sort of collapsed.'

'Was the doctor there? Has he managed to stem the bleeding, Liddy?'

Liddy shook her head.

'Liddy?' There was an element of hysterics entering into Bathsheba's voice as she shook Liddy. 'Tell me for God's sake woman!'

'He was too late. It happened so quickly.'

Gabriel poured a measure of brandy into three glasses. 'Drink this!' he ordered, swallowing his in one gulp.

'I knew she should have stayed at home. I told her to.' Bathsheba was sobbing silently. She had been so looking forward to this Christmas birth. Felt it would make up for her own loss somehow.

'God moves in a mysterious way.' Gabriel sat down with his arm around his wife in a vain attempt to comfort her.

'The doctor wants to call the baby Gabriel, after his Godfather,' Liddy sniffed.

Bathsheba looked up at Gabriel. She had forgotten they had promised to be Godparents. It seemed so long ago.

'At least we can share in looking after little Gabriel,' she said to her husband. 'I shall go to Theodore in the morning and offer any help he may want.'

Liddy had recovered her equilibrium a little so Gabriel offered to see her back to Nest Cottage. He felt he could do with some fresh air.

'I'll look in on Theodore whilst I'm out that way, if you don't mind, Bathsheba?'

'I'd like that, Gabriel.' She touched his hand as he passed her chair, 'but please don't be too late back.'

Bathsheba sat for a while longer, gently rocking, watching the dying flames lick round the last bits of log remaining in the ancient fireplace, craving and finding a small degree of comfort in Gabriel's old chair. Strange to think that only a few hours ago they had all been sitting here discussing something as trivial as trade unions. But it wasn't trivial she told herself. Just different.

Bathsheba suddenly realised that they hadn't had the chance to read any of the "Experience" poems. Never mind, there was always another day, but it wouldn't be the same without dear Harriet.

Chapter Sixteen
Season of Goodwill.

IT WAS VERY LATE, nay, very early, and a carpet of glistening white frost lay spread over the Wessex countryside by the time Gabriel finally arrived back at Oakdene. After he had escorted Liddy safely home to Manor Farm Cottage, he had gone straight on to Theodore Melksham's home to offer his condolences.

The doctor appeared overwhelmed by what had happened and repeated to Gabriel over and over again, 'I asked her not to go out. I should have insisted she stayed at home.'

Gabriel didn't know what to say to console the poor stricken man. Never one for hyperbole, he had simply sat with his friend and let him do the talking, trying when the need arose to assure him he was in no way to blame for his wife's untimely death.

Baby Gabriel was in safe keeping at the home of the pre-arranged wet nurse, a distant cousin of the Melkshams who lived in the High Street, only a short walk from "The Elms', the house which had been in the Melksham family for many generations.

Theodore, sitting dazedly in his deep leather armchair, his head cradled in his hands, occasionally looked up, around the room, noticing the furnishings he and Harriet had chosen. Playfully, she had made a condition when she had agreed to marry him he now remembered; insisted she must have some bright new furnishings in the drawing room. He also remembered how he had laughingly said it was but a small price to pay for such a precious commodity as her love for him.

Apart from a few small changes, in the name of progress, in some of the other downstairs rooms, the old house was the same as it always had been. Tears pricked anew at the back of his eyes as he remembered Harriet's delectation when the gorgeous rose pink patterned chintz had been delivered, at about this time, last year. She was so thrilled that the drawing room would now be finished in time to show off to her family on their yule-tide visit.

Although they had been married for such a short time the couple had accumulated many memories and these were echoed throughout the house mostly in art form, pictures, hangings and ornaments. In days to come the doctor would be able to draw strength from those precious memories but now he felt almost numb except for a strange, deep resentment mainly aimed at the inanimate objects which surrounded him, most likely due to the fact that they were still here and his beloved wife was gone forever and he would never see her again in an earthly form.

Eventually, after persuading the doctor to take some of his own medicine in the form of a sedative, Gabriel helped him to his bed-chamber where his housekeeper's husband took charge, assuring Gabriel of his continuing care of his employer. And yes, he would let Gabriel know should Dr. Melksham require anything at all, no matter what time of the day or night.

With some reluctance, Gabriel took his leave, but with the thought that Bathsheba would be anxiously awaiting his return, he rode as fast as he could back to Oakdene.

Bathsheba had been in bed for several hours but had been unable to sleep. She was so pleased to see her husband she wept. 'I began to think you wouldn't return safely, Gabriel,' she said between her tears.

'Well, I'm here now so you can dry those tears and try to get some sleep. 'Tis the baby and Theodore we must think of now,' he reminded her gently.

'Of course. You're quite right, Gabriel. I'm being selfish, just thinking of myself. But Gabriel, I shall miss Harriet so much I can hardly bear it.'

'You must pray for the Good Lord to give you strength. That's all you can do.'

Gabriel snuffed out the candle and kissed his wife good night.

What an eventful day it had turned out to be. He hoped sincerely that the following weeks would yield up far less excitement and anguish than the previous days.

Soon it was only two days to go before Christmas and the Oak family were all ready in the Hall, waiting for Caleb to bring round the carriage, for they were off to visit Adam at Christminster.

Sheba and Jayne had arrived the previous day to spend the first half of their vacation at Oakdene, the other half was to be spent at the Devonshire home of Jayne, full of news of college life and especially full of excitement as they'd described the end of term Ball. It seemed both girls were very much taken with the young Mr. Westley although it was Sheba he had danced with most, Jayne informed them.

Bathsheba, still in a state of shock at losing her best friend, tried to join in with the festive mood but was finding it extremely difficult. However she was looking forward to seeing Adam and hoped he would be able to travel back with them. It would be comforting to have the family all under the same roof at this special time of year.

Although they had invited him, Theodore would not be joining them. At his late wife's mother's insistence he had gone into Devonshire to stay with them as soon as the funeral was over. Gabriel was relieved as he felt the doctor needed to get away from Weatherbury for a few weeks at least. He had left his new son in the tender care of the wet nurse who would be taking him into Devonshire as soon as he was old enough to withstand the journey. No one knew whether he would stay there with Harriet's parents. Only time would tell. Bathsheba hoped sincerely that Theodore would bring them back with him when he returned. In the meantime, she would be keeping a watchful eye on the young Gabriel, which came as no chore. He was a dear little thing, all pink and white and a credit to his late mother. Bathsheba loved him dearly already.

Surprisingly, the Godwins had decided to accompany them to Christminster. It was a sudden decision but, Sir Cornelius, having expressed an interest in the architecture of the colleges, said he would dearly love to visit with them. To this end he had commissioned a railway carriage for all of them and even arranged for a hackney carriage to meet them at the station in Christminster to transport the party to the college chapel.

If Gabriel felt any resentment at Sir Cornelius" "interference" then he kept quiet about it. In spite of and not because of his wealth, Gabriel admired the man and his wife and anything which would make life easier for Bathsheba at this difficult time he saw as a good idea. Certainly Lady Emma had been most obliging when she had visited Bathsheba the day after the dreadful news had been received offering to do anything she could to help.

The girls had taken extra care with their appearance, fashionable new gowns were very much in evidence, and they were very excited at the prospect of the visit. Sheba, appeared to her parents, to be well and happy. She had been out in the company of Bartholomew Westley several times of late and seemed to have forgotten George's lack of interest.

Jayne was an ideal companion for her; a lively bubbly personality was just what Sheba needed, being, like her father, of a rather quiet nature. Indeed it was what they all needed and Jayne, true to form, regaled them with amusing tales of life at the Exonbury college and life on her parents" farm in the depths of the Devonshire countryside, throughout the train journey to Christminster.

Although the weather had turned cold it had not yet snowed but so heavy were the clouds it would be surprising if it didn't snow before the party returned home, a fact which didn't worry them in the least. On the contrary they hoped it would snow soon, for Christmas was almost upon them.

Adam was waiting in the carriage when they arrived at Christminster station. He was accompanied by his room mate who he introduced as Christian de Lore the younger son of the Earl of Bardwitch. Gabriel laughed inwardly at the exalted company he kept these days. To think that long ago when he had worked at Weatherbury farm, and then later married his employer, he had been a struggling farm labourer, parading at the hiring fair along with all the other peasants. Life had been hard for him but it had also been good.

As the carriage drew up in front of the chapel the bells were ringing out to welcome visitors.

Inside, the chapel was resplendent with a profusion of lighted candles. The choir, assembled ready for their walk down the aisle to the stalls where they would perform the carols and anthems, wore bright red gowns topped by immaculate white ruffs. Each held a candle which lit up his face giving to each chorister something of an angelic appearance.

The chapel was already nearly full but Adam showed the party to reserved seats near the front, close to the altar where some students had set up a model of the nativity. Bathsheba was suddenly overcome as she saw the infant Jesus lying in the manger for all the world like a real baby. Gabriel passed her his large red and white kerchief as he had in the summerhouse at Martinsham Hall. She smiled her appreciation, determined to concentrate on the service and not allow her grief to spoil the occasion for everyone else.

The story of the nativity never failed to move her and she could see others around her who obviously felt the same. Carols were sung with gusto, students read the nine lessons, interspersed with more carols, the vicar read from St. Luke, even more carols were sung and then it was over.

Outside the chapel it had begun to get dark and the light from the old-fashioned naphtha lamps in the courts which surrounded the college threw the buildings into relief giving them an olde worlde Romantic air. In the event they had very little time to view the college but Adam insisted they at the very least look at his room and its environs, having travelled so far. In fact, it took very little time to be shown round and as refreshments had been laid on in the refectory they all made their way there before boarding the carriage for the railway station and home.

Adam would not be travelling with them after all, as he had a pre-arranged appointment to fulfil. He had had a stroke of good fortune, the poetry he had written was to be published in the New Year but there remained one or two minor details that needed his attention and could not be put off until after the vacation.

With some reluctance his parents and sister wished him farewell but as they would be seeing him shortly it was not with too much sadness. The Godwins were already in the carriage so with haste they set off for the train. Their train journey would take them first to the capital before they changed lines for Wessex.

As the train finally pulled into the station at Weatherbury it was in the early hours of the next day. A few flakes of snow started to fall and Sheba shivered. 'I hope Maryann has put plenty of logs on the fire, mama.'

Bathsheba put her arm around her daughter, 'I'm sure she will have.' She turned to the other members of the party, 'Perhaps we could roast some chestnuts?'

A cheer from everyone ensured it was a popular decision, Bathsheba turned to Lady Emma, 'Would you care to join us?'

Sir Cornelius answered for her, 'I'm afraid we must refuse on this occasion, Mrs. Oak. We have arranged to be met at the station and we wouldn't wish to keep the coachman waiting unnecessarily long in this cold.'

Cornelius Godwin was quite correct. The small flakes were growing larger by the minute and there was a definite, frosty chill in the air. Soon the layer of white would transform the countryside into scenery barely recognisable.

'Then we'll keep you no longer. Good night and thank you kindly.' Gabriel extended his hand.

The party said their farewells, promising to visit each other at sometime during the festive season, leaving the Godwins to continue their journey on the train until it reached Martinsham.

At Oakdene, Maryann had set out a buffet for them in the dining room and just as Bathsheba had predicted there was a blazing log fire to greet them. Matthew had waited up for them and was sitting close to the fire reading. Gabriel had been unable to persuade his younger son to accompany them to Christminster in spite of Bathsheba's silent prayer. She had hoped that if Matthew saw for himself what an excellent time Adam was having then he would eventually want to join him.

Matthew stood up as they entered. 'Mother, father, may I speak with you?'

'My, this sounds serious, Won't it keep "til tomorrow?' Gabriel replied smiling.

'It is, father and no it won't'

'Then you'd better come to my study after the meal, m'boy.'

'I'd rather speak to you now, Sir.'

Gabriel recognised the seriousness in his young son's voice and decided to go along with his request. 'Very well, Matthew. Bathsheba, you stay here with the girls. We won't be long.'

The two men went off whilst the ladies helped themselves to the tempting array set before them.

In the study, Gabriel invited his son to sit.

'What's this all about, young man?' Gabriel asked curiously.

'Father,' he hesitated and started again. 'Father.' What ever he wanted to say was obviously much more difficult than the boy had anticipated.

'Come on, son, out with it!' This was most unlike Matthew and Gabriel was concerned. What on earth had the boy been up to, he asked himself?

'I want to leave school, Sir.'

Gabriel stood up. 'Would you like to start at the beginning and tell me exactly what's brought this on?' Gabriel was concerned and he could imagine what Bathsheba's reaction would be.

Matthew stood up, drew a deep breath and began, 'I was out riding a few weeks ago and I met a rider from the Casterbridge barracks,' Matthew paused, still unsure how to tell his father what he had on his mind.

Gabriel paced backwards and forwards in spite of his weariness. This was getting more and more difficult as by now he had some inkling of what Matthew was going to say. He hoped he was wrong but tried hard to be patient, 'Go on, Matthew,' he urged.

'Well Sir, the gentleman was an officer from the Dragoon Guards who are, as you know, staying in Casterbridge. Father, I wish to join with them.' Matthew sat down again, exhausted at actually saying what he had been rehearsing for many days.

Gabriel walked over to his son. 'I thought you wanted to be a vetinary, Matthew. Why the sudden change of heart?'

Matthew explained as best he could how he couldn't bear to hurt animals even though it was for their own good and as for killing them whenever it was deemed necessary, he could never do that. As a dragoon officer he would have his own horse and that would do for him.

Even to his own ears it sounded weak but surprisingly, his father seemed to understand.

'I think the army is a good choice, Matthew, but I know your mother will never agree.'

'Please talk to her, father? She will listen to you, I'm sure.

Gabriel grimaced wryly. 'You have a faith in me which I think is unworthy, my son,' Gabriel said patting him affectionately on the shoulder. 'But I must ask you to say nothing until after the celebrations have finished. At least let your mother enjoy this special time. She's had a lot to put up with of late. She deserves some respite.'

Matthew reluctantly agreed to wait. If he had his way he would leave this very day but he didn't want to hurt his mother, or his father for that matter.

As they left the scene of the revelation father and son joined the others acting as if they had just had a chat about the weather. Gabriel knew his wife would question him about his conversation with his son but he thought on this occasion a small white lie wouldn't go amiss and prepared one accordingly.

'What have you two been talking about?' Sheba enquired as they entered the room.

Bathsheba looked up enquiringly. Gabriel thought quickly. 'Just men's talk.' He looked at Matthew and winked. Matthew took his cue from his father and responded with a grin.

Bathsheba wasn't satisfied with the compact answer but she could talk to Gabriel later. Now they could all sit by the fire, roast some chestnuts and perhaps later, if they could keep awake, they would sing some carols while she accompanied them on the piano.

Chapter Seventeen
Resolutions and Change.

As GABRIEL HAD PREDICTED, his wife had questioned him about his mysterious talk with Matthew which had taken place before supper just as soon as they were alone. 'Are you going to tell me what "the men's talk" was all about, Gabriel?' she had enquired, her curiosity edged with impatience.

Gabriel had given the matter a great deal of thought, had even considered telling his wife the truth but then decided it would too cruel and an economy with the truth would be kinder.

'Matthew wished to talk about his future career. I think he's feeling quite grown up now, Bathsheba.'

'Well, he's nearly sixteen. I suppose it's not too early to decide.' She paused as a sudden thought struck her, 'I must say I'm surprised he felt it was so urgent. After all, Gabriel, he's known what he wants to do almost since he could talk, don't you agree?'

'I think he just wanted to talk man to man, if you know what I mean. I rarely see him these days, what with one thing or another. I suppose he thought if he didn't say what he wanted to say straight away, the opportunity might not arise for a long time.'

'I think I know what you're trying to say, Gabriel, but surely it could have waited until after the Christmas celebrations are over or at least until our guests have gone,' she insisted.

'Bathsheba, Matthew doesn't see Jayne as a guest. She's just his sister's friend,' he laughed.

Bathsheba joined in his laughter. 'I suppose you're right.'

'It's good to hear you laugh, Bathsheba. I've been so worried about you since poor Harriet died.'

'Well, coming on top of our own sad loss, it was even harder than it might have been, but I am a survivor, Gabriel,' she reminded her husband, 'I'll be alright. It's only when I allow myself to wallow, you know, to remember Harriet and what might have been, that I get melancholic.' Her eyes filled with tears. 'Don't you worry about me.'

Gabriel nodded. 'I love you. Of course I worry about you.'

How he was going to break the latest news he wasn't sure but as his wife had reminded him, she was a survivor. He hoped she would not try to persuade Matthew not to join the military, for the wrong reasons. Sargeant Francis Troy had hurt her badly and the tragedy was bound to have an effect on her reaction.

Christmas at Oakdene was always celebrated in a true Christian tradition. Attendance at the Church service in the morning, huge excesses at lunch time followed by parlour games in the afternoon in which everyone took part without exception. Afternoon tea was served informally in the parlour followed by a mass exodus to Weatherbury church for traditional carol singing and nine lessons.

Adam had arrived on Christmas Eve afternoon much to his mother's delight for she had started to imagine something would prevent him from joining them. In spite of a brave face she was very concerned that another tragedy would befall them before they had decently recovered from the traumas of the last months.

Matthew appeared, to his watchful mother, restless but Bathsheba put it down to his being confined indoors more as the weather had worsened. A light flurry of snow had fallen on Christmas day but it was on Boxing day the sky had become so heavy that no one was surprised at the blizzard like conditions that occurred in and around Weatherbury, effectively making transport for visitors difficult in the extreme if not impossible.

By the next day, the snow so threatening yesterday, had all but disappeared except for slushy heaps at the side of the lanes and byways where folk had made a vain attempt to beat cold nature. But, it would be a long time before the fields returned to their rich green and the trees regained their leaves. Conditions now being reasonable, it was off to Acorn Farm to deliver presents which should have rightfully been exchanged the day before.

Sheba, knowing George would be there, had mentally prepared herself for the meeting. Jayne expressed a desire to meet with George, she'd heard a great deal about him from Bartholomew and surprisingly little from Sheba, and was as excited as a child on Christmas morning. Sheba had carefully pointed out that George was somewhat entangled with Bartholomew's sister Adeline but it mattered not a jot to the carefree Jayne for she so enjoyed meeting new people.

The festivities were in full swing when the party from Oakdene arrived at Acorn Farm. A huge red-berried, red-ribboned, holly wreath adorned the white-painted Georgian front door and the freshly decorated Hall was bedecked with holly and ivy in the latest fashion filling the air with its evergreen scent.

As they entered, Adeline was playing a lively complicated air on the piano and George was leaning over attentively. At the arrival of the guests he crossed the room in haste to greet them.

After formal introductions George spoke to Jayne, 'So you are at Exonbury with Sheba, Miss Hartsworth. Are you to take up the teaching profession when your studies are finished?'

'At the moment, I'm not at all sure, Mr. Abbot. There are so many exciting things to do and see that I'd not like to be tied down to one thing too soon.'

Adeline had stopped playing in order to join the young people.

'That's what I believe, Miss Hartsworth.' She glanced coyly at George, 'but don't you think it's a good idea for a young lady to be married before she sets out to seek adventure?'

'On the contrary, Miss Westley,' Jayne quickly replied, 'I should think a husband might be a positive handicap, if one wanted to see other countries for instance.'

'But surely one could visit together the Romantic countries. In my view it would be far less hazardous to be accompanied by one's husband. Don't you agree?'

Jayne thought, "this young lady is obsessed with being married. You would think she was afeared of being left on the shelf."

Not wanting to upset Adeline she merely pointed out to her that in this day and age where travel was so much easier than it had been in her own mother's time, she would be quite happy to travel abroad with only a good friend to share the delights, and a chaperone of course, implying that Miss Westley was out-moded in her outlook.

Sheba joined in, 'Perhaps we could go together, Jayne. I would dearly love to see Rome and Florence for myself having read so much about Italy.'

Adeline was not at all happy with the way the conversation was going. Sheba and Jayne together had somehow managed to make her feel small and unsophisticated. Not to be outdone she took George's arm with a proprietary air and led him to the piano. 'I shall play for you, George. What shall it be this time?'

George, fond as he was of Adeline, was clearly embarrassed at her blatant show of possessiveness, and said quickly.

'I think perhaps a dance tune would be in order. How about the Dashing White Sergeant, Adeline? Can you manage that?'

Not wanting to confess she'd rather dance than play, having just offered to play especially for George, she turned angrily back to the piano and commenced playing. To her chagrin, George went straight to Sheba and asked her to dance.

'Miss Oak,' he said formerly with a curt bow. 'May I have the pleasure?'

Miss Oak could hardly refuse without seeming impolite so she inclined her head and was led on to the floor by George, quickly followed by Jayne and Bartholomew. Several of the other guests quickly formed groups and soon the dancing was in full swing.

Adam skirted around the room avoiding as best he could the fast moving groups of dancers. Miss Westley looked quite fierce as she banged out the dance tunes and he wanted to find out the cause of her aggression.

'You seem to be enjoying yourself, Miss Westley,' Adam stated ironically.

Adeline looked up to see the tall, dark haired young man who had been introduced earlier as Miss Oak's brother from Christminster. She knew very little about Adam but he looked somehow different to the others. She couldn't make out whether it was the way he was dressed or the fact that he was so tall. Then she realised it was his hair. It was much longer than was the latest fashion. Indeed, he could have stepped out of the last century for his long curly hair was pulled back and secured with a velvet bow. Clearly he was no slave to fashion although his dress was similar to that of any young man of his age. Adeline admired people who were different and she determined to get to know this young man better. She took her foot from the loud pedal and looked up at Adam.

'Mr. Oak, I offered to play for George Abbot and he requested a dance tune. It is not my choice and therefore I must confess not to my taste entirely.'

'I'm sure everyone is enjoying themselves, Miss Westley.'

'Then that pleases me.' Adeline's words did not quite match her tone and Adam guessed there was more going on in her mind than he could fathom at the moment. What a pretty girl she is, Adam thought, I shall ask her to dance at the first opportunity. He excused himself and went across to his mother who was sitting watching the dancers.

'Mother, could I ask you a favour? Would you mind playing for us? Miss Westley is a little tired and would like to rest but she doesn't wish to complain on her own behalf of course.'

Bathsheba agreed at once. She welcomed something positive to do as she didn't feel like dancing or playing cards which was what everyone else was doing. Adeline was delighted to change places with Bathsheba and said so. 'It's very kind of you, Mrs. Oak.'

Adam guided Adeline to two vacant chairs in the corner where they could watch the dancers without being observed by anyone themselves.

'Why so much anger, Miss Westley?'

Adeline was so surprised at Adam's question she was almost lost for words. However she quickly regained her composure and denied she had been angry.

'I think the Dashing White Sargeant needs to be played with gusto, Mr. Oak. Don't you?'

Adam realised Adeline was not going to confide in him readily. He would have to get to know her much better before she trusted him enough to share her feelings.

Instead they talked of everyday kind of things and Adam told her about the poetry he had written.

'Mr. Oak, you're a poet! Would you let me have a copy of the anthology as soon as it is published?'

'Are you interested in poetry, Miss Westley?'

Adeline admitted to knowing very little about classic poetry but had a desire to learn.

'Then you must attend one of my mother's poetry evenings, Miss Westley. I'll speak to her if you wish.'

Adeline thought it would be a good chance to get to know this dashing young poet better and would give her the chance to make George jealous. She hoped it might stir George into making an offer. Something she had been angling after ever since she had met her brother's best friend.

'Thank you, Mr. Oak. I'll look forward to that,' she smiled hoping George was watching.

George had disappeared to the billiard room with his father and Gabriel but the look had not been missed by Jayne who was already a little in love with the handsome poet herself.

'How affected is that young woman, Sheba. Who does she think she is?'

'She is very handsome, Jayne.' Sheba answered as if the fact that Adeline was beautiful gave her the right to be flirtatious.

She was confused about her own feelings for George. He had been so attentive when she had danced with him and he'd been clearly embarrassed by Adeline's possessiveness. Did this mean that he didn't care for her or was he simply not ready to be committed to any one person yet? After all it would be several years before he would be sufficiently qualified in his father's eyes to take on a farm of his own.

Why was life so complicated, she asked herself? In all the classic novels she had read the heroine always ended up with the hero. If only real life could be the same, she sighed.

Jayne noticed the deep sigh and felt sorry for her friend. She had guessed soon after she had met Sheba at Exonbury that her new friend had run away from a problem at home and it hadn't taken much to discover the reason might be unrequited love. They had talked in the dormitory, after lights out, for many hours, and although Sheba had mentioned no names, Jayne had put two and two together and arrived at George. She vowed to do as much as she could to bring the two together.

During supper there was much talk of the annual ball to be held at Martinsham Hall on New Year's Eve. It was a huge affair and anyone who was anyone would be there. Bathsheba and Gabriel had never been before as they usually held a small celebration in there own home. This year, however, the Godwin's had issued an invitation and although Gabriel had told his wife he would prefer to stay at home he knew he it would be foolish to turn down such a prestigious invitation and it might be useful to cement the growing friendship as an aid to furthering more business transactions particularly with regard to the union debate which would no doubt gather momentum once the festivities were over.

Late that night, in the sanctity of Sheba's boudoir, the two girls discussed the evenings activities.

'How much do you like, Bartholomew, Sheba?'

'He's good-looking and entertaining. I like him.' Sheba answer was casual to say the least.

'What about George?' Jayne asked in corresponding tone.

'What about George?' Sheba's reply was defensive and told Jayne all she wanted to know. Why Sheba didn't admit her fondness for the man, Jayne couldn't quite work out and somehow felt Sheba was not ready to talk about her feelings.

'He's not as fond of Adeline as you led me to believe,' Jayne said pointedly.

Sheba laughed. 'Poor thing. He was quite embarrassed when Adeline dragged him away.' Sheba performed a similar movement on Jayne's arm and the two girls fell back on the bed laughing.

Jayne sat up suddenly. 'Sheba, tell me about the Ball at Martinsham. Who will be there?'

'I don't know much about it except that it has been an annual event for simply ages. We've never been before as father and mama have only fairly recently become acquainted with Sir Cornelius and Lady Emma. I'm so glad you're here, Jayne. You will come with us of course?'

'Will Bartholomew and George be going, Sheba?'

'Oh yes. Everyone who was at the Abbots today and many, many others.'

Jayne was pleased she would have the chance to encourage the friendship between George and Sheba although she hadn't expected the opportunity to occur this soon. To this end, she was pleased to accept an invitation to join the party at the New Year's Eve Ball to be given by the Godwins of Martinsham Hall.

Chapter Eighteen
Merrily, Merrily we welcome in the Year.

L OVE SEEKETH NOT ITSELF to please,
  Nor for itself hath any care,
But for another gives its ease
And builds a Heaven in Hell's despair.

The Christmas vacation was galloping along at an alarming speed for Oakdene's young and not so young alike. Gabriel had all his usual farming tasks to perform but with everyone lending a hand, including Jayne, he was able to spend more time at home than usual.

Bathsheba hadn't mentioned Matthew's career again so Gabriel decided to let sleeping dogs lie, at least until the new year which he realised now, as he sat by the window watching Westy play with the two young pups they'd kept, was only one day away.

Tonight it was the big party at Martinsham Hall. The women had already started preparing for the occasion. There had been much discussion about fashion and hair styles between them at the breakfast table. The men had merely chatted amongst themselves and got on with the more important task of eating.

It was good to see Bathsheba looking so well. True she still shed a few tears whenever she allowed herself to think about Harriet but she managed to keep those sad times hidden from everyone except her husband. On these occasions he could say little to comfort her but his presence was itself a comfort and as much as she seemed to need. Words would have been superfluous somehow.

The men, having finished their meal long before the ladies had even started their second cup of beverage excused themselves with the simple reason that there was work to be done. Not feeling the least bit guilty, Bathsheba, Sheba and Jayne continued the important discussion of the Ball.

Both young ladies had brought several new gowns with them, Gowns which had been made by the London dressmaker in Exonbury and would certainly not look out of place at Martinsham Hall making their only problem one of choice. For Bathsheba however, the concern was that her dinner gown was not quite suitable for such a grand occasion as she felt she must wear black in respect for Harriet. After Jayne suggested she add a rather pretty corsage of white silk camellias to the bodice of the black velvet gown, complimenting the outfit with a similar flower in her hair, she was satisfied.

'Thank you, Jayne. I shall try it and ask Mr Oak for his opinion.'

Jayne was pleased Sheba's mother had agreed to try her idea. Her own mother would have insisted she was too young and inexperienced to know such things. She vowed that when she had children of her own, she would always listen to them, no matter what.

The day passed in a flurry of preparation for the big event. As soon as the clock struck seven, Caleb arrived at the front door with the carriage. Surprisingly, everyone was ready and no one had needed to be called for. Bathsheba looked as elegant as Gabriel had ever seen her. He had assured her when asked for his opinion that she would be, without a shadow of doubt, the most attractive woman in the room, which pleased her and caused her to blush a little.

It was more than six miles to Martinsham from Weatherbury and some of the way was little more than rough track. Fortunately the weather had remained dry but the early evening frost promised far colder weather to come. The travellers hoped it would not snow later making the return journey difficult if not downright hazardous.

They could see the flares which lit up the Hall before the carriage reached the long tree lined drive. Lights had been placed at frequent intervals along the curving driveway making it easy to see where they were going. Naphtha flares along the length of the balustraded terrace had the effect of making Martinsham Hall look even grander and larger than it really was although it was one of the largest houses in the whole of Wessex.

Liveried footmen in blue and gold uniforms were waiting at the huge entrance doors to show guests into the house. As the party from Oakdene arrived two of the footmen stepped forwards to help the ladies descend from their carriage and escort them into the entrance hall. Gabriel and his two sons followed and when they had caught up the head footman stepped forwards and asked them to accompany him.

The double doors of the Great Hall stood wide open and as they entered they were each introduced by name,

'Mr and Mrs Gabriel Oak and their sons Adam and Matthew, their daughter Bathsheba and friend Miss Jayne Hartsworth,' he boomed.

Sir Cornelius, Lady Emma and The Honourable Sarah Godwin were standing to the left of the entrance where, each time there was a new arrival, they could step forward to greet each guest with a personal 'Good evening', and a shake of the hand.

Formalities over, the party was shown to a table at the edge of the floor where they could either watch the dancing or take the floor with ease. Neatly placed on the table was an agenda showing the evening's activities. These included a list of dances, entertainment in the form of music and song and an invitation to partake of a cold buffet in the small dining room at any time after eight thirty.

Sheba sat down between her brothers, Jayne sat next to Adam and Bathsheba was comfortably sandwiched between her youngest son and her husband. The highly polished, sprung mahogany floor was perfect for dancing and it wasn't long before the young people were taking advantage of the setting, the music and the presence of other like-minded beings who were intent on enjoying themselves.

'Would you care to dance, Bathsheba?' Gabriel asked his wife.

'A little later, if you don't mind. I'm enjoying watching the others. The young ones have so much energy, don't you agree?'

'Indeed they do!'

The Abbots were seated several tables away and as Bathsheba caught Louisa's eye she waved, beckoning her to join them.

Gabriel rose as Louisa and Joseph joined them.

'What a splendid gathering, Bathsheba. How are you enjoying yourself?' Louisa enquired.

'Very well, under the circumstances,' her friend smiled. She leaned over to Louisa and whispered, 'What enormous chandeliers. I keep wondering how those narrow chains can support all that glittering heavy glass. I fully expect that any minute there will be a great crash as they come falling down.'

Both women laughed loudly causing Gabriel to break his conversation with Joseph in order to ask what was the cause of such jollity.

When Louisa related the tale, Gabriel went into great detail of the mechanics of the chandeliers including the method of letting them down to re-light the candles.

The two women were certainly impressed by such knowledge and felt much happier about dancing under the magnificent arcades of light.

'In that case, Bathsheba, would you care to dance?' Joseph asked.

'I'd be delighted, Joseph.'

Gabriel looked across at Louisa. He didn't really want to dance. He loved music and played his flute at the first opportunity which arose but as for dancing, that was a different story. He was happy to do a jig at the Harvest Home or suchlike occasion but formal dancing was not to his taste. Louisa didn't mind a bit. Like Bathsheba, she gained an enormous amount of pleasure by watching the dancers and was quite happy to sit and converse with her neighbours.

It wasn't long before their host joined them.

'You're enjoying yourselves, I trust?' Sir Cornelius asked politely.

'We certainly are,' the two replied in unison.

'Won't you join us?' Gabriel suggested.

'As a matter of fact, I will.' Cornelius had, with his wife, been on his feet meeting and greeting guests for the past hour and a half and a little footsore by this time, was glad of the chance to sit for a while. Lady Emma had repaired to the small dining room to look over the spread Mrs Summers and her entourage had prepared. There was no real need but it was a habit she had started when they first entertained at the Hall many years ago and it gave her the chance to express her appreciation to the servants before the hard work of clearing up commenced. It seemed to work well for very rarely did they have to employ new staff and then it was usually someone of the same family who was already working at the Hall. It certainly made for good relations and made for a happy household.

As Matthew was about to sit down, Louisa stood up. 'If you're free, Matthew perhaps you and I will show the others how a polka should be performed.' Without further ado, she whisked him away to the middle of the floor.

Gabriel wondered what to say to Cornelius. He was never a one for small talk and even today's weather was hardly interesting enough to provide a topic for conversation. He need not have worried for Sir Cornelius had something he wanted to say.

'Gabriel. I hope you don't mind my broaching the subject of the work you and Mr. Tallboys are undertaking. I would not wish to spoil your enjoyment on this occasion? After all you were invited here to enjoy yourself.' There was an implied question in what Cornelius said and he waited expectantly for a reply.

'Not at all, Sir.' Gabriel was pleased for he had wanted to talk to this influential man about the union movement but felt that this was neither the time or the place. As Sir Cornelius had brought up the matter Gabriel felt he should make the most of it. 'I was wondering when it would be convenient to see how you felt. There was trouble in the Square a few days ago. The men are very concerned about the possibility of being branded trouble-makers if they so much as talk about joining a union.'

Sir Cornelius Godwin nodded 'I understand that. That's why I just wanted to say, that if there is any trouble, I'm on your side. I've heard talk from both sides of the fence. Most of the landowners in these parts have ruled the roost for so long now they won't take kindly to change. Especially if they are not the instigators.'

Gabriel was a little surprised at the man's statement. He was aware of Sir Cornelius" altruism, why else would he and his engineering firm have built the model village for his factory workers and made sure they were paid adequate wages? 'That's very kind of you Sir. If there is any trouble, I'll know where to come.'

'Good man!' His host shook him by the hand as he stood up. 'I must do the rounds now, socialise you know, or I'll have Emma after me.' He laughed as he left Gabriel a little bemused, gazing after him. He's not unlike myself, he thought.

As the dancing came to an end the young people joined Gabriel at the table. They had brought with them several other young people including the Westleys and George Abbot.

'All that dancing has made me hungry,' Matthew declared having returned his energetic partner to her husband.

'It's nearly nine o'clock and the agenda states the buffet is ready from eight thirty, so shall we go?' Bathsheba suggested.

En masse the party headed for the dining room on the other side of the main entrance. The spread was enormous. Never had Gabriel and his friends seen so much food displayed and so delightfully prepared. It was arranged on three long refectory tables which were set out to form an upturned U. In the middle of the meat table sat a boar's head surrounded by dark meat, white meat, pies and pastries filled with delicacies and the most amazingly delicate sandwiches they'd ever seen.

A huge, round richly decorated fruit cake had pride of place on the top table and this was surrounded by sweet pastries, tarts, biscuits, mousses, jellies and fruits including some they had never seen before and couldn't put a name to.

The table opposite the meat table was given over to dishes of salad and vegetables all prettily decorated for the occasion. On the large sideboard their hosts had thoughtfully arranged to have placed dishes of hot food and soup for those guests who felt the need for a warming meal.

In a side room yet another refectory table was laden with drinks and beverages. At intervals around the room, liveried footmen in the now familiar blue and gold uniform of the Godwin household, hovered, on hand to help anyone who was unsure about what to do. The party decided to fill their platters and make their way back to the Great Hall for it was nearly time for the entertainment which would begin with a quartet who were to play a little chamber music, followed by a boy soprano who would perform for the guests some popular carols.

On their return the youngsters made for the large table leaving the four adults to themselves. Jayne had suggested this while they were collecting the food and both the Abbots and the Oaks had agreed with alacrity.

Jayne had decided this was the night she would encourage the friendship between Sheba and George so when Adeline tried to push past her in order to sit next to George she waylaid her. 'Miss Westley, would you mind taking the seat next to Adam. I believe he has something he wants to ask you.'

Adam looked up surprised but he wasn't going to object to sitting next to the pretty young Adeline so he quickly replied, 'Yes, Miss Westley. Come, sit here,' patting the chair next to him.

'Well, Mr. Oak! What is it you wanted to say to me?' Adeline asked seating herself close to Adam.

Adam was never at a loss for words, especially where young ladies were concerned. 'I wished to say how lovely you look, Miss Westley. The scarlet of your dress is most becoming and makes you stand out in the room above anyone else.' Adam said in a low voice, aware that Jayne was watching him with a slightly quizzical look.

The compliment pleased Adeline and she fairly preened as she smiled and thanked Adam.

'Would you like another glass of wine, Miss Westley?'

Adeline, who did not usually drink alcohol having been told that it was bad for the complexion, declined politely and reminded Adam that the string quartet was about to commence.

Conversations were halted or at least quietened as the music began. Sheba, sitting next to George, was very much aware of his proximity and felt the old familiar thrill in the pit of her stomach she thought she had dispensed with forever. She was also aware of George's gaze. His chair was in such a position that he had to look almost directly at her in order to watch the musicians on the raised dias at the end of the room. She looked down at her hands and noticed a slight tremble. This is absurd, she thought, but there isn't a way for me to decently remove myself so I must concentrate hard on the music.

It seemed to work for almost at once she was in control gaining pleasure from the exquisite baroque music, soon feeling almost happy and relaxed. As soon as the music was finished, the boy soprano, with the help of the Martinsham church choir, entertained them with popular songs and carols, some new like Good King Wenceslas and some rather old as "God Bless the master of this house.' in which everyone joined in enthusiastically. The "Boar's Head Carol" was particularly poignant as the choir had sang it at the Christminster Carol Service. It was only later that evening when Adam confessed to his mother he had requested the carol especially for her that Bathsheba realised where she'd heard before. Then it was back to the dancing.

George was the first to stand, insisting Sheba partner him for a reel. Soon the Great Hall was a rainbow mass of dancers, all eager to enjoy the last hour of the year. As they stood waiting for their turn to promenade, George whispered to Sheba, 'I really did want to see Westy's puppies you know.'

Sheba felt her heart miss a beat. She looked up at her tall, handsome partner as if for the first time. His eyes showed he meant what he said but there was still the question of his close friendship with Adeline Westley. Sheba was confused. She didn't dare to hope, dare she?

'We kept two of them, George.'

'May I see them tomorrow?' he asked gently.

'I'm off to Devonshire with Jayne at noon.'

'Then it will have to be early. Shall we say ten thirty?'

Sheba nodded as she lifted her skirt in preparation for their promenade.

Soon it was midnight and as the bells rang out there was much hugging and kissing especially between Miss Oak and Mr. Abbot. For the first time Sheba wished she hadn't arranged to go with Jayne to her parents" house. What had seemed like a good idea at the time, was now proving to be something of a mistake. But, she couldn't let Jayne down so Sheba said nothing, which was a pity because Jayne would have been the first to insist she stayed within close proximity of her re-discovered love.

All was not completely lost, however, because the following morning, true to his word, George arrived at the precise time he had promised. Together they went to see Westy's now half grown puppies.

'Would you like one?' Sheba asked.

George picked up the smaller of the two. 'This one will do,' he laughed. 'It reminds me of you.'

Sheba was mystified. 'How?'

'She is small but not too small, pretty but not overly so, she looks intelligent and has a mind of her own.'

It was quite a speech and Sheba was flattered. She longed to ask whether the puppy also reminded him of Adeline, it was frisky and full of fun, but that would have to wait. For the time being she was pleased that she and George were back to normal. Deep down she wasn't sure he cared for her as she cared for him but they both had a great deal to do before there was any possibility of a commitment. Some girls did become engaged at a very young age but Sheba felt she was not mature enough to make such an undertaking even if it had been suggested. Tempting as it was for her to encourage the friendship, possibly forsaking her course of study in order to be near to George, but having made up her mind to become a teacher, Sheba was determined to follow her chosen career.

'I shall miss you, Sheba, when you go back to your college.'

Sheba leaned up and gave his cheek a quick peck. 'I'll look forward to the Spring vacation, George. We'll be so busy the time will pass in a flash.' She wasn't sure what she had just said was true but it seemed the right thing to say.

'I'm sure you're right. Bartie and I are in the middle of an exciting project. I should be able to tell you about it by April.'

I'll look forward to that,' Sheba replied her eyes telling George all he needed to know.

Jayne appeared in the barn to remind Sheba that it was nearly time to go. She was very pleased with herself for it took only a glance to see that her little talk with George had had some effect on the couple. What happened next was up to them. Perhaps someone would do the same for her one day.

Chapter Nineteen
From little Acorns...

WITH JAYNE AND SHEBA gone, Oakdene had quickly become a much quieter place. It wasn't that the girls created a great deal of noise. On the contrary, they were both well-behaved, well-brought-up young ladies who were a credit to their families. It was more an air of quietness, a stillness which served to enhance the dreadful feeling of loss that would haunt Bathsheba, often when she least expected it. Much as she loved her menfolk she missed the closeness of the relationship with her best friend Harriet and of course her daughter. She was fortunate to have the support of a loving husband, she reminded herself when the blackness was at its worst, and Louisa was tremendous with her sympathy and understanding when she could spare the time to visit Oakdene. Often Louisa would bring with her small gifts which she thought might help to dispel her friend's melancholy. On one occasion it had been some lavender water she had seen on an outing to Melchester, another time it was scarlet ribbons. It was a pity that Acorn

Farm was so far away on the other side of Casterbridge for Bathsheba felt the journey tedious now the weather was bad.

Sitting in the drawing room several days after the girls had left for Devonshire she had a sudden thought. Whilst it was reasonably quiet she would use the time to her advantage by having a talk with Matthew. Adam had gone to see George and Bartholomew. Although not mechanically minded he had expressed a desire to see how far the students had progressed with their project before he returned to Christminster at the end of next week.

Bathsheba had seen Matthew go into the library so she put down the needlepoint she had just begun and went in search of him. He was sitting by the blazing log fire gazing into the flames as if he were all alone on some deserted isle. In spite of the softness of her call, Matthew started like a guilty thing, upon a fearful summons.

'I'm sorry if I startled you, Matthew.'

'It's alright, mama, I was miles away.'

'And where may I ask, were you?' his fond mama enquired.

Matthew wondered when his father would speak to her of his plan to join the military. Obviously he had said nothing yet or he would have heard about it. 'I was watching the flames burn pictures into the logs, mama. Look, can you see how those two logs together take the form of a cave?'

If Bathsheba was surprised at this unlikely response from her usually level headed son then she didn't let it show. She peered into the flames trying in vain to see what he meant. Not wanting to let on she couldn't see the cave she encouraged him to tell her what else he could see.

'It's how I imagine Hell to be. All glowing red and hot and deep.' He laughed suddenly. 'That got you going, eh mama?'

Bathsheba joined in her son's laughter but not without a dreadful feeling of unease. She decided to change the subject completely. 'Matthew, it won't be long before you start you're apprenticeship with John Cooper, the veterinary, will it?'

Matthew's head snapped up. He didn't know what to say. This was awful. He couldn't let his mother continue to think he was going to stay in Weatherbury, become an animal doctor, as he had always led her to believe

'Mother, there's something you should know, have the right to know.'

'Yes, son, what is it?'

Matthew couldn't bring himself to confess the whole truth. On the other hand he couldn't lie.

'I'm not sure about studying to become an animal doctor,' he began.

'So, that's what you wanted to tell your father the other evening, Matthew. That's alright. We wouldn't wish you to do anything which would make you unhappy. Have you thought what you might like to do? Will you work with your father, here at Oakdene? I'm sure he'll be so pleased. There's no need to worry.' Bathsheba patted her son's shoulder reassuringly.

'It's not the study that has put me off, you know?' He didn't want any misunderstanding, didn't want her to think he was unintelligent. If she thought he'd lost confidence she would very likely go to see his master at the Casterbridge Grammar school.

'Whatever the reason, Matthew, you are old enough to know what you wish to do and as I say, your father will be very pleased. It was always his dream that his son would take over the running of the farm when he grows too old.'

Matthew felt terrible. He was digging himself a big hole from which there would be no escape if he wasn't careful. He must see his father this evening and persuade him to tell his mother. If not the Lord only knows what he would do. He had visions of packing a small bag and leaving home in the middle of the night. He shivered at the thought.

'Are you cold, Matthew? It's rather warm in here. Perhaps you are getting this awful chill which is going around.'

Matthew assured her he was alright. 'It was just someone walking over my grave, mama,' he laughed.

'Don't ever say that, Matthew, not even in jest. I've always thought what a dreadful saying it is.' Bathsheba knew she had over-reacted but it had just come out.

'Let's go and find Maryann. She'll make us a beverage. Will chocolate do?'

They went together, arms linked, to the sanctuary of the kitchen where Maryann, with seeming second sight, had just made a huge pot of chocolate.

They sat down in the ladderback chairs and waited for Maryann to place two steaming cups of chocolate before them. 'Would you like a slice of seed cake with your chocolate, Master Matthew?' Maryann enquired. It had always been his favourite and to refuse would cause his mother to be even more convinced he was sickening so he grinned at Maryann, 'Of course!' Then remembering he was in the presence of a parent revised his answer to, 'Yes please, Maryann' which made them all laugh.

'And when do ye go back to school, Master Matthew?' Maryann asked throwing more coal on to the fire before she sat for a minute to enjoy her chocolate and a chat with her Mistress.

Matthew, who didn't know quite what to say, thought for a second then answered, 'Not yet, Maryann.' It was the best he could manage in the circumstances.

Maryann turned her attention back to Bathsheba. 'How many for supper tonight, Mrs. Oak?'

'George is bringing some young people back with him so let me see, that will make six altogether.'

Matthew was pleased to hear they were to have company. He made up his mind to have words with his father immediately after supper. The inevitable could be delayed no longer. Whatever the outcome he felt ready to face up to it. His determination to join the military grew more each time his future was mentioned and that seemed to be a great deal of late.

Excusing himself with the wish to visit Prince and ride, as the weather was fine with no sign of snow, he left the two women to discuss the supper menu. He needed to get outside, to breathe the fresh crispness of the winter day. How stifling Oakdene can be, he thought as he took the reins from Caleb. 'I shall ride as far as Acorn farm, Caleb. I might meet the George and the others on their way back.'

'Right-O, young master. But you be careful now. The ground is hard where the frost lies deep in the shadows.'

Matthew clicked with his tongue, and Prince responded immediately. Soon they were galloping as one, across the rough scrub of heathland which separated the richly cultivated land of Weatherbury Farm and its neighbours from the busy market town of Weatherbury. On a sudden impulse he changed direction. He wouldn't go to meet his brother and his friends; he would go on to Casterbridge. He just might bump into the officer from the dragoon guards, if he were lucky. At the very least he could ride up High West Street, past Top o'Town where the entrance, grey and turreted, to the garrison building stood looking for all the world like an ancient castle, and admire the red-coated soldiers who paraded up and down on guard.

As he reached his destination, he sat back in the saddle and watched the men busily going about their duties. A small band was practising a march in the courtyard, their breath steaming in the coldness of the January day. Matthew was suddenly hit by a desire so strong he marvelled he had never felt such an urge before. He must play an instrument in the marching band. He could already play the pianoforte a little and his father had given him some tuition on the flute so it should not be too difficult to secure a place in the company.

He turned Prince in the direction of the town. He could not wait to tell his mother or anyone who would listen. He had never felt so sure, so excited, about anything. When his mother realised how he felt she would be glad for him. With all apprehension gone, he trotted sedately through the town, past the Corn Exchange where the colonel's wife had declared its use as a tea and coffee room for the military in the previous decade, but once over Grey's Bridge he kicked his heels against Prince's side and soon they were galloping as they'd never moved before, across the water meadows, on to the heath, across the solid ruts of the ploughed fields until he reached Oakdene.

Caleb was still in the stables. 'Yu'm worked "im "ard, Master Matthew. He's fair sweating and so are you.'

'Give him a rub down, Caleb. He's done me proud this afternoon,' he instructed, patting the horse's neck with grateful affection.

'Had a good ride, did'e sir?'

Matthew decided on the spur of the moment to take the elderly man into his confidence. He felt he had to tell someone or he would burst. He followed Caleb into the stall.

'Caleb, If I tell you something, will you promise it will go no further, at least for the time being?'

Caleb nodded as he started to remove Prince's tack.

Matthew turned so that he could see the man's face as he told him his news. 'I'm to join the military, Caleb. I'm going to be a soldier.'

Caleb nearly dropped the saddle he was about to hang on the wall so great was his surprise. 'Does tha" mother know that?'

'Not yet, Caleb. Why do you ask?'

'"Tis not for me to say. Ye must ask her.'

'But you are pleased, aren't you?'

'If it's what you want young sir. You'll be knowing your own mind better "an I, I daresay.'

Matthew knew that for some reason he wasn't going to divulge, Caleb was not pleased. He wished that someone would tell him why his mother would be so against the idea. Well, tonight he would find out. He could not and would not go on in this fashion any longer.

Leaving Caleb to finish off in the stables, Matthew went to the house. It was very quiet so obviously Adam and the others had not yet returned. Bathsheba came out of the drawing room as he was about to ascend the stairs.

'I thought I heard someone come in. How was your ride?'

'Splendid, mother. Mother, may I speak with you?'

'This sounds serious. I'm just about to rest for a while before supper. Would you like to come with me? We can talk while I'm resting.'

Matthew followed Bathsheba upstairs rehearsing what he would say. As soon as his mother appeared settled and relaxed he began, cautiously at first, limiting the subject matter to affairs of the farm.

Bathsheba could sense her son was not getting to the point so she reached over and put a hand on his shoulder, 'Matthew, Matthew, please say what it is you want to tell me for I can stand the suspense no longer.'

'Alright, mother.' Matthew took a deep breath, took his mother's hands in both of his and said simply, 'I'm going to join the military.'

Bathsheba sat bolt upright and snatched her hand from her son's intense grasp. 'Is this a cruel joke, Matthew? Who's put you up to this? Tell me, tell me at once!'

Matthew sprang up and moved quickly across to the window. The curtains not yet drawn against a wintry sky, he was surprised to see that everything outside looked quite normal. It was almost quite dark but in the light from the moon he could pick out the last remaining, deep red berries on the holly bushes which flanked the gateposts.

He turned slowly to face his tight-lipped mother. She sat upright in her chair with a look of anxious enquiry on her pale face.

'It's not a joke, is it Matthew?'

'No, mother, it most certainly is not a joke. I've never been more serious in my life,' he replied tersely.

'I don't know what to say. Does your father know?'

'Yes. I believe he meant to tell you this evening.'

'How long have you known, Matthew? Why haven't you said anything before?' There were so many questions Bathsheba wanted answered and yet she didn't really want to know, could not take in what her youngest was telling her.

'A few weeks, now mama. Father said he wanted to wait until the time was right, said you've had it rough these last few months. I just wanted to do what was right.'

At her son's last statement, Bathsheba nearly exploded. 'Do what is right?' she asked incredulously. 'Becoming an animal doctor, working on the farm, that's what is right. What on earth has possessed you to come up with such a foolish idea? The military! I've never heard anything so ridiculous, so unsuitable in my life.' Bathsheba uncharacteristically burst into tears.

Matthew was horrified. This was worse than anything he had anticipated. He moved across to his mother's chair so that he could put an arm around her, to offer a little comfort.

She pushed his arm away with force. 'I'll not let you, Matthew.' Concerned because he thought his mother was on the verge of becoming hysterical he fairly ran out of the room on the pretext of going to fetch smelling salts.

Running quickly down the stairs as if Beelzebub himself were after him, he very nearly knocked his father over.

'Steady, boy! Where's the fire?' Gabriel laughed putting a restraining hand on his son's shoulder.

"Please go and see mama. I think she's going to faint,' a panic stricken Matthew explained to his father.

'Whatever's going on?' Suddenly the penny dropped. 'You've told her. You young fool!' Gabriel took the steps two at a time. No wonder he'd heard such a commotion as he'd opened the door. Why the whole of Weatherbury must wonder what's going on, he exaggerated to himself on his flight up the wide oak staircase.

Bathsheba had recovered a little when he arrived in the room. Recovered enough to insist on an explanation.

'To tell the truth, Bathsheba, it came as much as a surprise to me. He told me he had talked with an officer whilst out riding and had made up his mind, just like that.'

'Then you can talk him out of it, "just like that',' Bathsheba said sarcastically. She was behaving quite out of character for she was not easily ruffled and not normally of caustic wit.

Gabriel sat down next to his wife. He didn't know what to say to make the situation less tense. That's why he had put it off for as long as possible. He took her hand gently. 'Bathsheba, do you remember how we agreed to encourage the children to be independent, think for themselves and ultimately make their own decisions?' He looked into her dark eyes and could see clearly the deep unhappiness within. He longed to comfort her in the only way he knew how but this was neither the time nor the place so he sat quietly and waited for her answer.

"What you say is true, Gabriel. Her eyes filled with tears once more, 'but I cannot let Matthew go away to war, to fight, to be killed more than likely.' Her voice rose as she imagined the horrors of war.

'But there is no war, Bathsheba.' He tried to lighten the situation. 'He'll have a fine old time playing at soldiers, you see, and I dare say he'll soon get fed up with it and come home, carry on with his animal doctoring like he always said he would and we can forget all this.'

'Does he know about Troy?'

It was a simple question but it had the desired effect.

Gabriel sat back in his chair. 'No! He doesn't and there's no need.'

Bathsheba disagreed. 'I think you're wrong. Tell him and let him hear for himself the kind of "gentlemen" who are in command of a regiment.'

'That's not fair, Bathsheba. Frank was no good but you can't judge the whole of the military by him. It's noble to fight for one's country surely?'

'It's no good, Gabriel. You must go now and tell Matthew he cannot join the army and especially not the dragoon guards. That's my final word.'

Bathsheba left the room and went down to the kitchen. She would tell Liddy about it, she would understand. Liddy had promised to help with the entertaining as Maryann had needed to visit her sick sister. Sure enough Liddy was there with Temperance and Soberness. The latter made themselves scarce when they saw the pained look on their mistress" face, with the excuse that there were urgent jobs to be done in the scullery.

'Those two have become quite perceptive with maturity, I'm pleased to say,' Liddy said noting the redness of eye her employer was displaying.

Bathsheba was disappointed at Liddy's reaction at the news. 'It were a long time ago, weren't it? You should let bygones be bygones that's all I can say.'

'But you don't understand, Liddy. It's not only Sargeant Troy who has turned me against the military. I've seen pictures of soldiers fighting at the front in the Crimean war. In Mr. Johnson's gallery, in Casterbridge, hang the most dreadful pictures of scenes from Balaclava and Inkerman and Sebastopol. I couldn't bear my kind, gentle Matthew to be involved in the likes o'that. How could any mother in her right mind?'

'Mrs. Oak, it's what men do,' Liddy replied simply.

If Bathsheba hoped for sympathy from Liddy Bateman then she was sadly disappointed. There was a time when the good woman would have agreed with anything she said but times change, and with it, people.

'Have you tried telling him all this?' Liddy enquired.

'No, I haven't.' Bathsheba replied with a tremor in her voice.

'Then I think you should,' Liddy replied kindly.

Bathsheba left Liddy to attend to the last minute arrangements. In less than an hour the expected guests would arrive and she must re-collect herself before then. She went back to her boudoir where only such a short time ago Matthew had dropped his bombshell. The chair still stood in the same position but the curtains had been drawn against the winter draughts by a thoughtful servant. As Bathsheba performed her toilette, her mind was seething with memories of long ago. He had deceived her, her dashing red sergeant. She had fallen head over heels in love with the handsome officer only to be let down over and over again. She couldn't let her beloved son follow in such treacherous footsteps but it seemed inevitable. All she could do was tell him, warn him even, and then let him make up his own mind. If she didn't then she might lose him for good, she knew that.

Chapter Twenty
Pictures at An Exhibition

B ATHSHEBA HEARD VOICES IN the Great hall and guessed it must be Adam and his friends arriving back from Acorn Farm. She had remained in her room since talking with Matthew, not wanting any further confrontation just yet. Better to organise exactly what she was going to say before she talked with her son once more. If she had any hope of persuading him not to join the guards she must sound absolutely convincing and that would take a deal of careful preparation. Tonight she would say nothing, act as normal and let the whole situation cool a little.

However, proverbially, the best laid schemes of mice and men often go awry. Gabriel's pronouncement certainly disrupted Bathsheba's intention.

'So, he's told you then!' Gabriel stood in the doorway, his face a strange contrast of anxiety and question.

Bathsheba sat down in the chair so recently a spectator to the stormy scene between mother and son.

"Yes,' she replied simply.

'I gather, from him, er, Matthew, you were none too pleased.'

His seemingly careless, almost hesitant tone infuriated Bathsheba. 'What did you expect? Ah, there, there, Matthew. What a good idea! I am pleased!' Tears stabbed at the back of her eyes but this time she would not allow herself to show her true feelings.

Gabriel moved across the room with the intention of trying to comfort his wife.

'Why didn't you tell me? Matthew said he'd asked you to.'

'I'm sorry, Bathsheba.' Gabriel stopped his journey across the room and held on to the bed post as if he himself needed some support. 'I was waiting for the right time.'

'Right time, right time! There could never be a right time as far as I'm concerned. You must have realised that.'

Gabriel was at a loss. He had known she would be upset, justifiably so, but he hadn't been able to think of anything he could say that would be of any help or comfort. 'Bathsheba,' he began.

'Gabriel, listen to me. Please?'

Gabriel sat on the edge of the bed.

'Of course. Go ahead m'dear.' He couldn't even hazard a guess as to what might be coming next.

'I'm going to tell him.'

Gabriel had a good idea about what, but thought it politic to ask, 'Tell him what?'

'About Frank, about his deception, about Fanny Robin, everything. I want him to know just how awful the "fancy" dragoon guards can be.'

Gabriel thought it was highly likely Matthew already knew a large part of his mother's past as it was common knowledge hereabouts and happenings of that magnitude are not forgotten quickly. They tend to be passed down from one generation to another so it was unlikely Matthew knew absolutely nothing about the handsome guards officer and the lady farmer.

'Is that wise, m'dear? Shouldn't we let him find out for himself what the army's like? I doubt whether he'll listen to you anyway. He wouldn't listen to me. He's made up his mind good and proper, or so it seems.'

'Maybe you're right. I don't know. But Gabriel, let's say nothing tonight. I don't want everyone joining in the discussion. 'Tis a family matter, I know, but I don't want Adam involved until after I've talked again with Matthew.'

Gabriel agreed. A time lapse would give everyone the opportunity to calm down a little.

Although there was a certain amount of tension between mother and son, the evening was spent congenially, George and Bartholomew telling tales of college life, at times making everyone roar with laughter. It was amazing how they managed to get any real work done but there was a serious side to their nature and it was shown by their enthusiasm when discussing the special project they were working on. If they were rather secretive about their work this only lent to the seriousness of it. Gabriel was intrigued.

'I wish I'd had the chance when I were a lad, young George. Why, it was all I could do to keep myself employed. Did I tell you about the time I lost a flock of sheep over the edge of Norcombe Hill?'

There was a chorus from Adam and Matthew, 'Yes, father. Many times.'

'I don't think I've heard, Mr. Oak. It sounds disastrous.' George was teasing him and Gabriel, not realising at first, was about to launch into the sorry saga of his mad young sheep dog, the son of old George, a reliable old dog if ever there was one, who chased his newly acquired flock of sheep. Believing he was doing his master a favour, in his enthusiasm he forced the poor defenceless creatures to break through the hedge. The sad result was they went over the edge of a chalk pit, which killed each and every one of them, and all whilst the farmer slept.

'And them not yet paid for,' Adam finished for him. Even Bathsheba managed a smile. 'Well, that was a long time ago and it took your father more years than enough to pay off that debt.'

There was more laughter. These days the young people took so much for granted and Gabriel thought about reminding them, but things being as they were with young Matthew, he changed his mind. It was swampy ground, as dangerous as shifting sand and not wanting to be the one to instigate trouble he offered to play his flute for them.

The offer was accepted and everyone sat back to enjoy the performance. Several times during the meal, Matthew had glanced across at his mother. He wasn't at all sure how she would react next. Perhaps she had come to terms with the idea. Perhaps his father had been able to reason with her when he himself had failed miserably. Matthew hated to be the cause of so much unhappiness but his mind was made up and nothing was going to change it. He felt sure, with the arrogant certainty of youth, that when his parents realised just how serious he was then they would be as excited as he was. He settled back with the others to enjoy the rest of the evening.

'I am not arguing with you, I'm telling you, Matthew!'

Mother and son were once more having a heated discussion about Matthew's career. Immediately after breakfast the following morning, Bathsheba had ordered her son to the library. There she had sat face to face opposite him, the round, rosewood, Benson table betwixt them emphasising the wedge which now separated them, and insisted he listen to all she had to say, brooking no interruption from him.

She had told him in great detail the story of her romance with the dashing young guards officer, leaving out nothing of relevance. She was particularly graphic when describing the scene on a ferny bank when she was all but pared alive by the deftness of her lover's sword. The blame for Fanny Robin's untimely death in the workhouse, Bathsheba laid entirely at the feet of Troy. When told about the death of Troy's child which Fanny had been carrying, Matthew behaved in a most unmanly fashion; only a short, sharp blow of his nose into his handkerchief allowed him to gain control in time thus saving him from an embarrassing situation not to be expected of a future guard's officer.

Bathsheba spared no mercy for Sargeant Troy, in her telling of how he deserted her and the farm, for a life with a circus, leaving her to think he was dead.

Although it was all new to him, for Gabriel had been wrong in assuming he would have heard about his mother's previous marriage, Matthew could not relate what she was telling him to his wanting to join the regiment and said so as soon as he dared to interrupt.

'Mama, not all soldiers are the same. Surely there are as many different men in the military as there are working on the farm.'

'I must beg to disagree. It is a certain kind of person, Matthew, a pugilistic, aggressive, wild type, who is attracted to the military. Surely you can see that.'

Matthew shook his head. His youth gave him an entirely different perspective to the one his mother was portraying. Where he saw light she saw shadow, his bravery and courage was to her, foolishness and bravado. To him the army meant excitement, travel, and a sense of serving one's country, an honourable career.

There could be no compromise for either of them. They each stood on different sides of the same fence. It was stalemate.

Bathsheba was unable to understand how her normally, peace loving, nature loving son who wouldn't hurt a fly, would often go out of his way to help a sick animal, had turned into this complex character who was now saying he wanted to go off to fight. Surely he didn't know himself what he was doing.

She tried once more. 'Matthew? Will you come with me to the gallery, in Casterbridge? This afternoon?'

Matthew was not a little surprised at his mother's apparent change of heart. 'May I ask why, mama?'

'Mr Johnson has some very interesting pictures hanging there. I should like you to see them before you finally make up your mind.' She had been going to say "do something silly" but she had no wish to antagonise the boy further.

Matthew, who had of course already made up his mind, agreed at once.

'Of course, mama. I'd like that. I was told at school the exhibition is worth a visit but not being truly interested in the arts I haven't yet been.'

'I think you'll find it very interesting indeed.' It was Bathsheba's last hope and she prayed fervently the gory pictures would convince Matthew once and for all that a soldier's life was not for him.

Caleb brought the carriage to the front door almost immediately after the midday meal was finished as Bathsheba had requested.

Mother and son sat in silence for most of the journey to the county town. Neither wanted to enter into any discussion which was likely to make things worse between them so there was a quietness, born of unease, in the carriage. Matthew was still perplexed at what he saw as his mother's change of inclination. He was convinced he would never understand the mind of the female of the species. How changeable they seemed.

At the same time, Bathsheba wondered at the sudden change in Matthew. She could not stop herself from comparing him with Adam although she knew she shouldn't. How ironic life could be thought the mother, for if she had been inclined to predictions or foresee any problems with either of her sons she would have said Adam, with his artistic temperament, would be the one to challenge her presumptions.

The Gallery was newly opened and stood on the corner of High West Street and Trinity Street almost opposite to St. Peter's church. Bathsheba looked across the road at the entrance to St. Peter's and thought perhaps they should spend a few moments on their knees after they had viewed the pictures.

It was a Monday afternoon and it not being market day, there were very few people in the gallery. It was quite small with only two long rooms open to the public. John Johnson had told her on her last visit that he planned to open the upstairs rooms but it looked as though he had not yet achieved his ambition. The important thing though was the paintings and engravings Bathsheba wanted Matthew to see which formed part of an exhibition called, "A Lesson for Humanity." These were situated in the far room, a decent distance from the main entrance.

The couple spent some time in the entrance room admiring the work of several Wessex artists. Entitled "The Picturesque Countryside" the pictures were mainly landscapes of the local countryside, almost all in the style of Constable. Someone, whose name Bathsheba did not recognise, had bravely tried to emulate Millet's "The Gleaners" and had achieved some success, so much so she felt inspired to buy it and later to have a try herself at the art. She said so to Matthew, momentarily forgetting the sole purpose of their visit.

In the next room, under the title "A Lesson for Humanity" the contrast was sharp and to the point. Among the scenes of death and destruction was a particularly poignant picture, in the style of Delacroix, which showed in graphic detail the result of war. Among the dead and dying cavalry a horse lay writhing in agony, its rider, dying himself, unable to put it out of its misery. Nowhere on the canvas was a ray of hope. There was so little sign of life it was like Armageddon.

Bathsheba looked at Matthew. He was plainly disturbed. Mr Johnson had prepared the exhibition with excellent taste. The viewer was lulled into a sense of security in the first room only to be confronted with such scenes of mortality only the most hardened person could fail to be moved by.

Matthew turned to go. 'I've seen enough, mama. Shall we go?'

Bathsheba took her son's arm, 'Have you Matthew? Are you sure?'

Matthew didn't answer. He wanted to remove himself from the gallery as quickly as possible. If that was what soldiering was all about he wasn't sure if it really was what he wanted. In his mind's eye he had visions of clean living. The muck and filth of the battlefield hadn't been part of his images. He was most moved by the stark pain in the eyes of the horse. Could he bear that?

'Shall we take some refreshment Matthew?' Bathsheba interrupted his dark thoughts.

He nodded. Out in the bright light of the sunny winter day the images were beginning to fade. Those pictures were of some foreign field; there was no war at the moment; Matthew started to rationalise. Those officers he'd watched the other day appeared happy going about their business. Matthew felt confused. He drank the tea his mother ordered for him without noticing its smoky flavour, ate the sweet cake without tasting its richness. He wanted to be back at Oakdene, in the sanctuary of the stables. Most of all he wanted to talk to Prince for he was the only one Matthew felt would understand his point of view.

As soon as the carriage pulled into the stable yard, Matthew begged to be excused and leapt from the coach with the speed of a young hare. Bathsheba put out a hand in order to restrain him but failed so to do.

Bathsheba put her head out of the carriage door to instruct the driver to pull round to the front door of Oakdene. She thought after all it might be best to leave her son to think through the events of the afternoon. He had appeared to be horrified by the scenes portrayed in the gallery. Yes, best leave him alone for the time being.

In Prince's stable Matthew sat huddled in the corner eyeing the horse with a new vision. How would he feel if Prince were to be shot at in battle, he asked himself? Finding he couldn't talk to Prince after all, he left the stable and made for the orchard.

The trees were quite bare now and it was difficult to imagine how beautiful the blossom would look in just a few short months. Suddenly the youth felt as if a prayer had been answered. He knew what he must do. How could he have been so uncertain? He felt as he had when he'd seen the guards working at the barracks. It was a feeling so strong it could not be ignored. So, he reasoned, a few sad pictures had distracted him for a while but they were only an artist's impression after all, no more than pictures at an exhibition. Never mind, if he was going to be a soldier then he'd have a lot more than a disagreement with his mother to withstand. For the first time in his life he felt like a man.

Chapter Twenty One
A Friend indeed.

Bathsheba, alone in the drawing room, took up her needlework and absently began to pick at the stitches. Matthew had not yet come in and it would soon be supper time. Gabriel had put his head around the door In greeting but was anxious to change into some clean, dry clothes as he'd been caught in a sudden icy shower. He hadn't even asked how the afternoon had gone.

Hearing footsteps hurrying up the stone steps from the basement kitchen, she rushed to the door expecting and hoping to see Matthew. Instead it was Maryann with a message.

'Young master "as ridden over to "is school friend's house in Weatherbury, ma'am. Said as how you weren't to wait supper as he'd more "an likely eat there.'

'Thank you, Maryann.' Bathsheba made an effort not to show her disappointment. She knew deep down that if her son couldn't face her over supper, it could only mean one thing. She carried on with her needlework, giving it the same lack of attention as when she had begun it, stabbing the needle in and out, in and out, the monotony of the motion and the insipid colour of the pale blue sky on the canvas, its own panacea for her disturbed mind.

With Adam soon going back to college there was only one thing she could do she decided and that was to throw herself whole-heartedly into her work here at Oakdene.

In her mind, Matthew had already gone. When he told her, it would be something of an anti-climax, she smiled to herself, wryly.

In a way Bathsheba felt peculiarly excited at the prospect of having more time to spare. For as long as she could remember, at least since she had taken over the running of Upper Weatherbury farm, life had been so busy, hectic even, she had never found time to do all those things that her friends seemed to find time for. Louisa was on a committee which organised outings for the poor of the parish. She also organised parcels for the sick and needy. Of course Bathsheba had contributed goods and suchlike but she'd never been directly involved.

Also, Emma Godwin had invited her to join a circle of ladies who were campaigning for better conditions at the hospital. That sounded like a worthy cause. Then there was the desire she had to paint in oils and her piano practice could be improved. Her poetry evenings, which she organised to take place once a week, could now be more frequent. With a sense of achievement, Bathsheba found she had successfully cheered herself up. She felt much happier now she knew her time could be put to good use. She certainly wouldn't have time to miss Matthew or worry about him.

This she told to Gabriel after supper that evening. He was pleased his wife was much more cheerful and reminded her that she had promised to help out the doctor when he returned to Weatherbury.

'That reminds me, Gabriel. I bumped into Theodore's housekeeper this afternoon. She informed me that the doctor would probably return to The Elms during the second week of January. I told her to be sure and let me know when he arrives.'

'Has she heard from him them? Did she say how he is?'

'A few days ago, apparently. His health is good but he remains a bit low in spirit, she said.'

'Well, 'tis only to be expected. What a dreadful business it all was. I only realised the other day, Bathsheba, 'tis the second wife the poor man's lost in childbirth.'

They were interrupted by Adam who burst into the room as though being chased by a painted devil.

'I saw Matthew a while ago. He told me he's to join the Eleventh Dragoon Guards as soon as it can be arranged. I must say, I was absolutely confounded.' He paused momentarily in order to catch his breath. 'Did you know?' he asked his parents, looking first at his father and then his mother.

Gabriel said he did know. Bathsheba merely fiddled with her sewing, inclining her head slightly so her son wouldn't see her sorrowful expression.

'Why didn't anyone tell me?' Adam was obviously put out and not a little angry that no one had bothered to inform him.

Gabriel stood up and walked over to the fireplace where he knocked out his pipe on the side of the inglenook. 'To be honest, Adam, we didn't take him too seriously at first. We thought the least said the sooner he'd get over it.'

'Well, he hasn't, has he! Fancy, our quiet little Matthew going to be a fighting man. Who would have believed it?' Adam was unusually brusque and his mother perceived this was to cover up how he really felt.

Bathsheba answered him quietly. 'It was a shock for your father and me too, Adam.'

Adam dropped to his knees and took his mother's hand in his. 'I'm so sorry, mama. Of course you're concerned. I should have stopped to think.' He paused and the silence in the room, save that of the spitting, crackling logs, said more for their feelings than a million uttered words.

After a decent interval Adam continued, 'Shall I have a talk to him, father? I could try to persuade him to join me at Christminster, when the time is right.'

Here we go again, Bathsheba thought. Why does everyone want to wait for the right time when it seldom if ever happens to be "the right time"? She stood up. 'I think not, Adam. But thank you for offering. I shall prepare for supper now,' she said, leaving the room.

Father and son faced each other. 'Have you talked to Matthew, father? Told him how very upset mama is?'

Gabriel walked back across the room so he could sit in his chair. The gentle rocking action often helped restore his equilibrium in times of conflict and he found himself gently rocking now, as he talked to Adam. He explained to his elder son exactly what had taken place between mother and younger son over the past few days.

'I'd have thought those pictures in the Johnson Gallery would have done the trick, father. I've seen them and they are truly horrific.'

'Well, that's what your mother hoped. In fact she was quite positive they would have the desired effect but it seems she was wrong.'

The two men sat in silence once more. There wasn't much left to say and only time would tell if Matthew was right for a soldier's life. Adam was glad it wasn't himself. The thought of fighting, maybe even having to go to war was abhorrent to him and until today he could have sworn Matthew felt the same. In spite of his mother's advice, he made up his mind to seek out his brother and find out exactly what was at the back of his apparently sudden decision.

What with Sheba going off rather hastily, Gabriel wondered what the family was coming to. One minute they were all at home, their futures safely mapped out before them, knowing exactly what they wanted to do, the next minute all three offspring had had a change of heart.

Adam disturbed the quietness by rising from his chair to walk over to the fireplace as his father had done, both seeming to seek some degree of comfort from the radiated warmth, the difference being he couldn't tap out his pipe on the marble surround as he hadn't yet started smoking, although he'd had thoughts of starting from his room-mate, Christian de Lore. Adam suspected that the Earl's son smoked more than tobacco, as some rather strange smells emanated from his direction late at night but he hadn't liked to ask for fear of being thought naive.

Gabriel looked across at his son and marvelled at the difference in his three children. Once upon a time he could swear he knew what they were thinking, could often predict what they would say next, but these days they were grown apart, had become part of a new generation Gabriel felt he knew little about.

He wasn't quite right. His children were going through the process of growing up and in a few more years parents and children would become like friends.

That knowledge was of little use to any of them at the moment. They had somehow to survive the traumatic years of adolescence, bear with each other until they were as equals, until they eventually reached the time when the child would become father to the man.

At the first opportunity, Adam talked to his younger brother, demanding to know why he had made his decision to become a soldier. Matthew's reply was far from eloquent or adequate and did nothing to convince Adam that he'd thought it through or thought of the possible consequences.

'It just came to me, Adam. At the risk of sounding odd, I sort of felt it was the right thing to do. Do you know what I mean?'

Adam tried hard to envisage a time when he would take notice of something, which appeared to be on the surface, unseen and unheard. Matthew was right about one thing. It did sound odd. On reflection, at a much later date, Adam was to admit it was where most of the inspiration for his poetry came from; out of the blue, from the great big yonder.

'Matthew, if it sort of came out of the blue, perhaps you ought to wait and see. You know, it might disappear just as suddenly, this, er, notion you felt.'

Matthew did not agree and refused to discuss the matter any further.

'Father could refuse to let you go, Matt. Have you thought of that?'

'O, father's alright. He doesn't mind. It's mama who's making all the fuss. She thinks I'm about to go off and get shot or something.' Matthew laughed. It seemed to him that everyone was taking the whole issue far too seriously. Adam thought how much his brother had changed of late and all in the few months he'd been away at Christminster.

He thought he'd have one last try.

'Matthew, you didn't come to look round the college with the others. How about coming back with me next week and I'll show you round properly, introduce you to some of my friends if you like? Then, when you leave the Grammar school, the college will be familiar to you.'

Matthew shook his head. 'University's not for me, Adam. Anyway, I'll be busy getting ready to go off to training college, probably in Melchester. Thanks for the offer though.'

Adam gave up. How strong his little brother had become. Well good for him, if that's what he wanted.

He took his hand and shook it heartily. 'Well, Good luck, Matt. Remember where I am if things get a bit.., well, you know.'

Matthew smiled. 'Thanks, Adam. I'll remember that.'

Adam was pleased he'd spoken to his brother. He now had more respect for his decision than he'd felt previously. Although he wholeheartedly disagreed with him about fighting and the military as a whole, he had to hand it to him, he seemed totally committed. If he could convince his mother to see Matthew's chosen career in that light he felt she would be more able to bear her youngest son's departure.

Chapter Twenty Two

In Our Opposed Souls to Persevere - A Farewell.

I N NO TIME AT all, or so it seemed to the Oak family, the youngest son had been safely delivered to the barracks in Casterbridge. Then in less than a month, Matthew was transferred to Melchester, a barracks twenty miles north of Casterbridge, where he would receive further training which would equip him for a musical career within the regiment.

In his letters, Matthew was full of enthusiasm for his new life and now appeared to have more friends than he'd ever had before. Within the year, he wrote, he hoped to gain a place in the marching band and then if he were lucky enough to be amongst the chosen, would be sent abroad. At present it seemed very likely he would spend the next year at Melchester.

Before Adam returned to college he had spoken to his mother about Matthew's vocation. He had tried hard to put forward the good points of having such a distinguished career, placing great emphasis on the need our beloved country had for protection against any future enemies. Rather surprisingly Bathsheba had agreed with him although she insisted categorically that, in her own personal view, her youngest would have made a far better veterinary than a soldier.

After speaking to his mother and seeing for himself her positive response, Adam was able to return to Christminster secure in the knowledge that she would not be pining too much over her missing brood.

Now, as the sun rose earlier with each new morn, the trees and hedges responded in their own particular way. The once stark, dark wintry bareness began now to be overlaid by a wash of the palest green, heralding spring's brighter deeper tones.

The winter had been unusually harsh with frosts as hard as iron and on some days only the minimum of essential work had been carried out on the farms, leaving repair work and non essential jobs to be done when the weather improved. Now that time had arrived and the fields were alive with the sight and sound of workers busy mending fences, sowing seeds and all the usual activities of Spring.

Baby Gabriel was a delightful child, with his mother's fair complexion and his father's large hands and feet. Bathsheba adored him and visited whenever she could find the time often prising him away from his nurse in order to take him on some expedition or other which as yet he was far too young to appreciate fully. True to her plan she had joined in with community good works and was pleased and not a little surprised to find she derived a good deal of pleasure from her activities and appreciated her freedom from the humdrum domesticity that is the lot of the matron.

Perhaps the most surprising outcome was the formation of a committee to support the wives of union men. It was whilst Gabriel was explaining to her about Benjamin Tallboys" difficulty in persuading the farm workers of his reading group to become members of the union, that she had come up with the idea. Gabriel had felt it might possibly be of some use but had humoured her rather than actively encouraged her, forgetting how much a woman's support can mean to a man.

The committee, calling itself simply, "The Worker's Support Committee" or WSC, consisting of Louisa, Liddy, Lady Emma, (she had volunteered as soon as she'd heard about the group and was the Chairman), the vicar's wife, and a few tradesmen's wives from Weatherbury, had only been meeting for a few weeks and there was already a notable increase in membership of the union and a corresponding increase in the number in Mr. Tallboys" class at the vicarage.

With free access to the Martin and Godwin's printing press, Lady Emma had given Bathsheba a free hand to print any posters and pamphlets she deemed necessary, trusting her implicitly. So, the day after the committee had sat, Bathsheba and Louisa had drawn up a plan. The posters they designed were simple and to the point, advertising the fact that Benjamin Tallboys was at the vicarage every Monday evening from eight until ten where he would be happy to give advice on any matter causing concern. Those wishing to attend would be offered tuition in reading and writing. There would be some light refreshment, Lady Emma had offered to subscribe to this but only if they would guarantee no publicity as she didn't want Sir Cornelius or the firm to be directly involved. During the interval for refreshment there would be time to ask questions about union membership, this would be encouraged, and any other topic of concern. In large letters at the bottom they had put, FREE to all.

'That should attract some attention.' Bathsheba congratulated herself on the design of the poster.

Louisa laughed. 'Bathsheba, haven't you forgotten something?'

'No. Have I?'

Louisa laughed again. 'If the men can't read, how are they going to read the advertisements?'

'O, no! I never thought of that. What shall we do?'

The two women sat and looked at each other, neither could think of a solution.

Suddenly, Bathsheba stood up and paced about the room. 'We'll have to have a meeting in the square, Louisa. We'll pass the word around orally, go into the shops in Weatherbury, go to market, tell the menfolk to tell their workers if necessary.' Bathsheba became quite carried away in her enthusiasm.

'It's a daring task, Bathsheba. But you're right you know. We'll do it!'

'Shall we start tomorrow? It's market day and I can be free in the morning.'

The two women agreed to meet outside the King's Arms the very next morning. They had decided to say nothing of the content of the campaign to their husbands for the time being for fear of disapproval. It wasn't something a lady would normally do but needs must when the devil drives and they were determined to be successful in their campaign.

Once Louisa had gone, Bathsheba decided to visit Liddy. It would be as well to have some back up and she knew her old friend would be keen to help in any way she could.

'O, no, Mrs. Oak. I don't think that's a good idea, at all. I can't imagine Mr Oak will approve, nor Mr. Abbot neither.'

'But Liddy, what else can we do?'

'I don't think you should do anything. 'Tis up to the men themselves to sort out whether they want to join the union, or not.'

"Tis not only the union, Liddy, as well you know. Many more should be able to read and write.'

'That's as may be. O, I agree with ye, but 'tis not a woman's place to point these things out, now is it?'

Bathsheba failed to make Liddy see the importance of the meeting in Weatherbury. Although her friend agreed in principle, she was reluctant to get involved with any activity which might lead to confrontation.

Bathsheba could not or refused to see any danger at all and she left Liddy, somewhat displeased with the outcome of her visit. "I would have thought her to be more understanding" she thought on her way back to Oakdene.

It was a beautiful spring morn and standing outside the King's Arms, Bathsheba could feel the warmth of the sun through her bonnet although it was only early April and Easter more than two weeks away. It seemed like all the world and his wife were enjoying the Spring sunshine, milling about around the small market town, in and out of the shops, bartering in friendly argument on pavements or simply standing chattering in small groups. It wasn't long before she was joined by Louisa.

Soon the two women had set up a couple of tables loaned by the kindly landlord of the King's Arms, had spread their pamphlets before them and had fixed their posters to the wall. At first people passing just glanced across at them, no doubt thinking they were collecting for charity, but as one or two more extrovert characters with a curious disposition started asking questions, more and more joined in. Handing out the pamphlets, Bathsheba and Louisa explained what they were trying to achieve. A few locals seemed a little concerned about possible repercussions but many expressed an interest. Some travellers from as far away as Kingsbere and Casterbridge promised to take the pamphlets to their spouses to try to persuade them they should join in with the forward looking sage of Weatherbury.

On the whole it was a good morning's work and the two women were well pleased. All they had to do now, they thought, was to sit back and wait for results.

Chapter Twenty Three
The Lamb Misus'd Breeds Public Strife.

'IF YOU'D ALL LIKE to take a seat I can see how many more chairs we need.' Benjamin Tallboys was trying hard to keep some sort of order in the front room of the vicarage. Instead of the usual twelve or so regular pupils there were more than twice that number and still more were trying to gain admission to the pleasant bay-windowed room.

He'd thought of asking the vicar if he could use the church hall initially but as numbers were generally small he hadn't felt more space was necessary. Now the choir were using the hall for their rehearsal of the Messiah due to be presented on Good Friday and as that date was only a few days off, there was no way they could be persuaded, nor would Ben dream of asking, to give up their valuable time.

Vicar Hansworth came bustling importantly into the room. 'Well, what a turn out we have, Mr. Tallboys. Nearly as many as attend my service on Sundays.' His broad smile could not disguise the anxiety in his eyes. Most of the time he kept on good terms with the peasants of his parish but tonight he was able to detect a hint of aggression in the air. Not that he could put his finger on any particular deed or action which might suggest there could be trouble. No, it was more an atmosphere, something intangible, but nevertheless present.

Eventually all the men were seated and Benjamin Tallboys stood up, on an old oak footstool, in order that the men should all be able to see him as well as he all of them.

He held up his hands and immediately an expectant hush settled upon his audience.

'First let me welcome you all, especially the newcomers.' There was a buzz of assent and many heads nodded towards the new mentor.

Ben continued, 'As you are probably aware, you will all be at differing stages of literacy.' One or two nudged each other and grinned wryly. 'But I shall come round and speak to you all eventually. In the mean time we'll sort you into groups. You may be able to help each other. May we begin then by separating you into those who can read a little and those who cannot read at all? If you can read a little go and sit on my right, the others to my left.' Benjamin drew an imaginary line down the middle of the room with his arm.

After much shuffling about Ben was surprised to see that a good third of the students sat on his right hand. At the front of the room, Ben had propped up a huge piece of grey slate which he used as a blackboard. On it he had already written the letters of the Alphabet followed by his name.

'Right gentlemen,' he began, I want to assure everyone that by the time they leave this room this evening he will be able to write at least his own first name.' There was much muttering until Ben raised a hand to call for silence. It would be a huge undertaking to teach all these people but having promised to do so he set about his task with ardour.

Those pupils, who had already attended his classes and now knew enough to be able to read and write a little, he paired with any of the new students who were totally illiterate. The remainder he arranged around the improvised blackboard for their first lesson.

Starting with the first man, whose name was Jacob, Ben went painstakingly through the alphabet until he came to the requisite letter. Then he asked Jacob to step up to the slate and attempt to write. Fortunately, Jacob had attended school on the odd occasion, when his mother could afford the small fee, so he had handled chalk and slate before. However, when he tried to write his name he found the action much more difficult than he thought and the squiggles he produced bought a few smiles to the faces of the other students who knew that when it was their turn the laugh would be on them. To this end they progressed at a surprisingly rapid rate.

After about an hour and a half, refreshments were served, much to the relief of Wilberforce Wheeler who cursed his parents for not calling him John or something equally simple to spell and write.

'Do you think I could stick to plain Wil, Mr Tallboys?' he asked earnestly.

'I think it important you should be able to sign your full name, Wil.' Ben replied in the same tone to show his student he took his question seriously.

The others laughed. Those with simple names, especially the biblical kind thought how lucky they were and how considerate their parents had been for many recognised the spelling of the names from constant reference to the bible at Sunday School. The actual writing of the letters proved to be much more difficult however.

The lesson was proving to be more enjoyable than they had anticipated having had only the experience of a very strict school mistress to draw on for their previous learning, and that for various reasons had been very limited.

'If there are any questions anyone would like answered I shall be happy to reply.' Ben sat supping his ale, enjoying the success the overflowing room portrayed.

One of the men from the back of the room stepped forward. He was a giant of a man with dark hair, his beard giving him the look of man's ascendant.

'You don't know me, Mr. Tallboys. Name's Luke Welland. I work casual like, up at Twogates Farm mostly. 'Tis part of the estate owned by Lord Exonbury.'

'I know the place.' Ben put out his hand in greeting. "'Tis good to meet you, Mr. Welland.

Luke pumped his teacher's hand in response, pleased at the familiarity.

'I have a question, Sir.' He hesitated, not sure how to ask, but knowing he spoke for several of the others continued, 'Mr. Tallboys, 'tis very good of you to take the time to try an teach us to sign our names and the like but what's it all for? When are we likely to use this new knowledge, Sir?'

Luke Welland sat down in a chair opposite to Ben. He hadn't asked what he had intended and was now uncomfortably aware that he had let his colleagues down. Before Ben could answer he spoke again.

'That's not what I intended to say, Sir. I meant to ask about this new union business. There, I've said it.'

There was a general buzz of excitement as Luke voiced what was in the minds of most of the men present.

Quick to grasp the opportunity, Ben stood up on his stool once again, pleased the vicar hadn't joined them for refreshment. He would have felt not a little inhibited with a man of the cloth present although he knew that a true Christian spirit would want to see fair play no matter what a man's background was and no matter what it cost.

Seeing the rows of upturned faces all staring at him expectantly, Ben felt like the shepherd he indeed was but with a difference. The men now looking to him were his new flock.

He must lead them safely, making sure they did not run into danger, steering them gently along the path of righteousness and equality.

'I know some of you here tonight are against joining a union. I also appreciate your reasons. Firstly, I want to assure you that it is entirely your choice. Secondly, I want to assure you that I am here principally to teach. Thirdly, I want to assure you that whatever decision you come to I will be your representative. Finally, if it is the wish of the majority, I am willing to be your leader.

There was much applause and Ben sighed with relief. That was the first hurdle over. All he had to do now was convince this sea of faces that it was in their best interests to have the force of a union behind them. They deserved at least that.

By the end of the evening most of the congregation had agreed to join the union with the proviso that should there be any trouble between employer and employee, Ben would speak for the one in dispute. This was backed by Gabriel Oak who had joined his friend just after refreshments had been served.

Altogether, both men felt the evening to have been a great success and they looked forward eagerly to the next meeting. Sadly it was not to be as simple as it first appeared. Lord Exonbury, on hearing his employee's proposal to join a union had him dismissed instantly, leaving Luke Welland, his wife Matty and their five children without means or a roof.

It was late on Thursday afternoon, less than a week after Benjamin Tallboys" successful meeting that he was accosted in the main street in Weatherbury. Ben knew something was amiss long before a word was uttered for the stance of the assembled labourers in the square was unmistakably aggressive. Having an inkling about what they were about to say he squared his shoulders to meet the leaders, prepared to fight as necessary with them, not against them, for freedom and truth.

'Here he comes,' a voice was heard above the general hubbub.

Ben stopped in his tracks, not frightened, more apprehensive.

'What's going on? Would someone care to explain?'

Someone pushed Luke Welland forwards. 'Tell "im, Luke!'

'Tell me what, Luke? What's wrong?' Ben could see that whatever was troubling the man was serious. He took him by the arm and drew him into the shelter of the King's Arms.

'I've lost m'job, Sir, and m'cottage. Me an" the wife and kids is "omeless.'

'Did your employer give a reason, Luke?'

'Oh yes, sir. He said as "ow if I joined the union he couldn't use me any more. I tried to explain that I "adn't joined yet but "e wouldn't listen. Just said I "ad to go. Said "e'd given my job to someone else.'

Ben was only a little surprised. He'd expected some sort of reaction like this and that it came from the Exonbury estate came as no great surprise. But as the man's livelihood was at stake he knew he must move quickly.

'You must come and stay with me, Luke, until we can sort something out.'

As Luke was about to decline the offer, Ben insisted. 'You must Luke, if only for the sake of your wife and children. We can't let these landowners get away with such dogma. That's what the union has been set up to combat.'

Reluctantly, Luke agreed to stay with Ben as a temporary accommodation. 'You're right, Mr. Tallboys. If I didn't agree with ye I'd never "ave listened to ye in the first place.'

'Good man, Luke!' Ben slapped him on the back. 'We'll beat them yet. You see if we don't.'

Both men went back outside to inform the others what had been decided. There was much muttering as the small crowd dispersed, each going their separate ways.

'Go to my cottage, Luke,' Ben advised. 'I've someone to see before I go home.'

'Very well, Mr. Tallboys.' He turned to his wife, 'Bring the little "uns, Matty. We're going to stay with Mr. Tallboys tonight.'

As Luke and his family went in one direction, Benjamin turned to go in the opposite direction. His first port of call was a visit to Oakdene. It was right that Gabriel should be aware of what was going on. Maybe he could suggest the next step. One thing was certain, Benjamin Tallboys would not be content to see a man unjustly treated. This was the latter part of the nineteenth century and it was time some of the arrogant landowners in these parts were made aware that their "rule" was about to come to an end. They'd had their own way for far too long.

As Benjamin drove rapidly along the white path which led to Upper Weatherbury farm he had an idea. He wasn't sure whether Gabriel would agree with him for it was rather radical. However, Sir Cornelius Godwin had offered his help if needed and as Lord Exonbury was such an important and powerful man in Wessex they would need some force behind them. Yes, that's what they must do. Get Sir Cornelius involved. He only hoped Gabriel would agree. After all, why not make use of a man with such power if necessary? He had agreed to help. Now was the time to see if he was true to his word.

Benjamin whipped up the horse. He felt quite excited at the prospect of the forthcoming battle. If he had his way, it would be landowner against landowner. Now there was a turn up for the book. He laughed to himself as he reined in the horse, handing him to Jacob, who appeared to be waiting for him in the courtyard.

In reply to his question, Jacob replied, 'Mr. Oak said to expect you sir, in view of the trouble with Luke Welland.'

'News travels fast, Jacob. How did you hear?'

Mrs. Archer was in the market square an" she heard the men talking. Right angry, she said they were. So, she "urried back to tell Missus Oak.'

'Is Mr. Oak at home now, Jacob?' Ben asked as Jacob led the horse into a stable.

'Yes, Sir. Like I said, he's expecting you.'

'Good! Then I'll get to see him right away.'

Chapter Twenty Four

Too Much Knowledge For The Sceptic Side?

BATHSHEBA HAD SPENT MOST of the day minding and playing with baby Gabriel. He was an angelic child in looks and manner. In some small way he helped to compensate for the loss of her own once expected child and her recently departed siblings and with the tremendous range of activities she now found herself caught up in, Bathsheba was once again restored to her old contented self. Her grown up children were happy on their chosen career paths. Life was settled and good.

Although she heard the sound of the front door knocker, reverberating throughout Oakdene like a blacksmith's hammer on anvil, she was reluctant to enquire who the caller might be. The baby Gabriel had quite exhausted her and she was glad of the chance to sit back for a minute or two before it was necessary to prepare herself for the evening meal.

Picking up her poetry book she opened a page at random. Blake was her current favourite and the sensitivity of his work never failed to amaze and move her. She wondered idly whether great poets were born or made, coming to the conclusion that as there weren't that many it must be a God given talent. It hardly occurred to her that a great deal of talent must be wasted simply because some people never had the chance to express themselves, never mind see their work in print. That piece of philosophy would hit her much later on.

Now she read,

'The sun descending in the west,
The evening star does shine;
The birds are silent in their nest,
And I must seek for mine.'

As she read through the poem she felt its soft and rhythmic cadences both soothing and inspiring to her receptive mind and was the sole reason for her decision to ignore the caller at the door. It was with some degree of surprise and irritation to her when her husband burst into the room followed by Benjamin Tallboys, neither man stopping to apologise for the intrusion.

'Excuse us, Bathsheba,' Gabriel requested without even looking at his wife. 'Mr. Tallboys brings news of strife within the work force and feels we may be partly responsible.'

Bathsheba reluctantly put down her poetry book and turned to look at the two men. She could deduce that something was very amiss by the seriousness of their physiognomies. She had recently studied Mr. Hogarth's thoughts on the subject and now felt herself to be something of an expert.

'Shall I call for tea, Gabriel?' his thoughtful wife suggested.

'Thank you, Bathsheba.' He nodded and pulling out a chair for Ben joined him at the table.

'Tell me about your idea, Ben.'

'I think we should go to the top, Mr. Oak.

'You don't get much nearer the top than Lord Exonbury,' Gabriel jested semi-seriously.

'Well, there is someone you know, who has volunteered to assist in a crisis. Sir Cornelius Godwin!'

Gabriel was a little taken aback. He didn't know Sir Cornelius all that well. True, they'd met several times and the gentleman had offered assistance if and when Gabriel ever needed it but Gabriel wasn't at all sure if he had really meant it or whether he was just being polite.

'I'm not sure, Ben. I think it most likely he's a friend of Lord Exonbury. They do move in the same sort of circles, ye know, so he wouldn't want to be on the wrong side of him.'

'What then, Mr. Oak? I promised to support the men in the cause. I can't let them down at the first hurdle.'

Gabriel thought for a minute. 'I could give Luke Welland a job. I need help with the lambing. 'Tis a bit late this year due to the severe winter and I could use an extra pair of hands.'

Ben Tallboys was not happy with Gabriel's solution. He felt he was avoiding the vital issue and he said so.

"Tis very kind of ye to offer the man a job, Mr. Oak, but there be far more at stake than that,' Ben insisted.

Gabriel realised he wasn't going to give in easily and felt deep down Ben was quite right. Giving the unfortunate man a temporary job would help in the short term but what then? And, how many more would be dismissed because they had the good sense to join a union. He certainly could not offer everyone a job. Ben was right. He must go and see Sir Cornelius. After all, what could he lose?

'Alright, Ben. I'll go and see Sir Cornelius. As soon as possible.'

The man sitting opposite Gabriel gave a huge sigh of relief. He'd thought for a moment he was on his own and if that were the case knew his chances to be very small.

Bathsheba spoke for the first time. 'Lady Emma is on the committee, Gabriel. I feel sure she'll support us in this.'

'I think we'll keep the ladies out of this, m'dear. It might get a bit nasty and I wouldn't want Lady Emma involved as I'm sure Sir Cornelius wouldn't neither.'

Bathsheba wasn't happy with her husband's decision but decided to say nothing. She'd speak with Louisa at the first opportunity and together they could decide the best way to help.

Gabriel was a little surprised Bathsheba had agreed with him so easily. He hoped she was feeling well. Her little sojourn to Theodore's today must have tired her, he thought.

Benjamin Tallboys interrupted his thoughts.

'When will you go to see the gentleman, Mr. Oak?'

'As soon as he can see me, Ben. I'll send a message first thing in the morning. With a little luck he'll see me straight away.'

'Then I'll bid ye goodnight, Mr. Oak.'

'Would you like to stay for a little supper, Mr. Tallboys?' Bathsheba enquired politely. She didn't really know this friend of her husband's but already she had decided she liked him.

'Another time, Mrs. Oak, if you don't think ill o" me for declining your kind offer.'

Bathsheba smiled. 'Of course, Mr. Tallboys. Another time then.'

Gabriel saw Ben to the door with the promise to let him know of any developments as soon as he could and his friend agreed to do likewise.

Gabriel was extremely concerned, his furrowed brow exhibiting the fact, and he explained to Bathsheba. 'I'm affeared that now one employer has dismissed a worker many more may follow suit.'

'I suppose you're right, Gabriel.' She didn't feel like discussing Gabriel's impending visit to Sir Cornelius. She'd had a busy day and thought it highly unlikely that gentleman would be able or even willing to do anything. After all, he paid his workers a decent wage so he wouldn't want to be drawn in to something which could only lead to unnecessary trouble and as for not wanting Lady Emma involved, Bathsheba wasn't at all sure. She knew Lady Emma would rather say for herself whether or not she wished to be involved. A visit to Louisa first thing in the morning was called for. Then the women would decide what they would do.

Bathsheba smiled causing her husband to ask what she was thinking.

Looking a little like the Mona Lisa, Bathsheba shook her head. 'Nothing of import, m'dear.' And with the instruction not to be too long coming up to bed, Bathsheba took her leave of her husband.

'I was expecting you, Bathsheba.' Louisa patted the seat next to her. She had only just finished breakfast and now invited her friend to join her in the drawing room where coffee was about to be served.

'You've heard the news, I suppose, Louisa.'

Bathsheba had removed her bonnet before starting to speak. Now she placed it on the small table beside her.

'I've heard Mr. Welland is staying with Mr. Tallboys temporarily. Is this true?'

'Yes. At least the family is housed for the time being.' Bathsheba leaned forward and cupped her head in her hand. 'Louisa, we have to do something. We women I mean.'

'What can we do? Have you thought about it?'

'Well Louisa, I've been thinking about it half the night and here's what I suggest.'

Bathsheba took out her note book where she'd made a list of possibilities.

'Number one. We call a meeting of the WSC.

Number two. We make more banners stating that we support the Union members.

Number three. We parade through the streets of Weatherbury and if we have to, we'll march in Casterbridge too.'

Louisa was amazed. 'You really have given it some thought, Bathsheba.' She stood up. 'I'm not sure how Joseph will feel if I start marching in the streets, though. What does Gabriel say?'

Bathsheba stood up and began pacing the room.

'You haven't told him!' Louisa began to laugh.

Bathsheba ceased her pacing and joined in. 'No, I haven't. Why, only last evening he said as how he didn't want the "women" to be involved. Who is it that has to make ends meet when there's not enough cash? Who is it who has to face the tradesmen when they come calling for the bill to be paid? Who is it who has to tell the children they must go to bed hungry?' Bathsheba's face was growing pinker and pinker as she became more and more incensed with the injustice of it all.

Louisa held up both her hands as if to ward off the incorporeal blows.

'Stop! Oh, please stop, Bathsheba. You'll bring on an apoplexy.'

Bathsheba sat down once more and faced her friend. 'Louisa, dear, we manage very well. Yes we work hard and over the years we have made good, 'tis true, but there are so many who work just as hard and don't seem to see anything for it. Mainly because the wages are so poor. I must admit I haven't given it much thought until recently. I suppose I've been too busy with my own family to have time to think. Now, I do have the time and I'm not prepared to sit back and do nothing.'

It was quite a speech and Louisa found herself agreeing with everything her friend had said.

'In that case, I'd better fetch my cloak and bonnet. We have things to do and the sooner the better.'

The two women joined arms, the link as strong as iron, sealing their vow. They would start their campaign with a visit to Martinsham Hall.

Chapter Twenty Five
A Woman Oweth To
Her Husband!

GABRIEL HAD TOLD HIS wife of his arrangement to see Sir Cornelius that day so assuming the meeting would take place at the offices of Martin and Godwin, Bathsheba conjectured it to be quite safe for her and Louisa to visit Lady Emma at the Hall.

As they drove along the long winding drive which led to the front entrance of Martinsham Hall, Bathsheba kept a keen lookout for any sign of her husband. Although it was highly unlikely he would visit Sir Cornelius here, they couldn't be too careful. Both women knew for certain that if either of their husbands were to discover the reason for their visit they would not be best pleased and might even go so far as to try to stop it. So, what the eye couldn't see, they reasoned, the heart could not grieve over.

They were taking a calculated chance that Lady Emma would be "at home" but Bathsheba remembered her telling her when she had stayed at the Hall that she would be welcome any time. Now was the time to put the good lady's words to the test.

Leaving the small governess cart with the stable hand, Bathsheba and Louisa crossed the courtyard, walked along the gravel path at the front of the house, then made their way quickly up the stone steps to the huge doors. Louisa picked up the shiny brass knocker and hammered it down two or three times. The door was so sturdy they could hear no sound reverberating through the house as they would have done at Oakdene. The two women stepped back from the door a little in awe of their surroundings, half expecting there to be no reply but knowing deep down there would always be someone at home in the great house.

In the event they didn't have more than a few moments to wait. The door was opened by the woman Bathsheba immediately recognised as Mrs. Summers the housekeeper.

'Can I help?' she asked without smiling, her huge frame blocking the half door which was all she had needed to open.

'We wondered if Lady Emma is at home.' Bathsheba stated.

'Is she expecting you? It is rather early for visitors, madam.'

'No. That is, Mrs. Godwin said I may call at any time, Mrs Summers. Would you ask her if this is a convenient time, please?'

'Yes, Madam. Would you care to wait in the small dining room whilst I see if she is available?' The housekeeper, smiling now, looked pleased that the caller had remembered her name.

Louisa and Bathsheba were shown into the small dining room which looked out over the panorama of splendid lawns and trees at the front of the house. Louisa nudged her friend when Mrs. Summers had disappeared up the wide staircase. 'If this is small, whatever is the large dining room like?'

Bathsheba grinned. 'Enormous!'

They sat down somewhat apprehensively to await the news of the lady of the house.

In a few short moments Mrs. Summers returned with an invitation to join Lady Emma for coffee in the drawing room. They followed the housekeeper back through the Great Hall, down a wide wood-panelled corridor and into the palatial drawing room, although as both women had their minds taken up with what they were about to say, they did not really appreciate the elaborate decor on this occasion.

Lady Emma, unlike most women of her status and breeding, was evidently ready to receive visitors even at this early hour for she was wearing a becoming grey grosgrain morning dress in the latest London fashion. As they entered she rose to greet them, her silks rustling luxuriously as she extending her hand in welcome.

'What a pleasant surprise, Mrs. Oak. And Mrs. Abbot. Please sit down and tell me what brings you calling at this hour.' She glanced at the smiling face of the Grandfather clock in the corner as she spoke. 'From your expression, may I assume that it is something of a serious nature?'

Bathsheba apologised at the earliness of the hour before she proceeded to explain the reason for the call. Going into great detail she explained what had happened and what they hoped to do about it, taking great care to emphasise the fact that the menfolk knew nothing of the visit.

'I'd be grateful, Lady Emma, if you would say nothing to your husband of the reason for our visit here today.'

Emma Godwin was a woman who knew her own mind. Not one to act on the whim of others she agreed not to divulge the details of the visit but insisted she needed time to think it through thoroughly.

'I can promise you funds because I'm sure you'll both agree, little can be achieved without means to support such a scheme. Will you leave it with me for the time being? I'm busy for most of today. I have appointments which cannot be deferred but come back tomorrow afternoon, say two o'clock and we'll make some definite plans. Is it possible to bring others of the committee?'

The two women agreed to try.

Leaving the stately home, they took a short cut through Martinsham woods. It was such a beautiful spring day the brightness seemed to transfer its message to their inner souls; they were so uplifted with the weather and Lady Emma's promise, that they felt they could do virtually anything they set their minds to.

'What a very pleasant lady' Louisa commented. 'How I do envy her beautiful dress. How I would like to be able to afford such a garment.'

Bathsheba reminded her quickly of the course they were set upon and reprimanded her for her thoughtless talk. 'Louisa, compare yourself for one moment with the likes of Mrs. Welland who has only the clothes she stands up in and no roof over her head to speak of.'

It wasn't like Bathsheba to speak harshly so Louisa knew she was deeply concerned about the plight of the labourers.

'I'm sorry, Bathsheba. I'm afraid I spoke without thinking. But it doesn't do to become so involved; it affects your own well-being,' Louisa reminded her friend.

They were nearing Weatherbury Upper Farm by this time and as Bathsheba drew up in the courtyard where Louisa's own carriage was waiting she asked how George was progressing with his project.

'They say very little about it, Bathsheba and I'm reluctant to ask for fear they will think I'm over curious,' she paused for a moment unsure whether to say what was in her mind.

'Is something bothering you, Louisa?' Bathsheba had noticed the sudden furrowing of her friends brow.

'How is young Bathsheba these days? I've been meaning to ask but events seem to have taken over of late.'

'She's very well. I expect her home for the holidays shortly.'

'Bathsheba, George tells me his thinking of asking Adeline to marry him. Do you think Sheba will be at all troubled by this?'

Bathsheba smiled. 'On the contrary Louisa. I think she will be very pleased. She used to be very fond of George, I know, but I think she has come to regard him as much like a brother as anything else.'

'Well, that's a relief. I would hate her to be upset or hurt. She's such a lovely, kind-hearted girl. I must admit I had hopes for George and Sheba. They would make a handsome couple of that there is no doubt but Adeline is rather sweet, in her own way.'

'I know Gabriel thought that way at one time, Louisa, but having been away at college for some time she is quite recovered from her infatuation with George, I'm sure.'

Bathsheba was not at all sure her daughter did not have feelings that were more than brotherly for George Abbot but it was not in her place to say, especially not to Louisa. She would write and tell Sheba this evening so she was prepared when she arrived home.

'I do hope Lady Emma is full of ideas tomorrow, Bathsheba.'

'We'll just have to wait and see,' was the quick reply, her thoughts now on more familial things.

They arranged to meet at the Square after noon on the morrow, both women agreeing to visit as many committee members as possible in order to persuade them to Martinsham Hall for the meeting.

Gabriel and Benjamin sat facing Sir Cornelius across his vast mahogany, leather-topped desk in the office of Martin and Godwin. A large poster on the wall behind announced they were Steam Engine Manufacturers. Neither farmer nor shepherd knew much about the workings of the great firm but both appreciated the power of its owners.

Sir Cornelius had already heard rumours of the troubles and it didn't take long for Gabriel to put him fully in the picture.

'So you Sir, we wondered if you could help?'

Sir Cornelius stood up and walked round the desk..

'You'll appreciate I'd rather not be directly involved at this stage, I'm sure.'

Both men nodded.

'Lord Exonbury is an acquaintance of mine, certainly, but he is no friend,' he said smiling. 'Nevertheless, I wouldn't wish to be on the wrong side of him. We do have business associates in common and to upset the man would cause disruption throughout the works. I'd hate to put any of my employees" jobs at risk. It would simply make matters worse.'

Benjamin looked grim but Gabriel nodded understandingly.

'Could you advise us on the best course of action, Sir?' Gabriel asked.

'How long can you employ the unfortunate labourer Mr Oak?'

'Several weeks, I should think.'

'Then I suggest you do that and wait to see what happens. If the troubles escalate it will certainly be in the next few weeks. Carry on with what you're doing. In the meantime I'll confer with my partner and some colleagues and try to come up with something but I think essentially it is important not to react in such a way as to makes matters worse.'

Gabriel was happy enough with that but as they left the building Benjamin expressed his discontent.

'Are you sure he's on our side, Mr. Oak? Seems to me he is not going to back us.'

'Well, I can't be sure of course, Ben, but I believe he is on our side. I can't quite put a finger on it but I get the distinct impression he doesn't like Lord Exonbury.'

'I hope you're right. We don't stand a chance against the bigwigs without at least one of them with us.'

'Now, Benjamin Tallboys, that's not like you to talk like that.' Gabriel slapped him playfully on the back. 'Where's your fighting spirit?'

Ben grinned. 'Went into hiding for the minute, Mr. Oak. Don't worry. 'Tis back now!'

'How about a little refreshment at The Nags Head, by way of fortification?' Gabriel suggested, reining in his horse outside the inn.

"Twill make a change from The Kings Arms and we might find out a few bits of gossip.'

As they entered, two men, obviously farm workers from their style of dress, were talking loudly.

'How many's that then?' The man leaning on the bar was heard to say.

'Another three from Lord Exonbury's Estate and two from a neighbouring farm.'

'Why, "twill be only you and me left working at this rate, Seth.'

The man called Seth laughed heartlessly. 'Well you won't catch me having anything to do with that union. I'd rather starve and still "ave a roof over me "ead. What say ye, Joseph?'

'Aye, so would I.'

The two men noticed the arrival of Gabriel and Ben. They both pointedly ignored them, picked up their tankards and went to sit in the far corner, as far away from the new arrivals as possible.

'It's not going to stop, Mr. Oak.'

Gabriel looked concerned. 'You're right, Ben. But it gives us all the more reason to go on. Somebody's got to do something and we've started it so 'tis up to us to see it through.'

Gabriel heard himself committing himself with his fine words but inside there was an element of doubt. He hadn't the strength or might to fight these influential landowners on his own, he knew that. They desperately needed help from a higher source and although both men believed in the power of prayer they knew it would help to have something a little more practical and down to earth on their side. He just hoped Sir Cornelius Godwin wouldn't let them down.

Chapter Twenty Six
A Letter Gives Cause For Concern.

BATHSHEBA WAS GLAD SHE had arrived home before her husband. She was in no mood to be questioned about the day's activities, for Gabriel always made a point of asking politely whether her day had been a good one or not. What she needed now was some time to herself to sort out her thoughts. How strange she reminisced, as she took out her writing implements, that she'd thought she would be lonely without her offspring milling about as they used to. In fact she was busier and more fulfilled than ever and certainly had more than enough to occupy her mind.

The priority now was to send word to Sheba of the coming betrothal of George and Adeline. How strange it was that he had decided to wed the precocious little Adeline. She certainly had her fair share of good looks and charm but Bathsheba had reckoned George to require more than that in a wife. Adeline was such a scatterbrain. Hardly the kind of wife who would knuckle down and help on the farm when required.

Bathsheba wondered if her own critical attitude was just sour grapes. Louisa hadn't said very much about the young lovers. Maybe she had misunderstood the signs. Nevertheless in thinking this Bathsheba knew she was clutching at straws. She must repeat exactly what Louisa had told her in the courtyard. George was "thinking" of becoming betrothed to Adeline. No more and no less.

There was plenty of other news to tell her daughter so she had no need to dwell on bad news. So much was happening and she knew Sheba would be interested in the progress of baby Gabriel. She really must persuade Theodore to have a miniature painted of his small son as he was almost certain not to have thought of it himself, or, if not a painting then a photograph so she might have one as well.

'I am looking forward to seeing you at Easter which, I'm pleased to say, is only two weeks away', she wrote. "You will be bringing Jayne with you, won't you? We shall be more than pleased to see her if she can spare the time and will not be too bored in the country. Adam sends word that he will also be at home.

Your ever affectionate,

Mother."

Having written the letter, Bathsheba felt relieved. The next job was a list of committee members for tomorrow and possible suggestions for the meeting. The small community seemed to be at a crossroads, with the work force unsure which way to go. Bathsheba tried to imagine what it would be like to know your husband was at risk of losing his job just because he wanted a fair wage. It was easy for her, in her large farmhouse, her own future was secure enough but what if she were in danger of losing everything? She offered a short prayer of thanks to her Maker, thankful she was not born of a lower class.

Liddy must be the first port of call. She was bound to be interested and want to help. Mrs Hansworth would definitely want to be included. She wanted to be in on almost everything going on in Weatherbury and she certainly would not want to miss a chance to visit Martinsham Hall. Louisa would persuade some of the members from her side of the county. Bathsheba reckoned that altogether there would be at least seven members present but she had not allowed that Emma Godwin would invite anyone.

'I shall be out all day tomorrow, Gabriel', Bathsheba informed her husband after they had dined. 'There is to be a committee meeting at the Hall so I expect to be occupied for most of the day. What will you be doing?'

Gabriel explained what Sir Cornelius Godwin had suggested at their meeting. 'Wait and see, he advised! Well I don't think we can m'dear. The troubles seem to be gathering momentum and I fear violence may break out before long.'

'Is it really as bad as that, Gabriel?'

'Oh yes, indeed. It would seem a lot of the employers are getting in first. They don't want to pay higher wages so they're getting rid of workers before they have a chance to make trouble.'

'Do you expect our workers to join in?'

'No, they know which side of their bread is buttered. As you know we pay slightly over the odds and of course Martin and Godwin, them being manufacturers pay even more than we do.'

'I've heard tell, Gabriel, that in the large towns, fortunes can be made at some of the larger manufacturing plants. Can it be true?'

"Tis true, Bathsheba, but only if there is skill involved. Some of the labourers earn a pittance and are no better off than farm workers and of course they don't even get a tied cottage nor an allotment.'

'What will you and Ben do now?'

'I shall go back and see Sir Cornelius. When he knows what's happening he may think of something. My suggestion will be that he'll call a meeting between the local employers, put it to them what is happening and see if he can persuade them the union is not out to cause trouble. All the men want is a decent living wage and somewhere decent to live. Surely that's not too much to ask of anyone.'

Bathsheba agreed but decided to keep the content of her forthcoming WSC meeting a secret. There was no sense in giving Gabriel more to concern himself about. It seemed he had quite enough but she thought he ought to know about George.

'Louisa tells me George is to marry Adeline Westley.'

'But I thought our Sheba and George had patched things up.' Gabriel was plainly surprised and not a little pained at the news. 'It's a bit sudden isn't it?'

'Well it's not for certain, so don't you go saying anything yet to George. Louisa only mentioned it today but I thought I should let Sheba know. Fore-warned is fore-armed so they say.'

'I agree. Of course she should know. Won't she be upset, Bathsheba? I thought she was very fond of the lad in spite of her protestations when I teased her about him at Christmas.'

'I thought that way too but she never really confided in me, Gabriel. Sometimes I think how little I know my own children. Take Matthew for instance.' An expression of anguish crossed Bathsheba's face whenever she mentioned her youngest son. Although she had accepted his choice of career she could not bring herself to approve, although she never let it be known to anyone but her husband.

'Well, he seems happy enough. In his last letter he said the platoon was practising sword drill somewhere on Melchester Plain. Music appears to have taken second fiddle of late,' he said smiling at the pun he'd inadvertently made

Bathsheba shuddered involuntarily. She had no need to explain to her husband the reason for her discomfort for he knew all about Sargeant Francis Troy and the escapade on a ferny bank when she had been all but pared alive. It had been so exciting, exhilarating even, at the time. Now she wondered at her own naivety.

She looked up and smiled at her husband of many years and thanked God for her good fortune. He saw her looking and walked over to kiss her cheek, offering up a similar prayer. He wished he could put wise heads on the shoulders of his children but knew it wasn't possible. They had to live their own lives, make their own mistakes sometimes and then if they were as lucky as their parents they would end up content enough.

It was Friday morning, the day the post was often delayed owing to the post boy having to help sort the newspapers before he delivered the mail so it was late afternoon when Sheba received the letter from her mother.

She and Jayne had been studying the works of the Lake poets for most of the day and both girls were in mellow mood.

Sheba sat on the window seat and gazed out into the garden beyond before she opened her letter. Seeing the daffodils nodding in the breeze, she remarked to her friend, 'How I would love to see for myself the "host of golden daffodils', Mr. Wordsworth wrote about. Do you think there were "ten thousand, at a glance', Jayne?'

'That's what he said but I suppose we must allow him some poetic licence, Sheba,' she laughed. 'They say Ullswater is particularly beautiful at this time of the year.

'Beside the Lake, beneath the trees, Fluttering and dancing in the breeze,' Jayne quoted as she danced around the room with an imaginary partner.

Not receiving a reply from Sheba, Jayne turned to prod her playfully but was stopped in her tracks by the sight of her forlorn expression.

'Whatever is the matter, Sheba? Is someone at home not well?'

Sheba shook her head. 'No, it's nothing like that, Jayne.' Her face, usually a very healthy lustrous pink had turned as pale as a snowdrop and her head drooped likewise, mimicking the delicate flower.

'Would you like to tell me what has happened, Sheba? If you'd rather not...' Jayne sat next to her friend touching her arm in consolatory fashion.

'Read this!' Sheba thrust the cause of her consternation at her friend.

Jayne read quickly through the letter before she exploded, 'I cannot believe this to be true, Sheba. Please don't think I'm suggesting your mother is telling you something which is untrue, but I do think there may be some mistake. You and George patched things up between you before you left. He gave no inclination of this event when we were last at Oakdene,' she paused to take a breath, 'did he?'

Sheba shook her head. 'He said nothing in his last letter either. But, Jayne, Adeline was flirting outrageously when we were last there. Don't you remember how we remarked about her? I must say I thought George to have more sense.' Here she burst into tears.

'I can't believe it, Sheba! Adeline is such a ...' Not wanting to be deliberately offensive to the young lady of short acquaintance, Jayne was at a loss for words which would adequately describe her feelings for Miss Westley, for she blamed her almost entirely.

Her tears somewhat subsided, Sheba declared, 'Jayne, I won't want to go home for the Easter holidays now. I'm sure mother will understand. Would it be at all possible to go to your parents in Devonshire?'

'I'm so sorry, Sheba, my parents are abroad so the house is closed. That was one of the reasons I accepted your invitation to spend Easter at Oakdene,' she reminded her friend. And to see Adam, she thought, but she hadn't yet told Sheba of her deep admiration for the young poet and now was certainly not the right time.

'Well, I suppose I'll just have to put up with seeing the young lovers together all the time.' Sheba stood up and looked out onto the garden. The daffodils were still there, golden and glowing in the early spring sunshine. A red squirrel ran carelessly down the elm tree and crossed the lawn before disappearing into the woods beyond.

'Jayne, you will help me through this, won't you?' she pleaded.

Jayne walked across and hugged her friend. 'Of course, Sheba. And, don't forget, Bartholomew will be at Acorn farm.'

The two girls smiled at each other. One's heart was filled with joy at the prospect of seeing her beloved; the other's as heavy as though hung with frost.

Chapter Twenty Seven
Expostulation and Reply.

ONCE AGAIN, BATHSHEBA AND Louisa found themselves knocking on the huge door of Martinsham Hall. On this occasion they were expected and were shown without delay, into the drawing room where several other members of the committee were already assembled.

Lady Emma rose and extended a gloved hand. 'Good morning, Mrs. Oak, Mrs. Abbot. May I introduce my adopted daughter, Lady Sarah Godwin?'

A voluptuous lady who had obviously been a raving beauty in her youth, now, only a few years younger than Lady Emma but no more than five feet two inches tall with beautiful dark brown hair rather similar to Bathsheba's own, stood up and smiled a greeting. Her morning dress bore a remarkable resemblance to her mother's and it was obvious even to the untrained eye they were both served by the same expensive and talented dressmaker.

'Sarah has expressed an interest in the recent turn of events and wishes take an active part in this morning's proceedings. I trust no one has any objections?' Lady Emma exuded such an imperious air of authority that no one in the room would have dreamed of raising an objection. There were a few mutterings from the members present, mostly because they had never before met the aforesaid Sarah and they had a natural distrust of strangers. They were also loathe to admit a new member at this critical stage.

Bathsheba, not wanting the mutterings to be taken as dissension spoke up for her colleagues. 'I'm sure we welcome all the help we can get, Lady Emma.'

'Then we will continue. Sarah will be working completely independently, you must understand. I have not told Sir Cornelius the content of this morning's meeting as I was asked specifically not to,' she glanced quickly at Bathsheba and Louisa who nodded in appreciation. 'However, I do not think it is fair to him for me to become involved directly with the troubles, as I have a certain responsibility to my husband's firm. I'm sure you will agree.' She looked around and was pleased to see several heads nodding.

'I've explained to Sarah all that has happened thus far so now I shall leave you and allow Sarah to take the Chair.' Lady Emma smiled, bowed her head slightly in Sarah's direction and left the room.

Sarah stood up and picked up a sheaf of papers from the table beside her, looking for all the world as if she were about to deliver the Queen's speech at the opening of parliament.

'Before we continue I'd just like to tell you a little about myself for I cannot expect you to trust me if you know nothing about me.' She smiled again at her new colleagues.

'I was born into a working-class environment many miles from here.' There were gasps of surprise at the idea that this elegant lady could be connected with the labouring classes. If Sarah had wanted to gain their undivided attention she had certainly chosen the correct opening words. All faces were now gazing intently in her direction. Bathsheba already knew a little about the story but she hadn't given it much thought until now.

'It is a very long story,' Sarah continued, 'but I can tell you that I have both seen and felt much suffering in my time so I do assure you, I can and do feel an empathy with the plight of the poorly waged farm labourers who have often to live and work in the most unsatisfactory conditions. But the difference between them and me is, I was fortunate, for whilst still in my youth I inherited a considerable fortune from a close relative who until his death had been unknown to me. Now, I am involved with several business projects, some of which are abroad, which take up a great deal of my time.' Here she paused but as no one made any comment, she continued, 'In case you are wondering if I ever married, no, I have not.' In case the ladies present thought her to be dry and spinsterish she explained, 'I was in love once but I chose to keep my independence.'

There were again gasps of surprise. Here was a lady with a difference. So powerful was her charming personality that she had won over her audience easily with just a few carefully chosen words. They all, without exception, agreed for her to be accepted on to the committee and admitted she would indeed be an asset.

'As I am to take my mother's place on this committee, are you happy that I should take the Chair?' Sarah enquired.

There was a chorus of assent from the members.

'Good! Then we can proceed with the real business. Here's what I propose:' She paused and shuffled her papers.

'As it is important for us to continue to support the men financially in times of hardship I suggest the fund-raising continues as before but with even more effort on our part.'

There was a chorus of 'Hear, hear!'

'We must also continue to put out pamphlets informing the men of their rights.'

Louisa whispered to Bathsheba, 'She hasn't said anything new yet.'

Bathsheba put a finger to her lips with an implied Shush!

Sarah continued, 'Finally I have a plan which will be of some practical use but I must stress that I wish to remain anonymous. Can you agree to my anonymity?'

Again there was a chorus of assent which far outweighed Mrs. Hansworth's mutterings. She could not for the life of her understand why this important lady should wish to remain anonymous. If it were herself, she sat thinking, I would want everyone to know.

'Well, this is it. I shall donate the sum of twenty thousand pounds for the purpose of building cottages in the form of almshouses, but, with a difference. Each cottage shall have enough land to enable the tenant to grow his own food. There will be no ties and no tithes; just a nominal rent. The only stipulation is that the tenant must work on the land or be connected to the same and agree to keep his designated property in good order.'

Bathsheba was the first to recover from this amazing announcement. 'It sounds impressive, Lady Sarah, but who will maintain these cottages?'

'It will be a condition that the tenant is responsible for the maintenance and upkeep of his cottage and his reward will be a guaranteed tenancy for his life or the life of his wife. Hopefully, the children of the tenant will want to continue with the tenancy thus keeping a sense of continuity and stability, the very components that seem to be missing at the present time.'

Mrs. Hansworth couldn't keep quiet any longer. 'My husband, the vicar, may wish to have some say in who is suitable to have one of your new cottages Lady Sarah. May I explain to him what you propose?'

'Could I ask you all to address me either as Sarah or Miss Godwin, whichever you feel most comfortable with, whilst we are in private? It is less formal and it would please me very much.' Sarah smiled again causing Louisa to whisper to Bathsheba, 'Do you think she is always so happy and smiling?'

Bathsheba told her friend not to be silly.

'In answer to your question, Mrs Hansworth, I really must stress the importance of my remaining anonymous. Therefore I cannot allow you to inform your husband of our plans. You do understand, do you not?'

Mrs Hansworth flushed a dull red and merely nodded.

'I would just like to explain,' Sarah continued, 'I have considerable experience in the field of architecture and building. I was fortunate enough to help, if that is the right word, Sir Cornelius and Lady Emma to plan and build the village of Godwinstone several years ago. I also have experience abroad. I'm explaining this to you so that you have no need to be concerned about my capabilities in that direction.'

Liddy nodded like a clockwork automaton newly wound up. She hadn't said a word throughout the meeting, feeling a little out of her depth. Now she felt impelled to say a word or two. 'I think what you're going to do, Miss Godwin, is wonderful.' She blushed at her own courage.

'Thank you. Mrs. Barnes, isn't it? I can assure you it is no chore. In fact I feel honoured that my mother gave me the opportunity to become involved.'

A knock on the drawing room door heralded the arrival of refreshment. The discussion continued and it was arranged for more pamphlets to be printed and delivered, fund-raising and collections to continue leaving the architectural details for the cottages in the hands of Lady Sarah.

As the members left Martinsham Hall they took with them a buzz of excitement. There were happenings afoot and the sooner they got things moving the better.

At the offices of Martin and Godwin, Gabriel was having a much less successful time. Sir Cornelius" policy of wait and see remained unchanged.

'But Sir,' Gabriel pleaded, 'If we don't do something to stop these unfair dismissals I fear there will be severe reprisals.'

'Surely not, Gabriel. The men have more sense than to jeopardise their own well-being with petty fights amongst themselves which will serve no useful purpose,' the Gentleman had replied.

'Could I suggest that you to go and see Lord Exonbury, Sir? If you warn him he just might pass on the word to other employers especially if you stress your own workers belong to a union and you have no trouble.'

'Our mill workers are paid more than farm labourers, as I'm sure you are aware, so there can be no fair comparison, Gabriel.' Sir Cornelius sat back in his captain's chair and thought for a minute.

'I'll tell you what I'll do, Gabriel. At the next meeting of the Wheel Club I'll put what you suggest to the members. That way it will not appear that I'm pointing an accusing finger in one direction. How's that?'

Gabriel nodded and stood up. 'Then I'll leave it with you, Sir.'

The two men shook hands pleased that they had managed to reach a tacit agreement. One left to discuss with his Lady wife the next step in the proceedings; the other to Oakdene where he would say little to his wife for fear of her becoming too involved and therefore endangered.

Had he but known, Bathsheba was already heavily involved and was about to become even more so.

Chapter Twenty Eight

With Trumpets and Flaming Fire.

THE NEXT WEEK HERALDED no surprises although, not entirely unexpected in the circumstances, there was an air of tension among the farm labourers, they not being certain whether they would have a job at the end of each day but at this time of year when Spring lay just around the corner, not even the powerful Lord Exonbury could afford to lay off workers. Lambing-time could not be delayed even for the mighty landowner and naturally he wouldn't want it to be, for it would eat heartily into his profits.

The WSC carried on enthusiastically with their pamphleteering and fund-raising and felt they were at last beginning to see some positive results. Membership of the Farmworkers Union now showed an almost daily increase. Bathsheba was suddenly hit with the bright idea to start a sewing circle for the women of Weatherbury which made clothes for children from discarded adult garb. She, Louisa and Liddy made a tour of the grand houses in the area collecting unwanted items of clothing which for a reason known only to the lady of the house had not been offered to the servants first. The cloth, coming as it did from the well-to-do was of excellent quality although Bathsheba found the work of unpicking a little tedious. The newly made garments were then passed to any deserving family who had fallen on hard times. The receivers accepted gladly as they didn't look on the idea as charity having been given the chance to help in the manufacture themselves and they knew the deed would be reciprocated if and when their situations improved.

Benjamin Tallboys was also a happy man. His class was now always well attended and all of his students bar none could now read and write albeit some had a rather childish hand and it would take several more months for them to have the right to say they were at all fluent in the art of the written word. The main thing was they were improving and keen.

At the meeting of the Wheel Club, Cornelius Godwin had put it to the members that they should, in their own interest, at least think about what membership of a union would mean to their workers. He stressed that there had been no trouble at his mill, at least not due to union membership. In fact when there had been a minor dispute it had been a positive help because it meant a small delegation had asked to meet him and Nathaniel Martin, and between them they had managed to reach an agreement with very little acrimony.

The members of the Wheel club agreed to think it over with one exception. Lord Exonbury condemned the idea outright with the bald statement that workers should know their place and stay in it. He refused to discuss anything to do with workers rights because quite simply he didn't believe they had any. He said he was doing them a favour by employing them at all and that was the creed he had lived by and would most certainly continue to do so.

'If there's any trouble,' he had said wagging a fat finger at Cornelius, 'then they know what'll happen to them. They'll go! It's their loss, not mine. They've more to lose than me. Why, farm-labourers are two a penny.' He had thrown back his head and laughed raucously at his unfunny pun, his fat red jowls wobbling for all the world like poorly made raspberry jelly.

As Cornelius had remarked to his partner Nathaniel later that day, 'I've never felt such disgust for a fellow since the days of Sir Arnold Walpole.'

Nathaniel knew all about that particular aristocrat as Sir Arnold Walpole had been responsible for Sarah Godwin's illegitimacy, him carrying on with her mother up North, whilst already married with a family, all living at Martinsham Hall. How fortunate that when Cornelius had made the discovery that Sir Arnold Walpole was Sarah's father, rather than face the music he had decided rather quickly to go and live on one of his plantations in the West Indies and how fortunate for Sarah he had died soon after, leaving her a large share of his enormous fortune.

Sarah Godwin had never forgotten those hard times and whenever the opportunity arose she made use of her fortune to help the less fortunate, hence the idea to build cottages for the homeless.

The plans had been drawn up reasonably quickly for she had used part of the plans Cornelius had designed for the village of Godwinstone, built for mill workers at the same time as the mill was built. The new cottages, brick built and rendered in as was the local custom, were on a much smaller scale, consisting mainly of a two up, two down style and in a terrace of six. There would be four of these, making twenty four cottages in total. It was only a start but Sarah hoped there would be more built if the scheme proved to be successful.

It was on Maundy Thursday that Sarah met with Bathsheba and Louisa at the new site, just on the edge of the forest between Weatherbury and the Athel Hall acreage, to see how the foundations were progressing. The fine weather had allowed the work to proceed without delay for the builders were working from dawn until dusk.

The ladies, pleased with the progress made, could envisage the time when families would be living there which they expected could be well before Christmas.

Now, however, Easter approached and all the ladies had family commitments which would take priority over their charity work.

'Is Sheba arriving tomorrow, Bathsheba?' Louisa asked politely although in view of the circumstances with George and Adeline, she half expected her friend to say her daughter had made other plans.

'I expect her, and Jayne, late this afternoon, Louisa. May we expect you for supper on Saturday, as usual?'

Louisa nodded. She hoped she was worrying unnecessarily about young Bathsheba Oak. George hadn't mentioned his betrothal to Adeline since the day she had talked with Bathsheba but he was still seeing rather a lot of the pretty young maid.

The boys had finished their barn project and all that was left for them to do was the written analysis. Louisa gathered, the idea which had seemed such a good one at the outset, hadn't worked out quite as they'd hoped but the important thing was they had worked on it and got some pleasing results, enough to satisfy the professor at college anyway, so George had said.

'Would you care to join us on Saturday, Lady Sarah?' Bathsheba enquired. 'Your step-mother and father will be present.'

'They did mention it, Bathsheba. Yes, I'd like that. I'll see you on Saturday then.' Lady Sarah climbed into her carriage and was driven off at speed.

'She has such vitality, don't you think?' Louisa commented.

'I certainly agree, Louisa. And, she's such a pleasant person. I feel as if I've known her all my life.'

'So do I. I think it has something to do with the warmth she exudes wherever she goes. Even the workers on the building site seemed to have become more animated than usual when she spoke to them.'

'I suppose some people have it and some don't,' Bathsheba laughed. 'Well I must go, Louisa. My offspring will arrive home to an empty house if I don't make haste.'

'Bathsheba you exaggerate, my dear. Maryann will welcome them in your absence, I'm sure.'

'You're quite right, Louisa. I do rather forget they are grown up and have the capacity to live without a mother's constant care.'

Louisa put her hand to her mouth. 'Bathsheba I nearly forgot to tell you. I bumped into Theodore Melksham yesterday. He asked me to tell you that his eldest son is to be married this weekend in London. He will bring his new wife for a visit after the honeymoon and then he's to be his father's new partner.'

Bathsheba clapped her gloved hands. 'Louisa, I'm so pleased. It was what Theodore had been hoping and praying for ever since Harriet passed away. Do you think the new Mrs. Melksham will be taking the responsibility for baby Gabriel's care?'

'Theodore didn't say and I didn't like to ask.'

'Well, I shall ask him when I see him. That baby needs a mother's love and who better than his new..' Bathsheba paused to work out the relationship. 'Baby Gabriel will be Mrs. Melksham's brother-in-law.'

The two women laughed. 'Well, it doesn't matter. Age is neither here nor there. As long as she is old enough to be his mother, so be it.'

Bathsheba and Louisa departed for their homes happy with the new arrangement, both pleased that the baby Gabriel would now have someone to nurture him in a proper fashion.

When Bathsheba arrived home there was a letter waiting for her. She recognised her youngest son's hand and ripped it open before taking off her bonnet.

'My Dearest Mother," he wrote.

'Good news! I shall be home to help you and my family celebrate Easter. It will be so good to see you all and I cannot wait to catch up on all the Weatherbury news at first hand."

The remainder of the letter described his life at the barracks and told of new friends and the various escapades they had been involved in. He finished with the startling news that he had been given a permanent place in the Marching Band which he would take up on his return to the barracks after his leave.

'I shall be on leave for fourteen days in all, mother, so I shall probably spend some time with Adam at Christminster. I'm sure you won't mind?"

Such a long leave, Bathsheba thought as she made her way to the kitchen to inform Maryann of the extra visitor for the holidays.

Maryann was overjoyed at the prospect of Matthew being home on leave for such a long period.

'Does this mean he is to go abroad soon after, Madam?' Maryann enquired.

Bathsheba sat down in the rocking chair and stared into the fire whilst Maryann continued.

'My cousin's boy did that, Mrs. Oak. They let "im come home seeing as how it would be a long time before he would see "is family again. So excited "e was. I expect Master Matthew will be in a rare state of excitement too.' Maryann looked up from rolling out her pastry and stopped when she saw the stricken look on Bathsheba's face.

'I'm sorry, Mrs. Oak. I didn't mean to speak out of turn like.'

'It's alright Maryann. I just never thought of it. You're quite right. I expect that is why Matthew's leave is a long one. He didn't mention it in his letter though.'

'Perhaps it be secret then, madam. Why, sometimes they don't know where they be going "til they gets there, so 'tis said.'

'Well, Maryann, it's not as if there's a war on at the minute. No doubt he'll tell us all about it when he arrives tomorrow.'

When Gabriel arrived home, he tried to convince his wife there was no need to worry and although she agreed she had a little nagging doubt at the back of her mind that things were not quite as they should be.

Chapter Twenty Nine
Converging Courses

EASTER, A TIME FOR sorrow for our Lord was crucified, a time for joy because He rose again.

Maryann had been quite correct in her prediction. Matthew was sailing to India with his regiment at the end of his two week's leave and in stark contrast to his mother's apprehension, was as pleased and excited as a dog with two tails. It had soon become obvious he had inherited his musical ability from his father, but, as Bathsheba had shown some latent talent having become an accomplished pianist since Gabriel had bought her the piano he'd promised when first he proposed marriage to her, he could easily have inherited a little of her talent too.

Although Matthew said he would have preferred to be a drummer in the band, he had in fact been chosen to play the cornet and now was as proud of his instrument, as a mother is proud of her new born offspring, and couldn't wait to show off with it.

Now, in the sunny drawing room at Oakdene, he took out the instrument from its gleaming dark brown leather carrying case. The sun, catching the metal body of the instrument, was dazzling to the eyes of the onlookers.

Maryann was clearly impressed. 'What a bright gleam it do have. Do they make "e polish that instrument yourself, Master Matthew?'

'Yes, Maryann. I'm entirely responsible for it.' Matthew looked pleased at the compliment, more so than if she had said he looked polished himself which, resplendent as he was in his scarlet uniform, its silver buttons shining nearly as brilliantly as the instrument, would have deserved the same praise. He blasted a few notes just to prove he could play it.

Bathsheba covered her ears. The sound, it could hardly be referred to as music, in the confined indoor space of the front drawing room was rather deafening to the listeners.

Matthew apologised but reminded them it was sometimes used to wake the military. 'And if you don't mind Maryann, I'd prefer you to call me Lance-Corporal Oak as is my rightful title as of yesterday.'

'Certainly, Lance-Corporal Oak', Maryann replied smiling and bobbing a curtsey.

'Congratulations, Matthew!' Gabriel shook his youngest son firmly by the hand. 'The military must be mighty pleased with you to give you such a title after only a short period of training,' he jested.

'Father, I've been training hard for many months now,' Matthew replied seriously. 'Anyway,' he felt obliged to explain, 'it's a military tradition that when a soldier becomes a full member of the band he is automatically promoted.'

Bathsheba had said nothing. Now she added her congratulations. 'Well done, son.'

'Thank you, mother.' He kissed her cheek knowing how difficult it must have been for her to assume an air of pleasure, especially after the news that he would be going abroad shortly.

The family, greetings over, dispersed, Matthew to his own room so he could take a much needed rest for, despite his obvious enthusiasm for the army, he had worked harder in the past few months than he'd ever had to work in his life before, even when they were harvesting here on the farm.

As he lay on his comfortable bed, what a difference to his army bunk, he reflected on the past months. There had been odd times he had thought his mother had been quite correct when she had declared the military was not for him but they had been transitory moments and soon forgotten in the new hectic life style.

He was however a little apprehensive about going to India for he'd heard stories from his colleagues that would chill the heart of any die-hard never mind his own mother. He wasn't at all sure whether the stories were true but had decided to keep quiet about the trip and make the most of Easter here at Oakdene and ride Prince, whom he had missed more than he would care to admit to anyone.

Bathsheba, feeling a little low because Matthew would shortly be crossing to what she felt was the other side of the world went with Gabriel to Weatherbury station to meet Sheba and Jayne.

Their train was on time as usual and soon the four were making their way back to Oakdene.

'Is Adam at home, Mrs. Oak?' Jayne asked blushing a little.

Bathsheba was taken by surprise at the unexpected blush. Surely Jayne wasn't falling in love with her eldest son? She looked again at Jayne before she replied carefully, 'He's expected early tomorrow, Jayne.'

Jayne bent her head down. She had felt herself blush and now felt rather foolish. Obviously Adam hadn't said anything to his mother about her but then she had no reason to believe he might. Although he had seemed fond of her when last they met he had given no indication that he wanted to be more than a friend.

Sheba hoped Adam was more than fond of Jayne for she would like no one better than Jayne for a sister. It was a topic of conversation they had discussed on several occasions after the lectures of the day at Exonbury college were finished. Sheba did not know how her brother felt about Jayne but she was determined to find out, to ask him outright if necessary, at some time during the holiday.

'How is Matthew, mother?' Sheba enquired as much to take the focus from Jayne as anything else.

'He's well, Sheba. Of course you won't know, will you?' Bathsheba hesitated, finding it difficult to actually put into words the news of Matthew's posting.

'His regiment's off to India the week after next, Sheba,' Gabriel informed her.

'How wonderful!' Sheba was nearly as excited as her brother. 'What a marvellous opportunity to see how others live.' She could see her mother wasn't nearly as impressed with the news as she was so she tried to make light of it.

'I've heard some wonderfully exotic tales of the East, mother. All those delicious curries and fragrant spices. And all that wonderful sunshine! What a time he'll have.'

Bathsheba didn't share her daughter's enthusiasm and merely smiled her Mona Lisa smile.

As they approached Oakdene a horseman, who had overtaken the carriage as they left Weatherbury station, appeared to be waiting for them at the entrance gates.

"I thought that were Ben Tallboys who overtook us at the turnpike,' Gabriel remarked to no one in particular. 'Wonder what he wants.'

He leapt down the steps of the carriage and made his way over to where his friend, who had dismounted and was allowing his horse to crop the grass verge, was standing in impatient mode.

'Don't you ever take a holiday, Ben Tallboys?' Gabriel questioned laughingly. He was in jovial mood at the prospect of having all his family round him if only for a short time.

'Sorry to bother you, Mr. Oak. I've had news of trouble over on t'other side of Weatherbury.'

'You'd better come in, Ben.' Gabriel's previous joviality had turned abruptly to anxious curiosity.

Once in his study, Gabriel invited Ben to sit. 'Well, my friend, what's going on?'

'There's been a bit of a difference of opinion over near the Martin and Godwin mill. Apparently a gang of Lord Exonbury's thugs threatened some of the mill workers as they left their evening shift. No one was seriously hurt, more hurt pride and a few bruises than anything else. But, they threatened to come back and do serious damage if the cottage building wasn't stopped.'

'I don't understand, Ben. Why pick on the mill workers. They've nothing to do with the building. Is that all you know?'

'Yes, Mr. Oak. I couldn't make much sense of it either.'

'I'd better ride over and see Sir Cornelius straight away. Maybe you've misunderstood, Ben and 'tis nothing to do with the cottages.'

Gabriel didn't really think his friend had misunderstood the situation but there was no doubt there was some misunderstanding somewhere along the line. He made his excuses to his family, promising not to be long.

'Sir Cornelius and Lady Emma will be here tomorrow evening, Gabriel,' Bathsheba quickly pointed out, 'You can discuss it then, surely.'

'I'm afraid this can't wait, Bathsheba. I'll be back in an hour, or two at the most.'

As soon as he arrived at the mill it was obvious Sir Cornelius was expecting him.

'Go straight on up, Sir. 'Tis the first door on the left at the top of the stairs,' a tall dapper gentleman instructed.

The door was slightly ajar and on hearing his approaching footsteps a voice requested he enter.

'Sit down Gabriel,' Cornelius invited after shaking his hand. 'I can guess what you've come about.'

'I must admit to a little curiosity Sir. What is going on?'

'To cut a long story a little short, Gabriel,' Sir Cornelius explained, 'Lord Exonbury got wind of the cottage building, put two and two together and came up with a massive ten.'

Gabriel laughed at the absurdity of the sum.

'However, I've already sent word that I wish to see him but as he's away until after Easter I can do little.'

Gabriel sighed audibly. 'So we can do nothing for the time being, Sir?'

'That's about the top and bottom of it, Gabriel. My advice is; go and enjoy the holiday with your family. We'll sort this out once and for all come next Tuesday. Suffice to say I am not pleased about the occurrence.'

Gabriel was relieved in the sense that he need do nothing for the time being but he would have liked to have sorted out the misunderstanding straight away so it was over and done with.

'I'll go then Sir. "Til tomorrow evening.' The two men shook hands each looking forward to the social occasion on the morrow.

Gabriel found that Adam was already there when he reached Oakdene. He was sitting close to Jayne and they seemed to be having a rather animated conversation. Gabriel wondered idly what it could be about. He looked across at his wife but she was locked in a similar deep conversation with her daughter.

From upstairs came the sound of the cornet. So, Matthew had finished resting. He would go and see him.

Adam had asked Jayne if she would care to listen to some of his latest poetry which was due to be published in a slim, leather bound volume, just after Easter. As she had responded in such an agreeably fast manner they were now arranging a suitable time and place for this event to take place.

Bathsheba had taken Sheba to one side in order to discuss the latest situation between George and Adeline. To her surprise, Sheba seemed unconcerned at the prospect of George's forthcoming betrothal.

'I shall never understand these youngsters', Bathsheba thought as she remembered so clearly, how ardently she had felt for her first husband, Francis Troy, and how upset she had been when she had discovered he had loved another more than he could ever love her. I suppose times change and I must try to keep up with them, she decided.

She couldn't have been more wrong. Deep inside, her daughter was crying as though her heart would break but not for anything or to anyone would she admit this almost uncontrollable feeling which threatened to engulf her at any minute. Instead she begged to be excused, 'If you don't mind mama, I'll rest a little before supper.'

Bathsheba agreed it would be a good idea and said she would do the same. Gabriel hadn't said anything about the trouble he had needed to hurry to Martinsham to discuss with Cornelius Godwin so she assumed everything had been sorted out satisfactorily.

How good it was to have her family and their friends around her once again she thought as she lay back in the peace of her boudoir, eagerly anticipating the party tomorrow, pleased that Sheba had taken the news of the betrothal so well.

I really needn't have worried at all, she thought happily.

Chapter Thirty
Let Time be the Healer.

SO LIFE THIS EASTER, was for the Oaks a mixture of fleeting joy and passing sorrow, for as we are all aware, people who on God's earth do dwell must, without choice, live a life of transient mixed emotions, oft times only recollected in moments of tranquillity which then remain with us as spots of time.

Easter celebrations were always jolly in Weatherbury and so it was at Oakdene this year. Several mutual friends and their families had gathered together, after early evening Easter Day service at St. Mary's Church, to celebrate Christ's rising and the imminent arrival of Spring.

It was customary to hold the gathering at Oakdene so when it had been suggested by Lady Emma Godwin that the gathering might take place at the palatial Martinsham Hall as there was more room, the Oaks had refused the offer politely, explaining that they felt it was important to uphold tradition if and when at all possible. To their surprise the Godwin's agreed with this and let it be known that if they were to be invited to the celebrations then they would be delighted to accept. This particular Easter tradition, although relatively new as it had only started in the first year of Gabriel and Bathsheba's marriage, already showed signs of becoming a lasting affair. As the Oaks proudly pointed out, family traditions must begin somewhere and far too many were becoming lost to progress, especially of late.

'Take the music in church,' Gabriel was often heard to say, 'why, in my young day, we had proper music played on proper instruments; violin, oboe, piccolo and clarinet. They were all up in the gallery. Now what do we hear? Some small manual organ!' To which Adam would reply, 'Well, father, at least 'tis better than that barrel organ we had to put up with when I was a child.'

Gabriel agreed but still shook his head in disapproval.

As at Harvest time, there were two camps. The labourers celebrated on the Green if the weather was fine; if not then it was the local tavern. The more well-to-do were apt to share their celebrations in one another's houses. The Oaks were no exception and now on this glorious Easter day a fair crowd had gathered together in the large drawing room of the old manor house.

Bathsheba had arranged the usual entertainments but this time there was an addition item, for George and Adeline were to duet at the piano prior to making their announcement. When Louisa had spoken of their plans she had asked if Sheba would mind her friends" betrothal taking place at Oakdene as they were quite content to wait until the following day rather than risk upsetting someone of whom they were both fond.

Proudly, Bathsheba had been able to reassure Louisa that her daughter would not be upset, making it quite clear that Sheba had other plans which at the moment did not include settling down simply to become a wife and mother. Louisa had looked a little put out at her friend's reply but, having known Bathsheba for a very long time, and feeling she might be covering up her innermost feelings, said nothing.

In one corner of the room the men had assembled, each eager to talk about the recent trouble at the Godwinstone Carpet Mill. Cornelius assured them vehemently that as soon as the Easter celebrations were over and Lord Exonbury was restored to his estate, he would personally go to visit him to find out exactly what the man's intentions were and if indeed he was responsible for the trouble although there seemed little doubt about that.

Gabriel noticed his wife beckoning to him so he excused himself from the circle and went across to join her.

'What are you all talking about,' she enquired with blatant curiosity. 'You look as if you are planning the next gunpowder plot,' Bathsheba laughed merrily, determined to enjoy these celebrations no matter what.

'Men's talk, m'dear,' Gabriel replied, tapping his nose with his forefinger suggesting a conspiracy.

'Seriously Gabriel, what is going on? I assumed you had sorted out that small problem Ben came to see you about yesterday.'

'Not quite, Bathsheba. Sir Cornelius has a plan which will I'm sure, put paid to any further disturbance at his Mill.' Gabriel's manner was so assuring that Bathsheba felt it unnecessary, even unwise, to pursue the matter.

'Then perhaps you will accompany me on the piano?' She took her husbands arm and led him over to the corner where Sheba had placed the music in readiness for her parents" performance.

They had chosen a section of Handel's Water Music, a very popular piece, which earned them much applause and a request for an encore. They obliged with a rendition of another work by Handel which seemed to please the audience who by this time were becoming a little noisy having sampled the excellent champagne the Godwin's had brought along to the party.

Gabriel led his wife over to Louisa, Sarah and Emma Godwin who were eager to congratulate them on their performance.

'Won't you play for us, Lady Emma?' Gabriel asked.

'I'd be delighted, Mr. Oak, but I see the young people are about to play.'

'Perhaps afterwards then?'

Lady Emma nodded and smiled.

Adeline started off by playing and singing, the gentle ballad, "The Banks of Allan Water', her ebony ringlets bouncing as she nodded her head in time to the music. It wasn't long before George joined in the chorus inviting the audience to join in if they knew the words. At first the company seemed reluctant to concede. It was not something they were used to and they felt a little uncomfortable about it.

'It's what they do at the Music Hall, so I'm told,' Lady Sarah informed them in a loud whisper. As soon as it was seen that Lady Sarah felt it wasn't below her station to join in, it wasn't long before all the ladies joined George in the chorus and a few of the men as well.

With everyone in such high spirits, The couple was urged to continue with more popular ballads but George held up his hands,

'Please! I thank you for your appreciation but I do have something of importance to say.'

There was an immediate hush and everyone looked at George expectantly.

'Adeline and I, that is, Miss Westley and I,' George suddenly felt tongue-tied for the first time in his life.

"Go on son,' his father urged from the back of the room.

George gazed down at Adeline with an adoring look. 'I want you to know that Miss Westley has agreed to become my wife.'

There was a burst of applause. They made a handsome couple, he tall and brown-haired, she petite and raven-black, and they had become popular in their close circle of friends.

Gabriel stood up. 'Well, I'm not your father, George, but as this is my house perhaps you will do me the honour of allowing me to propose a toast.'

Joseph Abbot, sitting with his wife nodded at Gabriel.

'I must say I had hoped to become your father-in-law George' he jested but as he caught sight of his wife with a finger to her lips he carried on quickly, 'but as 'tis not to be, well,' he raised his glass managing to avoid looking at his wife and daughter. 'To Miss Westley and George.'

Once the applause and congratulations had abated, Bathsheba went to find Sheba who had escaped quickly to her boudoir on the pretence of a sick headache.

She was sitting at the window, her eyes red, her face pale. Bathsheba walked across and put her arms around her daughter. Sheba burst into fresh tears and Bathsheba found it difficult to stop her own tears from flowing freely. She swallowed hard and concentrated on what her daughter must be feeling. It was up to her to be strong. Sheba needed her now, perhaps more than ever before.

'Sheba, all I can say to you is, Time is a great healer. You will find someone else, you know,' she paused knowing nothing she said would console her child in her unhappy state. 'I'm very, very sorry.'

Sheba looked up. 'It's alright, mama,' she said sniffing in a most unladylike manner. 'I didn't really want to get married. Not for years and years, anyway. I'm going to be a teacher.' Then as an afterthought, 'Anyway, Lady Sarah isn't married and she is happy and fulfilled.'

'Yes she is, Sheba.' Bathsheba had to agree but chose not to add that Sarah Godwin had a large fortune and didn't need a man to support her but this was not the right time to remind her daughter of such facts. That could be said later if necessary. What was important now was to see that Sheba got through the next few weeks with as little suffering as possible.

'Are you ready to come down, my dear?'

'If you don't mind, mama, I would rather not, if you'll excuse me.'

Bathsheba accepted her daughter's excuse and left her to rest. I'm so glad I'm not that young, she thought, as she made her way back to the noisy, happy throng she had left a short while ago.

Lady Emma had played her favourite Beethoven Sonata and was now playing a beautiful melodic piece, which seemed to express the very essence of Spring,

(later she told Bathsheba it was a brand new piece by the Norwegian composer, Eduard Grieg), and the noise and merriment had been replaced by an awesome quiet. Bathsheba, standing for a moment in the doorway heard the sound of a bat's wings high against a window pane reminding her of a poem by William Collins she'd read recently;

Now air is hush'd, save where the weak-ey'd bat,

With short shrill shriek flits by on leathen wing.

She couldn't remember the rest but it reminded her of George in some obscure fashion for wasn't he, she reasoned, as blind as the proverbial bat. Why couldn't he see that Adeline was so unsuitable for him? Thinking of her own youth and the way she had been infatuated with the young scarlet-tunicked officer, she felt herself shiver. Why was life so problematic? Why did one have to make so many mistakes before arriving at the truth? She felt a hand on her shoulder,

'Come and sit down, m'dear,' Gabriel whispered leading her to a chair at the back of the room where they could converse without disturbing the performance.

Keeping his tone low, he asked, 'How is she?'

Bathsheba smiled. 'Rather upset just now, but I'm sure she'll be alright in a few days.'

Gabriel patted his wife's hand. There was very little he could say to console her. Then he had an idea; 'We'll arrange an outing to Budmouth tomorrow. That'll cheer her up, I'm sure.'

'Are you sure you can you spare the time, Gabriel?'

Gabriel had forgotten momentarily the problems at the Mill. 'Sir Cornelius will sort that out, mark my words. We've no need to worry on that score.'

'Then it shall be arranged.'

Later that evening just before the guests left for their homes, Sheba made a brief appearance. She looked a little pale but found enough courage to congratulate the happy pair.

George had the good grace to look a might uncomfortable but Adeline more than made up for his reserve.

'We are probably to be married in the Autumn, Sheba. Would you care to be my bridesmaid?'

'I'm sorry, Miss Westley. I shall most likely be out of the country at that time of the year. Jayne and I plan to travel you know.'

Adeline looked surprised. In her world, to be married was the be all and end all. She imagined Sheba to be making an excuse because she was envious of her newly acquired state.

'Then I hope you will enjoy your travels, Miss Oak,' she replied with a somewhat caustic edge to her voice.

'Where do you plan to go, Sheba?' George asked politely.

'We've yet to arrange the details, George, but probably France and Italy.' She held out her hand to congratulate him.

George took her gloved hand, lifted it to his lips and kissed it gently. 'I envy you, Sheba. I almost wish I were coming with you,' he jested. His eyes were serious though causing Sheba to feel once more the intense pain of unrequited love. She still didn't understand his involvement with the immature Miss Westley and quickly made her excuse to leave the couple.

Bathsheba thought how well her daughter had dealt with the situation and was justifiably proud of her. It had been a rather mixed evening what with all the emotion involved. She for one was glad it was almost over and she knew Sheba would feel the same. When the outing to Budmouth had been suggested, Bathsheba had thought her daughter would decline to go but surprisingly she had agreed.

As the last guest left, she breathed a sigh of relief. They could now, begin to get on with the rest of their lives and as Sir Cornelius's son was to be present at the outing perhaps Sheba... Bathsheba stopped herself from her forward planning. Time must be allowed to take its course. She had had high hopes and expectations before and look what had happened. Fate, predestined or not, was in the lap of the Gods.

Chapter Thirty One

It Is The Nature Of Extreme Self-lovers, As They Will Set A House On Fire.

IN NO TIME AT all, or so it seemed to those who remained at the old manor, Oakdene resumed its air of the well-built empty nest. Sheba and Jayne had returned earlier than planned to their Exonbury College although it must be said it was at Sheba's insistence. Jayne had displayed a considerable degree of reluctance before she had finally agreed to accompany her friend. Saying farewell to Adam had brought a lack-lustre sparkle to her usually bright eyes. If appearances were anything to go by, Bathsheba thought, whilst watching the young couple take their leave of one another, and if she were correct in her assumptions, Adam would be speaking to the young lady's father quite soon.

The outing to Budmouth had been pleasing to all. Even Sheba had let down her hair in the end and enjoyed the latter part of the day to the extent of making full use of young Cornelius Godwin's attentiveness. He was staying at Martinsham Hall on a short vacation before starting the Grand Tour with two friends from his University.

Sheba had not mentioned George and Adeline since the poignant talk with her mother after the party and seemed to have put all thoughts of George completely from her mind. Her plans for the future were concentrated almost entirely on an expedition to Europe which she and Jayne were in the process of arranging with members of the college staff who had, on a previous occasion several years ago, done the very same journey. It would be an arduous journey for they meant to visit France and Italy in order to gain cultural knowledge, knowledge of the language and experience of foreign teaching methods and be away for some considerable time; probably in excess of four months, starting in June.

News had arrived from Matthew from his regimental base in India and his first letter was full of enthusiasm for the old, exotic country although he did complain a little about the heat.

'We are regarded with esteem, mother, and the natives are very polite and friendly', he wrote. "Some of the food is a little strange for it is often hot and spicy. As the weather is so hot, one would have thought it appropriate to eat only cold foods, but no, they say hot food cools! Can you believe it? If they are correct, then perhaps we should consider eating cold fare at Christmas in Weatherbury?"

He had gone on to describe the band's attainments and his own prowess which seemed to be improving daily, and finished the letter by promising to write at least once a fortnight with all the news and begged his parents to do likewise.

'Do you think he misses us, Gabriel?' Bathsheba and her husband were enjoying a rare quiet evening together, at home, which seemed to be rather infrequent of late.

'Well, he's hardly likely to say so, is he?' Gabriel laughed. 'He's a soldier now. 'Tis not the done thing to own up to missing the family.'

Bathsheba agreed. 'I suppose you're right. India is such a long way away, though. Still, he will benefit from his experiences there, I suppose,' she added reluctantly.

Gabriel nodded and carried on reading. Ben had lent him a new book about the Trade Union Movement and he wanted to finish it before the two met on the morrow.

There had been no more trouble from Lord Exonbury and his cronies and everyone hoped fervently they'd heard the last of it. Ben was coming to the end of his stint with the labourers. Now the evenings were lighter the men were eager to work out of doors, in their allotments and gardens in order to have a goodly supply of vegetables for the coming winter. Spring wasn't the time to be spent with heads in books, or so they said.

The brightly coloured ribbon-bedecked Maypole stood proudly in the middle of Weatherbury Green. Children had already gathered there with eager anticipation, for the arrival of the musicians was imminent. The crowning of the May Queen and the subsequent festivities had been carried out for many years and many generations had enjoyed the spectacle, especially the free flow of alcohol which accompanied it.

Indeed many a village woman had found herself with child after such celebrations. Some said it was the sole purpose of the ceremony. Others said that if it were true they'd do well to keep away. Whatever the decision and whether it was true or not most of the citizens of Weatherbury were on the Green that sunny May afternoon.

As the shadows of evening began to fall across the riotous throng, mothers collected their offspring, urging them to hurry before the bogey man leapt from the moon and carried them away. It was the only way to persuade them to leave without trouble such was the excitement of the day.

Slowly in ones and twos, the men drifted off to the King's Arms or the Nag's Head according to their station. Although the ale had flowed freely all afternoon it was part of the May-Day tradition to extend the celebration well into the night.

Gabriel and Ben, striding purposefully in the direction of The King's Arms, talked animatedly of their success with the Trade Union Movement.

'I didn't think we'd get this far, Mr. Oak, "specially when old Exonbury set his men on to the poor Mill workers.'

'We've Sir Cornelius to thank for that, Ben. He never told me what he said to the man but it certainly had the desired effect.'

'There was a rumour going about that old Exonbury had some dark secret that Sir Cornelius knew about and threatened to tell. 'Tis hard to believe but something must have happened.' Ben stroked his chin thoughtfully as they sat down at the familiar table just inside the door of the Inn. 'He is in the running for the Lord Lieutenant's position, Gabriel, so he wouldn't want any skeletons to appear out of his cupboard now would he?'

Both men laughed. They'd heard rumours about what the aristocracy got up to and for the most part it was ignored. After all they held the power by virtue of their money and land. What could the peasants do but get on with what work was offered and keep their noses out of what didn't concern them.

'Ben, have you ever thought of standing for parliament?'

The question came out of the blue but Ben was not taken aback. It was something he had thought about and it had been for a long time a deep seated ambition, which he never thought to fulfil.

'Do you think I'd have a chance, Mr. Oak? I must say it's something I've often thought about.'

'Certainly I do, Ben Tallboys. Why not? You're an educated man who can speak up for himself.'

Ben's fingers quickened on his chin as he became excited at the prospect. 'Where do I start? Who shall I see?'

Gabriel put down his now empty tankard. We'll go to Casterbridge in the morning and see the mayor. He'll know what to do and who to see.'

The two men rose simultaneously. Shaking hands they bid each other Goodnight with the promise to meet on the Road to Casterbridge on the morrow.

Deep in thought they didn't notice three shadowy figures passing down the alley between the Inn and the Blacksmith's forge. If they had they might have been able to stop the terrible fire which engulfed many innocent labourer's cottages in Weatherbury that fateful night.

The fire had started on the new buildings. The wooden shell, the only part yet complete went up like an inferno and was almost burnt to the ground before the fire brigade had arrived from Casterbridge. They were able to prevent the fire spreading which was some small consolation as the building was adjacent to the forest, nevertheless some of the thatched cottages to the west of the building site had caught light, there being a strong easterly wind that night.

Lady Sarah, although angry and put out about the fire which she was certain was started deliberately, a fact which the firemen had confirmed, assured the committee that work would start again immediately and swore to get to the bottom of the cause of the trouble.

True to her word, the very next day, workers were busy clearing the site in order to continue the building without any further delay.

There was much whispering and speculation as to who could be responsible. Some blamed high spirited revellers, others felt differently. Sir Cornelius determined to have another quiet word with his adversary, Lord Exonbury.

There was no further trouble and life resumed normality in Weatherbury, the quiet spring giving way to a gloriously hot summer, the second in a row.

Chapter Thirty Two
Sursum Corda, The Summer Has Arrived.

BY THE MIDDLE OF July, the new cottages began to spring up again like the phoenix from the ashes. Lady Sarah who had visited the site the day after the fire to see for herself the damage caused by a person or persons as yet unknown, although visibly shocked by the devastation she saw, still managed to encourage her workers to carry on as if nothing had happened. As usual her charm had cast its magic spell and the men had responded accordingly but it had taken several days just to clear the site of the smoke-blackened debris. Once that was done, the men set to work with a will, picks and shovels flying until the foundations were ready once more. They were determined not to be put off by rumours they'd heard, that the fire had been started deliberately. When one of the apprentices had been heard to say, 'What if they do it agin?' he was quickly reprimanded by a clip round the ear and told to "get on with it and mind his own business".

At the meeting of the Wheel society, the last before the summer recess, most of the members had given full support to the new building and there were whispers of "very commendable" and "good show". Sir Cornelius Godwin had not quashed the rumour that it was he who was responsible; he simply remained silent on the subject. He hadn't felt the need to go into details and thought it might serve to protect his adopted daughter from any undue aggression if the community in general thought it was he who was responsible. When the deed was done then he would own up to all and sundry that his beloved Sarah was the one to be praised and congratulated, but until then he would say nothing.

He had meant to have a quiet word with his old adversary but Lord Exonbury was once more away on business. He seemed to spend rather a lot of time away at present. Cornelius wondered why; what was his next move? Any further trouble and he would have to get heavy and had already made plans to that order. He would not allow Sarah to be compromised or be in any sort of danger if he could help it.

The Godwins were to be away for two weeks in August and had invited Gabriel and Bathsheba to join them. Apparently, so Lady Emma had told Bathsheba in one of their more intimate moments, they had spent a rapturous honeymoon in a cottage on the South coast, in a picturesque hamlet called Bethel Bay. Cornelius, who could be surprisingly romantic at times in spite of his worldly image, had bought the cottage soon after, improved it greatly and given it to his wife for their first wedding anniversary and now the couple spent as much time in their idyll as possible although this could not be as often as they would like, Godwin and Martin being so very busy all of the time.

Gabriel and Bathsheba had discussed the invitation and after careful consideration had declined the offer on the grounds that their own family might be home sometime during the summer and Bathsheba definitely wanted to be there for them.

In the event, only Adam spent his summer vacation in Weatherbury and then only for a short time as he'd made arrangements to spend several weeks in Devonshire with Jayne and her family. Sheba had decided to stay on in Rome where she had been joined by two of her teachers from college. Bathsheba was dreadfully disappointed but agreed with her daughter it was probably for the best in the circumstances.

George, home from his course at agricultural college had not brought Adeline with him. She was, so Louise explained, a little under the weather and was being taken to a well known spa town to spend some time taking the waters.

'Is she very ill, Louise?' Bathsheba had asked, concerned at the news.

'Oh no, Bathsheba. Between you and me, I think it is an excuse to join in the parties and dances there. When I saw her a few weeks ago she seemed perfectly well. Of course she was always a little pale but I put that down to her meagre appetite. She pecks at her food like a little bird.'

Bathsheba smiled. 'Is George very disappointed?'

Louise shook her head. 'He doesn't seem to be particularly concerned. Not like a newly engaged gentleman should be. In fact, he and Bartholomew have decided to travel abroad during August. I told them it would be too hot; reminded them that they would need to work to pay their for their expensive travel, but they ignored my advice and said they were tough and could take it.'

'How typical. Have they set a date for the wedding yet?'

'No. George has a further year at college so I should think he will finish his examinations and establish himself here before he takes on the responsibility of a wife.'

Bathsheba nodded her head in agreement. 'I think he's very wise. Will I see you at the poetry evening tomorrow, Louise?'

'Of course! I wouldn't miss it for the world, you know that.'

'Then I'll bid you good day.'

The two women went their separate ways. Bathsheba had need to visit the surgery. It was several days since she had seen Gabriel the younger and he was reaching such an interesting stage of his development. She loved the child as if he were her own and felt slightly jealous of his new "mother"; although she was his sister really she would be a good mother to the child. Theodore's new daughter-in-law was beautiful, intelligent and had a pleasing personality. He was extremely pleased with his son's choice of bride.

When Bathsheba arrived at "The Elms', Alice and the baby were sitting together on a woollen blanket which was spread out on the lawn at the back of the house.

'Come in, Mrs. Oak. I was hoping we would see you today.'

Bathsheba pleased at the welcome sat on the elaborate wrought iron seat beside the two and watched Alice and the baby playing with a soft ball until she suddenly realised someone was missing.

'Where is Nanny Brown, Alice?'

'That's what I wanted to talk to you about, Mrs. Oak.' Alice's furrowed brow told its own story.

'I know she's been with the family for years, Mrs. Oak, but I'm afraid I told her she could go.' Alice paused to observe Bathsheba's reaction. When she saw she wasn't unduly shocked Alice carried on. 'It's not that Annie is too old you understand although she is in her seventies, but she's so old-fashioned. I tried telling her not to be so hard on the little one as he's only a baby but she wouldn't listen, just put her nose in the air and carried on as if I wasn't there.'

Bathsheba didn't know what to say. She had brought her children up in what would be now called an old-fashioned way and it hadn't seemed to have done them any harm.

'Would you like me to talk to her for you, Alice? You really need some help with baby Gabriel.'

'Thank you Mrs. Oak but I don't think that will be necessary. The doctor has given me leave to employ another nanny and I was hoping you might know someone.'

Bathsheba's first concern was for the old redundant nanny.

'But what's happened to Annie? Where is she?'

'To tell the truth, Mrs. Oak, after she'd spoken to the doctor and realised he could manage without her she was much relieved, said she was pleased but she hadn't wanted to admit the baby was a little too much for her now. She's gone over to Kingsbere to live with her son and his wife.'

Bathsheba was relieved. She hadn't wanted to be drawn in to a family dispute. She'd known Annie for a very long time and it would have been very awkward indeed to have to take sides.

'Hasn't Dr. Melksham any preference, Alice?'

'He's left it entirely to me, Mrs. Oak. He trusts me implicitly.'

Bathsheba thought long and hard before she replied.

'I can't think of anyone at the moment but I have an idea. Would you leave it with me and I'll let you know within a day or two?'

'Of course. Now won't you join us for lunch, Mrs. Oak?'

Over lunch, Bathsheba took the opportunity to invite Alice to her poetry soiree the following evening. 'It will give you the chance to meet some of the Weatherbury folk, that is if you enjoy poetry, Alice.'

Both doctors were out on their rounds but Alice said as long as her husband agreed then she would be pleased to attend. As she spoke of her new husband her eyes lit up like the sun and it was obvious she was very much in love with him.

'Then I shall see you tomorrow, Alice. Do try to come.'

'I'll look forward to it. Will I have need to bring a book? A great many of my possessions are still in London and I'm afraid that includes most of my books.'

'We're reading Blake and I have a spare copy so please do not concern yourself with the simple matter of a book, Alice. Just bring yourself.'

The two women, one at the beginning of her married life and the other drawing near to her silver anniversary, bade farewell. Both realised they had struck a chord with each other but at this stage was not sure quite how and why. Sometimes it can be quickly recognised that one is a kindred spirit. In their case it was the beginning of a very long and close friendship, one which would enable Bathsheba to be something of a sister and mother to the doctor's wife.

'Alice reminds me a little of Harriet, Gabriel.' Bathsheba explained to her husband later that evening. 'Not so much in looks. More in her personality, her way of expressing herself. Do you know what I mean?'

Gabriel nodded. 'I think so. I haven't yet met the young woman. Am I soon to have the opportunity, Bathsheba?'

'She is probably coming to my poetry evening tomorrow but I suppose you will be out?' It was more of a statement than a question.

Again Gabriel nodded. 'Mm, I've arranged to meet Ben Tallboys. Did I tell you he means to stand for parliament?'

Bathsheba's mouth opened wide before she replied, 'No. Do tell me about it.'

'We went to see the mayor of Casterbridge today and he was most helpful. He explained to Ben what he must do. It's a little complicated but I'm sure we'll get there in the end.'

'We?'

'Well, not we exactly. I shall provide the moral support and attend the necessary meetings with him. More his agent so to speak.'

'That will keep you both busy. Say Good luck to Mr. Tallboys for me, Gabriel.'

'Indeed I will.'

It had all gone splendidly when they had been to see the mayor. He thought Ben had a good chance of being elected as long as he was prepared to put in a great deal of work canvassing. As he was already very well known in this part of Wessex and known for his good work with the labourers it would stand him in good stead when it came to the election. He could be certain of their votes at least. The rest of the electorate would just have to be won over and this is what Gabriel intended to help him to do.

Chapter Thirty Three
A Surprise Meeting In Rome

I T WAS THE VERY last day of August, a month of contrasts, for the weather which had begun rather wet and humid with two or three violent thunderstorm was now dry, bright and sunny with temperatures as high as in the previous year.

Around midday the mail-cart had arrived with a bundle of letters, mostly for Gabriel for the campaign was well under way and he would frequently receive a heavy parcel of mail for himself and Ben Tallboys. Today however, there was a blue envelope which stood out from the rest. Bathsheba instantly recognised it as having come from Sheba. Opening it quickly Bathsheba read that her daughter planned to be home within the week. Not having time to read it in its entirety, she had put it into the pocket of her day dress with the idea of reading it at leisure in the comfort of her own room before dinner. Events had taken over and she had forgotten about it until she had started to change for the evening meal. A swift glance through the contents showed that it would take more than a few minutes to digest the epistle so she decided to take it to the drawing room where she knew Gabriel would be relaxing before the evening meal.

Sure enough, he was there, deep in thought.

'We have received a letter from Sheba, Gabriel. Would you like me to read it to you?'

'That would be very pleasant indeed,' he answered, stretching out his legs and wriggling his toes, as was his wont.

'Sheba says it has become unbearably hot in Rome, even hotter than she had been led to expect and much as she adores the city, it will be with relief that she will leave Italy for the cooler climes of home.'

Bathsheba, now reading the letter for the second time, read out excerpts now and again to her husband who had just returned from an exhausting day harvesting and was now seated contentedly in his chair, rocking gently as he listened to the latest news of his beloved daughter.

'It will be good to see her again. What else does she have to say?'

Bathsheba continued with her reading. "I had the most amazing surprise, mama and papa, when I was visiting the Vatican ten days ago. We had fairly fought our way through the crowded palace and finally reached the Sistine Chapel and oh how breathtakingly beautiful it is, when guess who I literally bumped into? No, I know you can't possibly guess so I shall tell you. George and Bartholomew! Can you believe it?"

Bathsheba shook her head in disbelief, noting Gabriel doing the same. 'The poor girl. Travelling all that way to get away from her unrequited love only to find he has unwittingly followed her. Please carry on Bathsheba.'

'There I was, walking along with the Misses Smart and one of their Italian friends, a Signora Maria Feroldi, with whom we are staying incidentally, admiring the painted ceiling, when bump, two rather tall good-looking English gentlemen, heads also tilted backwards in order that they should be able to view the stupendous ceiling, collided with us. Their apology was so profuse that they didn't recognise me at first, nor I them. Imagine the mutual surprise when we did recognise each other!'

'I can imagine.' Gabriel put in somewhat sharply.

'To make sure their apology was fully accepted, they insisted on treating us to afternoon tea at a small cafe on the Via Bella Rosa. Mama, papa, it was delightful. I do wish you could have been here. We were treated to the most delectable gelato I have ever tasted. An enormous quantity of soft, sweet and oh so chocolatey, bowl of delight, topped with delicately flaked and roasted almonds. What a pity I cannot bring some home for you to experience. After that we all returned to our respective abodes only to find that George and Bartholomew are staying in the next street."

'How convenient!' Gabriel was sceptical.

'Gabriel, I'm sure they didn't know. I don't see how they could. Anyway, let's not forget that George is betrothed to Adeline.'

Gabriel remained quiet, fearing he would say something he might later regret.

'I shall carry on,' Bathsheba declared unperturbed by her husband's scepticism.

'There is another amazing coincidence, mama, papa. We found we all had tickets for the same concert so of course we arranged to meet there. I'll tell you all about the concert when I return home. Suffice it to say that it was an Italian composer and the music was baroque - can you guess?

Since that day we have met the gentlemen several times as Signora Feroldi offered to be their guide as well as ours. I must admit I was at first a little dubious as to the wisdom of the meetings but it has worked out splendidly. Rome seems to have put on a different face now we have someone to share the glorious antiquities."

'There's not much more, Gabriel except she expects to arrive in Casterbridge on Friday afternoon and would be grateful if we could meet her as she seems to have accumulated a great many souvenirs.'

'Well, she seems happy enough, Bathsheba. Let's hope it lasts once the magic of the Eternal City has worn off.'

Bathsheba tucked the letter into the bureau, agreeing with her husband. Life was so strange sometimes, she thought. You may try to avoid something or indeed someone only to find when you turn round there it is or they are, staring you in the face.

'What do you make of the meeting with George? Do you think he planned it, Bathsheba?'

'It certainly seemed like it at first but now I've had time to reflect I suppose it is possible to meet someone accidentally even if it is many miles from home. It is not such a strange coincidence is it?'

'It's not that which bothers me too much; it's how Sheba feels about the fellow. I do so hate to see her unhappy and surely that must be the outcome with things as they are.' Gabriel was very concerned about the latest development in his daughter's life. If only it were Sheba, George was betrothed to. How much more simple it would be. For the umpteenth time he rued the day that Bartholomew's sister had been introduced to George Abbot.

'She'll cope, never fear.' Bathsheba was not as sure as her positive tone suggested. Secretly she had hoped her daughter might be introduced to some other traveller from England who the Misses Smart might know and strike up a friendship. It would seem that was not to be. Perhaps she, after all she was her mother, ought to try a little match-making.

Suddenly she had an idea. Dr. Melksham had told her his youngest son was due home from his studies abroad any day now. She would arrange a party to celebrate Sheba's return and invite the young doctor, Teddy Melksham

'Why are you smiling in that enigmatic way, may I ask?'

'I thought a small party might be in order. To celebrate Sheba's return, y'know.

Gabriel agreed. 'Good idea. That should cheer her up.'

Bathsheba decided not to say anything about young Teddy Melksham's return. She'd make the party quite small with just a few close friends but not the Abbots this time for obvious reasons. She would invite Alice and Albert Melksham, the Godwins and perhaps Lady Sarah and the young Cornelius if he were free. Adam and Jayne would be arriving shortly but they hadn't given her a definite date, "just for a few days before we return to college" was the information about their impending visit she had received a week ago. They had said how wonderful Devonshire was at this time of the year and Adam had eulogised over the scenery, had even admitted writing some poetry based on his surroundings. Bathsheba had wondered how much inspiration was due to the countryside and how much to his companion because it had become obvious from the letters Adam had written over the past weeks that the couple were deeply in love.

Whether they arrived or not there would be just enough guests present to make the party a rather intimate, informal event. It was a pity she had forgotten the Godwins were away on holiday so there were even less present than she anticipated. Bathsheba decided to go ahead as planned in the certainty that it would all turn out right in the end. Had she been the possessor of a crystal ball she might not have bothered herself with all the preparation for the party.

Chapter Thirty Four

Remember Days That Have Gone Past, I Am Home Again.

THE LONDON TRAIN WAS expected at ten minutes past four o'clock and as always, arrived right on time. Gabriel was otherwise engaged so Bathsheba had brought the trap to collect Sheba and her luggage. The station was busier than usual. Obviously other travellers were expected, Bathsheba thought, as she sat on the wrought iron bench waiting for the screeching brakes to quieten and the smoke and steam to subside.

At first she thought Sheba must have missed the train but then she caught sight of her alighting with some other travellers. To her dismay she recognised George and Bartholomew. The poor darling, was her immediate thought. Fancy having to travel all the way home with him.

As soon as Sheba saw her mother sitting on the seat she dropped her hat box on to the porter's carrier and ran to greet her.

'How lovely to see you, mama. You've no idea how much I've missed you and papa, and Oakdene. It's so good to be back.'

Bathsheba hugged her in return noting that she looked well but rather thinner than when she'd left England a few weeks previously.

'How are you? Was the journey pleasant? Are you hungry?' The words came tumbling out as, excited, she held her daughter away from her to make sure it really was her, and that she was not fading into a shadow of herself with all the foreign food she'd had to consume in the past few weeks.

'I am very well, mama, and yes and no to the other two questions. We ate in London, at a rather elegant restaurant near to the station, by way of celebrating the end of the holiday, and the train was reasonably comfortable, compared to the foreign trains anyway,' she laughed, 'but I must admit the journey was a little tedious.'

Bathsheba could remember when it was a great adventure to board the train for a trip to London. Now her daughter had visited not only the great capital but the capital cities of France and Italy as well. It was getting to be a smaller world all the time.

'I've the trap waiting in the yard if you're ready.'

George and Bartholomew had been talking to the station porter and now having sorted out their luggage had joined the others.

'Could we give the boys a lift please, mama?'

Bathsheba hesitated, unsure of her ground. She didn't know whether her daughter was simply being polite or whether she genuinely wanted to he helpful.

George spoke up, 'Thank you, Mrs. Oak but I'm expecting papa to meet us. He should be here by now. Perhaps he's been held up.'

'Well, if you're sure, then we'll be on our way,' Bathsheba put in quickly.

Sheba looked disappointed. Bathsheba wondered what was going on and meant to find out as soon as possible. Although George had chosen Adeline over Sheba, Bathsheba was still fond of her old friend's son. That would end if she found he'd been toying with Sheba's affections whilst they were abroad. She grimaced a little as she planned what to say if she found it to be true.

Sheba linked her arm with her mother's arm as they made their way to the trap. The porter had loaded Sheba's luggage and there was barely enough room for them both.

'I should have borrowed the landau from the Godwins,' Bathsheba joked.

'I have accumulated rather a lot of presents and souvenirs I'm afraid.' Sheba looked pleased with herself. Evidently she had enjoyed herself even though she had said it was good to be home.

As they approached Oakdene, Caleb came running from the stables, eager to help and to see the daughter of the house who he'd missed more than he would ever admit.

Maryann was on the steps to greet them.

'What's all this?' Sheba was pleased at the unexpected welcome she was receiving. 'It really is good to be home, mama. Where is papa? At work as usual, I assume?'

'I'll tell you all about that as soon as you've changed from your travelling garb. There will be plenty of time before dinner. As soon as you're ready, Sheba, come along to my boudoir and we can have a quiet talk before we change for dinner.'

Sheba knew her mother wanted to know about meeting George and how she was coping and she was oddly reluctant to discuss it. She wasn't sure herself how she felt. The party in Italy had simply concentrated on enjoying the experience of the Eternal City and that had pushed all other thoughts from her head. Strangely though, George hadn't mentioned Adeline the whole time they were in Rome and Sheba wasn't sufficiently interested to enquire. She'd assumed that Adeline wasn't fond of travelling and had no reason to think otherwise.

She took off her outer garments and lay on top of the patchwork coverlet which had been a present from her mother when she had reached twelve years of age and was deemed to be grown up enough to want an elegant boudoir rather than the nursery room she had been sleeping in since birth. How long ago her twelfth birthday seemed she thought, her eyes closed, remembering the day as if it were yesterday. It was the first of her mother's sewing projects, Bathsheba had not been an accomplished needlewoman, having always been so busy with managing the farm. She simply hadn't had the time to become proficient in the art. It had taken a full two years to complete and Sheba watching it grow hadn't realised it was intended for her. Bathsheba had been as pleased with the result as if it had been awarded a prize in the Great Exhibition. Of course it was nowhere near up to that high standard but Sheba had been so pleased and touched that her mother had made such a stupendous effort on her behalf that she'd treasured it ever since.

Swinging her legs over the edge of the bed, Sheba sat up and gazed out of the window. The sward of lawn was remarkably green for the time of the year. It must have rained a great deal whilst she been away. France had been dry but there had been several short sharp thunderstorms whilst they had been in Rome. Pity they had missed the trip to see the Tivoli gardens because of the rain. She must return one day.

They had met George and Bartholomew that same evening with the intention of seeing the sights together. In the event they had dined at a rather grand restaurant called the Temple of Jove and had been entertained by some travelling players whilst they ate. She had sat opposite George and he had been as attentive as a lover. She had simply enjoyed the experience, not feeling even a little bit guilty. It was as if they were inhabiting a different world, a world which consisted of sun, music and history and stupendous antiquities, the likes of which they had never seen before. Certainly not the world of Weatherbury and life on the farm. It was different and entirely separate. Now she was back, life would go on as it always had but she'd always have the memories.

A tap on her door brought her back to reality and she stood up and called, 'Come in.'

'I've brought you some hot water, Miss. Your mother requested it and said you was not to hurry but to go along to her room as soon as you're ready.'

'Thank you, ...er Rose isn't it? Will you tell her I'll be along in about fifteen minutes?'

'Yes, Miss. I know madam's dying to see you.'

Sheba smiled. 'I know! How are you settling in, here at Oakdene?'

The maid bobbed a curtsey, 'Very well, thank you, Miss,' and left the room. She was new to Oakdene and looked little more than a child. In fact she had just reached her fifteenth birthday and her delicate appearance was due to insufficient nourishment whilst growing up, a common sight in some of the poorer families and one of the main reasons for Benjamin Tallboys" quest for betterment for the labouring poor. Sheba wondered how her father was progressing with his campaign. She thought he would make a good politician himself, as he always had plenty to say for himself on whatever subject came up but especially on social matters. She would ask him at the first opportunity.

Bathsheba was reading one of her poetry books when Sheba eventually poked her head round the door of her mother's room.

'Sheba, come in dear. Come and sit beside me. I want to hear all about your travels and the wonderful sights you must have seen.'

Sheba sat down next to her mother. She had brought with her a present and as Bathsheba opened it her face lit up with delight.

'Sheba, it's beautiful! Thank you, darling.' She kissed her daughter.

'I hoped you would like them, mama.'

Bathsheba tried on the fringed silk wrap. The embroidered peacock's feathers took on a different hue whenever Bathsheba turned about as she did now, in front of the mirror. Sheba had also chosen long silk gloves in the same shade of turquoise as the wrap and together they were perfect.

'Like them? I adore them, Sheba. Thank you.'

It was obvious Bathsheba was well pleased with the present but it didn't manage to stem the curiosity which had welled up since she knew George Abbot had been a visitor in Rome and now she asked Sheba to tell her about their meeting.

'Mama, I don't know how it came about. One minute we were engrossed in the paintings on the Sistine Chapel ceiling and the next, there was George. It was as simple as that.'

'Mm. That's what you said in your letter. Well, tell me about those wonderful paintings which so overwhelmed you, you didn't see where you were going?'

'Where shall I start? There was so much to see, mama, you are right when you suggest we were overwhelmed. The ceiling is covered, literally covered, in works of art by Michelangelo and they are all wonderful but by far my favourite, and George's favourite by-the-way, was "The Creation of Man". I'll try to describe it but I know I can't possibly give it the justice it deserves.

The Creator and angels are set against a background of empty sky and the whole scene, figures and background, are painted in delicate hues. Two outstretched index fingers are the only point of contact between the figures, mama, the vivifying finger of God and the inert finger of Adam. From the outstretched arm of God flows a spark of life. It is exceptionally powerful. Oh, but, there is much, much more. The beautiful, "Delphic Sybil', "The Creation of the Sun, Moon and the

Plants', "Original Sin" and "The Expulsion from the Garden of Eden". I could go on forever.'

Bathsheba was intrigued. Her daughter's expression as she described the paintings appeared transformed. The experience must have been very special to have that kind of effect.

'Now tell me about your outings with George and the others,' Bathsheba invited.

There was a tap at the door and Gabriel's head appeared.

Sheba rushed across to greet her father. Talk about perfect timing. She couldn't have been more pleased to see him and she told him so.

'It's wonderful to be back, papa. How are you?'

'Well, m'dear. And you?'

The moment for intimate confessions was gone and Bathsheba realising this, suggested they dressed for the evening meal and could continue the conversation over dinner. She hadn't had time to tell Sheba about the party so perhaps it would be better to keep it as a surprise.

Chapter Thirty Five
The Winner's Shout, The Loser's Curse

THE GUESTS BEGAN ARRIVING just before seven on the cool, early September evening. Lady Sarah Godwin and Cornelius, he being her brother by virtue of her adoption by Sir Cornelius and Lady Emma, were the first to arrive.

Bathsheba had finally confessed to Sheba early that morning that she had asked a few of their mutual friends to dinner and Sheba's reaction was, surprisingly, one of pleasure.

'George and Adeline said they might drop in some time today, mama, so may I ask them to stay for dinner? I'm sure Maryann won't mind preparing for two extra.'

Bathsheba was nonplussed. That was the last thing she wanted but to refuse would appear churlish so she nodded her head in agreement, trying hard to disguise her displeasure.

Sheba sensed her mother to be uncomfortable. She had a fair idea why but said nothing. What could go wrong in a crowded room full of one's friends, she asked herself? And it really was time she showed her parents that George meant nothing to her these days except as a good friend.

'Who else have you invited, mama?'

'Oh, just the Melkshams and the junior part of the Godwin family. Sir Cornelius and Lady Emma are away at the moment. They did request your father and I accompany them but we wanted to be here when you arrived home from Europe. That's about all really.'

'I appreciate your being here, mama, but have you not asked Mr. and Mrs. Abbot to join us?' Sheba asked, feigning surprise, although she wasn't nearly as surprised as she would have her mother believe.

'No, my dear. Not this time.'

'Have you had words then?'

'No, nothing like that. Now, I really must go and see Maryann.'

Bathsheba hurried down the stone steps to the kitchen. She had confided to Maryann her plan. To her surprise Maryann had not thought the plan to be a good one. She'd thought that the young people would sort themselves out if they were left alone.

Sheba wandered out into the garden. The herbaceous border was beginning to fade now. Only the very tip of the tall hollyhocks and Canterbury bells showed any sign of the bright colours they had displayed all through July and August. The clump of budded Chrysanthemums would not disclose their glorious copper heads until the day-time was equal to the night-time.

How regular were the rhythms of nature she thought as she sat beneath the old oak tree which had stood solidly in the middle of the back lawn from what seemed like time immemorial. As it was a rare evergreen oak it didn't shed its leaves as the other oaks beyond the orchard did, so in that respect defied the common laws of nature, missing its winter sleep as it appeared to do.

When she was a little girl she had thought the farm was named after the oak tree and she must have been well past ten years of age when she had found out the real reason. It was strange to have the same name as a tree, she mused, twisting a blade of grass until the scent reached her nostrils, before throwing it carelessly to the ground. At school she had been teased a little about being an Oak, not unkindly, and not any more than anyone else with an unusual surname is, or so she supposed.

Suddenly she heard the rapid clip-clop of horses" hooves and the distinctive sound of wheels crunching on the dry dusty road which led to the front of the farmhouse. She looked up and saw in the distance what looked like the station trap approaching. Who on earth could this be, she thought rising and making her way quickly to the front of the house.

To her delight Adam leapt from the coach and turned to help Jayne alight. Sheba picked up her skirts and ran across the grass to greet them.

'Mother didn't say you were expected today, Adam.' She flung her arms around her brother's neck and hugged him with delight. 'And Jayne! How good to see you. How long are you staying?'

Adam laughed. 'May we tell mama we are here, my dear little sister?'

'Of course. Jayne, you come with me and tell me all about your time in Devonshire,' she invited.

The two girls linked arms and made for the summer house leaving Adam to explain to his mother why he hadn't let her know the precise time of their arrival.

As soon as they had made themselves comfortable in the summer house Jayne confided to her friend. 'Sheba, I'm sure you will have guessed that Adam has asked me to be his wife.'

Sheba hugged her friend again. 'I'm so pleased for you both, Jayne. Do tell me all about it. Was it frightfully romantic? Did he go down on one knee and all that?'

'Something like that, Sheba. Actually he wrote me some verses asking me to marry him and presented the paper to me whilst we were out walking in the park. We were alone at the time; mama had gone to purchase an ice as it was so hot. We sat in the shade of a tall weeping-willow tree and it was there he handed me the poem.'

'And you said, yes, of course?'

'Of course!'

'Mother and father adore Adam. I was a little concerned at first, with Adam being a poet, you know, but when he explained his prospects to papa everything was alright.'

'What did he say?' Sheba was intrigued.

Jayne smiled at the memory. 'He explained that one day he would inherit the farm and continue in his father's footsteps.'

'That's rather a surprise, Jayne. What did you make of that?'

'Well, I was as surprised myself as you are, as Adam hadn't discussed his plans with me. At least not long term. I know he has to finish his course at college and then he hopes to travel before settling down and I just may go with him if it can be arranged so as to be proprietous. We even thought you might like to be my chaperone, Sheba. Do you think your father will agree?'

'I'm not sure. I think so. Yes, he'll be delighted, Jayne. He thinks the world of you and he's quite happy to go on running the farm for years yet. He knows Adam's ambitious but I think he had almost given up the hope that he would run the farm one day. But what about the teacher training at Melchester? How does that fit in with your plans?'

'Let's hope you're correct in your assumptions, Sheba. I shall go ahead with my training as planned, as Adam has to finish his course at Christminster. There's no sense in wasting my place.'

Sheba laughed. 'Thank goodness for that. I thought for a moment I would have to go alone. Now Jayne, mama's arranged a small party for this evening. Will you and Adam announce your engagement then?'

'If your father agrees to our plan, then this evening would be an excellent time to tell all our friends. After that we will of course announce the engagement in a London newspaper.'

'Now I'm almost recovered from your splendid news, Jayne, do tell me about your holiday. I want to know where you've been and absolutely everything you've been doing.'

The two girls sat for almost an hour talking about their various tours and travels and the sun was beginning to sink below the horizon before they decided they had need to go inside and prepare for dinner.

They chose to wear almost identical dresses which they had purchased whilst they were visitors in the French capital. Sheba's shot silk, emerald gown was a of deeper hue than her friend's pale lime green, which as the candlelight caught the folds, assumed an almost lemony colour. The gowns were trimmed with black French lace both on the flounces and at the neck, showing off the girls" attributes to perfection. Each held a French lace fan which when open showed an exquisitely embroidered peacock in much the same pattern as Sheba had chosen for her mother's wrap and gloves.

As they descended the wide staircase, the party from Acorn farm was just being admitted. Hearing the rustle of silks they all looked up at the girls descending, George and Bartholomew with openly admiring glances, Adeline with a look of discomfort. Having been told it was a small informal party she had not bothered to dress in her best but had put on a somewhat dowdy gown of lilac satin which had very little in the way of trim.

Sheba and Jayne looked at each other momentarily each knowing what the other was thinking, not needing to say a word, then they carried on into the dining room where they greeted the other guests. Adam moved over to Jayne immediately and virtually took possession of her so attentive was he. Sheba wondered whether she would be comfortable with that sort of closeness and decided that Jayne must be very much in love with Adam and that if she were ever lucky enough to be that much in love then she would in all probability feel the same.

The announcement was due to take place immediately after dinner but everyone was already aware of the couple's intention not least by their behaviour towards one another.

'I believe you have lately been to take the waters in Bath, Miss Westley? How did you enjoy the experience?' Jayne enquired, not really wanting to know but much too generous in spirit to want Adeline to feel uncomfortable.

'Indeed I have. The experience was just as I had expected and I am now fully returned to good health, I'm delighted to be able to say.'

Jayne smiled and nodded. She found it difficult to converse with Adeline Westley for they had very little in common and was content to leave her to talk to Lady Sarah who was seated on her other side on the sofa which was placed to the side of the room for the comfort of the waiting guests.

Albert and Alice Melksham arrived with Teddy just as the boom of the gong heralded the start of the meal. Apparently they had needed to wait for the return of the good doctor, their father, for Alice was unhappy about leaving the baby Gabriel as he had the start of a head cold, although she had been assured by both her husband and her brother-in-law that he would be perfectly alright.

Everyone quickly moved to their allotted place around the long table as the soup course, a rich mock turtle, was ready to be served. Sheba found she had been placed between Teddy and Cornelius and opposite to Jayne who was seated between Adam and Bartholomew. Lady Sarah sat next to Gabriel who was of course in his familiar position at the head of the table with his wife on his other side. At the far end, Alice was opposite to George who sat next to Adeline, leaving Alice next to her husband. Bathsheba had planned the seating arrangements with care although not in the usual fashion. She wanted her daughter to have easy access to both Cornelius and Teddy without undue interference from Miss Westley so was quite content to have a husband and wife together and the recently betrothed couple side by side. If Adam was slightly put out by not being positioned at the head of the table opposite to his father he gave no inclination of the fact. His entire attention was focussed upon his beloved.

Conversation was slow to begin with and mostly dominated by Adeline's experiences in Bath. As soon as she had exhausted the subject the party round the table seemed to split into two groups. Gabriel and the top half got on to the subject of the new building and the trade unions whilst the other end talked about the benefits of holidaying abroad.

Teddy, who had missed all Benjamin Tallboys" activities in the village, begged to be told all about it. Cornelius, although aware that his sister was a figurehead as far as the cottages were concerned hadn't known she was entirely responsible for the financial part and turned away from the discussion on travel to learn more of Sarah's intentions.

Adam too had been away when the plan had been formed and he now turned his attention to what was going on. Not wanting to be left out, Adeline turned to George and said loudly, 'I'm pleased you're not interested in such stuff, George. I think those people are poor because they deserve it.'

At once all conversation ceased as heads turned towards Adeline.

'Would you care to elaborate on that, Miss Westley?' Lady Sarah invited stonily.

Never at a loss for words, Adeline tried to explain what she meant. 'They were born that way. They're a different class to us. I really don't know why there is so much fuss.'

George was clearly embarrassed and tried to change the subject but Sarah would not let go.

'Miss Westley, have you never heard of the saying, "There but for the grace of God, go I?'

'Lady Sarah, forgive me if I offend you but I could never imagine being like those poor folk you see labouring in the fields. Why, I just could not do it. I was simply not born to it.'

Sarah shook her head. Here was a woman who was sadly lacking in compassion and intelligence. She didn't want to cause any trouble as she was a guest so she shook her head once more and carried on eating her meal.

Gabriel had no such qualms. He addressed Adeline directly. 'Tell me, Miss Westley. What would you do if your father suddenly lost his fortune?'

Adeline threw back her head arrogantly. 'I should live with my aunt I suppose. Why do you ask?'

'And what if she had also lost all her wealth?'

Adeline looked uncomfortable and Sheba, feeling sorry for her, answered on her behalf. 'That's hardly likely father. Miss Westley's father is a highly successful businessman.'

'I know I'm being hypothetical in this instance, Sheba, but this is a "what if" situation. I'm just trying to clarify my point.'

George felt he should contribute at this stage. 'As Adeline is to marry me in the near future surely it is doubly irrelevant, Sir?'

Soon the conversation became heated as first one and then the other would give a different opinion about the subject of the condition of the labouring poor. Adeline was clearly in the minority and only George, who felt obliged to champion his fiancée, agreed with anything she was saying.

At last Bathsheba suggested they continue the discussion in the comfort of the drawing room, after the men had been to smoke.

Everyone was slightly relieved and agreed at once to repair to either the games room or the drawing room according to their sex.

To their dismay, Adam and Jayne realised they hadn't made their intended announcement.

'Don't concern yourselves. When we are all assembled once more there will be time enough then,' Bathsheba reassured them.

In the event, it wasn't until much later, for the subject which had delayed the announcement continued for a long time after the company were assembled again. All of the party with the exception of one had agreed to help and support the committee, doing whatever they could although the young people would not be in Weatherbury for long it must be said.

Before the discussion had ended, Adeline feigned a headache and begged to be taken back to Acorn Farm. George, feeling a little sorry for her agreed with alacrity for he had also become a trifle embarrassed at her obvious snobbery.

There was much clapping and cheering at Adam's announcement.

'When will you be married, Jayne?' Alice asked politely.

'Not for quite some time, Mrs. Melksham. We have some education to finish and some travelling to do before we settle down, don't we Adam?'

Adam agreed. He felt so lucky to have such an understanding fiancée. Most girls he knew would have wanted to be married straight away, he thought.

It was the end to a happy evening at Oakdene but not so at Acorn Farm. Adeline by this time had become very aggrieved at George's reluctance to agree with everything she said during the discussion and she had complained to him.

'Adeline, my darling, I just do not agree with your policies. I do think the labouring classes are hard done by and need to have their working conditions improved. I'm surprised you can't see it that way too.'

'Well, I'm afraid I can't!' Adeline declared with much emphasis on "can't", 'and I never will.'

George took her hand gently in his. 'Come now, Adeline, let us not argue about such a subject.'

Adeline snatched her hand from his. 'No George. I'm afraid I could never marry you knowing you have it in your heart to feel an empathy with a bunch of working men.'

George didn't know what to say. He hadn't realised Adeline Westley was such a snob. Certainly she was nothing like her brother. He and Bartholomew had frequently talked about the social aspects of farming and both felt if it was in their power they would improve conditions and they certainly agreed with union membership. It looked as if his engagement to the beautiful, capricious Miss Westley was over.

'I shall return home tomorrow, George. It would be better if we didn't see each other again so I shall leave early. Would you be kind enough to tell Bartie?'

She picked up her skirts and rushed up stairs. George sat down again. He was upset and rather shocked at the turn of events. He was still sitting in the same position when Bartholomew returned.

After explaining what had happened, George apologised to his friend

'Sorry to have let you down, old man'.

Bartholomew shook his friend's hand. 'No hard feelings here, George. I wondered whether you were doing the right thing when you announced your betrothal to my sister. I must admit I was a trifle concerned. Remember, I've known her a lot longer than you,' he grinned.

George grinned back. Nice to know that although he'd lost a fiancée, he still had his best friend.

Chapter Thirty Six
Bad News from Abroad.

WHEN SHEBA HEARD THE news of George's broken engagement she was overcome with a mixture of gladness and sorrow. Part of her rejoiced for she felt Adeline would not have made a suitable wife for him, could not possibly have made him happy, but at the same time, she realised George would be devastated by the rejection and she was far too fond of him to wish him the sorrow that enforced parting from a loved one brings.

Bartholomew had stayed with his friend, in the cosy, oak-beamed, sitting room at Acorn Farm, talking and listening, listening and talking as the need arose, until the early hours. Much as Bartholomew loved his sister he made no secret that he thought her an out and out snob. 'I'm afraid she takes after my mother, George. She is also beautiful and loving, an excellent hostess to invited guests and she's protective to her children but I'm afraid my mama has little time for anyone below her in class.'

George had realised that when he'd visited the country mansion but had thought it was mostly because Mrs. Westley was simply old-fashioned in her outlook. He hadn't realised that Adeline was cast in the self same mould.

'Well, Bart, I suppose we wouldn't have been happy in the long run but it'll take me a while to get used to the fact. To tell the truth, I'll be more than glad when we go back to college. At least it will occupy my mind sufficiently to ease the pain. I'm extremely fond of your sister y'know.'

'As that's the day after tomorrow, George, you've not long to wait.' He patted the other's shoulder in conciliatory fashion. 'I'm off to bed, if you're sure you'll be alright.'

George nodded. 'Thanks for listening, old man.'

As Bart went off to bed, George sat for a while, gazing into the dying embers of the once blazing peat fire. It had been an almighty shock to find out Adeline's true personality. She was such a beautiful woman; so poised, elegant, fun. How quickly he'd become completely besotted with her. George shook his head. He simply couldn't understand how he could have failed to see through her facade and wondered if he could ever trust his own judgement again.

His parents would have to be told and he didn't relish the idea one little bit. He knew who his mother had wanted him to marry, she'd often hinted what a splendid wife young Bathsheba Oak would make some lucky man, so he hoped she would not say, "I could have told you that Adeline wasn't right for you".

But, Sheba was more like a sister than a lover, wasn't she? He had to admit he felt an odd sort of chemical attraction whenever she was near but he put that down to a pleasing familiarity for it was nothing like the excitement of being with Adeline. Anyway, Bart found Sheba very attractive, he'd told him after their time in the Italian capital so surely it was only a matter of time before he started walking out with her. He had watched Sheba and Bart enjoying one another's company whilst in Rome and he had also noticed they had talked quite animatedly at the party last evening.

Pulling himself out of the deep leather buttoned armchair he slowly made his way up to bed. As he tip-toed past Adeline's room he paused for a second. He had thought she might be lying awake, tossing and turning, perhaps even crying, regretting having been so hasty. There was no sound. Well, he would just have to wait and see what happened next and get over his failure the best way he could.

Autumn came and went with Bathsheba having to be satisfied with letters from her three offspring for she could not hope for a visit from any of them until the Festive season. There was little chance that Matthew would be home but Adam and Sheba and possibly Jayne would be arriving at Oakdene around the twenty fourth of December and earlier if they could get away. Jayne's parents had promised to try to travel up from Devonshire for a few days during the season, if they possibly could, but at present it seemed highly unlikely.

She missed them all very much but was contented enough, finding satisfaction in running the sewing circle, helping on the WSC and organising regular poetry evenings as well as her normal work of running the farm.

Gabriel had arrived home one evening in late October to say he had met Sir Cornelius Godwin for their regular monthly business meeting. Weatherbury Farm was now supplying some of the Estate shops with produce, and he had said he'd been to see Lord Exonbury. Whilst not going into elaborate detail, it would seem that Cornelius knew something of the Gentleman's past which would do him no good whatsoever if released to the Casterbridge News.

'I didn't threaten him, you understand, Gabriel. I merely told him what I knew, how I knew it, and what would happen if there was any further trouble.'

'What did he say, Sir?'

Well, I can't reveal the details of our meeting, you understand,' Cornelius winked and smiled wickedly. 'Suffice it to say that it had to do with a young servant girl, if you know what I mean.'

Gabriel had smiled and nodded knowingly. It happened all too often. The girl would become pregnant and be sent packing. Surely Lord Exonbury wouldn't allow himself to become involved in such goings on? Gabriel assumed he must have been otherwise he wouldn't want it kept quiet. He couldn't help wondering how many young servant girls had given birth to babies with blue blood.

Bathsheba was outraged when she heard. She determined to talk to Lady Sarah. Perhaps at some later date, when the almshouses were complete, they might consider a project which would give shelter to such unfortunate girls.

'I appreciate your concern, m'dear, but you'll not mention any names, will you?'

'Of course not, Gabriel. You know I won't.'

Lady Sarah, after Bathsheba had told her of her idea, nodded enthusiastically.

'Yes, yes, splendid idea, Mrs. Oak. We'll start immediately. No need to wait until the almshouses are built. They're three parts finished and there's very little for me to do except oversee the final stages. We'll discuss it at the very next meeting of the WSC. Well thought of, Bathsheba!'

It had taken only a few months to organise help for young servants in distress. Mrs. Hansworth, the vicar's wife had offered to lend a hand until someone permanent could be found and was now virtually running the home single handed, at least, she was organising rather than actually doing the manual work it must be said. The committee had found suitable premises between Weatherbury and Casterbridge, an old tavern which had been unoccupied for so long no one could remember who it had originally belonged to. As it was on one of Martin and Godwin's tenanted farms no permission had to be sought so work had begun without delay.

When the question had arisen as to who should be in charge and live in the house, the project nearly came to an abrupt end. Who would really want to be associated with fallen women, for fallen women they were no matter what the reason? Surprisingly and somewhat ironically considering they were spinsters of the parish, Temperance and Soberness Miller had come to the rescue. Their mother, now elderly and in need of almost constant care, agreed to move with them. There they could look after her and do a fulfilling job of work. It meant Bathsheba would need to find extra hands at the farm but with the family away most of the time she didn't require as much help as she used to so she could employ as and when necessary. Besides, Fanny and Maria were now so competent they not only managed all the housework their mother put them to but helped with the kitchen garden as well.

Christmas came and went, then Easter with the usual celebrations and at long last, it was the summer holidays again. As in the previous year, the girls would visit Paris and Rome. Their French and Italian was vastly improved so, in spite of his protestations of the expense of the trip, Gabriel had finally agreed to let Sheba accompany her friend Then, when they returned to England the girls would spend a week or two in at each others homes. As far as Bathsheba knew it had yet to be decided exactly where and when.

However, as Matthew was due home on leave soon, Bathsheba had good reason for being especially pleased and excited. She took great pains to organise an elaborate party for the first Saturday in September when, if everything went according to plan, everyone would have arrived home and the family would all be together once more.

The day before, as Bathsheba was checking the menus yet again, there was cause for much alarm for a telegraph was delivered at around noon to say that Matthew had been unavoidably detained and would not be able to get home after all.

'What could have happened, Gabriel? Do you think he's all right? Maybe a war has started out there.' Bathsheba lived in constant fear that war would be declared in some outlandish place and Matthew would become involved so it did not take much of her imagination to fear the worst.

Gabriel tried to reassure her. 'If a war had been declared, then I'm sure we would know about it somehow.'

Bathsheba wasn't convinced and went about her chores that day at one time convinced she would never see her son again and the next minute excited at the prospect of seeing her youngest after so long.

When the young people arrived on the following day they were quick to allay her fears.

'You worry too much, mama.' Adam had put his arms around her shoulders comfortingly.

Bathsheba merely shook her head and said nothing. She didn't want to spoil the homecoming for the others so took great pains to hide her unfounded premonition.

It was during dinner several days later that the second telegraph had arrived. Maryann received it and passed it immediately to Gabriel. All eyes were on him as he tore open the missive and read its terse message out loud.

'Involved in riding accident. In field hospital. Will write. No cause for concern.

Matthew."

Bathsheba was to stunned to say anything. Adam was the first to speak.

'Well, he can't be too bad. He's managed to send us a note of explanation.'

Bathsheba had paled noticeably at the news but remained silent. Nevertheless, her anxiety had not gone unnoticed by Gabriel who felt he needed to reassure her again.

'No, you're right, Adam,' his father responded. 'At least he should be entitled to some sort of sick leave.'

Bathsheba brightened at that hopeful news. 'I hadn't thought of that, Gabriel. Perhaps he'll be home early in the New Year.'

Dinner was a fairly subdued affair after the sad news and Bathsheba was glad Jayne's parents had been unable to leave their farm for she wouldn't have felt like coping with extra guests. It was Christmas Eve on the morrow so surely that would cheer everyone up.

Chapter Thirty Seven
Fate Takes A Hand

IN SPITE OF THE worrying news from India, the family had managed to enter into the spirit of Christmas although Bathsheba was uncomfortably aware of the empty space at the meal table and the present she had made for her youngest son remained tucked inside a drawer in her boudoir.

Sheba had met George several times but only in the church and its environs. At the New Year's Eve Ball at Martinsham Hall they had politely but pointedly avoided each other which seemed strange to their families, as they had previously been such good friends. Both mothers were disappointed. Although not expecting George to rush to Sheba for comfort they both hoped their offspring would see more of each other if only in the course of village life. It was not to be. If there was ever any hope of the two getting together it seemed most unlikely now. George had taken his broken engagement very badly and although he was cheerful enough in conversation, it was apparent to those who knew him well, that he blamed himself.

No news was heard from Matthew until late January when three letters were delivered in quick succession. There were no intimate details of the accident but it seemed that he had been thrown from his mount during a training exercise. There would be no sick leave allowed as there was some sort of malaise going around and everyone was confined to camp which gave Bathsheba further grounds for concern.

Although disappointed that he would not be home, she said little. She had come to accept that her youngest son was now no longer a child and felt she must show him the respect he deserved by accepting that fact.

Letters from Melchester Training College assured her that the girls were happy and enjoying the course and excited at the prospect of soon becoming qualified teachers.

Adam had written from Christminster with the news that young Cornelius Godwin had secured a patron in Florence and would be leaving college, possibly as early as Easter, to take up the post of Tutor and painter to a well-known Florentine family.

'I wish I were going with him, mama, papa. It is a golden opportunity to gain valuable experience abroad. But I suppose it's easier to obtain such a post if one is an artist. I think I have chosen the wrong profession!'

'Surely he doesn't mean that,' Gabriel chimed in.

'If you'll let me continue, Gabriel!' Bathsheba was reading the epistle to her husband after his return from the cold, icy Weatherbury fields. Several fences had need of repair after the gale-force January winds had rent them asunder. Some of the young saplings they had planted to the east of Weatherbury woods had also been torn up and the ground needed clearing so it would be ready for re-planting as soon as weather conditions would allow. At least the old trees provided good firewood but the young trees were useless and meant the adjoining fields would now be exposed to the elements for the they had been planted solely to give some vital protection to the new crops which were destined for the Martin and Godwin shops.

The log fire was ablaze and the scent from the seasoned apple wood was particularly pleasing to the olfactory. The warmth wrapped itself around husband and wife in a comforting cloak, providing a protection and security from the world outside. They seemed lately, without any pre-planning, to have acquired a habit of reading the family letters by the fireside, immediately after dinner, she reading, he listening.

Bathsheba continued reading:

"Of course you will realise I jest. I could no more paint a recognisable picture than acquire wings to fly like Icarus. Nevertheless, I wish someone would sponsor me. Any ideas?"'

Bathsheba looked up as Gabriel shook his head. 'No, m'dear. We're doing very nicely, especially since we got the contract for supplying the Martin and Godwin shops, but to sponsor Adam would cost far more than we could afford.'

Bathsheba agreed. She did the books regularly and knew that what Gabriel said was true. She carried on reading.

'I believe Sir Cornelius Godwin is a very rich man, papa. Would you speak to him on my behalf?"

Bathsheba looked up again. 'Would you, Gabriel?'

'I don't know about that, m'dear. I don't think I could.'

'Then I shall speak to Lady Sarah. She'll think of something, I'll be bound.'

Gabriel was against the idea, not wanting to ask favours from anyone least of all the wealthy Godwins. But, if his wife felt she should, then who was he to argue. After all, she knew Sarah Godwin better than he did.

It was several weeks later that the chance to broach the subject arose. Lady Sarah had arrived early for the poetry evening and not wanting her guest to be uncomfortable, Bathsheba had sat with her leaving Maryann to show the other guests in as they arrived.

'Has Adam told you of my brother's new post in Florence, Mrs. Oak? I believe he is very excited about it and seems to have broadcast the news far and wide.'

'Indeed he has. In fact, Adam is quite envious.'

'Is he? I know Cornelius, is thinking of taking a companion. Do you think Adam would be interested?'

Knowing he could not possibly afford to travel to Italy without the prospect of a job when he arrived, Bathsheba didn't know what to say. She felt strangely embarrassed to admit that money was the problem and yet Lady Sarah must realise they were not rich people.

'I think he would be interested, Miss Godwin, but I think he would be looking for a patron and patrons for poetry are few and far between.'

'You're quite right, more's the pity. Never mind, perhaps he will think of something.'

As the other guests began to arrive the subject was dropped. It was a poetry evening and having reached the end of Blake's works they were to move on to Wordsworth, a popular choice from all accounts.

Lady Sarah, when asked by her hostess to choose the first poem, had been delighted to accept. Now she read in her beautiful melodic tone the words:

'She dwelt among the untrodden ways
Beside the springs of Dove,
A maid whom there were none to praise
And very few to love:

A violet by a mossy stone
Half hidden from the eye!
Fair as a star, when only one
Is shining in the sky.

She lived unknown, and few could know
When Lucy ceased to be;
But she is in her grave, and, oh,
The difference to me!'

Everyone clapped for all they were worth. Sarah had read with such sensitivity and feeling she had made the poem come alive.

After such an ovation, Lady Sarah felt the need to explain why she was able to read with such emotion. Apparently, way back in her youth, when she had attended for an interview as a lady's maid, the Lady of the house had thrust a book into her hand and demanded she read that particular "Lucy" poem. The Lady had been as moved, but rather more surprised at her fluency, as tonight's audience had been. Sarah vehemently believed that the poem had been indirectly responsible for her position today. Although, by her own admission, it was a hard and rough path she'd had to tread before she had finally reached the comfortable position in which she now found herself.

Before Sarah left Oakdene that night, she leant over and whispered to Bathsheba. 'Tell young Adam we'll think of something.'

Bathsheba smiled her acknowledgement. She didn't want to raise her son's hopes but next time she wrote she was able to be optimistic about the forthcoming trip.

'I haven't anything definite yet, Adam, but we are working on it. I'm sure something will turn up.'

Bathsheba realised she sounded like Mr. Micawber but unlike that sad gentleman for whom nothing ever did turn up, she felt deep down Lady Sarah could be relied upon to keep her word.

So, it came as no surprise when in the middle of May, a brief note arrived at Oakdene saying Lady Sarah Godwin would like to see Mrs. Oak as soon as she could manage it.

'Oh, Maryann, I do hope this is good news.'

'Well, you'd best go and see, Madam for ye won't know "til ye do.'

'Yes, yes. I'll go as soon as we've discussed the menus for the weekend, Maryann.'

There was to be a small gathering on Saturday evening. The Oaks and the Abbots had finally managed to arrange a date to suit them both. Both parties had made many excuses but having run out of decent reasons for not meeting, the two families were at last to get together for dinner. Bathsheba had met Louise in the ordinary course of their work for the WSC but they seldom met on any other occasion as they used to. There was no good reason for not meeting for a friendly chat except they were busy but if truth be known things hadn't been the same since George and Adeline became estranged. Somehow the relationship between George and Sheba had been affected which in turn had affected both families. Silly really, but it was so.

Lady Sarah was in the drawing room busy with some official looking papers when Bathsheba was shown in.

'I'm so pleased you could come so quickly, Mrs. Oak. I've some good news. Please sit down.' Sarah indicated a chair opposite.

Bathsheba sat on the edge of the chair, eager to hear what the good news could be.

Lady Sarah picked up a letter.

'This arrived yesterday form Florence. My brother Cornelius has settled in very well and sends his regards to everyone.'

Bathsheba smiled and waited for the real news.

Lady Sarah continued. 'As you know, he has a patron who is very pleased with his work and he confirms this in the letter.' Sarah looked so pleased that Bathsheba felt it politic to hide her impatience.

'He then goes on to say, "My patron, S. Valcelli, has asked me if I know any young Englishman who would be willing to come to Florence for a year in order to teach his son and daughter some English Literature. Of course I immediately thought of Adam Oak. I know he will be home quite soon for the summer vacation so rather than send word to Christminster I shall write to Oakdene to ask him."

'There, what do you think of that?'

Bathsheba clapped her gloved hands together. She wondered just how much Lady Sarah had to do with arranging such a post but she decided not to ask for fear of embarrassing the good lady.

'I'm sure I can speak for my son, Miss Godwin, so I shall accept on his behalf.'

Sarah smiled happily. 'That's what I thought you would say. I shall write straight back and tell Cornelius to expect Adam within the month. That's not too soon, is it?'

'No. Examinations are almost finished now so he'll be able to get away very soon. Thank you, Miss Godwin. I must say it is a weight off my shoulders for I didn't see how Gabriel and I could send Adam unless he had a job to got to.'

'I realised that of course. I'm glad to be of assistance.'

Bathsheba couldn't wait to get back to Oakdene to tell her husband the good news. Sometimes, she felt, fate was on their side.

Chapter Thirty Eight
A Wedding Takes Place.

BATHSHEBA WAS JUST ABOUT to make for home from the dusty, bustling market place when a very agitated Louisa grabbed her by the arm.

'Bathsheba, you must come home with me, please,' she begged.

Too astonished to raise an objection and concerned at her friend obvious distress, Bathsheba told Caleb to take her carriage home and to tell Maryann she would not be back for luncheon.

Louisa, very near to tears, sat in silence for the whole journey. Bathsheba seeing her friend so distraught kept her curiosity to herself, reluctant to ask any questions in case she made matters worse.

As soon as they arrived at Acorn Farm, Louisa gave instructions they were not to be disturbed and immediately made herself comfortable in the small sitting room, bidding her friend to do likewise.

'Now, Louisa, whatever is the matter my dear?'

'I simply cannot bring myself to tell you, Bathsheba,' she replied with the most unladylike sniff. 'Won't you read this letter, please?'

Taking the letter somewhat hesitantly, she read aloud;

'My Dearest Mama,

I have the most awful news and I hardly know how to tell you."

Bathsheba recognised George's writing. 'Should I be reading this, Louisa? Is it not very private?'

'Please read on. I know George will understand.'

'Although I am in the best of physical health I fear my mental state is a little disturbed. You see, mama, my news concerns my ex-fiancée, Adeline Westley. I hope you are somewhere private and are able to seat yourself comfortably for I shall come straight to the point. As you are fully aware, Miss Westley and I planned to be married in the not too distant future, that is before <u>she</u> decided I was no longer suitable for her. We became very amorous on several occasions, so much so, that the good lady now discovers she is with child!

As soon as I knew, which was but two weeks ago, I of course said we would be married within the month. But, horror of horrors, mama, she <u>refused</u> me yet again. I am, needless to say, both <u>angry and distraught</u> as I imagine you will be when read you this. But, mother, please try not to be too upset. There is a little good news, for Adeline at any rate. The curate, who she proclaims is the father, has a living on the Westley Estate in Hampshire. He is I am told, I don't remember as I met him only once, a few years older than I, and has asked her to be his wife! She has agreed!'

Bathsheba paused. Louisa had her head cradled in her hands. She wasn't crying but her taut posture suggested she was suffering a high degree of nervous tension.

'I don't know what to say, Louisa.' Shocked and amazed at Miss Westley's decision she felt an intense sorrow for George and for his family.

Louisa looked up. 'My first grandchild will be born never knowing who his true father is or his paternal grandparents. How can I live with this, Bathsheba?'

'I don't think she will go through with the marriage, Louisa. A curate, although he has a good living on the family estate will not be able to provide for the good woman in the manner to which she is accustomed, never mind support a child. You can be sure of that. Give her time. She'll come round and marry George. When is the baby expected?'

'What if her father provides for her. He is very rich and could surely afford to do that? Anyway, it is too late. They were to be married two days ago. The letter arrived several days ago but I couldn't bring myself to tell anyone.'

'Does Joseph know, Louisa?'

Louisa shook her head. 'What's the point? He'd only get angry and go to see the Westleys. George specifically asked me not to tell anyone, so I can trust you to say nothing, Bathsheba?'

'Of course you can trust me.' Bathsheba leaned across and patted her friend's arm. 'That's what friends are for.'

Secretly she thought Louisa was wrong not to tell Joseph but she could appreciate her friend's dilemma and was glad it was not her own.

Later, they were to find out that Adeline, once her parents had realised that there was a baby on the way, they had after all wanted her to marry George, had cast her off without a penny, vowing she would never set foot in her parental home again. For the sake of the child, they had allowed the curate to stay on in Hampshire in the small cottage next to the church.

Poor Adeline. How quick she had been to decry the lot of the poor. Now she could see at first hand what it was really

like to live at the mercy of one's husband's employer who was
of course her own father. Sadly there were no special favours.

At the beginning of July, Adam and several large trunks,
set off for the Italian capital. Cornelius was to meet him there
where they would spend some time seeing the sights before
settling down to work in Florence. Lady Sarah had already
made arrangements to visit her brother during the summer and
hoped to travel with Adam. Due to commitments connected
to the opening of the last of the cottages she had to put off the
trip until the end of the month.

'Surely you won't travel alone, Miss Godwin?' Bathsheba
had enquired when she heard of the delay. Sarah assured her
she certainly would not be travelling alone and was, in fact,
thinking of taking a companion with her.

'Do you think Sheba would be amenable, Bathsheba?'

'I cannot speak for her of course but I should think she'd
be delighted.' In the event, Jayne decided to go as well for
she was finding the prospect of Adam's prolonged absence
intolerable.

The following evening, after supper, the couple were
sitting at the back of the house, relaxing whilst watching the
sun, setting slowly in the west, cast its deep orange glow over
the tall, rapidly ripening wheat in the nearby field. Gabriel was
talking animatedly of Benjamin Tallboys" success in the local
election and it seemed there was a good chance he would now
be elected to stand for parliament in the very near future.

'What of the Union movement, Gabriel? Who will run it
if Mr. Tallboys goes away?'

'Luke Welland has been voted in. He's a good man for the
job. He'll see things keep running and cope with any trouble
which might crop up.'

'I'm pleased, Gabriel. He is a good man.'

Bathsheba thought it was a good chance now to raise the
subject of Sheba's trip to Italy. She told him of Lady Sarah's
suggestion.

'Have you any objection, Gabriel?'

'No, no of course not. "T'will do the girl good to get away.' He nodded as he spoke. 'And she can give us a first hand account of how young Adam is doing.'

Bathsheba decided not to reveal all that Lady Sarah had said. It would not do to let Gabriel stop Sheba from taking the post of governess which might be on offer although with Adam in the same house there would be no fears for her safety.

When all the arrangements were in place and there was but a week before the departure, Bathsheba had an amazing idea. If Lady Sarah would agree, and she could see no reason why she shouldn't, it might be possible to kill two birds with one stone. Of course the gentleman in question might not agree with the plan but Bathsheba planned to enlist all the help she could muster.

For that reason alone she set off the next day to Acorn Farm to see Louisa. She would need her help and she felt pretty sure she would give it in the circumstances.

Chapter Thirty Nine
Matchmaker, Matchmaker.

'THIS IS A PLEASANT surprise, Bathsheba. Please do come in. Would you care for a little refreshment?' The visitor was relieved to note her friend looked much improved on her recent state, her countenance conveying the welcoming smile of the old Louisa.

'That would be very pleasant, Louisa. Thank you.'

The two women made themselves comfortable in the small sitting room which had, only recently, been witness to the reading of such devastating news but which now seemed an aeon ago. It was mostly to do with the aforesaid topic that Bathsheba needed to talk to her friend.

'How is George, my dear?'

'If you can stay until noon you may see for yourself.'

So, George was at home. Bathsheba was pleased. This was even better than she'd expected. 'If you can spare the time, Louisa.'

'To tell the truth, I'll be more than glad of the company. Joseph is away for a few days for I do believe he and Gabriel have at last come to some agreement about the wretched steam engine; after much consultation with Nathaniel Martin I must add. George is well in himself but not altogether pleasing company for me just now. He's still a little low in spirit after his dreadful experience, Bathsheba.'

'I understand. I too was greatly relieved they've finally reached a decision about the threshing machine. Now labourers" jobs are more secure due, I must say, mainly to the support of the union.' The two women smiled a rather smug congratulatory smile at each other for they were proud to have had a hand in the support of the union member's wives at the crucial setting up of the membership when it looked as if there would be serious trouble particularly from Lord Exonbury and his minions. They had Sir Cornelius to thank for resolving that difficult situation and nasty as it was at the time, it had been worth the trouble for the labourers were a little better off, although not by very much, but it was a step in the right direction. They had not forgotten his intervention and neither had the men some of whom were now earning a considerably higher wage in the carpet factory. Not all the labourers had been tempted to take factory work for extra money. Since Lady Sarah's cottage scheme was now complete the labourers had some additional security for if they lost their job through no fault of their own, at least some of them would be offered a cottage with the means to keep themselves in food. They would never be rich but at least they could feed themselves adequately.

'It's partly about George that I am here today, Louisa. Shall we take a stroll and I'll explain as we walk.'

The two women walked slowly, arm in arm through the small, sweetly perfumed rose garden until they came to a stepped terrace. They climbed the steep steps where at the top stood a mellow stone seat carved in such a manner that it appeared to be part of the wall. Facing southwards, it gave protection from the cool south-westerlies, which were apt to blow in this part of the West country. It had withstood rain, hail and shine and been witness to many shared secrets. It was now to bear witness to Bathsheba's ingenious little scheme.

Louisa was finding it difficult to contain her curiosity, wondering what on earth her friend had thought up now and whether or not it involved her good self.

At last Bathsheba began to explain what she had in mind.

'Louisa, as I said, I have a plan.'

'Yes, Bathsheba, please do tell me about it. I am agog!'

'Very well. I shall tell you only if you promise not to interrupt until I have completely finished.'

'I promise.'

'As you know, Louisa, Sheba is to accompany Lady Sarah Godwin on her trip to Italy where she plans to visit her brother. They leave at the end of the month. Jayne is to go too. She wishes to spend some of the summer with Adam as is only natural. I'm sure you'll agree.' Not waiting for an answer but noting her friend nod her agreement, Bathsheba continued. 'I think you should persuade George to go along as well. He is, on your own admission, a little low in spirits at this time. What better way for him to gain a speedy recovery than to take a holiday abroad?'

Bathsheba looked keenly at her friend to see how she was taking the plan so far. If her expression was a reliable guide, and it could usually be relied upon to be the bearer of her friend's innermost feelings, then Louisa was showing a rather keen interest.

'Personally, and I would want this to go no further, you understand, I firmly believe George and Sheba to be made for one another and if I can do anything to get the two young people to come to their senses and get together then I can die a happy woman.'

Bathsheba continued. Now she had started, wild horses couldn't stop her.

'It's no good leaving things to chance, Louisa. George will go back to college and Sheba will do the same and for all we know they'll meet someone totally unsuitable, think of Adeline Westley for example, and may be unhappy for the rest of their lives. We have to do something and I think a holiday in the Eternal City could well be the answer.'

'May I speak now?' Louisa enquired smiling.

Bathsheba stood up, agitatedly smoothed some imaginary creases from her skirt, and sat down again. 'I'd be glad to hear your opinion, my dear.'

'I think your plan is an excellent one but how shall I persuade George he needs a holiday? He has no plans as far as I know.'

'I've thought of that, Louisa. What do you think of this? Tell him that travel is so dangerous for women alone these days that he would be doing Lady Sarah a great favour if he were to offer to accompany the ladies.'

'Yes, I like that.' Louisa laughed. 'I think he'll jump at the chance. Fingers crossed. I'll speak to him this very afternoon and ride over later to let you know what he says.'

'Thank you, Louisa. I'm sure it's in their best interests you know.'

The two women rose and walked slowly back to the house. It was one of those luminescent days, when sunlight evaded only the shadiest corners, when everything from the smallest blade of grass to the tallest tree appears brighter than usual. The velvety dark red roses took on a deeper hue and their summery perfume filled the air. The neat little faces of the delicate pink begonias were upturned as if to make the most of the heat from the sun. For Louisa and Bathsheba the heat was becoming a little too much and it was with relief they returned to the cool of the parlour.

Having enjoyed the promised refreshment, Bathsheba bid her friend farewell without having the pleasure of seeing the subject of her visit. 'You promise to let me know as soon as a decision has been made?'

'Of course. I hope it may be as soon as this very afternoon.'

Bathsheba pondered on the fact that she hadn't caught sight of George. Perhaps he had been delayed she thought as she headed back to Oakdene.

As she drove the trap along the winding lane on the west side of Weatherbury wood she took a deep breath of the good clean air. It was her favourite time of the year, not quite harvest time, the celebrations and thanksgiving prayers were yet to come, but it was well past the period when farmers wondered whether the good Lord would send enough sunshine for the crops to germinate and grow to their full height. The seed pods on the corn were filling out nicely and promised a bumper crop. The late-spring haymaking had gone well and there was enough hay in the barns to provide for the cattle in the coming winter regardless of whether the weather was cold and hard or not.

As the old house came into view, Bathsheba slowed the trap. She never failed to appreciate the wonder of the ancient homestead with its turrets and Gothic style windows. It looked imposing, not unlike some castellated fortress, and certainly appeared older than it really was. Thank goodness the fire had not destroyed more than the end gable. Looking at it now it was imperceptible so professional was the stone mason they had employed to do the repair.

The old evergreen oak stood proudly in the middle of the lawn and as she drew near a flash of pale blue and gold appeared as if from nowhere.

'Mama!'

Two arms waved frantically above the head of the figure in a desperate attempt to gain her attention.

Bathsheba turned the trap and headed for the front of the house instead of the usual stable entrance to the side.

'Sheba! What are you doing at home so soon?'

She helped her daughter into the trap so they could ride round to the stables together.

'I didn't expect you for another few days, Sheba. Is anything wrong?'

'No, no, mama. Everything is right. Jayne and I need some time to prepare for the trip. We leave at the end of the week, you know.'

'I thought it was the week after. Has Lady Sarah changed her plans?'

'It seems she is able to get away sooner so she said why waste time here when we can be in Italy. I agree, don't you, mama?'

Sheba was so excited her mother could only be pleased for her. Perhaps she would not mention the fact that they might have an extra travelling companion. Sheba would be silly about it, she was sure, and there was no sense in spoiling her joy of the occasion.

She handed the trap to Caleb and the mother and daughter made their way into the cool shade of the front parlour. Maryann had heard them arrive and now met them with a tray loaded with tea and Sheba's favourite ratafias. Jayne was comfortably ensconced on the window seat reading a book on the Italian language but she jumped up when they entered the room.

'Did you manage to arrange things then, Mrs. Oak?' Maryann enquired being as discreet as she was able with two interested persons looking on.

'I'll know this afternoon. Thank you for the tray, Maryann.'

Bathsheba put a finger to her lips with the intention of warning Maryann to say no more.

'Mama, what is going on?' Sheba was curious wondering what her mother was planning.

'Oh, nothing for you to worry about, my dear,' which suggested to Sheba that there probably was.

'Shall we show your mama the new dresses we have brought from Melchester, Sheba?'

Jayne sensed there was something Mrs. Oak did not want her daughter to know and not wanting to spoil any pre-arranged surprise pulled Sheba towards the stairs.

Sheba gave up. Whatever it was her mother was planning she was bound to find out sooner or later. She followed Jayne to the guest room where the new dresses were laid out in red and gold and blue and silver splendour.

The two girls were so excited at the prospect of the unexpected trip to Italy nothing could mar their joy. Trying the new dresses brought shouts of delight from both girls for they had not had time for a final fitting with the dressmaker.

'It fits perfectly,' Jayne pirouetted about the room so that the gold-trimmed, crimson frills danced and flashed their brilliance. She glanced occasionally in the cheval mirror to make sure the back looked as perfect as the front. Sheba, in lapis lazuli with silver trimmings on the lace petticoats, which peeped provocatively through the V shaped opening at the front of the skirt, wove in and out so that the pair appeared to be involved in some elaborately choreographed dance.

'Mine too! Oh, I'm so excited, Jayne. How glad I am that we don't have to wait until next week to travel to Italy. Jayne,' she paused in thoughtful contemplation, 'I believe Rome to be quite the most romantic city in the whole world.'

'Better than Paris? Surely not!'

'Oh, yes. Do you know, Jayne? I think....no, I'm sure, I shall meet Mr. Right, fall in love and live happily ever after.'

'Then I dearly hope your wish will come true, Sheba,' Jayne replied sincerely, happy in the knowledge that, for her, Mr. Right would certainly be waiting in the Eternal City.

Chapter Forty
Quod Semper, Quod Ubique!

AFTER SEVERAL FRANTIC DAYS of preparation, the girls were finally ready to leave for their trip overseas. Bathsheba had tried to help and advise at frequent intervals but to no avail. Unable to persuade the girls what they would need in the way of wearing apparel, they protested the fact that as she had never herself been to sunnier, hotter climes she couldn't possibly understand how uncomfortable thick underwear could be, she had left them somewhat reluctantly, to their own devices. To her surprise and chagrin, they seemed to have managed quite adequately without her.

Now, at the station with only minutes before the train would steam up to the platform and its noise and filth make intimate conversation impossible, she edged nearer to where the assembled travellers stood. She felt, quite illogically, uneasy about the trip and not a little envious. Hearing so much talk of Italy and its great Capital had whetted her appetite enough for her to feel a need to experience the sights for herself. It was just not possible at the moment though. As Gabriel had so rightly pointed out, they could not simply drop everything and go off, as some people seemed able to do.

Sometimes, especially at times such as she was experiencing now, Bathsheba wondered if it had been such a good idea to foster the friendship between them and the Godwins, allowing it to mushroom in the way it had. It was true the Godwins were, are, extremely pleasant, genial gentlefolk and the Oaks had enjoyed many a social occasion with them but the Godwins invariably moved in different circles to the farming folk and it was sometimes difficult not to be envious, in particular of Lady Emma's wardrobe and of the amount of travelling they did.

The loud shrill toot of the oncoming train broke into her reverie and she quietly joined her daughter and the group of travellers who had congregated together in a small close knit group, already at a distance from the people of Weatherbury.

Bathsheba put her arms around her daughter. 'You promise to write as soon as you arrive, Sheba.'

'Of course mama. You know I will.' She laughed, so happy to be going to see Adam, not even minding that George had been asked to join them.

Bathsheba had begged Lady Sarah to be the purveyor of the news that George would be accompanying them. Apart from being somewhat surprised, Sheba hadn't appeared to mind. As she explained to Jayne later, "It will do George good to get away. What Adeline did was so awful, Jayne, I cannot help feeling sorry for him. I shall be pleasant and certainly accompany him on social occasions, should I be asked."

Jayne had said little in reply. Her thoughts were entirely concentrated on the delightful thought of seeing her Adam again.

After an emotional farewell amongst the smoke and steam and hustle and bustle of the station, Bathsheba returned to Oakdene where she was met on the doorstep by an excited Maryann.

'Mrs. Oak, this telegraph arrived a short while ago. I think 'tis from abroad. India! I think.

Bathsheba took the envelope and tore it open. They hadn't heard from Matthew for some time and she had expressed her concern to Gabriel only the previous evening. Perhaps he was coming home at last. It seemed such a long time since they had seen their youngest son.

'The message was short and to the point:

MARRIED LAST WEEK. C.I.C.s DAUGHTER, ELIZABETH. SORRY CANNOT GET HOME, LETTER FOLLOWING.

MATTHEW OAK Sargeant at Arms.

Bathsheba sat down at this sudden unexpected news from her son. He certainly had not mentioned this woman before, at least not to her knowledge. She would have remembered something as important as that.

'Not bad news, I hope, Madam? You do look a bit pale.'

Maryann hovered over Bathsheba as if she expected her to take a fit of the vapours at any moment.

'Yes and no, Maryann. 'Tis a bit of a shock.'

'Can I do anything to help? Is everything alright in India?'

Maryann was clearly intrigued by the contents of the missive and was dying to know what news it contained. They had come to expect the unexpected from that part of the world and Matthew was often the subject of speculation around the kitchen table.

'A little refreshment, if you please, Maryann.'

'Yes, Mrs. Oak. A nice cup of that new Earl Grey will do you good I'm sure.' Maryann scuttled off, a little put out that her missus had not seen fit to divulge the contents of the telegraph. She muttered to herself as she descended the stairs to the basement kitchen. 'It can't be much or Madam would have been more upset...she might at least tell me... she must know I worry about young master Matthew. We all do.'

Bathsheba didn't know what to make of this recent turn of events. Matthew had been ill she knew that. That he was expected home to convalesce she had hoped, but not this. What was he thinking of? Suddenly the old house felt very large and empty. She put her head in her hands and in a fit of weakness gave way to pent up tears.

Maryann soon arrived with the tea and was concerned to see her mistress in such a state.

'What is it Madam? Is it bad news from abroad? Is Master Matthew alright?'

Bathsheba gave her self a mental shake. This was no way to carry on. 'I'm just a little tired, I expect, what with all the preparation for the girls" trip. I'll just lie down for a while. Don't concern yourself, Maryann. I'll be all right. Yes, Matthew is well but I'm not sure when he'll be able to get home.'

Not entirely convinced, Maryann poured the tea and handed it to Bathsheba noting how her mistress's hand shook as she took the delicate china from her.

'Yes, Madam. I think that's a good idea. Shall I call you when Mr. Oak gets in?'

'Yes, please. Tell him I'm resting and ask him to come up, will you Maryann?'

'Of course, Mrs. Oak.'

Maryann scuttled away still none the wiser but convinced something awful must have happened to upset her mistress in such a way.

By the time Gabriel arrived, Bathsheba had recovered a little but was still in a state of incredulity.

She showed her husband the telegraph and waited impatiently for his comment.

'Well, the young scallywag! What a surprise! No, I'll change that to shock.' He looked up to see how Bathsheba was taking the news. Having had a while to get used to the idea she was now taking it rather better than he expected.

'We don't even know the girl, Gabriel. What on earth has possessed him?'

'I can't answer that, m'dear, but it's certainly a bit of a surprise.' He sat down by his wife's side and took her hand in an effort to provide some sort of comfort but couldn't help feeling rather inadequate in the circumstances.

It was just over a week later that the letter arrived explaining how the marriage had come about. As usual, Gabriel was seated in his chair. Bathsheba was opposite waiting impatiently to read the day's letters to him. She had already read the letter from India and couldn't wait to hear what her husband made of the news.

'If you're ready, Gabriel, I'll start.' Her tone was a little caustic as she felt her husband had kept her waiting unnecessarily long, he having stopped off at the King's Arms on his way home and then insisting he ate his dinner before he would discuss the events of the day. He seemed strangely unperturbed at the prospect of the news from India and this made Bathsheba even more impatient than usual.

'My Dear Papa, Dearest Mama,

I expect you have been awaiting this letter ever since you received my telegraph message.

First let me assure that I am at last fully recovered from my dreadful accident and apart from the slightest limp in my left leg you could not tell I had suffered the injury.

No doubt you wish to know about my new WIFE! I shall tell you all about it without further delay.

We met in the field hospital where, the then Miss Elizabeth Corlyon, was visiting the wounded. If I say I was overcome at the sight of her beauty, I can assure you I am not exaggerating. She has the most wonderful deep blue eyes and gorgeous dark red hair. If I had to suggest who she most resembled then it would have to be Ophelia."

Bathsheba paused for a moment to see how her husband was reacting to the description of his new daughter-in-law. He merely lay back in his chair, rocked gently and looked pleased.

Bathsheba continued, "I know it sounds awfully trite, mama, papa, but it was truly love at first sight. Of course I did not realise who she was but by the time I found out it was too late. There was no going back, for me at any rate. I began to really look forward to her visits, nay live for her visits. They became the only thing that kept me going, my raison d'être, when I was in the midst of all that awful pain, when they thought I may lose my leg. My ardour did not diminish though, even when all danger had passed and I began walking out in the grounds. Miss Corlyon would accompany me for walks in the magnificent gardens and it was there we really grew to know and love each other."

Bathsheba paused to interject with her own thoughts. 'How romantic it sounds, Gabriel. No wonder he fell in love with the girl. I only hope it will last.'

Gabriel stopped rocking for a moment. 'The boy's made his bed, Bathsheba. He must lie on it.' Then in lighter tone. 'I see no reason why it won't last. He's a sensible fellow and I can't see that he would choose a partner who is any less sensible than he.'

'I do hope you're right, Gabriel. Shall I shall continue?'

'Please, m'dear.'

'At first I was concerned that her father would think me not good enough for her, he being the Commander-in-Chief, but as soon as Elizabeth told him how much in love we are and that I mean to make the Army my career he gave his blessing. And, what's more has suggested we live in a bungalow in the grounds of his house so that Elizabeth can still keep an eye on him (She has no mother. She died of a fever soon after their arrival here more than five years ago.)

I know you will think we married rather hastily but there was a reason and this is for your eyes only, mama, papa. Elizabeth is with child and expects to be delivered around Christmas time. Isn't this just splendid news! I can't believe it! Of course the child will be born "prematurely!" (Commander Corlyon knows of this) and no one will be any the wiser. We hope to visit England as soon as possible but I'm afraid this will not be in the foreseeable future as it will not be easy with a young baby as I'm sure you will understand. Although we shall have a nursemaid, Elizabeth will not even contemplate the thought of leaving the child even for a few weeks. She may change her mind of course after it is born!

My regards to everyone at Oakdene, particularly Maryann. Please give my love to Sheba but don't tell her all the details of the letter for I shall write to her telling all I want her to know.

Please take care of yourselves.

I remain, your ever-loving son

Matthew."

'Now what do you think to that, Gabriel?'

'Well, I must say I'm a bit surprised.'

'Is that all you can say? Our youngest son is married and about to become a father and all you can say is you're a bit surprised. Oh, Gabriel!' Once more Bathsheba gave way to pent up tears. It was seeming to become a habit of late and she was quite ashamed.

'I'm sorry. I didn't mean to do that,' she sniffed inelegantly.

'So, we are to become Grandparents, Bathsheba. That does make me feel old,' he laughed.

'I never thought of that. Me, a Grandmother.' Suddenly Bathsheba was all smiles. This was something she had looked forward to for some time and coming unexpectedly as it had did not detract from the joy she now felt at the prospect.

What had seemed at first to be something of a disaster now seemed to be a joyous occasion. Bathsheba felt like celebrating. Instead she stood up. 'I'll just go and see if Maryann is still in the kitchen. She was concerned about Matthew and will be pleased to hear he is all right after all. And, I might just mention the possibility that we might become Grandparents in the near future.'

Gabriel smiled knowingly. 'Yes, m'dear. I expect Maryann will be pleased to hear news from India. Matthew was always her favourite and I'm sure baby Oak will be high on her list of favourite people too.'

He continued rocking gently, his thoughts far away, somewhere on the Indian continent where his son was laying with a new wife. He hoped fervently he would be as happy and content with his wife as he himself was with his. As he gently rocked he remembered the far off days when Bathsheba was only a girl. He remembered the lamb he had taken her and the promises he had made of her own trap and a piano... and smiled gently and nodded, to himself as there was no one else in the room to observe his satisfaction.

Chapter Forty One
An Ambition is Finally Accomplished.

TRUE TO HER WORD, the message arrived from Sheba within the week.

Dearest Papa, Mama,

'Arrived safely. We are staying in Rome for a while before we go to Florence. Will write a long letter very soon.

Your loving daughter

Bathsheba."

Bathsheba was on her way to see Alice and baby Gabriel when the telegraph arrived. Her heart had leapt as if she had caught sight of Wordsworth's rainbow when she noticed the messenger boy turn into the drive; not with joy however but with unbidden apprehension. Fearing the worst, she simply could not get used to "the telegraph', she had paused, turned the trap and met him halfway.

Now fully composed and feeling a little foolish at her misgivings she made her way back down the leafy drive and headed for "The Elms" in Weatherbury.

Alice was overjoyed at seeing her. Ushering her quickly into the drawing room she perched on the edge of the chaise-longue with her hands clasped in a gesture of excitement.

Bathsheba caught her mood and smiled. 'Tell me, Alice, whatever has happened?'

'Oh, Bathsheba I am with child at last. Isn't that just the most splendid news possible?'

Alice was glowing with pride and to look at her you would not be mistaken in thinking she could have been touched by an angel, so ethereal was her joy.

'I'm so pleased for you, Alice. I expect', she laughed at the pun and Alice quickly joined in. 'I was about to say, I expect Albert is overjoyed at the prospect of becoming a father.'

'Yes, yes he is. At least I think so. He hasn't said a great deal, he being so busy with his doctoring and there's his research you know.'

Bathsheba knew instinctively that Alice was making excuses for her husband's lack of enthusiasm for the forthcoming event. Bathsheba felt she must offer some words of advice for fear Alice did not understand the male mind in such matters.

'Alice, my dear. Forgive me if I speak out of turn but from experience I must tell you that men do not always have the same sort of feelings for parenthood as we women. Please don't misunderstand me,' her speech became animated in her fear of being misunderstood, 'I'm sure Albert will make an excellent father but they, men I mean, derive their pleasure when the child is grown a little.'

Bathsheba was acutely aware that she wasn't saying exactly what she wanted to say. Somehow she couldn't find the right words to explain precisely what she meant. Alice however seemed to understand.

'I know, Bathsheba, what you're trying to say. I shall not expect too much from Albert until the child is born. Of course I won't.'

Oh dear, Bathsheba thought, now I've spoilt the moment. 'When is the child to be born, Alice?'

'Early in the New Year.'

I shall be a grandmother by then, Bathsheba realised, dying to tell Alice but knowing it was impossible. 'You must allow me to help you plan a layette, Alice. I should like that.'

Alice had regained her joyful expression and was soon in full flow, telling Bathsheba all the plans she had for her precious child.

After listening for what seemed a more than respectable time Bathsheba made her excuses to leave. It was almost intolerable to listen to Alice talk of her pregnancy without comparing her to her son's new wife. Watching Alice grow would be like watching a mirror image of Elizabeth. She wondered momentarily whether she could tell Alice if she swore her to secrecy but promptly abandoned the idea. It was not fair to expect that much from her especially in her condition.

As she drove the trap along the leafy lane towards Oakdene, she could feel the heat of the sun beating down on her head in spite of her heavy straw bonnet. She wondered if Sheba, in the heat of the Italian City was taking adequate precautions against the sun's rays. She worried needlessly however. Sheba was at that very moment about to enter the Pantheon accompanied by George, Jayne and Adam. Lady Sarah had decided not to stay in Rome after all. Her brother had been unable to be released from his duties in Florence so she had joined him there.

Before she had left she had made a proposition to Sheba. For some time she had been thinking of setting up a school for the young of Weatherbury and having finally found a suitable building which although in need of essential repairs, would be adequate for her requirements, and having been offered funds from an as yet undisclosed source she was ready to go ahead with her plans. It wasn't until she had heard Sheba and Jayne discussing what the future held for both of them that she had realised they could help her as she could assist them.

The two girls had laughingly said what a pity it was that Sheba had been offered the post of governess and not Jayne. Adam was to be in Italy for a further year at least and Jayne confessed how much they would miss each other.

'I just don't think I can bear it, Sheba. Adam can't afford to travel to England and I can't discern my parents paying for another trip for me.'

At this point Lady Sarah had joined in the conversation.

'Forgive me for butting in my dears,' she paused to see if they really did mind.

'Please go on, Lady Sarah?' Sheba invited.

Sarah briefly outlined her plans for the school and watched carefully for any reaction from the girls.

'I think it's a splendid idea, Lady Sarah.' Sheba looked at Jayne and realised immediately they were both thinking the same thing.

Lady Sarah not slow on the uptake herself carried on. 'I will of course be looking for a teacher and had in mind a man for the post. However, if one of you girls would like to apply, I can almost guarantee you will be successful.'

They were sitting in the lobby of their hotel waiting for their escorts to arrive. Sheba jumped up and clapped her hands causing many of the other guests to raise their eyebrows in disapproval. Sheba sat down again but her excitement was plain for all to see.

'I have just thought of a splendid idea! Jayne, you must take the governess" post here and I shall go and teach in Weatherbury,' she hesitated momentarily, 'that's if it would suit you, Lady Sarah?

Jayne's wide beam as she thought of the implications of staying in Italy turned to a wide-eyed apprehension as she waited anxiously for Sarah's reply.

'Excellent. That's what I hoped you'd say.'

The two girls were finding it extremely difficult to contain their excitement.

'You'll have to speak to your parents first of course but with their permission I'm quite agreeable to what you suggest.'

As soon as George and Adam arrived they were told of the plans. Both gentlemen were as pleased as punch but only one let it be verbally known.

Adam took Jayne's hand. 'That's absolutely terrific news. We can make our plans for our marriage together instead of hundreds of miles apart.'

'I'm sure the parents will do most of the arranging Adam but it will be wonderful not to have to live so far apart for the next year. I shall write immediately and ask for permission to stay and ask if I may take the governess" post but I'm certain they will agree when they know it is Lady Sarah who is overseeing the arrangements.'

In the event their plans finally came to fruition but not without several weeks of nail-biting anxiety. First there was the interview for the post which, being Jayne's first ever, threw her into a state of apprehension though not quite dread. Then there was the anxious wait for approval from the parents which, when it finally arrived, was filled with all sorts of advice and warnings. However it was all to prove worth it and the two were to spend some of the most enjoyable years of their whole lives in the historic climes of Firenze.

That was in the future and now the travellers were taking the opportunity to see some of the sights of Rome which is how they came to be about to enter the Pantheon whilst Bathsheba was on her way home from "The Elms".

'It is quite the best preserved piece of Roman architecture in existence today, so I believe.' Adam was airing his knowledge to his friends. He loved the Ancient City and spoke of its beautiful buildings and works of art as if he had himself been responsible for their very existence.

'Shall we go in, Adam, or are we to stand here in the porch admiring the Corinthian columns until it is dark?' Sheba enquired of her brother.

They entered the great unilluminated building unable to see the superb decoration at first, until their eyes slowly became adjusted to the gloom after the brilliance of the afternoon sun in the piazza outside.

The only light source seemed to come from a huge open-domed roof whose intention appeared to be that of providing light for the wide expanse beneath.

There were gasps of delight from the girls as they espied the tomb of Raphael for here was a statue of the Madonna and child by Lorennetti built to Raphael's own design. They had seen pictures but to actually see for themselves that which previously they had only read about was a source of great delight which pleased Adam as it was his suggestion they visit the great church.

As they could not possibly see everything there was to see in the city they had needed to choose very carefully the particular sights they simply could not afford to miss. George's wish was to see the Colosseum in all its glory and they were destined for there on the morrow. Although she had not showed any particular preference, Sheba also thought the Colosseum with all its history was a sight not to be missed. She looked forward to the next day with great anticipation and pleasure and now the excitement, which bubbled up inside her suddenly, became difficult to contain. As it turned out there was to be more pleasure than she could have thought possible.

A tremendous storm during the night with heavy and torrential rain threatened to put paid to their intended visit. Now, mid-morning quite miraculously the ground was virtually dry and the sun shone with as much heat as on the previous day.

The foursome strolled around the ancient tiered building admiring the mastery of the Roman architecture, noting the Doric, Ionic and Corinthian columns supporting the crumbling ruin.

'I've an idea,' Jayne broke the awesome silence. 'Adam and I will walk to the right and you, Sheba, can go with George to the left. Then we can meet at the opposite end and compare what we have seen. How does that sound?'

Sheba, realising Adam and Jayne wanted some time alone, agreed. 'Alright. We'll meet under that large arch opposite the entrance in about, say, twenty minutes. Is that long enough to walk all the way round?'

There was a chorus of assent and off they went.

At first Sheba and George said little, content to take in the atmosphere of the great amphitheatre and to admire their surroundings, gazing in awe at the mosaic scenes of the fighting between the gladiators and the wild beasts, imagining the brutality which had taken place in the arena long, long ago.

'George, would you like to have lived in Roman times?' Sheba asked curiously.

'I don't think so. I'm quite content with the way things are now. I know the Romans were a very civilised race in one sense but I really don't like to think of the horrors that went on in this place, do you?'

Sheba shuddered. 'No. I hadn't really thought of it like that. I'm afraid I was so impressed by the wonderful architecture and antiquities of Rome I never really thought about what really went on, what life was really like.'

They strolled along for a while in companionable silence until they came to a stone seat. Not really designed as a seat it was a large stone which had become separated from the rest of the wall but would suffice as a resting place. They sat down with little distance between them.

'I would love to see the Colosseum by moonlight,' Sheba mused. 'I wonder if the authorities would allow it?'

'We could ask,' George offered.

'Perhaps another time. We have our schedule planned for this holiday, George.'

Once again an easy silence fell between the two. People walked past them, there were people below and above them on the terraces, but the couple could have been alone. Suddenly Sheba realised that the heavy infatuation she had felt for George had turned now to a deep, deep love. As she turned to him to suggest they move on she saw he was looking at her. The intensity of his stare made her blush and she stood up to avoid looking directly at him.

'It's time to move on, George,' she said walking away from him.

'Sheba,' he called gently.

She turned to look at him noting how the intense look in his eyes made their usual mute brown appear almost black. She knew a miracle had occurred and offered up a silent prayer of thanks as she smiled and held out a gloved hand. 'Come George. We must find the others.'

Both knew what had happened. Both realised there was much to discuss. That was in the wonderful, exciting future, which lay before them. Now they could at last relax, and enjoy each other's company, and the glory that was Rome.

Chapter Forty Two
The Epilogue.

IT WAS A HUGE turn out for the christening of the Oak twins, Oliver and Christopher. The two cherub-like infants were now fast heading for their first birthday and their wailing as the cold water touched their foreheads proved to the attentive congregation that being born in foreign climes had not been at all detrimental; at least not to the lungs. Matthew and Elizabeth stood proudly by whilst the godparents, George and Sheba, took on the role they had agreed to undertake with surprised delight, when requested.

The family of five had been in England for two weeks and were due to return to India the following week. The change in climate had been something of a shock to the visitors as they were used to much warmer temperatures but such was the pleasure of being home it was a small price to pay.

A huge reception had been prepared at Oakdene so it was that Gabriel and Bathsheba led the way there. It was a distance the villagers were well used to walking, from the church to the house, but Matthew had insisted Elizabeth, Bathsheba and the babies use the gig.

'No, Matthew. It is your day. Yours, Elizabeth's and the twins". I'll walk; with Gabriel and little Ophelia; I insist!' Bathsheba was firm.

'Very well, mama.' Matthew had finally agreed.

It was four years since that fateful day when Bathsheba had ridden into Casterbridge with her son to try to persuade him to give up the wild idea he'd had of joining the military. But, how proud she was now of her son and daughter-in-law. What a splendid couple they made. It was a pity they had to go back to India so soon. Bathsheba was delighted with her new daughter-in-law and she'd been heard to declare 'I couldn't have chosen better myself.' Although Matthew had decided to stay abroad for the time being, he was now considering a posting nearer to England. Since the Commander-in-Chief had retired there was nothing to keep them in the East, unless the powers that be decided otherwise. Whether anything would come of it, only time would tell.

George and Sheba had been married two years ago in the self same church which had this very day witnessed a christening, and Deo Volente would be back there within the next few months to celebrate their own joyful event. If fate decided to play a part then Gabriel and Bathsheba would celebrate their Silver Wedding anniversary at the approximately the same time. What celebrations there would be when that day arrived.

As they approached the farmhouse a solitary figure stood in the middle-distance waving.

''Tis Ben. Ben Tallboys, would you believe?' Gabriel ran ahead to greet his old friend.

'Well, Ben, 'tis congratulations all round today sure enough,' Gabriel said, treating his friend's hand like the village pump. 'We've just, this very afternoon, christened the twins and we heard very recently that you're now a Member of Parliament.'

'That's right enough, Gabriel.'

'Why didn't you tell us you were coming, Ben? I would have met you off the London train.'

'Gabriel, a little bird told me you had a special event planned for today. I do keep regularly in touch with Sir Cornelius y'know.'

'Yes, of course you do. They, Lady Emma and Sir Cornelius, will be here this evening for the dancing so he'll be wanting to congratulate you himself then I'm sure. He does know I assume?'

'Oh, I should think he will have heard. He has friends in high places, don't forget.' Ben laughed. It was because of his mentor's influence that Ben Tallboys had been given the chance to stand for parliament. It has to be said though, he would have not got far without a great deal of intelligence and persistence and the fact that he was finally elected was almost entirely down to his own perspicacity and popularity.

As they entered the house followed closely by Bathsheba and little Ophelia, Elizabeth and Matthew's first-born, they could hear the sounds of instruments being tuned, coming from the direction of the old barn at the back of the house.

'The Weatherbury players still going strong, I hear,' observed Ben.

'True. They'll be in fine fettle this evening I hope for we're to have a dance after the feasting is over.'

'This is just like old times, my friend.' Ben looked as happy as Gabriel had seen him in a long time. It seemed so long ago when they had sat in the King's Arms plotting and planning. Now they were beginning to see the results of their labour.

There was now a regular school in Weatherbury and most of the younger children attended except at the busiest times of year such as Harvest-time. Sheba had enjoyed her two years spent as headmistress of the village school but since she was now married she could no longer be employed there. She often visited the school and taught in a voluntary capacity feeling a need to continue to take part in what she regarded as her own special project.

There had been great strides forwards in the Union Movement with many new members and although there was still a long way to go before conditions were ideal a vast amount had been achieved. Agricultural workers" pay was slightly improved, although it would never match Cornelius" factory workers', and the new model village had proved to be hugely successful.

With all the guests seated at the refectory table, Gabriel said a short prayer of thanks for his good fortune in having two new grandsons and after blessing the plentiful food before them invited his guests to 'tuck-in'.

As soon as the meal was finished and the babes" heads well and truly wetted there were calls for Gabriel to get up and play his flute.

'Follow me then?' he requested in the manner of the pied piper of Hamelin. Out they all went into the huge barn, which had been dressed up in traditional fashion. Bales of hay were strewn around the perimeter so that the weary guests could rest, as necessary, for the dancing for the most part was to be strenuous in the extreme.

The Weatherbury band quickly joined Gabriel in a lively jig. Matthew and Elizabeth were the first to lead the dancing as the celebrations were in their honour. Sheba was keen to join in but with her confinement but a few weeks hence, her gallant husband insisted she watch the strenuous dances but suggested perhaps she join in when the music was a little slower.

Noticing her mother in a far corner where the babies had been placed for safety, Sheba crossed the floor to join her.

Bathsheba glanced up as her daughter approached.

'How are you keeping my dear? I haven't seen much of you for the past week or so.'

'I'm very well, Mama. Dr. Melksham says as long as I take it easy from now on, there's no reason why everything should not go well at the birth.'

'And are you taking it easy down at Lower Hill Farm?' her concerned mother asked. 'I know how busy you and George have been in getting established.'

'Yes, mama. We've been at the farm for near on two years now and George is well pleased with the progress we have made. In fact he's taken on extra help so you've no need to worry about me working too hard.'

'Are you still helping out at the school, though?'

'There's good news about the school, Mama. I meant to tell you when we met at the market last week but with all the excitement of Matthew and Elizabeth, I completely forgot. There's to be another teacher starting in the autumn so hopefully they'll manage very well without my assistance.'

Bathsheba smiled. ''Tis a good day today, Sheba. One of the happiest I can recall. We've been through some hard and indeed sad times but now everything appears to have found its rightful place in this almighty universe, well Weatherbury, anyway.' She became more serious, 'I only hope it stays that way.' She crossed her fingers as she spoke not wanting to tempt fate.

''Tis a pity Adam and Jayne couldn't get home for the christening, Mama.'

'They'll be back before long, you mark my words. Adam is quite keen to help your father run the farm in spite of his success as a poet.'

There was a small commotion at the entrance to the barn as Sir Cornelius Godwin and his wife were announced. Lady Emma made her way through the crowd to Bathsheba and Sheba.

'I just couldn't wait any longer to see your grandchildren, Bathsheba. How delightful they look. You must be so proud.' Lady Emma handed a beautifully wrapped gift to her friend. 'I saw these little silver spoons in Casterbridge and just couldn't resist them. I hope Matthew won't mind.'

'He'll be delighted, I'm sure,' his mother declared.

Sir Cornelius joined Gabriel and Ben Tallboys who had seated themselves in a corner in order to take a little liquid refreshment. The music and dancing had paused for the players and dancers to take a much needed break.

'I hear congratulations are in order, Mr Tallboys.' Sir Cornelius clasped Ben by the hand and shook it vigorously 'Well done, man! You deserve to be elected after all the hard work that you have done.'

'Not without your help and guidance, Sir. May I take this opportunity to thank you heartily on behalf of myself and my team of helpers?'

'Not at all.' The gentleman nodded his head. 'It was my pleasure. Now if you'll excuse me I must go and congratulate the young parents.'

Gabriel and Ben Tallboys looked at each other. There was no need for words. Each knew how the other felt.

Gabriel stood up. 'Well, Ben, 'tis time I resumed my duties. My wife will complain if I don't dance with her soon. Why, I shall never hear the last of it.' He laughed knowing full well that Bathsheba was so enjoying herself with the family around her she would not mind in the least whether she danced or not. He looked across at the quartet in the corner of the barn. How happy they looked. Happiness being so ephemeral, Gabriel wished he was a talented painter. The scene upon which he now gazed deserved to be passed down to future generations, but for now he could only store it in his memory. It would be something to relate to his grandchildren and all being well, their children.

Printed in the United Kingdom
by Lightning Source UK Ltd.
135200UK00001B/225/P

DOAf